REMNANTS OF TRUST

ALSO BY ELIZABETH BONESTEEL

CENTRAL CORPS NOVELS

The Cold Between

REMNANTS OF TRUST

A CENTRAL CORPS NOVEL

Elizabeth Bonesteel

HARPER Voyager

An Imprint of HarperCollins *Publishers*

REMNANTS OF TRUST. Copyright © 2016 by Elizabeth Bonesteel. All rights reserved. Printed in the United States of America. No part of this book may be used or reproduced in any manner whatsoever without written permission except in the case of brief quotations embodied in critical articles and reviews. For information address HarperCollins Publishers, 195 Broadway, New York, NY 10007.

HarperCollins books may be purchased for educational, business, or sales promotional use. For information please e-mail the Special Markets Department at SPsales@harpercollins.com.

Harper Voyager and design is a trademark of HarperCollins Publishers L.L.C.

FIRST EDITION

Designed by Paula Russell Szafranski

Library of Congress Cataloging-in-Publication Data has been applied for.

ISBN 978-0-06-241367-3

16 17 18 19 20   RRD   10 9 8 7 6 5 4 3 2 1

For Alex

REMNANTS OF TRUST

T minus 8 years—Canberra

At least, thought Elena, *I'll die in a Corps uniform.*

She faced down the gun, looking not into the barrel but into the eyes of the man holding it. Keita had brown eyes, but in the frigid, rainy afternoon of this dying planet they looked jet-black and devoid of light. He had always—for as long as she had known him—looked angry, but she thought she saw something else as he stared at her through the gun's sight. Not fear, not that. Keita had never been afraid.

He looked *lost.*

The others were clustered behind him in the meager shelter of a crumbled cement wall. Savin was stoic as always, weight on one foot, but she saw his left hand resting on the grip of his pulse rifle. Jimmy had placed himself between Keita and Niree's prone figure, the medic shielding his patient. Elena knew his expression without looking. The loud argument, in a shattered alley next to a public square, was risking their exposure. Jimmy would be annoyed with her.

"Get the *fuck* out of the way, Shaw!" Keita yelled.

She did not move. "Stand down, Ensign," she said evenly.

"She killed the lieutenant! She set him up! You were there! You saw just like I did!"

Behind her, the girl she was protecting made a small sound, and Elena wanted to tell her to shut up. "She was a prisoner, Keita," she said. The child had been in chains, used as bait. Keita had seen it, even if they had been too late to keep the lieutenant from being gunned down. "Lieutenant Treharne was trying to save her, and now you want to kill her?"

The gun's barrel never wavered. "I will blow a hole through you, too, Shaw."

At that, Jimmy couldn't keep silent. "Keita—"

"Shut up, Jimmy."

She and Keita said it in unison, and she almost laughed. But it was time to bring the confrontation to an end. "You'll have to blow a hole through me, then, because I'm *not fucking moving*," she said. "Make up your goddamned mind. We don't have time for this shit."

Seconds passed. Elena could hear the girl whimpering behind her, and fought off irritation. What good were tears? Tears wouldn't make him put the gun down. Elena needed him to stop reacting and start thinking. She knew he could do it. She had *seen* him do it. She had served with him for six months aboard the CCSS *Exeter,* and despite his pretension of brainless thuggery, he was far more thoughtful than his usual manner betrayed.

"What about you, Savin?" Keita addressed the other infantry officer. "You with me, or are you going to listen to some fucking *songbird*?"

The nickname sounded ridiculous in context. But Savin, in his typically taciturn fashion, responded immediately:

"Songbird."

Keita's gaze faltered, and for a moment she caught a glimpse of pain in his eyes. Then he lowered his rifle, swore loudly, and stalked off.

The girl behind Elena began to sob openly. Elena ignored her, catching Savin's eye. "Give him thirty seconds," she instructed, "then get him back here." Savin nodded and trotted after his friend. She turned to Jimmy, who had witnessed the entire exchange with growing incredulity. "Can you move her?" she asked.

Jimmy looked down at the fifth surviving member of their landing party. Lieutenant Niree Osai, ranking officer since Treharne's death, was not unconscious, but she was in shock, blinking absently into the rain, her breathing shallow. Jimmy had used his jacket to wrap the remains of her arm, protecting the torn and ruined flesh from the acidic rainfall, but her color was awful, and she seemed to have no sense of where she was. Part of Elena envied her.

"She's not stable," he said. "She's in shock, her pressure's in the toilet, and she's not nearly unconscious enough."

"You misunderstand me." She locked eyes with him. "I didn't say *should* you move her, I said *can* you. Do you need help carrying her?"

"Lanie, she's had her arm torn off. Moving her like this could kill her."

She did not outrank him. She did not outrank any of them. She had no leg to stand on if she tried to give him an order. She wondered if Keita's tactic with the rifle would work better for her. "Jimmy, if we're not off this rock in seventeen and a half minutes, we lose our weather window, and we're stuck here for thirty-seven hours. You fancy our chances for another thirty-seven hours?"

He knew as well as she did that they couldn't survive it. Trained infantry or not, they were foreigners on this colony, and the natives who were hunting them knew every side street and abandoned building in the city. Starvation may have driven Canberra's settlers mad, but it had not rendered them stupid. Keita and Savin had been able to retrieve Niree from them, but over two nights and a day, none of Elena's team stood a chance.

Jimmy gave her a pleading look, but she did not shift. At last he sighed. "Yeah," he told her, resigned. "I can carry her."

"Get her ready, then. We'll move when Keita gets back." Jimmy knelt down by Niree, and Elena turned, at last, to the girl whose life she had saved.

She was fourteen, perhaps older. It was difficult to tell, sometimes, on planets where the children were chronically malnourished. She was short and thin and alabaster-pale, jet-black hair plastered to her cheeks by the soaking rain, and she had the sort of apple-cheeked prettiness that rarely bloomed into beauty with adulthood. She had stopped sobbing, but was still hiccupping, and her lips were blue. She stared at Elena with wide, frightened eyes.

"What's your name?" Elena asked her.

A spark of hope rose in those eyes, and Elena could follow her thinking: *perhaps I'll be rescued after all.* "Ruby."

"Ruby." Elena nodded. "If you slow us down, or give even the slightest indication that you are conspiring against us, I will shoot you myself. Understood?"

Those innocent eyes widened, and Elena saw tears filling

them again. But Ruby nodded, and Elena turned away from her. "Can you fire and carry her at the same time?" she asked Jimmy.

"How many arms do you think I have?"

Just then Savin returned, and marching next to him was Keita, rifle still in his hands, the nose pointed at the ground. He would not meet her eyes, but Savin looked at her and gave her a nod.

"Okay." She faced the others. "Two groups. Savin, you stay with Jimmy and Niree." Savin was a dead shot; she wanted him protecting their wounded. "Keita, you're with me and Ruby. We're heading back to the ship. We leapfrog each other, providing covering fire." She looked at them, one after another. "We're more than a kilometer off, and we've got less than sixteen minutes to get there, so nobody stops. For anything. Clear?"

Three nods, including the child. Elena stared at Keita.

"Clear?" she repeated.

His eyes came up, dark and deadly, boring angrily into hers. "Clear."

Jimmy and Savin went first, Jimmy slinging Niree awkwardly over one shoulder. He was a tall man, but slight—medics did not have to maintain the same fitness levels as the infantry, and with this planet's Earth-point-two gravity, it was slowing him down. Of course, mechanics didn't have to maintain infantry fitness levels, either, but she did it anyway, in part to prove to herself that she could, and in part to ensure nobody could accuse her of taking the easy way out.

If she had taken the easy way out, she might not have been a pilot as well as a mechanic. She might have missed this mission altogether. She might have been safe in *Exeter*'s engine room while her friends were running for their lives.

Better, or worse?

Shaking off the thought, she silently forgave Jimmy his high-gravity stumbles and beckoned to Keita, drawing her own weapon.

They proceeded through the ruined city a few hundred meters at a time, and Elena's universe contracted into a short routine: watch, aim, wait . . . then run like hell to the next bit of shelter. The gravity fatigued her with alarming quickness, and she could feel a faint sting developing on her skin from the long exposure to the polluted rain. She felt increasingly conscious of the time as the visibility contracted with the waning afternoon, but she kept moving—silent, methodical—Keita's footsteps solid and constant next to hers. It crossed her mind that she should not feel so comforted by the presence of a man who had just threatened to kill her, but there was no one else she would have chosen to be at her side in a fight.

It was almost a relief when the colonists started shooting.

She heard the pulse impact and Ruby's shriek at the same moment. They were still a meter away from the shattered storefront they had chosen as their latest shelter, and the shot blasted a fireball into the ground just before them. As one Elena and Keita dodged around it, their strides lengthening, and they dove into the dirt behind the wrecked building. There was another shot, and for a moment Elena thought they had lost the girl. But an instant later she scrambled in between them, arms over her head, abruptly willing to risk sharing the shelter of the soldier who had wanted her dead.

"Where?" Elena asked.

Keita nodded behind them. "That garage we passed, just after Savin's spot."

"Long range?"

He checked his ammunition. "I've got three."

"I've got five."

"You're a crappy shot with a rifle."

Fair point.

He took aim and squeezed the trigger. An instant later the roof of the garage blew apart, leaving a corner of the structure on fire. A volley of shots came their way, peppering the ground before their ruined shelter. The colonists were not terrific shots themselves, she reflected, but it was enough—Jimmy would never get Niree through that.

She aimed her own rifle and fired back conventional pulse shots as Keita took aim again. She heard him inhale, then exhale. An instant later the rest of the structure burst into flames. Five seconds, ten: no more fire. *Are they waiting?* She caught sight of Jimmy and Savin through the smoke and flames, running across the remains of the city block. Savin had placed himself between Jimmy and the garage, and was firing one-handed as they ran past.

She thought they might make it.

Elena kept up her shooting as they ran, although she never saw anyone hidden in the dense rubble of what was left of the city, never knew what she was aiming at. Ruby had grown silent, and the one time Elena looked at her she saw the girl's eyes had gone dull and cold.

Probably for the best.

At long last, with less than four minutes left, they caught sight of the ship, waiting in what had once been the town square. Four of the colonists swarmed around it, running their hands over it, and Elena swore.

Next to her Keita let out a chuckle. "Anything goes until they touch your baby, right, Songbird?"

Elena aimed at one of the colonists, then dropped the nose of her rifle and shot toward the ground. A chunk of cement erupted a meter in front of him. He started, and as he turned, she risked speaking.

"Get away from that ship or we will kill you!" It wasn't much of a threat, but there was little else she could do.

The man—boy, woman; she could not tell from this distance what the emaciated figure had been—shot toward her voice. The round exploded the corner of the building they were crouched behind. She swore again, then did what she had heard Keita do: she inhaled, exhaled, and fired.

The figure's chest burst with a brief flame, and he dropped.

Somewhat startled by having hit her target, Elena aimed at another, but the rest turned and ran, leaving their fallen comrade behind. She kept her rifle pointed at the motionless form, aware of Keita next to her doing the same. After a moment, Jimmy and Savin came around them, running for the ship, and it was clear Elena's target wasn't getting up.

She engaged her comm. "Open the door," she told the shuttle.

The door slid open. She saw Jimmy haul himself inside and begin to lower Niree to the floor. Savin took an instant to stop by the man Elena had shot—the man she had killed—and scoop up his weapon. Then he, too, jumped onto the ship, crouching in the open doorway to provide cover.

She straightened, ready to run; and only then did she notice Keita looking off to one side. He was frowning, his whole body alert. Next to him, Ruby was staring at their ship, her expression dazed and faintly hopeful.

8

"Keita."

"Ssh," he said brusquely. "Can't you hear it?"

She listened. She heard rain, Ruby's breathing, her own heartbeat. "Keita, we have to go *now*."

He turned to her. His anger was gone, replaced by something urgent and determined. "I need two minutes."

"We do not have two minutes!"

"Then give me what we do have."

He stared at her steadily, unwavering. She wondered, if she tried to order him, if he would listen to her. She wondered what she would do if she had to leave without him.

It was not her choice.

"We take off in ninety-six seconds," she told him.

In a flash he was gone, dashing off into the darkening city. Without looking she clapped her hand around Ruby's scrawny arm and pulled her forward, running full-tilt for the ship.

She released the girl as soon as they leapt on, heading for the cockpit. "Time."

"Eighty-four seconds," the ship told her calmly.

"Lift off at eighty-three and a half." She met Ruby's eyes and pointed to the bench along the far wall, where Lieutenant Treharne had been sitting when they arrived . . . forty-six minutes ago.

Christ.

"Sit down, buckle up, and be still," she commanded. Ruby did as she was told, and Elena thought her quick obedience had probably helped her survive this far. She stepped over to Jimmy, who had strapped Niree down onto another bench and was applying the ship's med scanner. "Will she make it?" she asked.

He looked at her, his expression unreadable. "We didn't do

her any favors, hauling her out like that." At her look, he acquiesced. "Yes, I think so."

"Strap in for takeoff, then."

She heard the engines igniting and checked the time. Twenty-eight seconds—he wasn't going to make it. They would come back for him, of course, for what it was worth, but not even Dmitri Keita was going to survive a day and a half in this place.

Climbing into the pilot's seat, she did a perfunctory preflight check. She keyed in the course home, compensating for the rapidly contracting weather pattern.

"Flight in this weather is not recommended," the ship told her. "Heavy turbulence is likely."

I know, I know . . . "Hang on," she called to the others. "This won't be comfortable."

At seven seconds, she heard feet outside the door and saw Savin tense. But then Keita was on board, drenched and covered in mud, something dark and wet clutched against his chest. "Go!" he shouted at her.

She was ready for him. She jerked the controls, and the ship jolted off the ground with three seconds to spare.

Normally Elena was a careful pilot. The infantry liked to fly with her. When there was turbulence, she would engage the artificial gravity just enough to temper the disruption of the atmosphere.

Today was definitely *not* normal.

She shot them straight up, as fast as they would go, allowing the planet's gravity to press down on them. She stared into the atmosphere, peering at the darkening clouds, looking for the fastest path out of the weather.

Through her concentration she heard a sound behind her, and she wondered if Keita's bundle was a cat.

Her viewscreen began to glow red, and her attention was dragged back to the task of flying. *Great,* she thought, *the planet's particulate atmosphere is ripping into our hull.* Elena whispered a quiet apology to the ship, thinking herself ahead twenty minutes, picturing herself home on *Exeter,* standing in the shuttle bay while her chief berated her for the state of her vessel. She would be days repairing it.

"Inversion in five," she told them, and counted down the seconds.

Moments later the artificial gravity engaged, abruptly reorienting them. She heard retching behind her; that was likely the girl. Elena usually took pride in gentle inversions, but today it had seemed slightly less important.

The night opened up before her, dark and pure and scattered with stars, and the glow of heat faded as the vacuum of space cooled their exterior. She sat back and closed her eyes. They were alive.

Most of them.

That sound again. She frowned. It wasn't Ruby—she could hear the girl alternating between retching and sobbing, Jimmy offering her quiet words of comfort. She turned around. Savin, still relaxed, was watching over Niree as Jimmy rubbed Ruby's back and held a bucket before her.

Keita sat in the corner, looking down at a bundle of muddy, sodden rags in his arms. She heard the sound again, and then a quiet response from him.

Is he singing?

She got to her feet and walked the length of the ship to stand over him. In his arms, wrapped in what looked like old shirts, was a baby. Elena knew little of such things, but she guessed it was no more than a few hours old. It was wide-awake, but it was not crying. Instead, it was studying Keita with enormous, somber purple eyes, that odd color some babies were born with. Every few moments it opened its mouth to make that small sound, a mew of greeting or protest; and Keita responded each time, rocking the infant gently.

"Jimmy should look at it," she said.

"Her." Keita's eyes never left the infant's. "And she's fine."

She stood for a moment, watching the incongruous scene, then retreated, making her way back to the pilot's seat. She would have to comm *Exeter*, let them know Treharne was dead and that they had rescued only two of the colonists. In a day and a half a larger crew would go down, more heavily armed, properly prepared after the report she would give them.

She wondered how many colonists would be left.

She closed her eyes, remembered aiming her rifle, her futile warning. On that planet, killing would have been a mercy. He had been emaciated, close to death, or at least close to the point where his companions would pull him apart to keep themselves alive a little longer. He had been trying to kill them, too; but really, she had done him a favor.

She saw the flame bloom in his chest, saw him drop.

Elena opened her eyes, sat up straight, and opened a channel to make her report.

PART I

CHAPTER 1

Orunmila

Guanyin was always amazed by how well puppies could sleep.

Samedi had slid into the narrow space between her pregnant belly and the wall, his body twisted like soft pastry, and was snoring blissfully into her ear as she stared at the ceiling. When he had first dozed off she had tried blowing on his nose. The first two times he had twitched, but the third time he was oblivious. She could almost certainly get out of bed without disturbing him, but she needed him as an excuse. If she sat up she would feel obligated to stand, and if she stood, she would feel obligated to talk to Cali about the warship Central Corps had just dropped in their backyard.

Cali would expect her to have worked it out, to have a plan of action. She had always looked to Guanyin for direction, even when they were children. Cali was three years older, but she had always been more comfortable as Guanyin's foot soldier than as her mentor. Guanyin knew many in her crew expected her to choose Cali as her second-in-command, and certainly she could trust Cali with her life. But for a first officer, Guanyin needed an adviser, someone who could help challenge her thinking. That was not Cali.

That was Chanyu, the ship's former captain, but he had retired. They had left him on Prokofiev's third moon, waiting for a shuttle to the Fifth Sector. She could probably find him if she needed to, but she knew what he would say. "You must find your own way, Guanyin. *Orunmila* is yours now. She lives or dies under your command. And remember, dear girl, she wouldn't be yours if they didn't believe in you. All you need to do is be worthy of them." Chanyu had raised her, and she loved him like a father, but she never could stand it when he spouted that sort of useless rubbish.

Guanyin was twenty-nine years old, pregnant with her sixth child, and captain of a starship that was home to 812 people. She had no second-in-command and no advisers, and it was down to her to figure out how to respond to a deployment buildup from the largest, best-armed government in the galaxy.

"It's only one ship," Yunru had remarked over dinner with their children. "It may not mean what you think it means." Which had occurred to her, of course. The CCSS *Galileo* was small for a Central starship, half the size of *Exeter*, the ship *Orunmila* most often dealt with. But unlike the equally small science ship CCSS *Cassia*, *Galileo* was unambiguously a warship. Central was not entirely inept at diplomacy, but they always felt the need to back it up with weapons. *Galileo* was spectacularly well equipped to do just that.

Not that she couldn't understand why Central would feel the need to build up their weaponry in the Third Sector. Numerous multiyear crop failures had led to an increase in intersystem squabbles and civil wars, and the Syndicate tribes, finding larger markets for contraband, were becoming bolder and more aggressive. But when *Galileo* had appeared a few weeks ago, contacting supply chains and shipping companies as if she had been in the Third Sector for years, Guanyin had found their polite diplomatic greeting entirely inadequate.

It had taken Guanyin very little research to remind herself where she had heard the ship's name before. *Galileo* had been credited last year with preventing an all-out war in the Fifth Sector. No less than Valeria Solomonoff herself, the Fifth Sector's most venerable PSI captain, had signed a treaty with Central through *Galileo*. *Galileo*'s captain, a man called Greg Foster, was widely considered to be an accomplished diplomat.

Guanyin disliked diplomats. She always found they were too good at lying for her taste. So when Greg Foster had contacted her, ostensibly to introduce his ship, she had been cold, unfriendly, and more than a little blunt.

"You waste your time with me, Captain Foster," she had told him. "It is the Syndicates attacking your ships, not us."

The last six months had seen a marked increase in Syndicate raider activity, and for the first time in decades they had included Central Corps starships in their targets. PSI, who had dealt with raiders for centuries, was the obvious place for Central to turn when formulating their own strategies for dealing with guerrilla attacks. A request for help Guanyin might have understood, the sort of short-term alliance PSI and the Corps had formed repeatedly over the centuries. She did not understand this amorphous buildup of Central's power, and it bothered her.

What is Central planning?

The baby rolled and kicked, and Samedi woke up, his wolf-ish face next to hers. She reached up a hand and rubbed him reassuringly between the ears. "Do you suppose they are trying to trick us, little one?" she asked. "Or do they fear something specific, and don't want to tell us what it is?"

Samedi gazed at her with his contented, worshipful eyes, and sneezed in her face.

Cali heard her roll out of bed, and came in from the sitting room to lean against the bathroom doorframe as Guanyin washed her face. "He's too young to be in bed with you," Cali said.

"When he's old enough he'll be too big."

"You slept with Shuja when he weighed more than you did."

"Shuja never weighed *that* much." Actually, Cali was right: Shuja had topped out at sixty kilos before he had started dropping weight due to illness and old age. Guanyin only broke fifty-five when she was pregnant. But she had been pregnant for half of Shuja's adult life, and she had grown used to having a dog curled up next to her expanding stomach. "Samedi will learn."

Cali crossed her arms and glowered.

"Your face will freeze that way, you know."

Not that it would matter if it did, of course. Cali was beautiful, and she knew it, breaking hearts without thinking much about it. Guanyin, who never doubted her own place in Cali's heart, yelled at her sometimes, but it made no difference, and she supposed Cali would have to grow out of it on her own. But Guanyin knew one of the reasons she had reacted to Captain Foster the way she had was because he reminded her of Cali, right down to the polite condescension.

Guanyin turned away from the sink. "Can I ask you something?"

Cali pushed herself off the doorframe as Guanyin walked past and asked *Orunmila* for some music. Guanyin settled back onto the bed next to the patient puppy, wide-awake now and wagging his entire body, trying and failing to resist licking her face. "No, love," she said sternly, and he backed off onto his haunches, waiting for her to change her mind.

Cali pulled up a chair and sat next to the bed. "Is this about the Corps captain?"

"He talked to me like you do, sometimes. Like I'm helpless, or too young to understand. He seemed to think I would find him persuasive and comforting, just because he has a nice smile, never mind the volume of weapons his ship is carrying into our territory."

At that, Cali grinned. "Did you swear at him?"

It was Guanyin's turn to glower. "Why do you do it? When you know I understand all this better than you do. Why do you treat me like a child?"

Cali shrugged and looked away. "Because I love you, I suppose, and I don't like that things are hard for you. I want to do it for you, even when I can't."

That was a surprisingly introspective observation for Cali. "Captain Foster doesn't love me."

"Maybe you remind him of someone else."

"Maybe he thinks, because I'm new, I'm a fool." She shook her head. "I don't understand. He dealt with Valeria Solomonoff in the Fifth Sector. You really think she let him get away with shit like this?"

"Maybe she doesn't like him, either."

"I spoke to her. She trusts him. She said, and I quote, 'He is fighting what we are fighting.' You know what she didn't say?"

"I wasn't there, Guanyin."

"She didn't say 'He is a good soldier.' So why is he talking to me as if there is nothing going on?"

Cali leaned forward, elbows on her knees. "You know, Guanyin, you could ask him. I mean, instead of trying to analyze what Solomonoff really meant, or poking at my character flaws."

She sighed, gently tugging Samedi's soft ears. "I was rude to him."

"They're rude to us all the time, and they've still told one of their captains to kiss your ass." Cali shrugged. "They want something. Find out what it is. Maybe we can get something in return."

Admittedly, that was not terrible advice. "What could they possibly want from us?"

At her words, Samedi launched himself at her again, and she had to close her eyes against his silky-soft tongue. "Hopefully puppies," Cali said dryly, and Guanyin laughed.

The comm on her wall chimed, and Aida spoke without waiting for acknowledgment. "I'm sorry to interrupt, Captain Shiang," he said, "but we're receiving a distress call."

She could hear it in his voice: tension and fear. She sat up, her hand resting on Samedi's head. "Acknowledge and reroute," she told him, knowing he would have started the process already. "Who is it?"

"It's a Central starship, ma'am," he said. "Captain—it's *Exeter*."

She met Cali's eyes. They had not seen *Exeter* in more than six months—since before Chanyu's retirement—but they had run countless missions with her for a decade. She had thought to wonder, just that morning, why Central had not had *Exeter* arrange for her to meet *Galileo*'s captain, instead of expecting her to accept the goodwill of a stranger. She wondered if Captain Çelik was still at *Exeter*'s helm.

She wondered if he was all right.

"What are they up against?" She swung her feet to the floor and stood, all her fatigue washed away by adrenaline.

"Syndicate ships, Captain. They're reporting twenty-seven."

Twenty-seven raiders. Against a Central starship. "How close are we?"

"Two minutes, eight seconds, ma'am."

"Get all weapons online," she told him. "*Orunmila,* call battle stations ship-wide."

The lights shifted to blue, and the quiet, repeating alarm came over the ship's public comm system. Cali fell into step behind her as she rushed out of her quarters into the hallway.

Raiders were often reckless—and occasionally suicidal—but attacking Central was a recent tactic. There had been three attacks over the last six months, always the usual smash-and-grab, and only one had been at all successful. So many raiders against a single starship . . . the Syndicates were never so bold. An attack so aggressive was insanity. Even if they scored against *Exeter,* who was well armed in her own right, Central could not let the attack stand. This battle, whatever the cause, was only the start, and the Syndicates had to know that.

She thought again of *Galileo*'s abrupt appearance, and wondered how much Central had known in advance.

CHAPTER 2

Galileo

Took on parts at Lakota, Greg Foster wrote. *Four days' travel en route to Shixin. Fucked up the latest negotiations with PSI.*

No. It was not the sort of report he would be allowed to file.

He swept a finger through the offending paragraph to delete it and stared, frustrated, at the nearly empty document. Realistically, writing the report should have taken no more than half an hour—less if he wrote in generalities—but he was fairly certain insufficient detail would cause Admiral Herrod to bounce the report right back with orders to do it over. Even with a proper level of information, though, he would need to take some care with his word choice. Allowing his frustration to bleed through onto the page would not help his shaky standing with the Admiralty.

Looking back on his conversation with the PSI captain, he couldn't blame her for being suspicious. *Galileo* was hardly a stealth ship—even before the blowup last year, Greg's ship and her crew had kept a fairly high profile in the squabble-ridden

Fourth Sector. And their first foray into the Fifth Sector had involved a set of incidents that had almost provoked all-out war between Central and the PSI ships in that region. He had known *Galileo*'s precipitous deployment to the Third Sector, done without so much as a polite forewarning for the non-Corps ships in the area, was likely to be misinterpreted. What he hadn't quite understood was how little his experiences in the Fifth Sector would matter here.

Shiang Guanyin, captain of the PSI ship *Orunmila*, had viewed *Galileo*'s arrival with hair-trigger paranoia, and he could not blame her. But even so, he had been surprised to find himself so far unable to open any kind of dialogue with her at all.

"Thank you for the introduction," she had said, her Standard enunciated carefully. "Should we find ourselves requiring anything at all from you or your government, we will let you know." And she had terminated the comm.

He did not have to review his diplomatic training to recognize she felt insulted, and by more than *Galileo*'s presence. Clearly something in how he had presented himself had put her off.

He had considered more than once just telling her the truth: that *Galileo*'s presence had nothing to do with PSI, or even the resource issues in the Third Sector. Central was indeed spread too thin, the supply chains delivering raw materials for construction having been constrained for years; but *Galileo* had been reassigned for an entirely different reason. He could tell Captain Shiang, he supposed, that he was only there so his superiors could make sure he remembered who called the shots. But he did not think that would inspire confidence in either him or Central Gov.

Although it would certainly torpedo what's left of my career.

Weary of his mind running in circles, he rubbed his eyes with a thumb and forefinger and let his attention drift to the window. There were no stars for him to contemplate, just the silver-blue brightness of the FTL field moderated by *Galileo*'s polarizers. They would be in the field another three hours before they stopped to recharge, and another five days before finally reaching their supply pickup. If he finished this damn report, he could enjoy some peace and quiet for a change. The last six months had been, in some ways, the most eventful of his fourteen-year career.

There was the court-martial and its outcome, of course, about which he was still not sure what to think. What had happened the year before had been too public for the Admiralty to cover up, and they had struggled to come up with charges that reflected the seriousness of the events but didn't alienate a public that seemed inclined to see both Greg and Elena as heroes. In the end they were charged with insubordination and destruction of government property, although the public record of the trial was coy about exactly what that property had been.

The final verdict—splitting hairs over specific charges, making them appear to be something between naively innocent and subversively guilty—had turned out to be strangely toothless. He and Elena had been taken off the promotion lists—her for a year, him for two—and they had each been assigned their own personal admiral with whom they were required to file monthly mission reports for the next half year. The most concrete changes were *Galileo*'s reassignment from her usual Fourth Sector patrol to the Third Sector, and the deployment of a dozen recent Academy graduates who probably shouldn't have made it past their first year.

Which meant that, yes, they had been sent a message. Just not one that made sense to Greg. Anyone who thought subtle insults would alter either his or her conviction that they had done exactly the right thing was unfamiliar with both of them to the point of absurdity.

But it was more than his professional life that had changed. For the first time in thirteen years—since he had deployed at the arrogant, self-assured age of twenty-four—he was unmarried and unattached, and he had not considered the impact that would have on his day-to-day life. There had always been people who saw his marriage as a challenge rather than a deterrent, but its absence had brought him a whole new population of admirers that he had no idea how to properly deflect. His usual techniques were not as effective on this crowd, and he often found himself caught flat-footed while trying to let someone down kindly. Having a wife had provided a buffer between him and the natural impulses of a crew that spent months in close quarters. He had been working to include himself more in their day-to-day lives, and many of them seemed happy to welcome him in without limits.

Jessica Lockwood, his newly minted second-in-command, had tried to explain it to him. "They're just happy for you, sir," she had told him, as if that explained everything. Jessica always put him in mind of his sister: practical and irrepressible, indulgent with what she perceived to be his shortcomings. Jessica would never come right out and tell him he was an emotional idiot, but he was pretty sure she thought it frequently.

And then there were the people who expressed sympathy

about his divorce—which he found equally puzzling. He did not doubt their intentions, but he did not understand how they could so thoroughly misread how he felt. Even Jessica tiptoed around the subject of Caroline, as if his ex-wife were a land mine or a raw nerve. In truth, he almost never thought of her, all the pain and resentment of their fourteen-year marriage having vanished for him even before the dissolution was finalized. Most days he felt light, more buoyant than he had felt since he was a child, and nobody seemed to notice.

Well, almost nobody.

Resigning himself to the impulse, he engaged his comm in text mode. "You up?" he asked.

A brief pause, and the word *Yes* appeared in the air half a meter before his eyes.

"You done yet?"

No.

He shouldn't ask. He had no business asking. Things between them had not yet healed. "You want to come finish here?"

A longer pause this time. Then: *Do you have tea?*

"I will by the time you get here."

She rang the door chime when she arrived. This was a regression—for years she had walked into his office unannounced, confident of her welcome. But showing up at all . . . that was progress. Glacial and frustrating, but progress.

He had *Galileo* open the door, and his chief of engineering walked in. Elena Shaw, his closest friend before he had blown it all up, still the person he trusted above anyone else. He had thought, for years, that what he felt for her was complicated, designed to trip him up when he least expected it. For a time, he had thought her presence was a curse. It was only recently, when faced with losing her, that he had recognized what he felt for her was simple. What was complicated was coping with it.

Oblivious to his ruminating, she dropped into the chair across from him and wrapped her fingers around the mug of hot tea. "So how far did you get?" she asked.

She was watching him with those eyes of hers, sharp and perceptive and bright with intelligence. Also dark and beautiful and so easy to get lost in. She was not pretty the way many of the women on his ship were pretty: her features were too uneven, the balance thrown off by her huge eyes and substantial nose. But there was an elegance about her, the way she moved, the way she spoke, as if she were some creature of earth and fire, liquid and molten. He often thought he could spend the rest of his days quite happily doing nothing but watching her.

In fact, he had said this to his father when he had visited last month. The older man had shaken his head, and said it was a damn good thing Greg had gotten divorced.

More proof he knows me better than I thought he did.

"Through last week," he replied to Elena's question.

She rolled her eyes, leaning back and lifting the mug close to her face. "I'm three weeks behind," she confessed. "I have too much work to do for this shit."

"It's not about the report. It's about reminding us who's the boss."

She knew that, of course. They had discussed the outcome at the time, and both understood the court-martial could have ended quite differently. The Admiralty would have been well within its rights to throw them out of the service entirely— saving the sector be damned. They hadn't, and the one conclusion he and Elena had come up with was that the Admiralty simply couldn't agree on what to do with them. "Some of them wanted to give you a medal," Admiral Herrod had told Greg shortly after the trial's conclusion. "Some of them wanted to separate the two of you." At that the old man had frowned, and for a moment Greg had the impression that the typically circumspect admiral was speaking entirely off the record. "Whatever else you do, Foster—don't let them separate you. And watch your back."

It was a precaution Greg had already thought about, but hearing Herrod suggest it, when he couldn't be sure where the man's loyalties lay, left Greg feeling even more uncertain and unsafe.

When he had repeated Herrod's words to Elena, she had only said, "Where does he think we would go?"

She was watching him now through the steam from her tea. "You should have Jessie do it for you," she told him.

"She doesn't write like me."

"You think Herrod gives a damn?"

"Why don't you ask her to do yours?"

She gave him a mock glare. "You promoted her over me, remember?"

"Okay, then get *Galileo* to do it."

"Which is not a terrible idea," she agreed, "apart from the fact that *Galileo* wouldn't write like me at all."

"So we can't get around this," he concluded, resigned.

She set the mug down on the desk. "Thirty minutes, no talking, we knock these out and we're done with it."

"And promise ourselves not to leave it to the last minute next month."

She grinned. "That too."

They both fell silent, and Greg returned to figuring out how to describe his discussions with PSI. He wrote and erased the section of his report four times, aware he was attracting Elena's attention. At last he leaned back, frustrated. "I don't know how to say this," he said.

"What have you got?"

"I just deleted it." At her look, he added, "I can't just tell him 'I said this, and she said that.' I know Herrod. He's not going to give me any leeway, not in an official document. The man doesn't like me."

"It's not personal. The man is doing a job, just like you are." When he said nothing, she extended a hand toward his document. "Let me try."

"You don't write like me, either."

"So wordsmith it when I'm done."

He let her tug the document to her side of the desk, watching her set her own aside. She read his last paragraph and frowned, then wrote rapidly for a moment. When she was finished, she pushed the document back over to him.

He read. "This is a lie."

"It is not."

"Negotiations are not 'ongoing.' I'm trying to figure out how I could possibly respond to her without sounding like an asshole."

"The most important thing about diplomacy," Elena said, "is not the goal. It's establishing communication. You've done that." He glared, and she shook her head. "How can you be such a good diplomat, and so lousy at managing your own chain of command?"

"I'm not a good diplomat. That's the problem." But he re-read her words. They were not bad. He reached in and reordered a phrase—she had nailed his voice pretty well. *If you use this,* he reminded himself, *you can be finished.* "Herrod will peg this for bullshit."

"Of course he will." She had turned back to her own work. "He's a bright person. But you'll have made the effort to spin it, and that's what he wants." She made a few notes, then sat back. "There."

"You wrote up three weeks already?"

She shrugged. "I'm a mechanic. My life is much less interesting than yours."

"Plus Admiral Waris likes you."

Elena's supervisor, Ilona Waris, had been a mechanics teacher when Elena was at Central's military academy on Earth, and Elena's aptitude had rapidly secured her place as the teacher's favorite. Waris had kept track of Elena's career, occasionally offering unsolicited advice, but Greg had always had the sense that Elena found the woman overbearing. Elena had no ambition—she would not even have been chief if *Galileo*'s old chief hadn't been killed—but she had enough political savvy to keep from completely rebuffing Waris's sporadic attempts to keep in touch.

Elena had paused, and was looking at him, her expression troubled. "She voted to acquit us," she said.

"Is that bad?"

"She said . . . how did she put it? 'Your careers shouldn't be hamstrung over one bad call in the field.'"

Bad call. He could tell from her expression she disagreed with the term as much as he did. "You think she's on the other side?"

The other side meant Shadow Ops, an organization within Central's official government that wielded far more power than most people knew. S-O had been knee-deep in the events that had ended with their trial. Not that they could prove any of it, of course. All of the physical evidence was gone, and S-O's public face was one of benign, largely ineffective bureaucracy. But they both knew differently, and he knew she was aware of the implications of Admiral Waris's statement. Acquittal would have meant Central could have sent them off anywhere, unsupervised. They could have been separated, isolated from each other, alone with their suspicions and without resources to pursue them. Or they could have vanished without a trace, just a couple of random, unrelated accidents, and no one would even have asked the question.

"I think," Elena told him, "that presuming on an old acquaintance would be incalculably foolish. So I will be a boring mechanic in my reports, and she can check off a box, and she and I can smile at each other with our fingers crossed behind our backs."

Trust was the biggest casualty of the events of the last year. Elena, despite her years of experience in the Corps, used to trust her superiors to be in the right, at least as far as their intentions were concerned. The loss was a small one, he suspected, but it was a loss all the same, on the heels of far too many others. "Elena," he began, "you know I—"

A high tone sounded, and the wall readout flashed red. He stood, but across from him Elena was already moving, sweeping away both of their documents with a wave of her hand and pulling up a tactical view of *Galileo*. Out the window the field dimmed and dissipated into stars, and they hung still for a moment as the ship changed their flight plan. Then the stars blurred and they were in the field again, and if he had not heard the alarm he would have thought nothing had changed.

A priority Central distress call.

All ships in the vicinity, help us.

"Status," he said tersely. Above his desk, his ship rendered a reconstructed tactical display of a starship similar in design to *Galileo*, only three times the size: a great sprawling eagle rather than a sparrow. The CCSS *Exeter*. He stole a glance at Elena, who was staring at the display, her jaw set. In addition to being the Corps ship that had patrolled the Third Sector the longest, *Exeter* had been Elena's first deployment. She still knew people who served there.

Emily Broadmoor, Greg's chief of security and infantry commander, entered the room as *Galileo* gave status. "CCSS *Exeter* reports being under attack by twenty-seven Syndicate raiders. Current readings count twenty."

Twenty-seven. He could not recall ever hearing of a Syndicate tribe so large.

"Additional status is available," *Galileo* added helpfully.

Jessica came in, trailed by Greg's medical and comms officers. He caught her eye. "Give us what you've got," he told his ship, as Jessica moved to stand beside him.

The display animated with twenty-seven small ships, replaying the status relayed by *Exeter*'s sensors. The small ships spiraled in eerie unison, blasting somewhat futilely at *Exeter*'s solid hull. *Exeter* was firing back with external weapons, but her response was sluggish, and the raiders looped and dashed and avoided more shots than they took. As they all watched, one raider split from the others, heading abruptly toward *Exeter*'s belly. *Exeter* shot at the small fighter, a single gun, over and over again. She missed each time.

The little ship pitched and yawed like a drunken soldier, and for a moment Greg hoped against hope that it would miss *Exeter* entirely. But as they watched, it sped up and lurched into *Exeter*'s side.

Greg's office was lit by the playback of the massive blast, and when it faded there was a flaming crescent carved out of *Exeter*'s side, debris flying out of the gap. One-third of the starship had vanished. That the ship had survived to send a distress call was a minor miracle.

Greg's fists clenched involuntarily as they watched the remainder of the reenactment. He knew it was already over, but he found himself waiting for the battle to go differently, for their gunner's aim to improve, for some impossible sign that *Exeter* would recover. Instead, a single raider flew, unmolested, into *Exeter*'s wrecked side and attached itself like a limpet to the open wound. The remaining raiders kept circling the starship, drawing *Exeter*'s meager fire. Five of the tiny ships flamed out in the path of the starship's crippled weapons. Someone with some skill had found their way to the targeting controls.

Or maybe, Greg reflected, thinking of the futile shots before the impact, *they were just luckier than they had been before.*

A moment later the reconstruction looped back to the beginning, and Greg dismissed it. "Audio?" he prompted.

A voice began to speak, garbled by digital artifacting. "Mayday, Mayday, Mayday," a deep voice said. Greg recognized Captain Çelik. "We are under attack. Syndicate raiders. We're down to one gun, no shuttles. All ships in the area, please respond. Emergency. All ships—"

The voice broke off.

Christ.

The Syndicates had never moved so boldly against Central. There were skirmishes, sure—over the past year, there had been a handful of swipes taken at Corps starships, but nothing remotely this aggressive. Their goal had always been theft and escape, not engagement.

What the hell could have prompted this?

But the why of it was secondary for now. "ETA?"

"Three minutes, fifty-eight seconds."

Too long. "Has anyone else acknowledged the Mayday?"

"The PSI ship *Orunmila* will arrive in one minute and seven seconds."

With *Orunmila*'s help, *Exeter* might stand a chance. *Thank God*, he thought, *for spiky, suspicious PSI captains.* He looked up. "I want two ships on deck for a boarding party. Two platoons, armored. That limpet likely means they were boarded. And Bob, I want a full medical team in with the infantry." Surely there would be survivors. Surely there would be some hope to salvage out of all of this. "Mr. Mosqueda, I want all comms in and out monitored, and I want to know what they heard before they got hit. Chief," he told Elena, "you're on weapons, and watch out for jammers. I don't know why *Exeter* couldn't defend themselves, but if those bastards try that same trick with us, blow them apart. Commander Lockwood, you're with me. I want this over fast, everyone. We're not losing anyone else."

He watched them disperse, all efficiency and purpose, and tried not to imagine the crew of *Exeter,* not three minutes earlier, doing exactly the same thing.

CHAPTER 3

E lena ran down the hall, thinking back to the last time she had been in a firefight. The battle had been on a much smaller scale, but the odds had been overwhelmingly against her, and the outcome had been far less certain. Strange how little she remembered of the actual shooting. Most of her memories were of her companion: levelheaded, experienced, strong, and good-humored, even in the face of what had seemed like certain death. He had stood with her, unwavering, despite the fact that she had brought him all of his trouble, that he had known her only a day. Here, diving into a fight to save what was left of *Exeter,* she thought of how invulnerable she had felt when she was with him, how she could fight anything. She let the memory flood her bloodstream, leaving her cool and determined. *You've done this before. You can do this again.*

She entered engineering, her eyes sweeping over her crew. They were already at their stations, subdued but composed, even the new kids who were dumped on Greg before they left Earth. She tried to remember how many battle drills she had done with them. She tried to remember if battle drills had helped her at all the first time she had been shot at. She didn't think so. Real-world battle had little to do with drills, and everything to do with who you were underneath.

She would have spared them this early test if she could.

Ted Shimada, her second, was waiting to take her aside, pulling her away from the others before she could reach the main weapons console. "What do you think we're facing here?" he asked, his voice low enough to keep the others from overhearing.

She studied his expression. Ted's reputation as a clown was not entirely undeserved, but she had known him for more than ten years, and she knew his clowning masked a sharp and observant mind. He was one of a short list of people whose judgment she trusted absolutely, and the only one—with the possible exception of Greg—whom she would trust to look after her engines. He would have noticed the same anomalies in the replay of *Exeter*'s hit that she had.

"Your paycheck and mine says the bomber was a drone," she replied, "although whoever was remoting the thing didn't know what they were doing. Most of the others are drones, too, but based on the flight pattern I'm guessing those are autopilot." That would give *Galileo* a tactical advantage; autopilots in drones that size were almost always less imaginative than human operators.

"Especially with most of those Syndicate bastards too cowardly to risk their own skins hitting a Corps starship." His jaw worked, and he looked away from her for a moment. "*Shit*, Lanie."

"Later, Ted." She put her hand on his arm, just for a moment. "Let's get them out of this first."

Easy enough to say.

She turned to the weapons console, taking in the bank of green indicators. She could see, in her mind, over and over, the replay of *Exeter*'s destruction. There might be survivors—if the ship's environmentals had survived to seal in the atmosphere—but there would be many, many dead. And she would know their names.

Not now.

She heard the engine's harmonic change as the field generator began to spin down, and then Greg's voice over ship-wide comms: "All hands, enemy engaged."

They dropped into normal space.

She had expected to see *Exeter,* to be facing its destroyed underbelly, burned and twisted metal over the exposed bones of the ship's structure. Instead, she saw a massive, unfamiliar flat bulkhead scattered with lines of windows, and a swarm of those Syndicate drones firing into the dark hull. She glanced over at the generated tactical view to find they had emerged on top of another ship, larger and bulkier than *Galileo,* its graceful, hybrid lines identifying it as the PSI ship *Orunmila.* She beamed a silent *thank you* to its captain. If *Orunmila* had not been so close, she was not sure they would have found anything left of *Exeter* at all.

"Launch shuttles," Greg was saying. "Emily, draw those snipers off the PSI ship. *Galileo,* head to *Exeter*'s other side."

Galileo moved upward until she cleared *Orunmila,* then sped opposite the PSI ship to *Exeter.* Elena watched *Galileo*'s troop shuttles appear on the tactical readout. *Exeter* was still fighting, albeit with only one weapons bank—automatic defenses, or did they have crew left to man her remaining guns?—but the bulk of the raiders were focused on *Orunmila*. Elena frowned. "Why aren't they protecting the boarding ship?" she asked.

And then she saw it.

Their flyby allowed her an unobstructed view of the raider that had attached itself, leech-like, to *Exeter*'s charred hull, and she swore when she saw where it was clamped. "They're over *Exeter*'s generator battery," she said grimly, her comm open so Greg would hear as well. *Galileo* couldn't shoot at the raider, because taking out that ship would take out the generator, triggering an explosion that would then take out *Exeter, Galileo,* and *Orunmila*—not to mention irradiate the travel corridor for weeks.

"I see it, Chief," Greg said. "Anything from *Exeter* at all?"

"Their comms are all dead." But they were still firing that single gun, and making more shots than they missed. She didn't think their traumatized automated system would be making such accurate shots. Surely there were still people inside, alive, fighting. People who could handle invaders on foot.

Then again, maybe it was only wishful thinking.

Elena saw half a dozen drones peel off *Orunmila* to follow Emily's shuttles as they docked on *Exeter*'s intact side. Ted tracked and shot two of them, and *Orunmila* three; the shuttles handled the last one, maneuvering themselves against *Exeter*'s dark hull. "Stay on them, Ted," Elena said, but Ted was ahead of her, taking out every drone that angled for an attack. One of the raiders caught the wing of one of the shuttles as it docked; she winced, but the shuttle fired in return, and the drone disintegrated in a silent flare.

Who's hurt? Who's hurt? Who's hurt? But there was no time for that now. "*Galileo,* what's the status of the limpet?"

"Engines are on standby," *Galileo* said. "Internal atmosphere and gravity normal. Field generator running two-thirds above recommended levels."

She switched her comm to the captain. "Greg, bring us around by that attached ship."

"We can't fire on her," Ted warned.

"Not until she detaches," Elena agreed. "But when she does, she's going to rabbit. She's half spun up already."

His eyes widened. "A ship that small? She'll pull herself to pieces."

"And save us the trouble," she said grimly. "She'll need to pull away from *Exeter* to build the field without the whole thing going up."

"Not a suicide mission, then."

"When have raiders had the nerve for suicide?"

He threw her a nervous grin, and hovered over the tactical readout. "*Galileo,* target that ship. As soon as she's minimum safe distance from *Exeter,* take her out."

"Minimum safe distance is undetermined," *Galileo* said calmly. "Calculation depends on unknowns."

Galileo meant cargo, and possibly fuel levels, not to mention potential booby traps. "Manual targeting, then," Elena instructed, meeting Ted's eyes. "Watch that ship. Watch how it flies. If we assume they want to survive, they won't take a risk. There'll be a tell."

She hoped she was right.

"The limpet is powering up," *Galileo* said helpfully.

"Ted," Elena began, "keep your—"

Before she could finish, all of the remaining drones turned in unison toward *Galileo,* and, like a flock of southbound birds, began flying with determined speed directly toward the ship's midsection.

She swore and fired, Ted next to her doing the same thing, but there were too many of them. *Galileo*'s weapons caught drones, over and over: twelve, eleven, ten . . . but they were firing too slowly, and her mind's eye saw *Exeter*: one second whole and intact, the next second flaming scrap. All those people dead, and here she was now with her own people, just the same . . .

. . . and the great, alien shape of *Orunmila* rose between *Galileo* and the oncoming raiders, so fast that fully five of them immolated themselves against her hull. Elena trusted the PSI ship's pilot to do her job, and kept firing, her eyes flicking among the remaining raiders, watching them flame into nothing one by one.

"The limpet has detached," *Galileo* said.

Four raiders.

Three . . .

Two . . .

One.

"Status of that ship!" she shouted.

"FTL field is powering up. Entrance in three seconds."

It was too close. The risk of discharge against *Exeter*'s remaining power sources was huge. So much for no risk, she thought, furious with her mistake. They would not be in a position to take a solid shot anyway; if they caught the ship as the field was enfolding it, they might all get pulled to pieces.

Galileo spoke again. "*Orunmila* is targeting the raider."

Blindly, Elena opened a channel to the PSI ship. "*Orunmila*, you can't fire on that ship! *Exeter*'s generator battery is on that side, and the field—"

But it was too late.

Elena watched, helpless, her eyes leaving the tactical read-out to look out the window. She saw the small bright projectile speed toward the escaping raider as the raider began to glow that familiar blue-white, the sharp edge of the developing field becoming defined around it. Maybe it would escape, and *Orunmila*'s shot would go wide, dispersing itself harmlessly into the vacuum.

I don't think this is going to be that kind of a day.

The shot connected, and Elena held her breath . . . for nothing. The field folded cleanly around the Syndicate ship, and it vanished.

An unfamiliar voice came over Elena's comm. "*Galileo,* this is *Orunmila.*" The woman's voice was warm and melodic, her accent subtle, all soft consonants and low vowels. "We fired a tracker. Our apologies for alarming you."

Suddenly Elena could breathe again. "Our apologies for doubting you," she replied. "And thank you."

"And you, *Galileo.*" The connection dropped, and it was only in the silence that Elena wondered if that musical-voiced woman had been Greg's irritable Captain Shiang.

Elena flew Greg, Jessica, and three computational experts in a shuttle designed to carry four. Ordinarily Jessica would have made an acidic joke about the close quarters, but Elena's usually irrepressible friend was silent, her normally sharp green eyes watching absently out the window as they approached *Exeter*'s carcass.

Which is what it is, Elena kept telling herself. Despite the oxygen and gravity still intact in pockets. Despite the fires still sputtering out from the shattered systems that still had a power source. A full third of the ship's structure was gone; the rest of her could have been in perfect shape, and Central still would not have elected to repair her. *Exeter* was fifteen years old, near the end of her expected life span; but even a newer ship would have been decommissioned and listed as scrap. Despite their reliance on technology and science, the Corps was not without its institutionalized superstitions, and nobody would ever knowingly serve on a ship that had lost a battle like this one. *Exeter*, just that morning humming and perfect and home to four hundred people, was as dead as if there were nothing left of her at all.

Elena had been bitterly unhappy during her deployment on *Exeter*. Her escape to *Galileo* had felt like fleeing a prison. But she had friends who had stayed behind, had thrived, had loved the place as their home, just as she loved *Galileo*.

She fixed her eyes on the schematic of *Exeter* that the shuttle had superimposed over the front window, looking for an open docking conduit. She avoided the urge to look over at Greg. She knew he was worried about her, but he would never say anything in front of the others. He knew all about her experiences on *Exeter*—well, almost all—and he understood the curious attachment that came with one's first deployment. He would know she was upset, too, know she wanted to run through the ship and find out how many of her friends had died. He would also know she would not indulge the wish, that she would do her duty to the best of her ability. And he would count on her to tell him if she couldn't cope, even knowing what the admission would mean to her.

She was recognizing more and more often lately how well he knew her, despite all the ways he did not know her at all. A year ago, before she had learned she knew nothing of him at all, the thought would have been comforting.

Greg commed Commander Broadmoor shortly before they docked. "Where are we?" he said.

"We've got thirty-seven survivors so far," the security chief told him. "No raiders yet. There are dead spaces between us and Control that we'll need to physically bridge. And the core is silent, which means we're stuck on external comms. The faster we can get past that, the easier it'll be to sweep the ship. Do you have Lock—uh, Commander Lockwood with you? We could use her expertise."

Up until seven months ago, Jessica had reported to Emily Broadmoor, and the security chief still sometimes forgot to address her with her new rank. Elena had been worried, in the beginning, that Emily would resent Jessica's being promoted over her, but as it turned out Commander Broadmoor was pleased. "Amazing hacker," she had confided to Elena, "but as a subordinate? What a pain in the ass."

Elena docked the shuttle, and one by one they lowered themselves into what remained of the CCSS *Exeter*. The corridor was dark apart from the dim light coming from the shuttle, and she pulled a loop of emergency lights from her toolkit, pressing the glowing blue strip to the wall. Here the corridor was untouched, the wall and floors undamaged, the only evidence of injury the stillness and the dark. She could hear the hiss of the environmentals, but none of the mechanical hum of the engines. Which made sense, she realized belatedly: the engines were gone. The environmentals were likely running on batteries, and she struggled to remember how big a bank *Exeter* carried. "The systems won't last more than twelve hours," she told Greg, doing the math in her head. "We need to pull some emergency packs over from *Galileo*."

He commed back to their ship as Emily came around the corner, a dozen infantry flanking her. She gave them a crisp salute, and turned immediately to Jessica. "Think you can get us talking, Commander?" she asked.

Elena and Greg left the technical people to their work and moved to the infantry. These were combat soldiers: broad, well-muscled, and well-armed, and Elena hoped they would be superfluous. Greg picked off half of them and put them under Elena's command. "I need you to get down to engineering," he told them, "or what's left of it. Chief, see what you can find there, if there's anything we can postmortem. And I want to know what that limpet left behind at the entry point. The quicker we can identify the tribe, the quicker we can shut the bastards down." He met her eyes then, for the first time since they had been sitting in his office idly writing reports. Ten minutes ago? Five? "You stay on the line, Chief. Understand?" He didn't wait for her answer, but turned to frown at the infantry. "All of you. Thirty seconds goes by without someone telling me what's going on, I'm assuming an emergency situation and we go after you, weapons hot."

Nods all around. Elena stepped into the group, feeling oddly slight despite being taller than four of them. She knew what worried Greg: *Exeter* had almost certainly been boarded. And without knowing why the raiders had come, they had to assume something—or someone—had been left behind.

CHAPTER 4

Exeter

Guanyin had never been on a Central ship before. Captain Çelik had offered once, when she was just twenty-one and in the early stages of her training with Chanyu. She had desperately wanted to go, but Chanyu had politely vetoed the idea, and Çelik had not asked again. Now, wandering *Exeter*'s dark, unfamiliar corridors, she wished she had pushed the point, had seen what this lifeless, colorless structure had looked like when it was functional. She might have been able to lead the mission without feeling like she was walking through a tomb.

She had eight of her security people with her, including Cali, who was following a resentful three steps behind. Cali had expended a fair amount of energy trying to convince Guanyin to stay behind, beginning with stating her value as the ship's captain, and eventually resorting to referring to her pregnancy. But that was not what had made Guanyin shut her down. When the appeal to Guanyin's maternal instincts had failed, Cali had gone for politics.

"You step on a Corps starship, you're sending a message,"

she had said, in front of the assembled landing team. "You're implying alliance. Commitment. Never mind Captain Çelik—have you thought about what their command chain is going to think?"

This, she thought, *is why you will never be anyone's first officer, Cali.* But even as the rational thought was running through her head, she lost her temper completely. "Who are you to tell me I should leave them to their own devices?" she had snapped. Aida's head had come up when she said it, and she realized he had never really seen her temper before. *A learning experience for him, then.* "They are in trouble, and like any other ship in trouble we will help them. And *we,* Lieutenant, means *me.*"

Cali had backed down. She had, in fact, said nothing at all to Guanyin since then. Guanyin wanted to shake her for her silliness. Protectiveness was one thing, but Guanyin was the ship's captain. If Cali had a problem with an order, the place to bring it up was not in front of the whole crew.

She had spoken briefly to Captain Foster before they arrived. All of his glib self-assurance was gone, replaced by a quiet levelheadedness that she liked much better. She had offered Aida's help in getting *Exeter*'s internal comms systems linked into the external network, and Foster had accepted without qualification. They were headed toward the bow of the ship to deliver Aida to the comms center, dependent on the schematic Captain Foster had sent over, which he had told her would likely be out of date. That should not have surprised her—*Orunmila* was being constantly reconfigured; no map but their own dynamically generated schematic would be accurate more than a few weeks—but she had not, she realized, thought of Corps ships as similarly living, changing habitats.

They came around a corner, and Guanyin caught the sound of distant voices. Instantly she halted the group, and snuffed out the lights; for a moment the absolute darkness blinded her, and then she caught a weak glimmer of light far ahead. She turned her own light on, very low, and began creeping forward again; Cali, cured of her snit in the face of her duty, moved in front of her, hugging the wall as she crept forward on quiet feet. Guanyin gripped her handgun—a lethal but short-range model her arms officer had suggested as useful for avoiding unintended hull breaches—and strained to make out words.

She recognized first that they were speaking Standard. Not entirely a guarantee of safety, but most of the raiders she had run across spoke their own dialects, cobbled together from a half-dozen local languages or more, and communicated in Standard or PSI dialects roughly and with thick accents. On impulse, she commed Captain Foster. "Captain, do you have anyone aft of Control?"

"Not yet, Captain. We've got vacuum between here and there. What have you got?"

She was quiet again, listening. "Possible survivors, I believe. I will let you know." She cut the comm, and nodded to Cali.

They all stopped, and Cali shouted, "Drop your weapons and stand down!"

A flurry of footsteps, the sound of weapons powering up, a series of shouts and murmurs. And then one voice, over the rest: "That's a PSI dialect, you shitheads. Stand the fuck down."

Guanyin placed the voice almost immediately. "It's all right," she told Cali and Aida. "They're *Exeter*." And striding in front of her friend, she rounded the corner.

There were eight of them, all standing on their own two feet, she noted with relief. Despite the stand-down order every one of them still had their hands on the bodies of long pulse rifles— no concerns about hull breaches here. As an afterthought she holstered her own weapon. None of them were in environmental suits, and instinctively she reached up and tugged her hood off. Instantly she was hit with the odor of burning electricals and ozone, combined with the pungent odor of human sweat. *Just like home,* she thought, and approached the tall man at the head of the group.

"Commander Keita, I believe," she said, and held out her hand. "I am Captain Shiang Guanyin, of *Orunmila.*"

She did not think he would remember her. She had met him briefly, two years ago, shortly after he had been promoted, during one of the supply missions they had performed with *Exeter.* He looked older than she remembered, but otherwise she was struck by the same things: his wide, thick-necked build that made him seem even taller than he was, the chiseled, almost cruel handsomeness of his square, dark-skinned face, the strange softness of his brown eyes that made her think of an artist more than a soldier. She recalled his smile, which had moderated his features considerably; he had been quick-witted, she remembered, friendly and professional in a way that had put even Chanyu at ease. She had liked him immediately, and she felt an unexpected wave of relief at seeing his face.

He took her hand, and a shadowy version of that smile passed over his lips. "Good to see you, Captain. And thank you for stepping into the battle when you did. Without you, we'd have been dust before *Galileo* arrived."

"I am grateful we were close," she said sincerely. Beside her, Cali was radiating disapproval. "This is Lieutenant Annenkov, in charge of my security, and Mr. Aida, my comms officer. We are trying to rendezvous with Captain Foster in the bow of the ship." She cast her eye over the rubble beyond his people. "It might be faster for us to go back to the shuttle and fly to the other side."

Keita's lips tightened, making him look grim again. "Captain Çelik is on the other side of that," he explained. "He was heading from Control down to engineering—or what's left of it—to find out what the fuck was going on with our guns, and we took a hit."

All of her relief vanished. "What do you need?"

"Beyond shifting all this debris? Structural support, I think," he said. "There's no vacuum on the other side, but this whole section got hit hard. We can't be sure we won't be pulling the whole ceiling down by digging out."

She could send back for some of her structural engineers, but the thought of the time it would take for them to fly over twisted the knot in her stomach. She commed Captain Foster again. "We have survivors," she told him.

She heard him exhale sharply. "How many?"

"Eight. Commander Keita is here. And . . . they tell me they believe Captain Çelik is behind this debris. Do you have any structural people with you? I suspect there is some urgency here."

"I'm going to connect my engineer," he told her; and then a moment later: "Chief? Where are you?"

A woman's voice, as calm and self-assured as his, responded. "We're about a hundred meters from Control. We haven't found anyone so far."

"Captain Shiang is down there, with some of *Exeter*'s people. They're trying to dig Captain Çelik out of some wreckage. Can you evaluate the structural situation?"

But the woman didn't answer his question. "Who's down there?" she asked, considerably less calm.

Guanyin opened her mouth to answer, but Commander Keita spoke first. "Songbird? Is that you?"

"Dee?" The woman sounded relieved. "My God, Dee. Are you all right?"

"I've got a fucking pulse, at least. Get your ass down here and help us dig the captain out."

"Right." The businesslike tone was back. "Thirty seconds."

"Captain," Guanyin put in, "I suspect there will be more need for structural evaluations. *Exeter* took a great many hits."

"Agreed." There was a hint of weariness in his voice now, as if his chief's urgency had drained him somehow. "Can we pick up the pace on the security sweep?"

"I have another hundred people I can bring over," she told him. "We should be able to clear the ship in thirty minutes." *Faster if you'd let him show me all those years ago,* Guanyin thought bitterly at Chanyu. She could have cleared *Orunmila* in ten minutes, she knew the corridors so well.

"I can send a medic your way as well," Foster offered.

It was on the tip of her tongue to refuse him. "I think that would be wise," she agreed. "I will also bring in a team from *Orunmila*. Captain Çelik will not, I think, be the last casualty we find."

As Cali commed back to *Orunmila,* relaying her instructions, *Galileo*'s people rounded the corner.

There were seven of them, all armed and armored, led by a striking woman with dark hair, as tall as Guanyin was herself.

In an instant of incongruous shock, Guanyin recognized her, and she realized she should have guessed the moment Captain Foster said *Chief*.

When she had finally thought to search the mainstream news outlets for information on Greg Foster, she had been surprised to find he had been part of what had happened in the Fifth Sector last year. The face of Central's involvement had been this woman's: Commander Elena Shaw, a mechanic who had laid her life on the line for love of a retired PSI captain. Which was the popular myth, of course; Guanyin, who had little sentiment around love, suspected the reality of it was both more mundane and more complex. She had seen a brief, much-reproduced vid of Commander Shaw shouting at some police officers, and while the woman had seemed passionate in her pursuit of justice, she had not seemed much like a romantic hero. Foster was much more the stereotype; but his was not the name that had ended up in the spotlight.

Here, her face lit by the cold portable lights, Commander Shaw looked even less the hero: she looked haggard and tired, and her worried expression seemed etched into the lines of her face. But as Guanyin watched, the woman's eyes hit Commander Keita, and her whole demeanor unwound in relief. Oblivious to Guanyin and her people, Shaw shoved her pulse rifle back over her shoulder and flung her arms around Keita. He embraced her in return, and Guanyin saw his eyes squeeze tightly shut. Shaw whispered something unintelligible, and for an instant, Keita's lips widened into something almost like a smile.

Then she pulled away and turned to Guanyin, her expression once again professional. "Captain Shiang?"

Guanyin straightened. "Yes. Commander Shaw, I believe."

Something passed across Commander Shaw's face—chagrin, Guanyin thought, at being recognized. And then her gaze dropped, just for an instant, to Guanyin's midsection. It was hard to tell in the dim light, but Guanyin thought she blushed.

They don't have children on their ships, Chanyu had told her years ago, his voice disapproving. *They are superstitious.* Guanyin had not believed him.

Whatever the reasons for her reaction, Shaw regrouped quickly enough. She held out a hand, aware enough of PSI etiquette not to salute, and Guanyin took it. "We can start shifting anything that's loose," she said, her eyes scanning the wall. "Anything resists, leave it alone for now. Give me a few minutes to analyze the structural damage."

Guanyin left her comm open, then pulled off her gloves, heading for the pile of debris. Behind her, she heard the slither of fabric as Cali and Aida pulled off their hoods and gloves. Cali was moving hesitantly—wary of Guanyin's trusting nature, she suspected; Cali had always had a much larger dose of Chanyu's skepticism—but Aida gamely stripped off his protective gear and lent his shoulder to the group. All the Corps soldiers were twice as wide as he was, but they moved aside and included him without comment. Guanyin moved in next to him, and she saw, out of the corner of her eye, Cali against the opposite wall, reaching for a collapsed beam along with Keita. Guanyin started at the bottom, shifting smaller pieces, while Commander Shaw ran a scanner along the ceiling.

They worked steadily in silence for what must have been a quarter of an hour, and then Commander Shaw took a step back. "Stay to the right," she said. "Greg? Can you add some gravity units to the supply list? Once we're clear we're going to want to shut off *Exeter*'s gravity and work localized. There's more structural damage here than we thought."

The group shifted to one side, and Guanyin began pulling at larger pieces of debris. At one point she found a solid length of steel that, with Aida's help, she was able to slide through the gap. Commander Shaw joined her on the other side, and the three of them levered a massive section of shattered bulkhead out of the way, revealing a meter-wide passage through the wreckage. Aiming her light, Guanyin stared anxiously into the opening beyond.

The gap opened onto the ruins of what had once been a large room, sparsely furnished. The interior walls had fallen in on themselves, table and chairs tossed around the room, in pieces on the floor.

And in one corner, against the wall, half under a massive tangle of sheet metal and electronic equipment, lay a very still Captain Raman Çelik.

Oblivious to the others, Guanyin stepped inside. She heard Commander Shaw's light step behind her as she crouched down next to Çelik's prone form. Focusing her light on him, she could see he was breathing, although his chest rose and fell too quickly, and she took a shaky breath. His appearance was appalling. His usually copper-warm skin had an undertone of gray, as if he had been rubbed with ash, and his right leg, trapped beneath the remains of a wall, was buried almost to his hip. There was a dark spot on his forehead, a mix of blood and bruise. "Xiao," she snapped into her comm, "where are you?"

"Two minutes out, Captain," Xiao said smoothly.

"Our doctor is on his way as well," Foster said in her ear. "He's alive?"

"He is." Guanyin heard Shaw whisper to the others, and they began to clear the debris away from the opening, careful not to disturb the wreckage pinning Çelik down. He began to stir, and Guanyin thought if he could be roused, perhaps his head injury was not as bad as it looked. His eyes still closed, he moved his head, and his eyebrows twitched together. Pain, no doubt. She wondered how much he could feel of what was trapped under wreckage. She wondered how much he remembered of what had happened.

Guanyin crouched down, bringing her face level with his. "Captain Çelik," she said, keeping her tone measured and formal. "Sir, you must wake up."

Çelik coughed, then cleared his throat. He winced, eyes still closed; his senses were coming back. Out of the corner of her eye, Guanyin saw a pair of legs appear, and then Commander Shaw crouched down next to her.

"Captain," Shaw said, her voice firm and sharp.

He opened his eyes. For a moment he looked at Shaw, unfocused, expression troubled and confused. Then he blinked, just once, and his eyes locked on Guanyin; and to her astonishment, he began to laugh.

"Well, fuck me," he said, his voice rough and damaged. "I've been rescued by the child prodigy."

Beside her, she felt Commander Shaw stiffen; but the relief she felt at the gibe was so intense she almost laughed herself. She fought to keep her expression neutral. "Do you know where you are, Captain?" she asked him.

He frowned irritably. "I'm in what's left of Control," he told her, "on my ship, the CCSS *Exeter,* which some execrable bastards who will soon be dying a slow and painful death have blown to pieces. I am forty-six years old, my mother's name is Nadide, and you have five fingers on your left hand. Are you satisfied?"

"For the moment." That was worrying; she would not have expected him to lose composure in front of her.

He blinked again, his eyes back on Shaw. "I know you," he said.

"Yes, sir." Shaw's voice was so composed it might have come from a computer.

"You worked for me."

"Yes, sir."

"Didn't they throw you out?"

"Not yet, sir." There was no mistaking the hint of annoyance in her voice; but Çelik looked satisfied.

He looked past Shaw to take in the rest of the group. "Keita," he said to his second-in-command, "what's our status?"

"We're still doing recon, sir," Keita said. "Twenty-six enemy ships destroyed, one escaped, but Captain Shiang hit it with a tracker before it entered the field."

Çelik's eyes, all their sharp intelligence intact, snapped back to hers. "Can we follow them?"

She shook her head. "It is not an in-field tracker. We must wait until they emerge."

"And if they don't?"

"Then our mission is complete, Captain."

He looked discontented at that. "I'd get up and scan for the damn thing myself," he growled, "but I seem to be immobilized.

55

Any reason you pack of geniuses are standing there staring at me like I'm a garden gnome?"

Under other circumstances, she would have asked him what a garden gnome was. "We are waiting for Doctor Xiao," she told him.

"Ah." No gibes for Xiao, at least. His eyes stole away from hers, returning to Keita. "How many dead?"

"Internal comms are down, sir. We can't be sure. We can't even bring up the duty rosters to validate who was on duty down there."

"Who's on that?"

"*Galileo* has sent their comms people," Keita told him.

"How many do we usually have on duty in the engine room?"

Keita paused. "Eighty-four, sir."

Guanyin did not think any of the others were close enough to hear the hiss of the quick breath Çelik sucked in between his teeth. He turned his attention back to Shaw. "You're still a mechanic, as I recall," he said to her. "Tell me: Is this a rescue mission, or is it salvage?"

Guanyin wondered if the woman would lie to him. "Salvage, sir," she said at last. "In my opinion."

The last Guanyin recognized as a kindness. She thought Çelik would recognize it as such. He ignored the words, and turned back to Guanyin. "Captain, how many of your people have you got on board?"

"We have brought forty so far," she told him. "Captain Foster has a similar number, I believe. I am bringing another hundred to clear the ship, and more when we are certain the raiders are gone."

At that, his eyes went dark and tired, and for the first time in the ten years she had known him, Guanyin thought he looked old. "You won't find anyone," he said. "They got what they came for."

Xiao came in then, quick and businesslike as if she were walking into her own infirmary, and stepped up next to Guanyin. She clucked down at Çelik. "You should have stayed away from the walls," she told him, pulling out her medical kit.

"I'll remember that next time," he replied dryly. "What's under that mess?"

Xiao frowned at the readout. "Your right leg is severed midcalf," she said, as if she was explaining an insect bite, "and your femur has a hairline fracture. You might do better to have it taken off at the hip. It would make for a cleaner joint when they grow you a graft."

Guanyin felt her gut turn over, and she laid a hand instinctively on her round stomach. She had always found Xiao somewhat tastelessly matter-of-fact about these things, but under the circumstances she thought Çelik might appreciate the bluntness. Indeed, a grin stretched across his gray features. "For now," he told Xiao, "I'd just as soon you leave me what parts are still attached."

Xiao heaved a sigh; he was making her life more difficult. She turned to Guanyin, and switched out of Standard. "We'll have to remove the debris quickly so I can cauterize the wound," she said. "He may bleed out if I don't. He might if I do, but it's our only option. And he's likely to pass out either way; the pain will be dreadful, even for a man like him. We'll need to immobilize him."

"Perhaps," Çelik put in, speaking Standard, "one of these brave souls could prop me up."

Guanyin had forgotten he could understand them. She took a step toward him, but next to her, Shaw spoke. "I'll do it, Captain," she said. Guanyin gave her a sharp look, and Commander Shaw must have guessed what she was thinking, because she softened her expression. "I outweigh you by a bit, I think," she added. Guanyin nodded, willing herself to take a step back and trust that others could look after him as well as she could.

They cleared as much of the debris as they could without removing the lifesaving pressure from his wound, and then, at Xiao's nod, Commander Shaw sat on the floor next to Captain Çelik, her back to him, bracing her feet against the wall. "On three," Xiao said in dialect. "One—"

"Wait," Guanyin said. She met Shaw's eyes; it was clear the woman didn't understand Xiao's numbers. "I will count."

She counted down in Standard, and when she finished, Keita—along with Cali, Aida, and the rest of the soldiers—heaved the remaining chunk of metal off of Çelik's trapped leg. The captain made a brief, strangled sound through clenched teeth and then fell silent. Guanyin forced herself to look at his face rather than Xiao's frantic ministrations. He was still gray, and with his eyes closed and his face slack he looked disturbingly vulnerable; but she could see him breathing, his chest rising and falling in shallow gasps. She caught herself breathing with him, and dug her fingernails into her palms, steadying herself. Xiao was a professional, and Çelik was strong, and she would have no more deaths today, thank you very much.

After interminable minutes, Xiao sat back. "That will hold," she said, to Guanyin's look. "The break was fairly clean, and he was burned as well. Without that, he would have bled out, even with the bulkhead cutting off his circulation." She frowned at Çelik's face. "His pressure is still lower than I'd like, but he's better off unconscious right now. We should transport him."

Guanyin nodded, and Xiao commed her team and began packing up her kit. Out of the corner of her eye, Guanyin saw

Shaw looking from Xiao to Çelik and back again; but it was Captain Foster, listening in on the exchange, who spoke in her ear. "With respect, Captain, he should be transferred to *Galileo*."

Guanyin had been expecting this objection. "Do you worry our medical team is inadequate?" she said icily. "Or do you believe we will harm him?"

She braced herself for more of Captain Foster's paternalistic rubbish; but his tone stayed steadily professional, and she thought he had anticipated her objection as well. "He'll want to be with his wounded people, Captain. And most of them will prefer the familiarity of another Corps starship."

Damn. He's right. Guanyin had been thinking about Çelik as an individual, not as a starship captain. That, and her own selfish worries. Chanyu's voice echoed in her ear: *It is how you make apologies that will show what sort of commander you are.* "You are quite right, Captain Foster. Would you object to Doctor Xiao accompanying him?"

Guanyin caught something flicker through Shaw's dark eyes; relief, perhaps. "No objection at all," Captain Foster said. "And if she's willing to stay and help, I'm sure our chief medical officer would be grateful for the extra hands."

Galileo medics arrived, and to their credit they did not blink even once at the mixed crew tending Captain Çelik. Xiao spoke with them, and a few minutes later they carried Çelik, still unconscious, down the corridor on an anti-grav stretcher. Guanyin had to fight the urge to go with them. Perhaps she would find an excuse to visit later; she still had to ask what it was the raiders had taken away.

And she did not think she would feel easy until she heard him snipe at her again.

CHAPTER 5

*C*aptain Shiang is pregnant.

The corridors leading to the gap that had been the engineering section were largely intact, and Elena and her team were able to move quickly. She unrolled light strips methodically onto the walls as they progressed, all of her movements on autopilot. Such an odd thing to fixate on, the PSI captain's round stomach; but with everything she had seen since the battle, that had been the most unexpected.

She felt herself growing angry with Greg. He should have known this; he should have warned her. But of course he would have no idea why such a thing would bother her, and it wasn't like she was prepared to discuss it with him now. Too much had changed between them, and she was still too uncertain of what they had become. She might never find the right time to tell him.

Only once before had she seen a pregnant woman on a starship, and she hadn't known it at the time. For those five days she had looked in the mirror each morning and noticed nothing different. Not until the pregnancy was lost and over had she known it had existed at all.

Stress, she told herself. *This is all distraction. Set it aside, deal with it later. Remember why you're here.*

The damage to *Exeter*'s engineering section had been relatively contained, the ship's modular structure keeping the adjacent corridors almost completely undamaged. They came across one section where the wall had gone missing, exposing the corridor to space; the ship's environmental system had managed to extend oxygen over the breach, although not gravity. Elena let Darrow, the platoon leader, leap over first. The soldier then extended her arm and pulled the others over, one by one, with Elena last.

She wondered if, under ordinary lights and populated by a working crew, she would find the halls familiar. She had spent a year of her life here, the turns and levels becoming second nature. But after almost eight years away, she found most of her memories were emotional: her hideous naiveté when she arrived, so certain that she had found her path, that she would serve out her career on board this ship; her realization that the hazing and the insults and the subtle acts of subversion were not an initiation, that Captain Çelik preferred his people insecure and off-balance. Less than six months into her first, coveted deployment, she had begun to search for a way off the ship.

And then Canberra had happened, and all her priorities had changed.

They walked the perimeter of the wreckage, alert for intruders; but all they found were more of *Exeter*'s crew. They stumbled on nearly three dozen of them, mostly techs and medical staff, holed up in an interior space, shivering in the dark and awaiting news. Greg promised to send a team for them, but Elena traded one of her infantry for a medic and left them behind with some of her temporary lights. Purely psychological, leaving them with one soldier; but in their place, she thought she would want the reminder that they were not in danger anymore. And she was hoping she would need the medic with her team.

But the others they found were beyond help.

They came across a group of six who had all been burned, a quick, white-hot flash leaving them unrecognizable. Elena wanted to scan them herself, wanting to know if she recognized a name; but she realized, as *Exeter*'s medic knelt before them, that they were not her dead. She watched as he slipped a gloved hand behind their burn-contorted necks to scan their ident chips. There was nothing in the charred flesh, in the holes where the eyes had evaporated, that the medic could have recognized.

"We'll collect them," he asked her, rising to his feet, "won't we?"

He was a little shorter than she was, and roughly the same age. She wondered if her eyes, like his, looked centuries old.

"All of them," she told him. He nodded, and they moved on.

The limpet had left a shuttle-sized hole in the wall of the corridor. *Exeter*'s automated system had done a good job of sealing out the vacuum, but managing a space that size would drain the batteries far too quickly. "Captain," she said, "we're going to want generators. A lot of them. It's going to take some time to seal this." Regardless of what she had told Çelik, she wasn't ready yet to give the ship up as lost.

There was a pause on the comm, and she tensed. "Shimada is pulling some equipment together," he said. "I'll have him add generators to the list."

"Is there a problem?"

"Not on an open comm, Commander."

Her first response was annoyance—*why does he always pull rank when I ask something important?*—and then she realized what he was saying: he had received confirmation from the Admiralty. They would not be sealing the breach. Her list of damaged equipment would be listed as salvage, and *Exeter* would be scrapped. It would have been obvious to anyone who was thinking clearly, but now was not the time to say it out loud.

"*Exeter* can hold the vacuum out for a few hours yet," she told him. Without waiting for him to give the order, she turned to Darrow. "I'm heading out. Sweep this area, and get any survivors behind the central bulkhead. Once we're sure it's clear, we can expose this section."

If Darrow had put together the implications, she kept her reaction to herself. She nodded to Elena, and led the rest of the infantry down the hall toward the brig.

Elena checked the seals of her environmental suit, and stepped forward to the blown-out hole. She could see vestiges of quick-drying foam sealant around the torn metal edges of the opening. It would have been easy enough to modify a standard consumer-model shuttle to secrete foam on impact; it would be a simple inversion of a land-model safety feature. Easy enough—low-tech, even—to make the shuttle a missile to punch through an exposed interior wall and create an airtight seal.

Somewhat less refined than the fleet of advanced fighter drones, but much more in keeping with the inept piloting of the drone that had hit the ship.

She attached her tether to the interior wall and stepped

through the hole, feeling a familiar lurch as she shifted out of the gravity field, and a strange sense of claustrophobia as her suit's interior began generating its own heat. Keeping one hand on the edge of the blown-out opening, she looked up and down the ship's exterior.

From a distance, she had seen *Exeter*'s build structure, all arched ribs and level separators at right angles. Up close it was chaos: scrap metal, polymers, and fiber, burned and torn as if some massive animal had pulled it apart in a rage. She reached out and tugged at a line; it came loose, and when she pinched it between her fingers it turned to dust.

Too much heat, she thought. "This is more than just a short-range generator explosion," she told Greg.

"Can you identify it?"

She pushed off along the hull toward another cluster of fiber. "I expect so. Standard incendiaries will leave residue." She took a handful of lines in her fist and tugged experimentally; these were less decayed. She pulled more steadily, and they came away from the hull. "If the drone had some kind of hybrid battery—*son of a bitch*!"

Reflexively she released her clutch of fibers and pushed away from the hull. What she had pulled away from the interior was a body, bloated and unrecognizable, its exterior covered in a thin sheen of ice. Regrouping, she tugged on her tether and brought herself closer to it, closing her hand around its arm to keep it from drifting free.

"Chief?" She became aware that Greg had been calling her name repeatedly.

"Sorry, sir," she said, as steadily as she could. "I believe I've run across one of the enemy."

Up close she could make out more details. The clothing it was wearing was dark brown, thick and sturdy cloth, but nothing like an environmental suit. Not a Corps uniform, which meant it was one of the raiders. Some kind of infiltrator caught in the blast? Piloting one of the ships she had thought was a drone? She tugged him forward, examining the alcove she had pulled him out of. She could see nests of fibers and polymer sheets moved to one side. The body had been shoved there after the blast. And from the look of the remains . . . he had been alive when he had been exposed to the vacuum.

She hooked her arm through his rigid elbow and pulled on her tether, hauling herself back through the opening. The abrupt gravity yanked the body from her grip, and she caught at him, unable to prevent him from dropping, stiff and undignified, to the floor. She stepped over him, leaning against the wall.

"I'm not a medic, but it sure looks like death by decompression," she told Greg. "If he hasn't got an ident chip, we're going to have a hell of a time getting a name."

"Don't go back out there alone, Chief," he said. "That's an order."

An emotional one, she thought, then looked down at the corpse. Inhuman, at this stage, distorted and hideous.

Murderer.

"Yes, sir," she acknowledged. She was far too close to all of this, and Greg knew it, too.

"Chief?" Darrow said. "You inside?"

"Yes. Where are you?"

"Aft. By the brig. We found two more bodies, ma'am, one raider, and one of *Exeter*'s people, but we've got one alive.

65

One of ours. Looks like he was guarding the brig, but it's been blasted open."

She began heading down the hallway. "Had it been inhabited?"

"Hard to tell, and the officer isn't talking yet."

She rounded the corner, and came across the raider first. Despite being free of the ravages of the vacuum, he was, in his brown uniform, as nondescript as the other one. She put his age at something between thirty and forty, but his slack skin was already sinking into his cheekbones. He could have been much younger. His features were neutral to the point of blandness: regular, symmetrical, echoes of a dozen different ethnicities easily projected onto his bone structure. She wondered if he'd had himself altered to be ordinary, or if his ability to blend in had led him to a life of theft and rootlessness.

No way to ask him now.

He had taken a shot directly in the sternum, and his chest had collapsed with the impact. She wondered if it had been a quick death, if he had blacked out and felt no pain. She hoped not.

She stepped over him to the other body, sprawled out on the deck, staring sightlessly upward, her unlined face forever stilled. *Young. Maybe new. Maybe not even out here a year.* This was not what she would have hoped for when she chose her deployment, the ship on which she would live her entire life.

Beyond her, Elena saw Darrow and the medic crouched before another soldier, slumped against the wall. Elena knelt down with the others. He was a sturdily built man around her own age, breathing but unconscious; the medic was administering something with a dermal patch.

The man shifted and his eyelids fluttered, and she felt her

heart thumping against her chest. She took a quick look at his uniform. "Lieutenant. Can you hear me? Open your eyes if you can hear me."

A small sound pushed its way through his lips. If the ship had not been so cavernously silent, she would not have heard him.

"Come on," she entreated. Cautiously she extended a hand and touched his arm; he shifted again.

". . . sorry . . ." he murmured. His eyes opened, staring at nothing.

"Lieutenant, do you know where you are?"

"Sydney," he said. His unfocused gaze had wandered to the dead woman.

"Is that her name?"

He swallowed. "Dead now."

"I know, Lieutenant. I'm sorry."

He did not respond, just kept his eyes focused over her shoulder. "Sorry," he said again; and as she watched, his eyes grew damp.

She rubbed his arm, helpless. "Just hang on. Help is coming."

He shook his head. "No help."

We came as fast as we could, she thought; but that was her excuse, and it gave him nothing. She kept her hand on his arm, hoping the contact would give him something to focus on, a reason to fight back.

"Who is it?"

Greg's voice in her ear, normal and familiar. The medic responded. "Lieutenant Farias," he said. "He took plasma fire. I think it was either him or Sydney who took out the raider."

"Ask him if the raider was the one in the brig," Greg said.

The medic gave Elena a look, but shifted to one side so she could question the injured man. "Lieutenant Farias, were you and Sydney on duty? Was there a raider in your brig?"

But he had started closing his eyes again, and she could not be sure he had understood her. "No help," he said again. "I'm sorry, Sydney." And he fell unconscious once more.

Elena stood and moved away, letting the medic tend to him. She could not see where he had been shot, and she wondered instead if he had been beaten, if he had taken a blow to the head. "Did you get that?" she asked Greg.

"Not much to get," he observed. "Will he live?"

Elena, who had not had the heart for such bluntness, looked at the medic, who nodded. "Can't say for sure," he equivocated aloud. "The concussion is pretty bad, but he's got no fractures. As long as he doesn't fall into a coma, he should recover in a few days."

"Not sooner?" Greg asked.

The medic's lips thinned with disapproval. "You want guarantees, Captain, you won't get them from me," he said shortly.

Greg was silent for a moment. "Chief, on a private line, please." When she changed over, he said, "Are you okay there?"

She knew what he meant. "I'm better off here than home chewing on it," she replied. "I want to get through this debris, and bring home some evidence."

It was Greg's turn to be silent, and she could see his face in her mind, knowing something was going on with her, uncertain of what he should do about it. *Kindness.* So often kindness from him, these days. She wished she could trust it.

In the end, he let it go. "All right, Chief," he told her. "Carry on."

She waited until they came to carry the injured lieutenant away, and then she reattached her tether and went back outside alone.

CHAPTER 6

"Ted," Jessica asked, "are you afraid of the dark?"

She was kneeling on the floor, running her magnetic scanner over *Exeter*'s data core, looking for echoes of information. The explosion that had taken out three levels and the entire engine room had sent a shock of heat and current through the system that had effectively shut it down, leaving nothing but the ship's autonomic functions in place. There was no dynamic data scanning, no seeking, no sorting; she had to read the raw data off the core and feed it to *Galileo* for analysis. Next to her, Emily Broadmoor, her old boss and a damn good hacker in her own right, had nearly finished patching through the base comm system, so at least *Exeter*'s internal messaging system would work, after a fashion. With the ship's brain offline, though, routing would be crude, there would be no records of anything, and the crew would have to route through *Galileo* for any kind of external services. Stone Age tech.

"I'm not afraid of anything," Ted's voice said in her ear.

She was transferring the echoes to Ted on *Galileo*, who was matching them up with *Exeter*'s last known data dump. With some luck, he would be able to help her pinpoint the weapons data, to see if there had been a malfunction. Greg had been talking about it as a given, but it would be a double-edged sword if she found something. Evidence of malfunction would exonerate deceased gunners; but it would open up an avenue none of them wanted to have to explore.

"That's bullshit," she retorted. She frowned at her scanner and slowed it down; the information was patchy here, and she did not want to miss any. *God, this job is going to take days.* "You're afraid of the captain."

"A healthy respect for authority isn't fear. That bit there, Jess—stop for a second."

She sat while he waited for *Galileo* to chew on the data. "I was always afraid of the dark," she confessed.

"You picked the wrong career," he said. "Okay, keep going."

"What was that?"

"Battery information, about three days old. We're getting closer."

Gently she nudged the scanner forward. "We'd get these long winter nights at home," she went on. "Dark twice as long as it was light. When I was little, I figured if someone got sick in the daytime, they might live; but if they got sick at night, they'd never recover."

"Have you ever considered therapy, Jess?"

"If you looked at the statistics," she reasoned, "more people got sick at night just because the nights were longer, so more of them died. The correlation was meaningless, of course; but I was a kid."

He paused, catching on. "You still superstitious?"

"I want," she told him, carefully teasing apart a particularly dense chunk of information, "to be back home in my room with the lights on, getting very drunk with someone lovely and very, very alive." She sat back, rubbing her eyes. "You should see this place, Ted. It's a crypt."

"That's one way of looking at it."

"Nearly a hundred dead, at least. How else can you look at it?"

"Like the ones who survived were pretty damn lucky. What do you think would have happened if that PSI ship had been further out?"

She thought back to the battle, watching the schematic at Greg's side, hoping he could not see her shaking. He had appeared level and composed through the whole thing. She wondered if that was something that could be learned, or if he just went cold in a crisis—if that was something unique to him. Jessica never went cold in a crisis. "I don't ever want to be captain, Ted," she said.

Ted was apparently accustomed to her random changes of subject. "Given how bad he is at staying out of trouble, you may have a problem."

"That was only once."

"And you had to save his ass. And then he promoted you."

"He's a bastard."

"You're the one who works with him all day; you'd know better than I would." He made a sound. "That's it, Jess. Weapons systems. Get me everything you can preserve, as dense as you can get it."

She spent the next half hour sorting through the magnetic shadows and memory imprints of the blocks Ted specified. She did not even have to lay it all out sequentially to see the pattern:

the excision of information, the lobotomizing of the weapons systems' connection to the ship's larger mind. And at the end of it, fragments of something else: a personal bio key, obscuring a shattered block of indecipherable commands *Exeter* had not survived to execute.

This was careful damage, done with thought, entirely different from the randomized destruction of heat and pulse waves. And it had been done much earlier.

"What do you think, Ted?" she asked. "Sixteen hours?"

"No more than seventeen, for sure," he replied. "Didn't their flight plan have them in the field seventeen hours ago?"

Despite its size, *Exeter*'s massive stellar batteries ensured it could travel for long stretches in the field. Elena had told her once, but Jessica could not remember. "What's she rated for?" she asked Ted.

"Nineteen hours, but she's done twenty-one without turning a hair," he recalled. "*Shit*, Jess."

Ted was not one to curse, but this time she was not surprised. The implication was clear to her as well. "Had to be someone on board."

"What about a delayed payload? Could someone have coded something like this?"

She frowned at the system. "Possibly," she allowed. "I'll have to take a closer look. But I don't think so, Ted. The timing would have had to be just right, or someone would have discovered it as part of a maintenance run or a drill. You don't just hack a payload into a Central starship. It'd be hard even for me."

He was quiet for a moment. "But someone did. And people died, Jess. Someone did this, and did it on purpose. Someone they *knew*."

She thought back over her career, over her schooling, over her early life on a planet where fully half of the children she knew had died before the age of fourteen. "Knowing someone," she told him, "doesn't mean they won't fuck you over."

Greg asked the same question Ted had. "How much skill would it take to seed something like this to execute later?"

She was leaning against the wall, eyes closed, head aching from staring at small pieces of data for hours. Emily had brought the emergency lights online, and they had given Jessica some energy, but they could not erase eye strain. "Given enough prep time," she said, "I might be able to code something, although I don't think I'd bet my life—let alone my career—on the thing working. The Admiralty might have someone, though." She thought of Shadow Ops, but did not bother reminding him of the skillsets present in that organization.

He knew more of those details than she did.

"How hard would it be for someone to do it in person?"

"Not hard. They'd need command codes and a little knowledge of weapons systems, but that's it."

He paused, and she imagined him rubbing his eyes. *He is going to be very nearsighted someday.* "Have you got enough left to find out whose command code was used?"

At last, an easy answer—but not one she wanted to give him. "No, sir. All the analytical memory is gone. Volatile storage doesn't even have echoes left. I found a partial bio key that was probably intended to wipe the evidence after the fact, but there's not enough to attempt a match." She fought a wave of depression. "We can't find out, sir. The information is just not there."

Another pause, then: "Okay." He had regrouped, just in those few seconds. "I want you back on *Galileo*. Get in touch with the Admiralty—Herrod, if you can get him, but otherwise anyone but Waris—and get this area quarantined. We'll need another ship for the wounded, but I want it clear this is a crime scene. Get him to agree to that."

"You think he will?"

"If he doesn't," Greg said grimly, "that tells us something right there. After you've talked to him, get a crew over here to finish the core analysis."

She felt a bubble of indignation. "Sir—" she began.

"Jessica." His voice was gentle, the way it got when he was about to tell her she was an idiot. "Is this job so delicate that you're the only one who can do it?"

"Are you telling me I'm replaceable?"

"I'm telling you you're the second-in-command, and you need to delegate, because you're not at *all* replaceable and right now I need you. Pick some people you trust, and get them on the job."

"I don't trust anyone." That wasn't precisely true. Emily had some damn good crypto people. None as good as Jessica was, but hadn't she just been thinking that what this job needed most was patience? "It feels wrong, sir," she confessed, "passing this off on someone else."

"I know." And that, of course, was the worst part: he did. "But right now that's your duty, Commander. We have good people. Trust them to do their jobs."

Within a few minutes, she was able to find a space on a shuttle back to *Galileo,* and she sat in silence next to a half dozen of *Exeter*'s crew, all with minor abrasions, all somber and still.

None of them seemed inclined to look at her, and she felt that strange indignation again. *Who am I to be heading home, to my bright room and my well-lit corridors and all the people I love? Why do I deserve that peace, when these people have lost everything in the space of a few minutes?* Because they had to know they would never be going back to *Exeter*. She wondered if they would have the chance to retrieve their possessions, and she resolved, if she had the power, to make sure they were given the time.

She wanted to talk to Elena. Elena always let her rant, and never tried to slow her down or tell her she was being silly. Elena was one of a very few people who had ever seen her cry. But Elena would be handling her own raft of shit right now—or, rather, avoiding it. She was just like Greg that way: she went stony, handling what was in front of her, all emotion shoved aside. But unlike Greg, the emotion eventually caught up with her, and she would flame out in a burst of grief and rage, days, sometimes weeks later.

Greg swallowed everything. Elena held on until she flew apart. As much as Jessica admired them both, neither was teaching a lesson she wanted to learn.

CHAPTER 7

Galileo

Nearly seven hours later, Elena finally flew home.

It had occurred to her, during the fifth hour she was floating outside going over the burned-out remains of *Exeter*'s decking, that she ought to pass the task off to someone else. Someone uninvolved, who had not been awake for twenty-five hours. But there was something in her that wanted the worst of it laid out starkly before her, so she could get on with the anger and grief and move beyond it. She hoped if she stared point-blank at the horror long enough, she could jolt her way past the leaden numbness in her stomach.

Everyone on the shuttle with her was ambulatory, the worst of the casualties having been moved hours earlier, and once she landed she left them to disembark on their own. She had it in her mind to head for her room and a long hot shower, but the halls were full of strangers. *Exeter*'s crew. Based on the crowds, possibly all of them. *Cassia* was still hours off, and she suspected her room, along with most of the rooms on *Galileo*, had been commandeered to be used as temporary quarters.

Nowhere to be alone, then. Of course, given her mood, perhaps that wasn't so bad.

The pub was both overcrowded and more subdued than she was used to seeing it. All the tables were filled, and soldiers stood in groups, drinks in hand, some talking in low voices, others just looking around or staring down at their feet. The pub's wide windows faced into the stars, the view uninterrupted by planets, space stations, or other ships. Greg would have done that deliberately: positioned them so the most popular common space on the ship would not be overlooking the wreck. He was always so careful about such things. How many hours since she had spoken to him? She could not remember. She could not remember much of the day, now that she was thinking of it. That numbness, more familiar than it should be.

God, I need sleep.

Instead she scrounged a cup of tea from the bar and wandered toward the windows, letting her eyes rest on the stars, willing the tension out of her body, trying to relax, muscle by muscle. But the stars were letting her down: all she could see, every time she blinked, was burned corpses, disintegrating filament, and the last Syndicate ship escaping into the dark. She closed her eyes, and she saw the dead woman again, and in her ear Farias whispered, "No help . . ."

"Songbird?"

That familiar voice, so hesitant. For a moment she felt something that was not despair. She opened her eyes and turned to face him. "Dee," she said, and almost smiled.

Even while shifting debris with him on *Exeter,* she had noticed how little he had changed over the years, although she supposed her memory was selective. Apart from his formerly shaved head—now covered in half of a tight-curled centimeter of black hair—and the utter exhaustion on his face, he could still have passed for twenty-six. His face was unlined and un-scarred, despite his battle experience, and his broad shoulders were still well-defined enough to show through his thick uniform shirt. She remembered wondering, when she had first met him, if any of it was fat; and then she had seen him training, half-dressed, his dark skin stretched over nothing but muscle and sinew. She remembered how his skin felt under her hands as she traced those muscles with her palm: smooth and cool, except when he woke at night, when it felt clammy, her palms sticking as she tried to soothe his nerves. The nightmares had lessened before she left, but they had not disappeared, and she wondered if he still had them.

She did.

Part of her wanted to embrace him again, just to prove to herself that he really was all right; but he was not on his own. Jimmy Youda stood next to him, looking less exhausted, but far more drunk. She gave him a nod, and a smile, and he waved his glass blearily at her. Uninjured, at least; she wondered where he had been during the battle.

He had aged less gracefully than Dee, although he had started out more handsome: lean, chiseled, striking—almost as head-turning as Greg, although without the sharp wit in his eyes. But he had more lines on his face than she remembered, more than men she knew who were older, and she wondered how his career had gone after she left. Dee had become second-in-command; not the youngest in the fleet, but still recognized earlier than most. Jimmy had acquired his M.D., and was a lieutenant commander on *Exeter*'s medical team. An average promotion run: not exceptional, but certainly nothing to be ashamed of.

He's in charge of Exeter's *medical team now,* she thought, remembering the quick look she'd had at the casualty list.

Jimmy had always handled his drinking impressively well, she recalled; anesthetizing himself at night seemed to leave him fit for duty during the day. She suspected he was close to numb by now. She couldn't blame him. If she were capable of drinking, she would have taken the same approach. Of course Jimmy always got angry, she recalled, before the anesthetic took proper effect. On this day she was not inclined to blame him. "How are you holding up?" she asked him.

Jimmy snorted something that sounded like a laugh, and stared into his glass. "Is that a joke?" he asked, tossing back the remains of the drink.

"No," she said, "but that sounds like an answer."

His eyes shot into hers, angry and resentful. "Still judging, I see."

"Come on, Youda," Dee said.

"But that was always your thing, wasn't it?" Jimmy went on, as if Dee had said nothing. "Tell us all what we should feel. How we should handle it. You going to tell me how I should handle *this*?"

His rage was palpable, and it felt strangely personal. "I'm not going to tell you anything," she replied, as gently as she could. Why would she try to tell anyone how to process something like this?

Jimmy fell silent, mollified, and Dee risked looking away from him. "I heard you got Farias out of the brig alive. Have you talked to him yet?"

She shook her head. "I just got back." And she suspected it would be some time before the man would be ready to talk to anyone. Still, while she had Dee's attention, she risked doing some fishing. "Dee, the way we found him—was there someone in your brig when you were attacked?"

"Why do you want to know?" Jimmy asked her. His tone was just short of being openly hostile, and she remembered, then, how he had behaved after Canberra, where they had lost only one man. Jimmy's usual, somewhat forced charm had disintegrated into prickly hostility, the reality of what they had been through removing most of his desire to get along with anyone. Canberra had knocked his legs out from under him; she could only guess what this incident had done.

She decided to be as honest as she could. "I was wondering about the dead raider I found outside," she said. "If he was the prisoner. If they might have been trying to break him out."

"Did a pretty shitty job of it if they were, didn't they?"

Jimmy had always been a good medic, and she had no doubt he was now a good doctor; but when he wasn't dealing with a patient, he could be tiresomely cynical. "Actually," she pushed, "it occurred to me they were executing him. It's possible he got caught in that alcove by accident, but I doubt it."

She had expected curiosity at that remark, or even defensiveness. Instead, Dee and Jimmy exchanged a quick glance, and she brought her chin up. "What is it?" she asked.

Dee said, "Nothing," just as Jimmy said, "None of your business, Shaw."

Shit. Like hell it's none of my business. "You know something." Her eyes went to Dee, who was looking away. "Both of you."

"We know it was a *waste*," Jimmy snapped.

"Shut up," Dee hissed at him, and shot her an apologetic glance. "He's drunk," he explained.

"Yeah, but *he's* talking to me," she said, turning back to Jimmy. "What was a waste?"

"He shouldn't even have been prosecuted, if you ask me," Jimmy declared, his thick tongue loosened. "He was following orders. He was a *patriot*."

Elena began to wonder how long he had been drinking. "The raider was a patriot? What are you talking about?"

Jimmy ignored her interruption. "They hung him out to dry because they didn't need him anymore, thanks to you. You never could mind your own fucking business, Shaw."

"Shut the fuck up, Youda. That's an order," Dee snapped.

"Fuck you, Keita. I'm the fucking chief of medicine now. You have no authority over med."

Elena ignored their squabble, her head spinning with blind confusion. "*My fault?* How could an attack in the Third Sector be my fault?"

"Youda, goddammit, I swear—"

"We wouldn't have been carrying him if you hadn't made yourself out to be a fucking *hero*," Jimmy yelled at Elena, "stopping a fucking war with some backwater pirates at the expense of every other fucking thing that mattered!"

And it came to her then, with ice-cold certainty, freezing away all of her exhaustion. His court-martial, unlike hers and Greg's, had been secret, despite the fact that his crime had been far more central to everything that had happened last year; and his punishment had lacked any mercy at all.

"MacBride. You were carrying Niall MacBride."

"*Were* being the operative word," Jimmy snarled, raising a mock toast.

She turned to Dee, dumbfounded. His face was shuttered. "Don't ask me," he warned her. "I'm under orders, Songbird, and I outrank you."

She felt as if someone had wrapped a fist around her stomach and twisted. Niall MacBride, court-martialed alongside her and Greg, but for vastly different charges: incitement to war. Although, from Jimmy's response, it seemed rumors of the truth were rampant. MacBride had been found guilty—quietly—and sentenced discreetly. And now, apparently, he had been sprung out of prison, the cost a mere ninety-seven trained Corps soldiers, and one starship.

"I think," she told Dee, "we need to talk to Captain Foster."

CHAPTER 8

Orunmila

All the way back to *Orunmila,* Guanyin stayed silent, listening to the others talking in subdued voices about what they had seen. She stared out the window as her ship, intact and safe, grew larger in the shuttle's front window. The last few hours had been a blur of faces, some injured, some panicked, all stunned, as *Exeter*'s surviving crew members had regrouped and recognized what had happened to their home. To her consternation she found herself cast in the role of savior, and more than once was subjected to a grateful and rather desperate embrace. One man, some years older than she was, had started to weep, and she had held him as gently as she could until Keita's people brought in a medic. Keita extracted the man from her arms with more compassion than she would have credited him with, and traveled with him back to *Galileo* with the other wounded.

She had thought Commander Shaw's assessment had been premature, but based on what she had overheard, the crew fully expected that *Exeter* was going to be scrapped. Another incomprehensible Central custom. Apart from the destroyed engine room, the ship had sustained very little damage. Guanyin thought her own people could have repaired it within two months, given the parts. But there was more to it than that, she learned as she absorbed snatches of conversation: it seemed Central was inclined to quietly retire ships that had suffered such devastating damage. Instead of harvesting older ships to repair *Exeter*, *Exeter* herself would be parted out and recycled; and Captain Çelik, regardless of how well he recovered, would likely be shuffled off to some sort of bureaucratic position.

And that, she thought, as Cali maneuvered the shuttle into *Orunmila*'s fore hangar, would be the end of him.

She unclipped her harness and rose absently to her feet, hanging on to the hand grip toward the ceiling. It was none of her business how they dealt with their officers. After ten years as second-in-command and six months as captain, she should have learned how to let go of anger over things she could not change. At least this time she could funnel it into something useful.

Yunru was waiting for her on the tarmac, his arms full of their two-year-old daughter. Lin's dark head lay against his shoulder, her round arms locked around his neck. Even from a distance Guanyin could see the child frowning. She quickened her step, leaving Cali behind.

"What is it, my little gumdrop?" she asked as she approached.

Lin turned and held out her arms, her face dissolving. Guanyin met Yunru's eyes as she relieved him of his burden, bouncing Lin gently and rubbing her back as she snuffled noisily into Guanyin's neck.

"She wanted to wait up for you," he said. "I told her no. She has been objecting for the last three hours."

Overtired and unhappy, just like Mama, Guanyin thought. "Lin, my love, I miss you, too. But you must sleep, dear. And you must listen to what your father tells you."

Still carrying Lin, she fell into step with Yunru. "I'll hang on to her if you like," she said. "You get some sleep."

He gave her a curious look. "You look like you need it more than I do."

"I may," she conceded, "but I'm too furious at the moment to close my eyes. And I have to make a comm."

There was a twinkle of amusement in his eyes. "Don't curse in front of her, okay? She's too good a mimic."

"It won't matter," she said, giving him a smile. "I'll be speaking Standard."

He leaned over to rub Lin briefly on the back. Lin made an angry sound of objection, and nestled herself more firmly against Guanyin's neck. Guanyin would have chided her, but Yunru just smiled and headed back to the suite they shared with the children.

By the time Guanyin reached her office Lin had stopped crying, and grown drowsy against Guanyin's shoulder. She shifted the little girl as she sat, and took a few minutes to whisper to her gently until she fell asleep. It was a bad habit to instill, she knew, letting the child doze off in her arms; but soon enough Lin would be too old for it. Cali always told her she was worse with the children than she was with Samedi. Which was, Guanyin reflected, perfectly true, and one maternal luxury she never intended to give up.

When she placed the comm to *Galileo,* she kept the vid turned off.

They had an officer filtering all incoming messages. He

85

sounded young, and appropriately intimidated when she identified herself, and she felt a little better. By the time Captain Foster came on the line, she had resurrected all of her outrage.

"Captain Shiang," he began, in that measured, polite tone of his, "on behalf of Central, I wanted to thank you for coming to *Exeter*'s aid. She would not have survived without your assistance."

Chanyu had spent a lot of time teaching her manners. She had never much cared for them.

"From what I have heard said," she told him, "*Exeter* did not, in fact, survive. Is my understanding correct?"

A pause on the line. "Yes," he said, and she was surprised at his candor. "But that doesn't change the fact that three hundred people are alive now who would not have been if they'd had to wait for us."

"PSI are not so cynical as you are, Captain Foster." Her rage felt cold; she wanted him to feel cold as well. "We do not let any ship fight off such an attack alone when we are able to help. We would even help *Galileo,* if it came to that. But now that the crisis is finished, we must leave you."

"Captain Shiang," he said, "if this is because of our earlier exchange—"

"It is not." Full points, though, she had to admit, for his being willing to shoulder the blame. She had read that he was an honorable man. It was the only consistent thing in all of the reports of him she had found. "Captain Foster, do you know how many people I have on my ship?"

"Eight hundred," he replied. He sounded resigned, and she wondered if he already knew what she was going to say.

"And are you aware that it is my personal responsibility to look after each one of those people?"

"I believe our respective services view the role similarly, Captain."

Do not try to ally yourself with me. "I will help any ship in distress, Captain, but I will not give assistance to an organization that has chosen to use subterfuge to obtain our trust, that has deliberately concealed intelligence, and that allowed us to enter a volatile situation with insufficient understanding."

There was silence on the line again, and this time she waited for him. But when he spoke, he sounded genuinely confused. "What are you talking about?"

She felt a sudden desire to shout at him. Captain Çelik would not have bothered pretending; he would have told her flat-out that he had lied to her—or better yet, he would have been up front to begin with. "Do not tell me that this attack was not anticipated," she continued over his objection. "You assign an additional Corps warship to this area, just before an organized Syndicate raider attack? On a scale that has not been seen in this sector in twenty years? Why is it that we were closer to *Exeter* than you were, Captain? Why was it that my people were first in the line of fire?"

"*Exeter* was first in the line of fire, Captain Shiang."

"I am not interested in your self-righteousness," she told him coldly. "I am not comming you to listen to more prevarication. I am comming you to let you know that once we have a tracker report from the escaped raider, we will be leaving this area, and you may pursue the criminal on your own."

There was a brief silence. "You're really going to ignore what happened here?"

Let him think she was foolish enough to let an organized attack pass without investigation. "Once we have given you the raider's location, we have no intention of engaging in further contact with you or your ship."

"Is that just *Galileo,* or Central in general?" She could not be certain, but she thought she caught a note of humorless dryness in his tone.

"I will accept reports on Captain Çelik's condition," she told him, without answering his question. "Should you find the accused raider and exact your *justice,* we will hear of it without your help."

More silence. "How many Central starships have you dealt with, besides *Exeter*?" he asked.

Damned if she was going to tell him that. "Raiders rarely have a range of more than twelve hours," she said. "I am expecting a signal before that time has expired. When we receive the information, we will transmit it to your ship, and our interaction will be concluded. Am I making myself understood?"

"Very clearly, Captain Shiang."

"And please tell your Admiralty," she added, "that they need expend no more energy trying to ease our concerns about their troop buildup here. PSI's allegiance is to each other. We will continue to battle the Syndicates and their raiding parties as we always have—by ourselves. Your allies are your own problem. Good evening, Captain Foster."

She cut him off and looked down to find Lin staring at her, her dark eyes wide open.

"I didn't mean to wake you, dear," she said gently.

Lin blinked. "Samedi?" she asked.

Guanyin carried the little girl through the interior door into her quarters. On the other side the rest of her children slept, and one room beyond that, Yunru was, with any luck, getting some hard-earned rest. Guanyin felt immeasurably better having had her say; she thought her gnawing worry over Çelik might settle enough for her to get some sleep herself.

Samedi, who had been dozing on the couch, looked up when she came in. She laid Lin gently next to him and went for a blanket. When she came back, the ordinarily irrepressible puppy had curled up against the little girl, who had hooked an arm around his neck. *I should let her train Samedi,* Guanyin reflected. *He is certainly more mindful of her than he is of me.*

She shook out the blanket and pulled it over the pair, then tugged off her own uniform to get ready for bed.

CHAPTER 9

Galileo

Raman Çelik was well-known as a pragmatic man. He always saw the reality of what was before him, with all its attendant possibility and detail, and had a knack for choosing the most efficient solution to any problem. He could fix a generator or defuse a bar fight, and he always knew when it was time to cut his losses and move on. For years people had said that Captain Çelik could turn straw into gold—or bullshit into steak. He found those descriptions tiresome. People who said such things about him tended to have slow minds and no imagination, and he almost always ignored them.

His own imagination was failing him at the moment. He supposed it was medication-induced grogginess. He had known when he woke, even with his eyes closed, that he was not on *Exeter*. The room smelled wrong. Even in the antiseptic confines of her infirmary—and his nose told him he was in *someone's* infirmary—he knew the odors of his ship.

The infirmary was on her starboard side, opposite the engine room. It would still be intact.

The engine room.

What had they been doing? His gunners were in the engine room. They had fired, and they had missed, but why? Something was wrong. They were all dead, of course, but there was something else. His own survival, perhaps. With his ship gutshot, he should not be here. Duty dictated that he go down with her. Perhaps he had, and this sterile, odd-smelling infirmary was some sort of near-death hallucination.

He opened his eyes and squinted into the bright light of the ceiling. "Fucking hell," he croaked, forcing his voice through his dry throat, "turn down the fucking lights."

A man's deep voice said something unintelligible, and the light dimmed, but not enough. A moment later, a head and shoulders appeared in his line of sight, silhouetted by the illuminated ceiling. "How are you feeling, Captain Çelik?"

Should he know the voice? "That's a stupid fucking question," he said. He had been drugged. He had passed out from pain and blood loss. He was supposed to be dead. Who was this idiot?

"Mentally fit, I see," the voice said, and Raman relaxed. "How much do you remember?"

Something had happened. *What had that PSI doctor said . . . ?* "I lost my leg."

"You did," confirmed the voice. "Doctor Xiao did a nice job of cauterizing the wound. We shouldn't have any trouble growing you a graft. But in the meantime, it's going to hurt like a son of a bitch."

And just like that, Raman's brain registered the pain: white-hot, nearly numbing, all the nerve endings screaming with nothing attached. He could feel his toes, the toes he did not have anymore. He had always thought that was a myth. "What about the rest of me?"

"Concussion, contusions, small femoral fracture, one deep cut on your back under a left rib. About what you'd expect for a firefight."

He liked this doctor and his dry practicality. "Who are you?"

"Commander Robert Hastings, chief medical officer, CCSS *Galileo*," the man said smoothly.

Raman frowned. The name was familiar. "We've met."

"Three years ago, on Aleph Six."

"Did we get on?"

"Not even a little bit."

That made sense. Raman preferred people who were not so easy to charm. "When can I get up?"

Of all things, that question made the doctor hedge. "The drug Doctor Xiao gave you is going to be in your system for a few more hours," he began.

Raman interrupted him with a snort. "Cut the shit, Doctor-Commander Hastings. If you don't know, say so."

"I don't know."

"Why not?"

Another pause. Raman was becoming annoyed, and it was clearing his head. "In cases such as this," the doctor said cautiously, "the psychological aftereffects of the incident are less predictable than the physical."

"The 'incident' being the crippling of my ship. The deaths of my crew."

"Yes."

"Did we talk long, on Aleph Six?"

"No, Captain Çelik."

"Then I forgive you for talking like a mealymouthed, mud-dleheaded psychiatrist. Please don't call it 'the incident.' It was an attack, a battle, and *Exeter* lost. That we will remedy that situation is not in question. Are we clear here?"

"Yes, sir." Hastings sounded unhappy, but he was, as Raman had guessed, a practical man.

"Good. Now when can I get up?"

"Six hours."

"I'll need a temporary prosthetic."

"I can't recommend that, sir."

Good Lord, he had forgotten how aggravating doctors could be. "Why would that be?"

"A prosthetic that is not specifically grown for your phys-iology will be uncomfortable, and by its nature not properly functional."

"That's acceptable for a temporary."

"Exactly, Captain. But if it stays on too long, or if it's dam-aged while it's grafted to you, we'd be looking at an above-the-knee amputation and a much more complicated growth for a permanent fix. Recovery time will be months instead of weeks, and you may never see full mobility out of the device."

"What's too long?"

Hastings shook his head, defeated. "Three days. Possibly four, if you don't damage it. But I can't give you painkillers while you're wearing it, sir. They'll interfere with the electrical impulses and you won't be able to control it."

Raman took a moment to let the heat of his missing leg wash over him, and his head swam. "Will it hurt more or less than it does now?"

"Less," Hastings said. "Probably."

"How long will it take you to attach it?"

"An hour, maybe a little more."

Raman nodded. "Proceed then, Doctor," he said, letting his eyes close again. "And when you're finished, and you can see your way clear to letting me get the fuck out of here, I will speak with my crew standing on my own two feet. So to speak."

He heard nothing for a moment, and then he heard the shuffle of feet as Hastings turned and walked away. Definitely practical, Raman thought. Practical people were so much more useful than empathic ones.

CHAPTER 10

Greg poured a generous measure of whisky into the glass on his desk, and nudged it in the direction of the officer sitting across from him. "Start from the beginning, Commander."

Dmitri Keita glanced briefly at Elena, seated beside him, before reaching out and lifting the glass. He sniffed it first, then raised his eyebrows and sipped. Greg was surprised; Commander Keita had not struck him as a connoisseur. Under the circumstances he would have expected the man to gulp the liquid, but even traumatized he clearly recognized quality. Greg felt briefly ashamed of the amount of the stuff he had guzzled unceremoniously when he was still drinking.

Quality had not mattered to him at all.

When Elena brought Keita to his office, Greg had resisted the urge to call the man "son." Despite being only three years younger than Greg, and fully as tall, there was something in his face: an earnest innocence that suggested vulnerability. Elena had hovered over him like a worried parent, which had puzzled Greg at first. All he knew of Keita was what he had read in her official report of the incident on Canberra, nearly eight years ago now. She had not seemed protective of Keita in the report. Indeed, she had emphasized the team's dependence on his strategy and marksmanship, and his bravery when rescuing the infant. Over the years she had spoken only obliquely of Canberra, and almost never of Keita, although Greg knew she kept in loose touch with him.

She perched on the edge of her chair now, leaning toward *Exeter*'s second-in-command, her eyebrows firmly knit together, fairly vibrating with focus on her old friend. An unwelcome thought wandered into Greg's head, and the urge to call the man "son" vanished, replaced by the need to keep the exchange professional and as brief as possible.

Keita took a breath and leaned back, his hand still curled around the whisky. "We were back on Earth three weeks ago, a little after you were," he said. "Everyone was still talking about you two, but nobody really understood everything that happened. At least nobody at my rank." He was quiet a moment, and Greg wondered if Keita thought he would elaborate. "Nobody much thought about MacBride—his trial was a lot less high-profile than yours, and he never had your . . . celebrity. Sir." Keita shifted, and Greg sensed disapproval. "But most of us figured, well, he'd screwed up, and someone was taking care of it. Right? Because that's what we do. We figure out how to punish people, and we do it, and it's sane and sensible and all in the interests of the Greater Good." Greg heard the emphasis in his bitter voice.

"And I wouldn't have thought about it at all anymore, but the day before we left Captain Çelik called me into his office, took everything off the record, and told me we were going to be transporting Captain MacBride to the prison system out by Xihoudu. I didn't understand why it needed to be secret, but I didn't ask."

Greg interrupted. "Who else was assigned to the task?"

"Initially, only me, Farias the brig officer, and Doctor Lawson, but Lawson had to pull in a team." He turned to Elena. "That's how Jimmy got involved."

"Why did you need a med team?"

Keita shifted and dropped his eyes, taking a moment to sip the whisky. "They transferred him to us unconscious, sir. Drugged. Told us he needed to be fed intravenously, because he'd been on a hunger strike."

That, Greg thought, made no sense at all. What could MacBride have hoped to gain from a hunger strike? "Did your doctor confirm that?"

Keita nodded. "But that's not why he brought Jimmy—Doctor Youda in. Lawson let the drugs wear off the first afternoon. Said he wanted to examine MacBride, and he wasn't going to do it while the man couldn't speak for himself. And . . . as soon as he woke up, Captain MacBride started ranting. Screaming about being set up, about injustice, calling the Admiralty a pack of cowardly murderers. That sort of thing."

Now that, Greg thought, *sounds like MacBride.* "Who heard him?"

"I did, sir. And Doc Lawson, and Jimmy."

"What did you do?"

"Doc Lawson drugged him again," Keita said, and Greg thought he disapproved of that as well. "He told me MacBride was a danger to himself. But he wouldn't look me in the eye when he said it."

Elizabeth Bonesteel

Lawson's name, Greg remembered, had been on the casualty list. If he had known more than Keita about what was going on, he could tell no one now. "What makes you think the attack was over MacBride?"

Keita's eyes met Elena's again, and Greg saw her nod, almost imperceptibly. "It's an anomaly, and I suppose I am assuming the anomalies are all related. Using a starship to transport MacBride, the Syndicate attack on a Corps ship, their disproportionate firepower—" He stopped there, and Greg wondered if he was including *Exeter*'s feeble attempts at self-defense in his mental list. Instead, he added something that required more imagination than Greg would have initially suspected of him. "And the timing, sir."

"Timing?"

"I'm not privy to most of it, sir, but Captain Çelik does talk." He exchanged another glance with Elena. "You being here in the Third Sector, after you were exonerated." Greg didn't correct him. "And nobody understanding exactly what happened out there with PSI, or even really what MacBride did or didn't do. Captain Çelik says nobody can even cogently explain why he was court-martialed."

"Incitement to war," Greg said automatically. In reality, of course, it was for disobeying orders; but the branch of the Admiralty who had given him those orders could not charge him with insubordination without admitting they had given the order in the first place.

Keita made an impatient gesture. "Whatever the charge, sir, are you going to tell me all of this is happening now for no reason?"

"Coincidences do happen."

"Bullshit, sir." His eyes blazed, and Greg thought under other circumstances he would like Keita. Instead of rebuking him for the outburst, Greg held the younger man's gaze steadily, and after a moment Keita shifted and dropped his eyes. "I'm sorry, Captain."

"Given the day, Commander, I'll let it go," Greg said. He avoided looking at Elena. "Why do you think it's bullshit?"

"Because . . ." Keita was struggling. "It can't be coincidence. Not like this. What happened to *Exeter* . . . you can't tell me that was for nothing."

Keita looked suddenly vulnerable again, and Greg felt exhausted. So many things did happen for nothing, but he did not think this distressed officer could stand to face that just now. He needed to get Keita out so he could unravel this with Elena. "Thank you for your time, Commander," he said. "You're dismissed."

Keita processed the abrupt order, but he did not lose his temper this time. He stood, saluted stiffly, and turned.

"Commander," Greg called after him. When Keita turned back, he held out the open bottle of scotch. "Take this," he said. "Share it with your friends."

Keita gave him a puzzled look, but wrapped his fingers around the bottle and nodded. "Thank you, sir," he said, and when he left he looked a little less stiff.

Greg sat down again, and ran his hands over his face and into his short-cropped hair. Elena was watching the door where Keita had gone, and he had the distinct impression she was avoiding looking at him. "Smart guy," he remarked.

"Yes," she said absently. "He always was."

"How long were you involved with him?"

She turned back, surprised. At another time he would have laughed at her; she was always startled by how transparent she was. "About three months," she said warily. "Maybe a little less."

"Do you trust him?"

At that she sighed and slumped back in the chair, exhaustion washing over her face. "I am not objective about Dee," she said unwillingly. "Which is to say that yes, I trust him, but I recognize at this point in my life that my instincts about such things are not always particularly accurate."

"Do you think he's telling the truth?"

She nodded. "But whether it's the whole truth, I don't know."

"He may not know the whole truth."

"Do you ever get tired of all this secret spy bullshit?"

He had grown tired of it the moment he had lost a member of his own crew to it the year before, and a single casualty paled in the face of what had been done to *Exeter*. "There's no reason Keita would be involved in this," he argued aloud. "No reason Çelik would be, either. Or anyone else on *Exeter*, really. But someone is. The coincidence that your friend doesn't want to see is not that it all happened now, but that it all happened at once. And maybe that *Orunmila* was close enough to defend. I'm not convinced there would have been much left of *Exeter* if they'd had to wait until we got there."

"I don't like PSI being pulled into this. Too many admirals in Shadow Ops are ready to use them as a catalyst for war."

"Not going to do much good when they're throwing their ships bodily between ours and the enemy, and shifting broken bulkheads to rescue our injured officers."

"It's awfully risky for them, though, isn't it?" she asked.

"Who? PSI?"

"Shadow Ops. Assuming they're the ones behind this. *Exeter*'s a well-known ship. To finance an attack . . . of course other ships were going to show up to help her. They couldn't possibly have been confident of a victory."

"Maybe not," he said, "but they got one, didn't they?"

"I'm just thinking it might be a coincidence after all."

He shook his head. "With what Jessica found in their weapons systems?"

"I know." Exhausted again. "I just—I'm not Dee, Greg. I want it to be an accident. Bad timing. A rogue Syndicate tribe, a random equipment failure, them grabbing a prisoner just for the hell of it. I know there has to be more to it, but God, it's awful enough without adding conspiracies on top of it."

The final list had been ninety-seven people. A full quarter of *Exeter*'s crew. Greg had sent the list back to Central, and had offered to help notify the families. Ordinarily, that would be Çelik's job, but Greg wouldn't hazard a guess as to when the man would be up to it. He was not sure he himself could be up to such a job, were it his own crew.

He agreed with Elena. He wanted Keita to be wrong as well. He wanted this tragedy to be one rogue, stupid Syndicate tribe, and nothing more. He wanted to take the revenge the Corps would demand, to pursue and destroy the tribe that did all of this, and ignore the tendrils that reached out into secret areas of his own government, areas half his own chain of command didn't know existed.

There were so few of them who knew the whole story, and only one person who had been through it all with him. And he needed her thinking clearly, instead of dwelling on the horror.

Which is more than I have the right to ask of anyone.

"We need more information before we draw conclusions," he reminded her. They were missing too many pieces. He had no doubt someone had gone after MacBride, but he couldn't yet understand why.

Elena's shoulders straightened, just a little, and some of the tension left her. "When will we hear from that tracker?" she asked.

He rubbed his eyes again. "Captain Shiang thinks somewhere in the next five hours or so."

"You talked to her."

"After a fashion. She commed me earlier to tell me to fuck off."

Elena's eyebrows shot up, and to his amazement she looked faintly amused. "You personally?"

"Kind of, yeah." He related the conversation, such as it was. "And you know, Elena? I hadn't thought of how it must look to her. One minute I'm playing the friendly representative of the Big Bad Admiralty, explaining to her that no, really, there's no special reason we've deployed an extra warship in the area, and the next someone's actually blowing the hell out of a ship she's worked with."

"It matters to her, doesn't it? *Exeter.*"

"I think if Central really cared about getting Shiang on their good side, they'd have had Çelik talk to her years ago."

She was silent a moment. "Greg, why didn't anyone tell us about MacBride? Why was the transport classified in the first place?"

It was a good question. "Your friend Jimmy Youda was a pretty weak link," he pointed out.

"Yes, but be fair: he wasn't in on it at first. And Jimmy gets spiky when he's upset. I don't think he'd be a security risk under ordinary circumstances."

And that thought bothered Greg. In the last several decades, Central had been fortunate: Corps deployments were often relatively uneventful, the kinds of troubles they ran into small, familiar, and manageable. But no Corps soldier should allow themselves to forget that extraordinary circumstances happened. He wanted suddenly to talk to Çelik about *Exeter*'s crew, and whom Çelik himself trusted. Greg shook his head. "This whole business stinks. I don't even know if I should comm back for orders. If it was Shadow Ops that grabbed MacBride, anything the Admiralty might tell us right now is probably bullshit."

"Greg," she asked suddenly, "do you think *Herrod* is part of Shadow Ops?"

Greg had spent the better part of a month pondering that question. "He may not be officially on the payroll, but he knows what they get up to."

"He gave us good advice," she recalled. "To stay together. To be careful."

It took Greg a moment to catch on to what she was saying. "You think he's on our side." He shook his head. "It's dangerous to assume that, Elena. Half of what he's said to me I have a feeling is off the record. We always need to assume when we talk to him we're talking to *them*."

"Still. I think if you contact him as part of the Admiralty—"

"—that he'll give us real orders?"

"As opposed to running us into another raider attack? I think it's possible."

" 'Possible' is a little hair-raising, Elena."

"So is what happened to *Exeter*," she countered. "Greg, they're going to expect us to find out about MacBride. If we don't comm back for orders, what are they going to assume?"

How do we live like this, he thought, *second- and third-guessing every single word anyone says to us anymore?* He rubbed his eyes. "Jessica's already filed the preliminary report. The Admiralty has agreed to quarantine the area. But I don't want to ask them for anything else until Jess finishes dissecting *Exeter*'s logs, and we get something back on that tracker. I don't want to risk getting sent off somewhere we don't want to go."

"Do you think you can still get away with that kind of thing?"

"What kind of thing?"

She gestured into the air. "This thing you do, where you get an order and you ignore it, until you decide how to convince them to give you what you want."

He blinked; he had never thought of it like that. "You think I disobey orders?"

"I think you interpret them creatively. Greg, after all this, they're going to be a lot more careful with you than they have been."

He had felt it already, the subtle shift in power that came from not being an unquestioned hero anymore. He had never cared much about his reputation, but now that it was damaged he was beginning to recognize its usefulness. "They can be careful once we know what's going on," he told her. He watched her haul herself wearily to her feet. "Where are you going?"

"I'm going to talk to Çelik," she said.

"Why?"

"Because as we stand here chatting about whether or not our

own people are after us, I'd just as soon have *Orunmila* on our side. And you said yourself Captain Shiang cares about *Exeter*. Maybe Çelik can talk her around."

"I've already sent Jess after him."

"You afraid of us tag-teaming him?"

She sounded mildly amused again, and the moment felt familiar, the way they had been with each other before everything had gone to hell. "I'm just suggesting that he might not be especially receptive to you just now."

He could order her to leave Çelik alone, and she would obey him; but he understood her thinking. She had a preexisting relationship with Çelik. He remembered the other captain's notes on her transfer orders: *If she doesn't learn to keep her mouth shut, she'll either get tossed out of this outfit, or be running it in less than ten years.* Even then, Greg had known enough of Raman Çelik to recognize the statement as a compliment.

"I don't need him to be receptive," Elena said, turning away. "I just need him to stay still long enough for me to yell. And I want to do it while I'm still too exhausted to care if he yells back."

CHAPTER 11

J essica had expected the infirmary to be far more crowded. All of the beds in the main ward were taken, and most of the seats in the waiting area; but most of the wounded she could see were alert and talking quietly. She caught the eye of Redlaw, the head nurse, and he came closer so they could speak without being overheard.

"The casualty rate is pretty low," he said. "Most of the losses were immediate, or shortly afterward. Çelik is the worst, although there are a couple of head injuries I'm keeping an eye on." He frowned at her. "You look like hell."

"So I've been told." She relented enough to give him a smile; all she'd had to face was a dead ship's core. "I'm sorry, Fran. This being in charge shit doesn't suit me all that well."

"Today isn't suiting anyone well, Commander," he said, and she remembered why she liked him. "You're on your feet? You're doing fine."

She moved slowly through the ward on her way to the private room at the end. Some of the soldiers were dozing—on their own or with assistance she could not tell—but most were sitting up, surrounded by people from both *Exeter* and *Galileo*. Despite the chatter, there was a stillness to the room, a hushed heaviness that clung to her skin like sweat. Jessica always hated the aftermath of tragedy. It involved far too much paralysis.

It reminded her far too much of home.

She headed for Doctor Hastings, who was studying a readout at his desk at the end of the ward. Beyond him, she could see the open door of the private room where Captain Çelik was staying. A small, cowardly part of herself was hoping he would be asleep.

"Is he up?" she asked Bob.

"He's been up for three hours," Bob replied, his expression sour. "He's clobbering the hell out of that new leg."

"Can't you stop him?"

"Is that a joke?"

Jessica stole a surreptitious look through the door of the private room. Çelik was walking around the bed—slowly—testing his balance on the artificial leg. Jessica had never seen a metal prosthetic before—grafts were much more common these days, although they took time—and she found herself impressed at how well he was doing with it. His gait was slow and uneven, and he seemed to test the odd, spidery, six-toed foot every time he set it down; but he made repeated circuits around the bed without hanging on to anything. He would never be graceful on it, but he would be able to move. She couldn't think of more than one or two officers who would be so tenacious and disciplined in this situation, and one of them she was already serving under.

What the fuck is wrong with the Admiralty, that they'd retire the man over this?

She swallowed her anger. None of this was her call, and feeling righteous wrath on his behalf wasn't going to make what she had to tell him any easier.

Jessica stepped forward into the doorway and stood at attention, waiting. Çelik, who had certainly seen her, did not alter his careful path across the floor. She felt a moment's uncertainty—should she wait for him to speak first?—before remembering her still-unfamiliar rank. "Captain Çelik," she said politely, "I have a report on what happened to your ship during the attack."

His eyes shot into hers, although he did not stop walking. "As I was there, Commander Lockwood, I'm pretty sure I don't need your report."

Oh, the rage that came with that look. She found it comforting, after a fashion. If he was angry, that meant he was likely to be still thinking, at least enough to help her out. "I'm referring to *Exeter*'s lack of defense," she clarified, never doubting he'd known what she meant.

He looked away from her again. She would have thought he would be watching his feet, but instead he stared straight ahead, gaze unfocused. "Do you know what the worst of it is?" he asked incongruously. "It's slow. I feel the pain in the stump where it's attached before I get the feedback from the foot and the ankle. It's not my balance that's the problem. It's my brain trying to decode nonsense."

She took his change of subject as tacit agreement to hear her report. "Your gunner isn't culpable, sir," she said. "Your targeting systems were taken out before the attack, probably at least sixteen hours earlier."

"Wasn't."

"Sir?"

"My gunner *wasn't* culpable. He's dead." His tone was icy, derisive.

He's angry with me. Jessica, who had a closer acquaintance with death than most of her crewmates, absorbed his fury without complaint. "Wasn't, sir," she corrected herself.

Stomp, clank. Jessica wondered if they couldn't make something a bit less robotic, even for a temporary. Çelik had enough oddness to deal with. "Why isn't your time frame more precise?" he asked.

"Parts of the core were damaged, sir."

"Any suspects?"

"No, sir."

"Why not?"

"Weapons are under command codes, sir, but not priority ones. They're not that hard to crack."

Another look, although this one was more calculating than angry. "Not for you," he said. "For the average Corps grunt?"

"Your people all have excellent reputations, sir, including the infantry. But if you're assuming someone figured it out on their own, then . . . no, sir, not for the average Corps grunt. Although I imagine most of your cyber people could have done it."

Stomp, clank. "You're saying it requires knowledge, but not skill."

"Yes, sir."

"Which doesn't eliminate anyone."

"No, sir."

"Well, then, the information isn't actually helpful, is it?"

"I don't agree, sir."

That stopped him. He turned to face her down, and she

looked up at him, careful not to react. Jessica was short, and most people made her feel tiny. But Çelik—wide and glowering and angry—made her feel like an insect. He had a reputation for being ill-tempered and intimidating, and Jessica was discovering it was not exaggerated. What was interesting was how deliberate it was, how much of what he was doing to her was designed to get her to respond. He was, in a way, the diametric opposite of her own captain. Greg turned everything inside, measuring and calculating before he moved. Çelik targeted everyone with laser-precise shots, daring them to react to him.

Jessica was used to people thinking they could intimidate her by making her feel small. It had never worked.

"How long have you been second-in-command of this ship, Commander?" he asked her.

"Eight months, sir." Eight long, bureaucracy-filled months—too many of them spent worrying that Greg was going to get demoted . . . or fired. He'd given her the job because he knew she could run the ship in his absence.

Never mind if I wanted to do it.

"And exactly how is it you feel entitled to tell me you know what the hell you're doing?"

Well, it was hardly surprising she had struck a nerve. "Because I do, sir. I was hacking computer cores long before I hit command. Are we going to keep arguing about this, sir, or are we going to discuss what we're going to do about it?"

He straightened a little, and she took a breath, realizing she had frozen under his looming gaze. "How's your security?" he asked her.

"On alert," she told him. Greg had ordered the heightened

security before they started taking on *Exeter*'s crew—even before she had proof that the battle had been anything other than one starship overwhelmed by numbers. They had people monitoring all of the strangers, but Jessica would feel better after they offloaded them to *Cassia*.

And how much do I hate myself for suspecting my fellow soldiers? She had mistrusted Greg's previous second-in-command, and with good reason, but suspicion always made her feel angry and irritable.

Çelik was looking away from her, frowning. That, at least, was a look she knew: Greg had it sometimes, when he had absorbed everything he could and was sorting through it in his head. "I need to speak to them," he said abruptly, "and then I'll talk with Foster." He focused on her again. "Where are the rest of my people?"

She escorted Çelik to the pub, reflecting that his slowed-down pace was just about perfect for her relatively short legs. Bob had shoved a cane into his hands, which he carried in one fist like a spear. The crew members they passed tended to give him first a look, then a wide berth. Jessica wanted to laugh at them. Their own captain had been known to tear furiously through the corridors, although lately he had been working to do less of that; but the studied scowl of Captain Çelik was far more alarming than anything Greg ever expressed publicly.

Çelik must have caught her look, because he slowed his pace a little and tried to arrange his features into something less horrifying. "How long have you served on *Galileo*, Commander?"

If he had read anything about her at all, he would know. "Almost seven years, sir."

"Did you want the job?"

"Yes, sir. I beat out sixteen people for it."

She felt him glance at her. "Selection is blind, Commander. You couldn't have known how many you were competing with."

Shows what you know, she thought. "Given my background, sir, I think you'll find you're mistaken."

"So you cheated."

"No, sir."

"You broke the law."

That was closer. "Technically, sir, yes."

"And Foster hired you anyway?"

"Yes, sir."

"Even knowing you could have fabricated your own history."

Greg had offered her the position, and after her enthusiastic acceptance, he had taken the discussion off the record and told her that if he ever caught her falsifying records or using privileged information for fraudulent reasons, he'd have her thrown in jail. Youth and inexperience had made her more angry than frightened. *I don't need to fake my talents, sir,* she had told him stiffly.

He had laughed.

"Captain Foster is almost as good as I am, sir," she said. "He would have known if I'd hacked the records."

"You have a strange sense of ethics, Commander. I could have used someone like you on *Exeter*."

Jessica absorbed the odd sensation of being complimented and insulted at the same time.

There was too much ambient noise in the pub for the sound of Çelik's artificial foot to be detected, but she was surprised it took so long for people to feel his presence. He filled the doorway, and as she stood to one side of him, she felt him change: he straightened, and all of the rage and frustration he had been radiating turned to calm confidence. She felt the hair on the back of her neck go up as the room slowly fell silent. He stood still for a moment, then walked past her to approach the bar, effortlessly becoming the center of gravity in the room. *That,* she thought, *is not a thing you learn. It's a thing you are.*

Çelik stood steadily on both feet, one real, one artificial, hands behind his back closed over the cane. His eyes moved from face to face, one at a time; she could see in their reactions that they felt the personal touch. "I'm glad," he said, his voice carrying effortlessly through the big room, "to see all of you.

"And I know you, like me, are thinking of our comrades who are not with us. Who were lost in this act of war against our ship, against our government. They fought with bravery and strength, as we all did. Every one of us. Why they were lost and we were not—" He broke off, and his next words were quieter. "There is no answer to that question. But I will tell you this: every one of you must take pride in how you responded today. Every one of you stood up, and did your duty, and so much more. I am proud to have been your captain today, as I am every other day. And I am humbled, constantly, by your focus, your talent, your dedication.

"We fought together. We fought bravely. We fought with strength and courage. We lost comrades, and that is a tragedy we cannot reverse. But we have not lost this war. Thanks to our allies aboard *Orunmila* and *Galileo,* we will find the enemy. We will thwart their plans. We will ensure that they will never again attack a Corps starship, that we will lose no more of our people. They will understand—completely and irrevocably—what fools they were today. What they have taken from us we will take from them a hundredfold. Why? Because we are strong. We are united. And we will not fail."

Cacophony followed this speech as he was rushed by his crew, clapped on the shoulder, offered drinks, salutes, and handshakes. None of them, Jessica noted, seemed to register his prosthetic at all. For her part she hung in the corner, away from the throng, aware of an atmosphere that was close to hysteria. It had been a rousing speech, hitting all the right notes of nationalism and revenge.

She might have fallen for it herself had she not just spent ten minutes explaining to him that he probably had a traitor in his crew.

Without a word to anyone, Jessica slipped out the door and left him to his subterfuge.

CHAPTER 12

And to think I was actually worried about him.

Elena watched from the entrance to the pub as Çelik lifted a glass, surrounded by his usual crowd of acolytes. He said something she could not hear, and they all laughed uproariously as he drank. He had not changed at all, apparently, not in the nearly eight years since she had worked for him.

Not that she flattered herself that she knew him. She did not think anyone could truly know a man like him. She was not sure there was anything genuine in there for anyone to touch.

She could not, from this angle, see the prosthetic, although she spied the cane Bob had told her about lying on the bar behind him. Bob had tried to talk her down from her anger: "However he acts, Elena, he's in considerable pain right now. That's not going to improve anyone's disposition."

She did not have to ask Bob why he had let Çelik leave.

"He is DEFCON-1 pissed off," Jessica had told her, catching Elena in the hallway before she entered the pub. "But he's thinking. Or at least he was, before they swarmed him after that speech. You think he believes his own bullshit?"

Elena hadn't heard the speech, but she could imagine it. "No," she said. "But I think he knows what they need to hear."

Jessica's eyes had narrowed then, and Elena braced herself for compassion. "What about you, Lanie?" she asked. "What do you need to hear right now?"

Elena inhaled, exhaled, smiled. "Mostly," she said, "that you'll stick with me when I finally have a fucking meltdown over all this."

Jessica had reached out and rubbed Elena's elbow, and for one moment she had thought about falling into her friend's arms and sobbing until she couldn't feel anything anymore. Instead she had put her hand over Jessica's and squeezed, then let her go.

She nudged her way through the crowd of men and women around Çelik, avoiding their eyes. The man himself watched her over his glass, gaze shrewd and sober. When he was off-duty, she recalled, he often had a drink in his hand, but it was usually the same one over several hours. She was not convinced she had ever seen him drunk.

He waited until she was directly in front of him. "Something I can help you with, Commander?" he asked easily.

Just like that, the others fell silent, waiting, and she felt her annoyance deepen. He was always surrounded by toadies, and she had never understood the appeal. He was one of the brightest people she had ever known; she had no idea why he wasted his time with such obvious gestures. "I'd like a word in private, Captain," she said.

Behind her someone snickered. She ignored it.

But Çelik, as he always had, took her seriously. "Leave us

alone, please," he said, and the others dissipated like so much smoke. He waited until they were gone, then took a sip. "Still brimming with judgment, I see. How've you been, Shaw? Managed to recover from your lousy career move?"

It took more resolve than she liked to admit to keep from arguing with him. She had argued enough at the time, albeit from a much more vulnerable position. He had thought moving to *Galileo* was a choice to take the path of least resistance. She had agreed with him. Where their opinions differed was on exactly what resistance she was avoiding. He had refused for nearly six weeks to sign off on her transfer request, but in the end, the reference he gave to Greg was not only honest, but complimentary. Çelik could be spiteful, but he was never unprofessional.

"May I speak with you candidly, Captain? There are some things I'd like to ask you that may seem rather blunt."

"Are there now?" He smiled, harsh and humorless, and his eyes grew hard. "And why on earth should I recognize your authority to ask me questions?"

Eight years later, and he was using the same tactics: rigidity and intimidation, but only when she hit a nerve. "Because we're on the same side. For now."

His eyebrows shot up. "Planning some more insubordination? In your shoes, I might give that a rest for a while." He shrugged, and sipped. "Speak as candidly as you like, Commander. Why the fuck do I care?"

At least I've made him curious. "Why were you transporting Niall MacBride?"

He did not look surprised that she knew. "That's classified. But I'm guessing you know that, or you wouldn't be so pissed off."

"He wouldn't even have been arrested if it wasn't for me," she told him.

"So I understand. By the way, I found it fascinating that he ended up losing his career for not killing people, while you managed to stay on your feet after—what did they call it? 'Unauthorized equipment damage'? I love military understatement, don't you?"

Privately, she did not disagree with him. MacBride could have followed orders and made his life much easier; instead, he did the right thing. "Why did they take him, sir?"

His eyes slid away from hers. "How the fuck should I know?"

"I'm supposed to believe that?"

"Do you think it matters to anyone what you believe?" He turned back to her, his eyes bright and piercing. "Why does it matter, anyway?" he asked, curious. "What is MacBride to you, except the guy that took the heat for you?"

"It matters," she replied deliberately, "because he's the reason you were hit. And you know it."

He watched her for a moment, eyes still bright; and then he relented, leaning one elbow on the bar. "Yes," he said, suddenly serious, "I do know it. And whether he was kidnapped or rescued, it's my responsibility, Commander. Not yours."

It crossed her mind, then, that he might be trying to do her a kindness. Along with all of his less pleasant personality traits, he had always had a streak of military honor—a calculated form of chivalry—that surprised her. For an instant she looked at him and saw beyond his abrasive persona to a man, nearly fifty years old, body badly injured, psyche nearly mortally wounded. His rank, his patriotism, his loyalty to his command chain would seem like lifelines right now. And she could respect that.

But she would also rip them away from him if she had to.

"Bullshit, sir," she said clearly. "You know as well as I do we're going to be told to pursue this thing. Right now, we're doing it blind. And on our own, now that you mention it, because Captain Shiang, not being a *fucking idiot*"—she emphasized the obscenity—"has no intention of having anything to do with this. She's saved your ass once; she's not going to risk her family again if we won't tell her what's really going on."

"If I had my ship, you'd be turning tail as well."

"Well you don't, Captain," she said bluntly. "You need us. And we need her. So what are you going to do about it?"

He raised his eyebrows. "What makes you think I'm not perfectly happy having *Orunmila* out of the line of fire here?"

"So you think there's a line of fire."

"Don't be coy, Chief. You do as well, or you wouldn't be here playing ham-fisted psychological games with me."

Ham-fisted my ass. "I think whoever wanted him was willing to kill a hundred people to get him."

"Don't underestimate them. They would have destroyed my entire ship."

"So we agree, then, that this isn't a bunch of rogue raiders."

He scoffed. "With twenty-six fighter drones? Any Syndicate tribe with that kind of money wouldn't have wasted it starting a war with Central Gov."

"*Orunmila* will get pulled in anyway," Elena argued. "Captain Shiang knows it, too."

"We can't let them deal with this blind." This was half to himself. She remembered that tone of voice, too; she had only heard it from him once, when he was debriefing her after Canberra. Curiously, he had been talking about PSI then as well. He shot her a suspicious look. "Why is she leaving?"

Interesting that he had assumed Captain Shiang would stay. "Because she knows we're lying to her," she told him bluntly. "And she is not in the mood to believe anything we say."

"Why don't you tell her anyway?"

Elena deflated. "She didn't give us the chance."

He stared at her a moment, and then he threw back his head and laughed, the sort of laugh he used to let loose in *Exeter*'s big cafeteria, usually at someone else's expense. "She hates you that much."

"She doesn't know us," Elena equivocated. "But she knows *you*. And apparently she trusts you."

"Your boss the Great Diplomat couldn't get through to her?"

She held his gaze, aware she was blushing, aware he would notice. "After this? She's wondering about the timing of our deployment here." *And so am I.*

Çelik let the laughter trickle to an end. "Let me tell you about *Orunmila*," he said. "She's the second-oldest Third Sector ship out here. The fifth-oldest PSI ship in all the five sectors. Half her crew, maybe more, is fourth or fifth generation. Chanyu Laoshang was at her helm for nearly fifty years. Smart as hell, but a paranoid son of a bitch. Insular to a fault. Shiang Guanyin, on the other hand—she wasn't born there. She was picked up at the age of five as part of the Llandro evacuation. Chanyu raised her as his own, but she's got twice his brains, and far more curiosity. Even so, he taught her what he knows, so she's still pretty damn narrow and mistrustful where Central is concerned. And who the hell can blame her?"

Elena, who knew something of the Third Sector political situation, agreed. "You have a good relationship with her, though, don't you?"

"I had a good relationship with Chanyu as well, but we kept it mission-based. Trade and rescue. We never once talked politics. Shiang . . . she was always more inquisitive. She didn't speak much when Chanyu was there, but when she got me alone, she would ask questions about colonization strategies, resource issues, distribution channels, that sort of thing. She wanted to understand how we planned all this, and how we supported our people."

Badly, Elena thought, and wondered if Captain Shiang had come to that conclusion yet. No, she probably hadn't. Central worked hard to maintain the impression that they were wealthy and over-resourced; that the distribution problems were due to great distances and the complexities of building and commissioning new starships. As a mechanic, she had learned which official excuses were intended to conceal financial or materials shortfalls. Early in her career she had not thought much about it beyond the annoyance factor.

Canberra had cured her of being blasé about anything at all.

"Do you think she's more likely to listen to you than to us?" she asked.

At this he looked away, and she could not read his expression at all. "I think she'll let me get the words out," he admitted. "Whether or not she'll believe me . . . I honestly don't know." His lips twitched, and to her shock she realized he was smiling. "Not a lot of people I deal with who are as smart as I am. Refreshing, finding someone you can't manipulate." His eyes locked with hers again. "Maybe you'll run into someone like that someday."

Ah, yes—Captain Çelik's famous backhanded compliments.
This one, though, was more about how much he disliked Greg,
and she let it pass. "Comm her," she suggested, "and tell her
what's going on."

A different smile this time. This one she knew: shrewd, inci-
sive, and deeply unpleasant. "Why is it I think you know better
than I do?"

Dammit. That was how he beat her, every time: he was
opaque, and she was transparent. She set her jaw, refusing to
rise to the bait. "Whatever I know, Captain Çelik," she said,
"doesn't matter. But *Orunmila* does. Get her back on our side,
sir. You know as well as I do that we need her."

CHAPTER 13

R aman Çelik watched Shaw leave. He had forgotten, in the years since she had left, what an appealing woman she was: a handsome and expressive face, and a set to her lips that was unconsciously sexual, especially when she was pissed off at him—which seemed to be most of the time. What made her extraordinary, though, was not her features, but her sharp wit. He had always enjoyed sparring with her; she could keep up with him, and he had not been lying when he had told her that was unusual. What she saw in Foster had always puzzled him. Looks would not have swayed her—his own appearance was generally considered extremely pleasant, and he had never had occasion to question that assessment—and after she left he had decided it was because Foster was never going to push her. She'd always had it in her head to be a mechanic, and nothing more. Foster would have let her languish forever as a low-grade mechanic had he not lost his old engineering chief in a battle. Raman would have pushed her into leadership, damn her foolish whims.

Seeing her make her way through his crew with such an

effortless assumption of privilege had reminded him how irritated he had been when Foster had accepted her request for transfer. He should have challenged the orders. The Admiralty would have understood, had he taken the time to explain it to them. And maybe she wouldn't have been caught up in the clusterfuck that was Niall MacBride.

He shoved aside the ruminations and got carefully to his feet—to his foot—retrieving the cane off of the bar. Leaving the remains of his drink, he made his way to the door, accepting handshakes and claps on the back as he went, forcing himself not to flinch from the sensory overload. His nervous system was completely fucked-up. Every time someone touched him he felt a flare of phantom pain, an entirely different sensation from the asynchronous mechanical signals sent through the nerves in his knee. He thought of borrowing Foster's office for the comm, but somehow he felt more comfortable heading back to his private room in the infirmary. Damned if he'd be beholden to the man. Better to be thought an invalid.

He ran another gauntlet as he lurched back through the main ward. He repeated his performance with the injured, offering words of support here and there. Raman carried guilt for all of them, but guilt was useless. Guilt didn't change the fact that he'd had no power to protect them, and now he had no power at all.

But that was different from being helpless.

He made it back to the private room and let the door slide shut behind him. Dropping the façade of nonchalance, he let the cane fall to the ground and leaned heavily on the bed, taking the weight off of the artificial limb. The pain came in two waves—knee first, then foot—and he squeezed his eyes shut, wondering for a moment if he would actually pass out. But after the wave the rhythmic throb of pain became bearable, and his heart caught up with his lungs again. For now, he would avoid collapsing onto the floor.

Tapping the comm behind his ear, he queried for *Galileo*'s main network. The connection was picked up slowly—pulling his ident, perhaps; but Raman would never have tolerated such a delay by his own people. "Yes, Captain," said a brisk voice at last. "What can I do for you?"

On the record, Raman reminded himself. *Every bit of this on the record. My choice, my action, no one else's.* "Connect me with Captain Shiang on *Orunmila*."

A pause. What the hell was wrong with Foster's discipline? This kid should have been jumping. "What's your name, son?" Raman asked.

"Samaras, sir." That came fast enough.

"Ensign?"

A brief clearing of the throat. "Lieutenant, sir."

"Recently?"

"Four years, sir."

"Not on this ship."

"No, sir. I transferred from *Arrarat* six weeks ago."

At least it had not been Foster who promoted the man. That was something. He'd never make lieutenant commander, this one. No initiative. "If you have a problem with placing the comm, Lieutenant Samaras, let's hear it. Otherwise don't waste my time with your dithering. This is a direct order. Make your choice."

Strictly speaking, of course, Raman had limited authority on board this ship. Samaras could have deferred to Foster and checked the validity of the order. With Shaw making her case with such fervor, though, Raman suspected Foster already knew what he would be doing. Too many more instants passed, and then the lieutenant said, "Connecting now, sir." The line went quiet as Samaras negotiated with the comms crew on *Orunmila*.

Much to Raman's surprise, Captain Shiang herself answered him. He wondered if her comms crew filtered without interference, or if she had been monitoring *Galileo* for messages. "Your comm signal is unsteady, Captain Çelik. Is everything all right there?"

"We're fine," he assured her. "The comms officer is new."

"What is it I can do for you, Captain?"

Never any preamble, not even after the day they had just had. "I'd like to discuss today's attack with you, Captain Shiang."

A brief pause, and he realized he should have insulted her if he did not want to tip his hand. "What is it you have found?" she asked.

She sounded apprehensive. *Off on the wrong track,* he thought, and frowned. "Can we do this with vid, Captain?"

Another pause, and then her head and shoulders appeared before him. She was, as always, neat and composed; but her long hair was out of its intricate braids, falling straight over her shoulders. She was out of uniform, too, wearing a simple gray tunic, and it came to him that he had woken her up. She regarded him with her usual composure, though, her eyes sweeping him up and down.

"You are looking better," she said.

"I am walking," he told her. "After a fashion."

"What sort of fashion is that?"

He almost smiled. "*Galileo*'s quack handed me a walking

stick after threatening me with further amputation. I wonder if he recognizes the absurdity of that?"

Her eyebrows went up, and her expression relaxed a little. "Is he a quack, then?"

"You like him?"

"I did not speak with him, but Xiao likes him. She says he does not defer. I find such an attitude necessary in a medical professional."

She had such a lovely accent, but it seemed unfair to conduct this discussion in Standard. He switched to dialect. "Between you and me," he told her, "I like him myself. Pragmatic, despite the bullshit. And given how deep the bullshit is around here, I suppose he cannot help it."

"I've been reading about Captain Foster," she said. "I don't think 'bullshit' is the right word. Perhaps . . ."

"Please do not say 'tact,' " he offered, and at that she did smile.

"Chanyu used to call it 'active personnel management.' Learning about people by being receptive rather than blunt. Listening."

"You think Foster is a listener?"

At that, she equivocated. "There are a lot of things about him that seem designed to irritate me. But I must entertain the possibility that he is an honorable man."

"The universe is full of honorable men," he told her. "I would rather have a dishonorable one who was straight with me about what he would and would not do."

"It seems to me you might not want to turn your back on a man like that."

"I do not turn my back on anyone."

She shook her head. "I think of myself as vigilant," she said, "but you exhaust me. And although I'm pleased you're feeling better—you're avoiding the subject."

"What is the subject?"

"You didn't comm me to discuss Captain Foster."

"Actually," he admitted wearily, "I did. At least in part."

He saw her shoulders drop as her spine straightened, and her expression closed. "Did he ask you to speak to me?"

"No. It was Commander Shaw."

At that she relaxed a little. *Interesting.* "She was the one involved in the Fifth Sector last year. The hero."

He caught himself smiling. "Is that how you are all seeing it?"

"To the extent that we have visibility into your side of it. Are we wrong?"

"I don't think so." He shrugged. "She does not like me."

"Is that so unusual?"

From a different person, the remark would have been flirtatious. "She worked for me a long time ago. Just for a year. She did not like me then, either."

"She holds a grudge?"

He shook his head. "Nothing for her to hold a grudge over. Just ordinary dislike."

Her eyes narrowed, and he almost smiled again. Watching her changing expression was almost as good as climbing inside her head and seeing her put it all together. "She left you for *Galileo,*" she deduced.

"I know that is not a thing that is done on your ships," he said. "On ours, though—"

"—your people do not grow up on board," she finished. "We do have people move around, a little. Wanting a new home,

falling in love with someone on another ship. Retiring, like
Chanyu. It sometimes feels like a rejection."

"She is hardly the only soldier to ever transfer off of my
ship," he said. Most, though, were screwups, children who were
misfits for the service entirely. But Shaw . . . she had been smart,
and had disapproved of him without apology. He could have
taught her, he thought; mentored her through her career. He
thought she could have taught him as well. He could never learn
a damn thing from people who rolled over and placated him. Or
mealymouthed politicians like Foster.

Despite his silence, Guanyin had seen it. "You see her as an
equal," she observed. "That's not usual for you."

"That," he conceded, "and she threw her career away."

"By choosing not to work for you anymore."

"You think I am arrogant."

"From what little I know of Commander Shaw, she seems to
have had a very fine career."

" 'Very fine' is good enough for some, I suppose."

Her lips twitched. "Be that as it may, Captain. She asked you
to speak with me, and she must have made her case, because
here we are. What is it she wanted you to say?"

The impossible. "She wanted me to tell you why we were attacked."

"Ah. Because then I'll help you."

He shook his head. "Captain Shiang, not that it is worth a
damn thing, but I would just as soon you get your family as far
away from this fucking mess as you possibly can."

"I see."

"Since you are acquainted with what happened last year, I
assume you know the name Niall MacBride."

She nodded. "Captain of *Demeter.* He was involved in an

attack on the Fifth Sector PSI ship *Penumbra*. Your people have labeled him a rogue, or so we're led to believe."

"He was arrested, tried, and convicted of incitement to war."

Her eyebrows went up. "We hadn't heard that. That's good. That will please people. Why did you keep it quiet?"

"I do not know," he told her honestly. "Foster and Shaw got all the media, and I do not know why." It should have been *bad* PR for the Admiralty, now that he thought about it. The public knew nothing of the refinery they had found and destroyed. The public only knew that they had stopped a misunderstanding between Central and PSI that could have led to war. That the Admiralty would have court-martialed them so publicly suggested there was more to the story than he knew. That was an unsettling revelation that he filed away to deal with later. "MacBride, though. What he did was incomprehensibly foolish."

"There's a rumor he was following orders."

Her intelligence was pretty good. "There are a lot of rumors. But incitement to war, that is—well, not the point in all of this." *Except that it might be exactly the point.* "The point is, he was on board my ship when we were hit . . . and now he is not."

"Those dead people outside your brig," she said. "That's what you meant when you told us they had what they'd come for." She shook her head. "Captain Çelik, you are not telling me everything you know."

"I am not," he admitted. Too much of what he believed was guesswork, and it was too soon for him to share it. "But here is what I can tell you: most people I have spoken to, Admiralty or otherwise, think MacBride's sentence was just. *Most* people. And the people I speak to are either Central, or commercial freighter crews. In MacBride's position, it is fair to assume he knew a lot of things that might be considered valuable. The list of suspects who might have wanted him dead is pretty long."

She looked puzzled. "But to kill ninety-seven people. Captain. That's—"

"Sociopathic?"

"I was going to say evil."

"A quaint concept."

"A very real concept."

"What do you know of evil, little girl?"

Her eyes softened. "Enough to know that what happened today could have no other explanation. Do you know so little of me, Captain, that you think I can't see that much?"

He felt a twitch of annoyance with himself. He needed her help; pointing out her inexperience wasn't going to get him anywhere. "The point, Captain Shiang, is this: I know those raiders were after MacBride, because there was absolutely nothing else on board my old, patched-together beauty of a ship that was worth that kind of carnage to anyone. But I do not know who paid them. Maybe they thought he knew something they could use; maybe they were hired by some corporation. Maybe he owed the wrong people money. Maybe he paid them himself."

"Or maybe," she said slowly, "Central itself believed his continued existence was too high-risk."

Clever woman. "You see my conundrum."

"And why don't you suspect PSI paid for this attack?"

Because it is not who you are. That was sentiment, based on childhood stories and old myths, and he stopped himself from saying it out loud. "I cannot imagine anything valuable enough to make you recruit Syndicate raiders to do your dirty work. If you wanted him, you would have taken him yourself."

As he watched, her dark eyes dropped closed, and she raised one hand to rub her palm over her cheek. "So if we become involved, you believe you're reducing the risk of sabotage by your own people."

"I do not really think *Galileo* would sabotage this mission," he said. "Foster may be humorless, but he has never been a company man. He will chase these raiders down until we find them. But what happens to them after that—well, that is not up to him."

"You think our justice would be different?"

"I think your justice would *be* justice."

"You have great faith in us."

"I have been out here fifteen years," he said. "Far as I can tell, my faith is warranted." He shifted forward, forgetting his handicap, and winced as his prosthetic pressed against the floor. "I meant what I said earlier, Captain. Get out of here. Leave us to our own bullshit. Your people do not need to get hauled into this. What happens to those raiders—what happened to MacBride— it does not matter. Ninety-seven people will still be dead." *Blood on my hands.* "Do not risk making it more, just because some little man bothered the wrong people." He meant every word he said, and he knew how she would respond to his sincerity.

He could see it in her face already: she would change her mind. She would help them. And when they found the raiders, he suspected she would stand next to him as he executed them, one by one, before all of their fellows, and know it would not be enough. She was smarter than Chanyu, but the real difference was her heart: open, accepting, a powerful weapon all on its own. He had known, once he told her, that she would not abandon him, and she would not abandon his dead.

Shaw, he thought, had been right to flee from him.

CHAPTER 14

W̲e can take all the wounded," Captain Vassily told Greg, "including Çelik. We've got a graft tank on board—three of them, actually. The virtue of traveling with scientists." Her professional expression grew grim, and she looked away from him. "After that we can take maybe twenty more, if people are willing to double up. But we don't have room for everyone."

CCSS *Cassia* was a little larger than *Galileo,* but she carried more equipment than personnel. Her original charter had been research and exploration, but over the years *Cassia* had turned into a de facto mobile hospital for the Third Sector. Andriya Vassily had embraced the role wholeheartedly, which had not surprised Greg. He had known her a little back at Central Military Academy—she had been a few years ahead of him, and one of the few students whose academic record matched his own—and she had always been passionate about her duty. There was something familiar in the way she stood here in his office, radiating effortless competence as she scanned the list of wounded.

With a start, he realized she put him in mind of Elena.

"We can start transport immediately," he told her. "Commander Lockwood will coordinate with Doctor Hastings to shuttle people over in groups. We're still waiting on some intel on our destination, so there should be time to do it properly."

She gave him a shrewd look. "This is your PSI intel?" When he nodded, she said, "I don't like that we're so dependent on them here. We got nothing off of *Exeter* at all?"

He felt a twinge of disappointment at her response. He'd spoken to enough of his fellow captains to know that opinions about PSI ranged all over the map, and Andriya, in charge of a science ship, wouldn't have had much of a chance to interact with them on rescues. But her sentiment suggested an unfounded bias, and he suspected an argument wouldn't get him far.

"What we have from *Exeter* is going to take us some days to sort through," he told her, keeping their sabotage theory to himself. "With all the places the Syndicates have to hide, you're damn right I'm depending on PSI intel. I wish I could depend on more." At that moment, his comm chimed quietly in his ear. "Excuse me," he said to her, and kept the audio private. "Yes?"

"Captain," Lieutenant Samaras said, "I've got a comm coming in from *Orunmila*. Asking for you."

Greg turned to Captain Vassily. "I'm sorry, Andriya, I've got to take this."

"Of course." She nodded graciously. "I'll coordinate with Commander Lockwood. We can touch base before I leave."

He waited until she had left his office before returning to Samaras. "You can put it through, Lieutenant."

"Yes, sir . . ."

Greg swallowed impatience. Samaras was a decent comms

officer, but his constant need for reassurance was wearing under the best of circumstances. "What's the problem, Samaras?"

"A little while ago, sir—Captain Çelik had me put a call through to them. To *Orunmila*. He—I should have asked you, sir, but—"

"That's perfectly all right, Lieutenant," he assured the man. Count on Çelik to make an officer feel guilty doing something Greg would have given him permission to do anyway. "I thought he might. You can put Shiang through, and thank you for letting me know."

There was a pause, and a brief digital hiccup, and then Captain Shiang's voice was in his ear. "Captain Foster," she said. He did not know her well enough to know if her hesitance was real, or just the language barrier. "We have received a communication from the tracker. It is . . . unexpected."

"Unexpected in what way?" If the data was erroneous or incomplete, this would become a very different mission.

"That passenger raider—it's a typical design. We see a great many of those—cheap to manufacture, easy to repair unless the hull infrastructure is damaged. It is not new, or durable, or particularly high-tech. Certainly not powerful. But according to the tracker . . . it has traveled—on a single charge, in this short span of time—thirty-six light years."

Greg wondered if Shiang was translating the number wrong in her head. "Say that again?"

"Thirty-six, Captain. Three times the distance such a small ship should have been able to make."

He made his way around his desk and sat down, his mind working furiously. "Extra batteries?" he suggested, but even as he said it he knew that wasn't enough. An extra battery on a ship so small would add weight, reducing the benefits. They might expect to pick up twenty or thirty percent, but . . . *thirty-six light years*. "Someone gave them more than just the drones," he concluded.

"It does seem likely their range is due to further borrowed technology."

"Is this normal for them?" he asked her. "Not the nature of the tech—but to procure specific equipment for a strike? Maybe take on a partner, or"—and wasn't this an alarming thought— "even a commission?"

"A partnership would be extremely unusual," she told him. "And I have not seen them work purely as mercenaries, although I believe sufficient payment would motivate them."

"Would the tech they used be considered payment?"

"If the tech was their payment, they would not have wasted it on such a risky attack."

There was so much more about the raiders he needed to ask her. "Captain Shiang, I know what you said earlier. Under the circumstances . . ." He stopped. "I don't know what Captain Çelik said to you. But this entire situation is awfully personal, to all of us. Central, the Admiralty, all the officers who seem to think they know what I should say to you—can we put them aside? Can you help? Because in truth, Captain Shiang, we need your assistance here."

He waited.

"I do wonder why you Corps soldiers opt for formal diplomacy," she said at last. "You are far more persuasive when you speak for yourselves."

"Is that a yes, Captain?"

"I have conditions."

Of course. "All right."

"First of all, I want it understood that this is a joint mission. When we find these perpetrators, we will agree—together—on the appropriate punishment."

"Assuming any of them survive to be charged?" he asked.

"Just so."

"I don't know about PSI," he told her, "but we do try to stick with the innocent-until-proven-guilty idea."

"That is why we will agree together, Captain," she said smoothly. "Neither you nor I will have veto power. But no one will be remanded to Central's sole custody without my agreement. That is the first condition for my assistance. Do you understand?"

He should be protesting the implication, he knew; but if she and Çelik opted for summary executions, he was not sure he would make the effort to object. "Go on."

"Sharing of intelligence related to this investigation must be reciprocal and complete."

It was an entirely reasonable request . . . and he did not have the authority to grant it. "Anything else?"

"Captain Çelik will be transferred to *Orunmila* for the duration of this mission."

That one surprised him. "Did he agree to that?"

"He did." She paused. "You may consider him an ambassador, if you wish, or an intermediary; but I will not be a part of this without his presence on my ship."

And wasn't that an interesting statement. He had not believed they knew each other so well. "As we're being honest, I'll tell you flat-out I don't have the authority to unilaterally agree to any of this."

"Nevertheless."

Everything out here was negotiable. Central made rules, and starships filed reports; but even with priority comms, there were times decisions had to be made without Admiralty approval. If the outcome of those decisions was positive, any discipline by the Admiralty was largely symbolic. If the outcome was more ambiguous . . . he had firsthand knowledge of that. For years he had been given a fair amount of leeway. But last year—after the incident with *Demeter*—he had run out of credit. He could agree to all of Shiang's terms, but if they came back empty-handed, there was a very good possibility he would lose his ship.

Without his ship, his life was nothing.

"All right, then, Captain Shiang," he said. "We're agreed."

"Excellent." He thought she sounded relieved. "I have sent you the telemetry on the tracker. Our engines are charged, so once Captain Çelik is transferred, we can leave."

"It'll take us another couple of hours to transfer the wounded to *Cassia*," he told her as he studied the telemetry. *Wait . . . that couldn't be right*. "Captain Shiang, this location." His stomach knotted. *Anywhere else*. "Are you sure of this?"

"The signal was quite strong," she replied. "They transmitted nearly four minutes before they hit the atmosphere."

"It's uninhabitable."

"They've used it as a temporary base for years," she said. "They never stay longer than a few weeks. You were unaware of this?"

"We don't track the Syndicates that closely." On top of everything else, everything Elena was dealing with, he was going to have to add this to her burdens. "You're sure?"

"Quite sure," she told him. "The raider that hit *Exeter* has landed on Canberra."

"How is Canberra a Syndicate base?"

Jessica was standing in front of his desk, animated and agitated. In contrast, Elena, standing at the window, was staring out at the stars, her expression blank.

It is never a good sign when she gets so quiet.

"Apparently they've used it for years," he told Jessica, keeping half an eye on Elena. "They had frequent trade with the colony before it crashed, and Captain Shiang says they kept using it as a stopover after the climate took over. They can't stay on the surface long, of course, but as a temporary base—"

"No one would bother following them down," Elena finished for him. She did not move.

"No one would bother," Jessica returned, "because it's insane going down there to begin with." She glared at Greg. "How did our intelligence miss this?"

But she was only venting—she knew as well as he did. Canberra had been given up, the reasons for the colony's failure flagged as tragic but uninteresting. And Central, with what Greg was beginning to recognize as typical shortsightedness, had assumed no one else would have an interest, either.

Elena knew it, too. "Until the Syndicates began attacking us," she said, her thoughts mirroring Greg's, "we didn't care where they were going."

She sounded so bitter, and he couldn't tell her she was wrong. "Jess, can you give us a minute?"

Jessica was looking at Elena, her eyes full of worry. She

turned back to Greg, shooting him a *Be careful with her* glare, and left his office.

"Tell me what you remember," he said.

She kept staring out the window, posture stiff, expression unchanged. "It was just a recon job." Her hands gripped her elbows. "We were supposed to go down, contact the locals, evaluate how much equipment we would need to evacuate everyone—that sort of thing."

"Did you have any intelligence at all?"

"Very little." He saw her fingers tighten. "Canberra was isolationist. They almost never contacted Central, and they sure as hell never asked for anything. The only reason we knew there was a problem was because PSI had sent us a vid. They had been doing a food drop, and it nearly caused a riot. The colonists were aggressive. The cameraman—the vid ended with him falling down."

"That's why Çelik sent infantry."

"Four infantry, one med tech. I was just supposed to fly." She looked over at him. "Do you know, Çelik offered to let me off? We had a rotation, and it was just chance that it was my turn. He said for my first I could wait for something safer. I was insulted." Her fingers twitched again. "Treharne was joking with Niree on the way down. I still remember when he stopped. I was coming in high, figuring we'd start with a flyover, since they hadn't been answering any comms. The city was nearly demolished. Debris everywhere. Fires. Treharne asked if I was up on my target practice. My original orders were to stay behind with the ship, but with what we were seeing, I was happy to have them overruled. I didn't want to be left to defend the ship on my own."

She turned around, leaning against the window, releasing her elbows. Her hands closed into fists. "We landed in a town square, or what used to be one. There were fragments of buildings here and there, suggestions of structures. I thought—" She broke off for a moment. "There were no people. No birds, no animals. All we could hear was the wind, and the distant sound of crackling fire. And the smell—" Her nose wrinkled in memory. "Did you know I wasn't a vegetarian before that day?"

He had not known. He had grown up vegetarian, and tended to assume others had, too, unless he specifically saw them eat meat. "Did you figure out what it was?"

"There's no other smell like it. But we didn't understand, not at first. Crematoriums are a safe way to dispose of bodies if you don't have the space or the time to bury them. It wasn't until we saw the bones . . . Jimmy figured it out. He said . . . human teeth leave different marks than animals'."

Dear God. That certainly wasn't in the official reports.

"Why didn't you abort?"

"The weather was hideous," she told him. "We only had forty-six minutes to land, recon, and come back. Aborting would have meant the colonists would have gone two days longer without help." Her smile this time was bitter. "If we'd known, we would have left right away. But if we'd known, Greg, we never would have gone down with such a small team in the first place.

"We found this block of buildings that was mostly intact, and then we heard someone crying. It—she sounded like a child. She was down an alley, this narrow space, closed on the other end. Like something out of a bad vid." She shook her head. "She saw us, and she started screaming and telling us to go away. Treharne—I think he thought she was afraid of us. He kept talking to her, speaking really calmly. I remember thinking he'd never been so nice to any of us. I wondered if he had children, or what his extended family was like. I was wondering all of that, and then—

"They shot him from the roof. Laser rifle. Clean shot, shoulder to hip. Cut him right in half. He must have bled out in seconds, but . . . it seemed to take forever. And that girl, she kept screaming and screaming. And then they came out, all around us, and grabbed Niree, and we all started shooting, even Jimmy. Jimmy hates weapons. He always said shooting when he was a medic would make him a hypocrite."

We're all hypocrites under fire, Greg thought.

"They got her away from us, but we could hear Niree screaming, so we went after her."

"You left the girl behind."

She nodded. "And Treharne. His body. We—"

"You went after the one you could help," he said gently. "It was the right call." So easy to say, and he knew she would never believe it. He wouldn't, in her place.

"Savin and Dee went in shooting, and Jimmy and I circled behind to pull Niree out. I think . . . I can't remember how many there were," she said apologetically. "We all talked about it, when I was writing up the report. Jimmy thought maybe fifteen; Savin thought it was only seven. More than us, either way. And they were . . . inhuman. Shouting, taunting, growling, snapping at us like crocodiles. No language at all. I don't—it was probably just to frighten us."

"So you got Niree away."

She unclenched her fists and knitted her fingers together. He thought she wanted something to do with her hands. "We got her away. She was walking, after a fashion, and we were able to run, sort of, Jimmy and me holding her up between us. We found a corner where we could rest so Jimmy could look after her. They—" She swallowed. "Her right hand was gone. Bones taken off at the wrist, skin cauterized at the stump. And most of the flesh of her forearm was missing. Torn off. More teeth marks. After that, we figured there was no point in going back to look for Treharne."

"And that's where the girl found you."

She nodded again; and then her eyes slid away from his. "There was a part we left out of the report," she told him. "About Dee."

Uh oh, he thought.

"When she appeared—she startled all of us. We all drew our weapons. Jimmy stood in front of Niree. But she was so small, and clearly frightened, we all stood down . . . except for Dee. He said we had to execute her, because she had killed Treharne."

"He thought she was in on it."

He saw her jaw set. "You can't blame him." He didn't, and he wondered where her defensiveness was coming from. "But she was unarmed, so I shoved her behind me and told him to back off. And . . . he threatened to kill me, too."

That bastard drew *on her?* The same wounded, vulnerable soldier she had been *defending* earlier that day? *Not a good time to start yelling again,* he told himself.

"I reasoned with him, and he came around, and we made it back to the shuttle. You know the rest."

He took a breath to steady himself, but the pressing need to point out the madness of the situation won out over sympathy. "Elena, do you have any idea what you're telling me?"

"I know what you're thinking, Greg," she said wearily. "That's exactly why we all agreed to leave it out of the report."

They all agreed. Good God. "This isn't some random act of insubordination," he told her, getting to his feet. "He *drew* on you. He threatened to kill you. I don't care what kind of war zone you were in, that should have ended his career! And after all that"—how did any of this make sense?—"how in the hell did you end up *in bed* with him?"

Her eyes flashed. Apparently that, of all things, was going too far. "Are you mad about the omission," she snapped, "or about me sleeping with yet another man who isn't you?"

He turned away from her, seething. *Damn—ran right into that.* She always knew where to hit him, every time, and it didn't help a bit suspecting he deserved this one. "Let's start with the omission," he said tightly.

"Dee was never going to shoot me," she said evenly.

"You knew that how?"

"I knew *him*."

"Circular logic, Commander."

Her lips tightened. "We all, every one of us, reacted differently down there. Savin went matter-of-fact. Jimmy got protective. Niree—she just removed herself mentally, and who can blame her? Dee lost his compass. He's an idealist. A cynic, and a smart-ass, and an egotistical jerk, but an idealist. In those thirty minutes down on Canberra, he had every ideal he'd ever had torn away from him. I couldn't let him kill a civilian, Greg. It would have destroyed him. And I knew he wouldn't kill me. Dee is Corps down to his chromosomes. I was the only thing that could have stopped him, and I did."

He closed his eyes. *God.* He'd thought this not-thinking

problem of hers was recent, that flinging herself into space with no suit and no lifeline and no actual plan was a habit she'd picked up later in her career. "And it was on you. Just you." *Always just you.*

He wasn't sure she caught the sarcasm in his voice. "I needed him, Greg. We already had one person we had to carry. If he'd shot that girl, we would have had to carry him, too, one way or another."

An escape plan, then. He wondered if he ought to be concerned that it was beginning to make sense to him. "You were fixing him," he said aloud.

"I was patching him up long enough to get him off the planet," she corrected. "That's all I could focus on—getting back to the ship and getting home. Nothing else mattered." Her face shuttered again, and he remembered how the mission had ended. She had shot a man dead to get her crew safely to their ship.

He ran his hands over his face, dropping back into his chair. "Was there anything left down there afterward?" he asked.

"Nothing," she told him. "By the time the next crew went down, the rain had become so acidic they had to wear full suits just to walk around. We swept the surface, but there was nothing recoverable. Even the terraformers had been wrecked. We retrieved some bodies—most of them didn't have any known relatives anywhere else, but we tried to identify as many as we could. After we sent the report, Central gave the planet up as lost."

"What happened to the others?"

"Jimmy and Dee you know. Niree—she stayed on *Exeter* for a while. I lost track of her. She's been gone for about a year—transferred, retired, I don't know."

"Were you friends?"

"Before." That miserable look again. "She was a mentor of sorts. We would sit and talk sometimes about what a horrible influence Çelik was on everyone. And after Canberra . . . she fell in with him for a while. I expect it was rather like me and Dee, but I judged her for it. I was an idiot. And any friendship we had just dissipated."

"Savin?"

"He left the Corps shortly after I transferred off *Exeter*. He works as an artist now, living on Akkadian. I think Jess has a few of his pieces."

"What about the children?"

She rubbed her eyes. "The baby went to a closed adoption. If anybody knows where she is, it would be Dee, but I expect he let her go. Ruby," she said, and he thought she sounded cooler, "immigrated to Earth and went to school. Iceland, I think. About three years ago she bought a ticket to Aleph One, and I haven't heard anything since. We never knew if Dee was right and she was in on the plot to lure Treharne. I've been over it thousands of times in my head, and I really can't tell. If she was . . . she was a kid. Not even fifteen yet. And if it was participate or get ripped apart by those bastards, I can't really blame her."

"But you do."

She shrugged. "Makes me a hypocrite, too, I suppose." She was silent a moment, then added, subdued, "The body of the man I killed was gone when they went back. I'll never know who he was."

Greg had been responsible for death. He had shot down attacking ships, had made calls during a battle that caused his own people to die. He was responsible for every death under his command, even the ones he told himself had been unavoidable. He carried them under his skin, always a part of him. But he had never killed anyone face-to-face, never had to make the choice Elena had made. "You did him a favor," he said, knowing his words were useless.

Her eyes snapped into his, angry. "He doesn't have the luxury of being grateful for my choice, does he?"

Hell. All her old fractures pried open over this. "You want off this one, Elena?"

Something almost like a smile passed over her lips. "Are you insulting me, too, Greg?" She shook her head. "If I can help by remembering something—terrain markers, familiar streets, anything—that's a bonus. That's extra. But it doesn't matter to me where they are.

"It just matters that we get them."

CHAPTER 15

Exeter

The pilot's name was Tumen, and he spoke dialect with the same lilting, sibilant pronunciation as Guanyin. He had been cool and formal when he emerged from the shuttle in *Galileo*'s hangar, but when Raman had greeted him in his own language, his stiff posture had relaxed. Just like that, Raman became one of his own. Tumen's nod to Jimmy Youda was an afterthought, which was just as well; Youda spoke no dialect at all, and would not have accepted any gestures of friendship anyway. Raman had been surprised when Youda, never one to take chances, had volunteered to accompany him as his medical supervisor; but Youda had always felt strongly about his medical duty. He was a humorless bastard, but a decent enough physician for the job.

As long as Raman didn't have to share a room with him.

The shuttle was an oft-refurbished Fender, as ubiquitous in the Third Sector as fireflies had been at home. He had asked his mother once why their ancestors had brought fireflies, among all of the other more useful insects they had imported from

Earth. She had smiled—not the most common expression for her—and said, "Because they thought they were pretty."

> *Beauty is truth, truth beauty,—that is all*
> *Ye know on earth, and all ye need to know.*

His mother loved poetry. Raman, more often than not, found it to be self-indulgent bullshit.

Foster had broken out a clean uniform to say his farewells, and brought his first officer with him. Raman had to admit the other captain had made a good show. He had greeted the PSI pilot with polite deference, and managed not to act surprised when he found the man had come alone. Apparently Foster knew enough to understand that any PSI representative on a Corps starship—first Doctor Xiao, now Pilot Tumen—represented an act of trust and diplomacy on their part. Well, Raman had always heard Foster was a good diplomat. Guanyin's dislike said more about her perceptiveness than Foster's failings.

"You don't have to agree," Foster said, when he told Raman about his agreement with Guanyin. "I'll come to some other accommodation with her, or we'll do without her help."

Raman had arched an eyebrow at him. "Some reason you think you should be the only Corps captain ever hosted on a PSI starship?" Foster had looked away, irritated, dropping the subject, and Raman was disappointed. He wouldn't have minded one last argument before he left.

With some care, and with most of his weight on his still-flesh foot, he came to attention before Foster and Commander Lockwood and gave them both a courtesy salute. "I'll let you have your ship back now, Captain," he said.

But Foster was done being baited. All he did was return the salute, and say "Safe journey, Captain Çelik."

Çelik dropped the salute and turned briefly to Commander Lockwood, bowing ever so slightly. "It has been a pleasure, Commander Lockwood."

She lifted her chin a little, measuring him with those careful eyes. "Good luck to you, sir."

He liked that word, *sir*. He could still remember the first time he had heard it: the first day of his second year at CMA, running into a new cadet on his way into the dorm. *Excuse me, sir.* She had been taller than he was, and years older; her words had been protocol and nothing more.

The reason hadn't mattered to him at all.

He turned away and climbed aboard the Fender, leaving Youda to his perfunctory farewells. He had the impression Youda had spent most of his hours on *Galileo* in the pub, and was probably not fully recovered, despite the availability of sobriety aids. It was a pleasantly humanizing idea, thinking of Youda with a hangover. Raman had long since given the man up as a lost cause.

The journey to *Exeter* took only a few minutes. Tumen was a deft and relaxed flyer, and he docked on *Exeter*'s far side with practiced ease. When they were secure, he turned to Raman. "Would you like me to come with you, Captain?" he asked.

Raman shook his head. "I won't be long. I don't have much." He looked back at Youda. "You can wait here, too, Doctor," he offered.

Youda looked vaguely alarmed, and glanced at the pilot. "No, thank you, sir," he said stiffly. "I'll come with you."

"Fine," Raman said. "You can carry this." He handed Youda

the cane, and propped himself up on the Fender's walls to make his way out of the hatch.

It didn't look at all like his ship, he thought, as he leaned one hand against the wall and limped down the corridor. Most of the systems were still offline—forever offline—and the lighting was a combination of emergency spots and those strips of portable lights that *Galileo*'s crew had pasted to the walls throughout the ship. It didn't sound like her, either. He heard the faint hiss of the air, and the low hum of the gravity generator, but the sound of the prosthetic hitting the floor clanged against his eardrums at an unseemly volume.

But when he inhaled . . . yes. That smell. Despite the residual scent of burning and the ozone of overloaded circuits, he recognized the odor of his ship. For more than fifteen years of his life, his first conscious breath every day had smelled like this. Given time, his mind would lose the olfactory memory. Smell brought things back better than any other reminder, but it also was the first thing the brain lost.

Not me, he told his ship. *I will not lose you. Not until the day I die.*

His office and his quarters were around the corner from their docking port. Youda trailed him like a disapproving shadow. He had asked, before they left *Galileo,* why Raman was not using the cane, but he would not ask again.

Raman stopped at the door. "Wait here," he told Youda.

"Sir," Youda said, "don't you need help carrying your things?"

Raman didn't bother to answer.

The rooms were dark, but otherwise had weathered the battle unscathed. There was his desk, the chair pushed neatly beneath it, the place where he had written reports and taken comms. Behind it a cabinet—real wood, this one, a gift from a colony governor. Limping more slowly, he moved around the desk and pulled it open. Three bottles of good bourbon there. He took one, tucking it under his arm, and left the others.

He crossed the room and went through the open door into his quarters.

Most Corps soldiers kept few possessions. Soldiers were expected to be able to decamp quickly, in case the Admiralty needed to reassign them. Many who stayed in one place managed to acquire a small collection of souvenirs, though. Niree had collected shot glasses, especially the kitschy sort sold to tourists on various Alephs. Raman's own collection of objects was considerably more diverse, and also smaller. He was counting on being able to fit all of it into a single bag.

He opened a drawer and pulled a duffel out from under a stack of uniforms. Almost as an afterthought he pulled two changes of clothes out with it and tossed them in, wrapping the bottle of bourbon in a black-and-gray jacket. Then he crossed the room and sat on the bed—waiting out the throb of pain that hit with the pressure change against his injured knee—and opened a cabinet.

He had been wrong; he would not have room. There were too many. He had only kept one item from each soldier lost, but he had not remembered the number. The names were different. He would always remember the names.

Well, if he had to choose, he thought chronologically would be best.

He packed one item at a time, tucking each memento carefully into his bag, wrapping anything fragile with a piece of his clothing. A crystal snowflake, a knitted stocking, a small

turned wooden box. A deck of cards, worn and bent from shuf-
fling. Those had been Treharne's. Treharne had been a terrible gambler, but he could do card tricks that Raman still found
mystifying. A book of old poems; a Standard-PSI dictionary of
obscene phrases. All of these people whom he had lost, whom
he had failed.

Plus ninety-seven more.

He thought to leave the glass Niree had given him behind,
but he found, in the end, that he couldn't. She was not like the
others, of course. She was alive and well, and it had been both
a joke and genuine sentiment when she gave it to him. "Cheap,
fake, and useful," she had said, and given him a treasure from
her collection: a mass-produced shot glass from Aleph Naught
that she had bought when she was a teenager.

Picking it up, he stood, and limped back to his dresser. He
opened a lower drawer and pulled out a thick insulated under-
shirt, the sort he wore only when they were headed down to
a particularly cold planet. Laying the shirt out on the bed, he
rolled the glass up in it, folding as he went, until he had created
a soft, secure cylindrical home for it. Then he tucked it into a
corner and zipped the bag up.

His knee twinged, and an instant later he felt that odd, flat
pain signal from the prosthetic. He had stubbed a toe on the bed
frame. *One advantage of being in constant pain,* he thought,
as he breathed evenly through the wave, *is that a little extra
doesn't make much of a difference.* The sensation blinded him
for a few moments, motes appearing before his eyes as his nervous system coped with the overload. Because he was alone, he
hung on to the edge of the dresser and took a few extra seconds
to recover. Then he lifted the bag and turned, leaving the room.

Youda was waiting outside the door, trying and failing to mask his impatience. He moved as if he was going to reach out to take the bag, but he must have seen something in Raman's face because he froze, and then shrank back a little. Raman had been wrong: he should have found a different medic. He had never been overly fond of Lawson, but at least the man cracked a joke once in a while.

He took his time heading back, Youda trailing sullenly behind him. The pain was slowing him; that was it. He was having trouble balancing. Stupid pride keeping him from using the cane, perhaps; but he needed to learn to do without it. It would have no place in his responsibilities in the days ahead. He pushed off the wall and made himself walk without assistance: short steps, careful balance, keeping his weight on the prosthetic as briefly as possible as the pain jolted straight up his spine and into the back of his neck. Don't touch anything; just walk.

But as he neared the docking port and the Fender, he let his fingers open, let his hand brush the wall. Cool polymer, sturdy and strong. Out of assembly fifteen years earlier, and directly into Raman's hands. He had flown her, helmed her, commanded her, and finally sacrificed her. She had never belonged to any other captain. She had never belonged to anyone else.

And she never would.

He turned to Youda. "Anything you need to retrieve, Doctor?" Raman asked him.

Youda looked briefly surprised. "No, sir. Thank you, sir."

Raman waited a moment, then sighed and gestured with his hand. "After you," he said pointedly.

Youda startled a little, then composed his features and headed back through the docking port. If the kid was that superstitious about PSI, Raman thought, he was going to be jumpy as hell for the next three days. Ah, well. He had volunteered; it was on his own head.

When Youda had vanished through the port, Raman turned around, looking one last time at the dimly lit hallway. Unfamiliar. Dark. Dead, or very nearly. This was not his ship. His ship was in his memory. His ship was strong, and he was strong with her. He would be as strong as long as he needed to be. And then, like her, he could stop.

He turned back to the docking port, and left *Exeter* behind.

CHAPTER 16

Orunmila

Guanyin watched as the shuttle settled on the hangar floor and powered down. Tumen emerged first, leaving the door open, walking around his ship for the usual postflight examination, his relaxed hands caressing the little ship's nose. The next person to emerge was not Çelik, but a tall, slightly built man carrying a medical kit, his wary eyes sweeping the hangar. Çelik's doctor, her one concession to diplomacy. He stepped onto the floor, looking around uncomfortably, and she was not sure if he was pleased to be off the shuttle, or worried about where he found himself. His appearance was ordinary enough—he might even be called handsome—but everything in his restless posture suggested someone alien. As she watched he straightened, turning back toward the shuttle's open door, and held out a hand.

Çelik emerged, ignoring the offer of assistance. She noted, however, that he was, in fact, holding a cane. He lurched gracelessly out of the shuttle, the artificial foot hitting the deck with a metallic clang that echoed through the cavernous space. The medic jumped, but Çelik himself ignored the sound, his eyes scanning the hangar floor to ceiling. Eventually his gaze came to rest on Guanyin, and he stepped forward, his gait uneven, the cane still grasped, unused, in his fist. "Permission to come aboard, Captain Shiang."

"Granted, Captain Çelik. Welcome to *Orunmila*."

"You don't change much around here, do you?" he said to her.

"You remember it." It had been more than five years ago, she recalled: Chanyu had let Çelik bring one of his shuttles on board to transfer some large cargo. Chanyu's guards had been careful not to let anyone from Central leave the hangar.

"I never forget a deck," he said. He flashed a charming grin at Cali. "I don't believe we were properly introduced back on *Exeter*," he said, holding out a hand.

Guanyin stole a glance at Cali, standing at attention beside her. Her friend looked flustered, off-guard, and Guanyin wasn't sure if she was pleased or annoyed. He had figured out Cali already, and Cali—usually the aggressor in these situations—had no idea she was being manipulated. "I am Lieutenant Annenkov," she said, taking his hand. "Cali to my friends."

"You kept your name," he observed, holding on to her hand longer than necessary.

"I didn't know you understood our naming conventions," Guanyin put in.

He let go of Cali, conquest completed, and returned his attention to Guanyin. "I don't," he told her candidly. "But Lieutenant Annenkov has a different accent, as well, and with the mismatched last name, I drew a conclusion."

Cali was clearly impressed by this parlor trick. "I didn't come on board until I was almost ten," she said. "I never did lose the accent."

Guanyin cleared her throat, then stared pointedly at the medic. "You have not introduced your doctor," she said.

"Ah." Çelik gestured carelessly at the slight man. "This is Doctor Youda. He's insisted on hovering over me. Any chance you can find him some quarters on the opposite side of the ship?"

Briefly shocked, Guanyin took a moment to realize that Doctor Youda had not registered anything that either of them had said. "He doesn't speak dialect," she said.

"He speaks the intergalactic language of healing," Çelik said dryly.

Guanyin thought a moment. "The barracks are a few levels down from where I had planned on putting you. He'll be able to look after you, but he won't be underfoot."

"An equitable compromise," Çelik agreed. "Lead on then, Captain Shiang."

She turned and led them away, allowing Cali to escort the cagy Doctor Youda. Çelik's mood was strange, elusive, and she wondered what was bothering him. Her ship, perhaps, unfamiliar to him, alien and inhospitable? She could not believe him so susceptible to his surroundings, but she supposed being away from his home would be uncomfortable no matter where he was.

She waited as Cali led Doctor Youda down a different corridor, then looked over at Çelik. "Why did you bring that one?"

"He volunteered."

"So you did this out of generosity."

He caught her eye. "Why not?"

She sniffed. "I think you're laughing at me."

He was silent for a moment. "Doctor Youda," he told her

more seriously, "has always felt strongly about treating the wounds of my crew. And with the others leaving with *Cassia*"— here something shifted in his eyes, and she looked away from him—"he finds himself without anything else to do."

Sentiment was unlike him. "I'll see that Cali looks after him properly."

A brief smile touched his lips, and she thought his eyes lightened a little. "Don't be *too* generous," he said.

They reached his rooms, and she left her security detail outside the door. As they walked in, Çelik's eyebrows shot up, and his expression shuttered. "Is Youda's room like this?" he asked.

She couldn't blame him for being surprised, she supposed. The room was the nicest they had, outside of the officers' quarters: spacious and well-furnished, with a set of wide, floor-to-ceiling windows looking out on the stars. There was a bathroom that boasted both a sunken tub and a standing shower, and a separate bedroom with an oversized closet and a family-sized bed. Guanyin's own bed was not so big; she didn't like having that much space. She suspected that, as part of the Corps, he wasn't used to such luxury, either; but she had not had time to swap out the furnishings.

"The barracks are more . . . military," she apologized. She stood next to the door, one hand absently on her stomach, watching him as he prowled the rooms. He stood in the bathroom door for a long time, staring down at the bathtub, and she wanted to ask him what he was seeing. When he turned back to her, his face was wooden.

"How long did it take you to put this together?" he asked.

"These rooms have been here for quite some time. Is something wrong?"

He gestured at the bathroom. "A tub with handrails? No stairs anywhere? Nothing mounted too high, or too low? I'll bet your glassware isn't glassware, either." He reached out and picked up a water glass from the sink, then dashed it to the ground. It shattered, and he picked up a large shard of glass, running the edge against his palm. Unharmed, he opened his fingers and let it fall to the floor. "Candy glass. The nice stuff, too. Quite a luxury item for a PSI ship."

All at once she realized what he was thinking. "You believe I had this room prepared for you."

"Unless you find yourself with a lot of crippled visitors."

The only thing crippling you, she wanted to snap at him, *is your foul mood.* Instead, she dropped her arms to her sides and walked into the room, crossing around the sofa to stand in front of the big window. "As the story is told," she said, "*Orunmila's* fifth captain commissioned this room, about two hundred years ago. It is said he found his long-lost brother acting as a dictator on a starving colony. The citizens wanted the dictator killed, but instead our captain brought him back here. They say he lived out his days in this room. The captain visited for three hours each day, but nobody knows what they talked about."

To Guanyin's satisfaction, Çelik was gaping at her. "You're saying this room is a prison."

"It might all be rubbish, of course. There are so many old stories that nobody writes down, just tells over and over again until they make no sense. How the captain would have known he had a brother when he came to us as a baby nobody knows. But this room is intended to be entirely self-contained, providing comfort without requiring any sort of maintenance."

"And the candy glass?"

"We use it everywhere we can, so we don't have to give the children special dishes."

"And you don't have to worry about houseguests cutting their own wrists."

She cocked her head at him. "Actually, I think the concern is more with attacking the guards. But you make a fair point as well." He kept frowning, his eyes lighting on everything in the room, never resting. "If you wish," she added, "I can move you into the barracks, and still place you away from Doctor Youda. But the barrack rooms are much smaller. Even I wouldn't be comfortable in those."

His eyes connected with hers. "At this point I don't imagine you're comfortable anywhere, are you?" he asked, and she wondered how many pregnant women he had seen in his life. Grudgingly, he relented. "I'll stay. I'll admit, it's nice to have a bedroom door to close against the world." He walked over to stand next to her by the bar. "Can I pour you a drink?" he asked.

She smiled and shook her head. "I am on duty, Captain, but I thank you for your hospitality."

He opened one of the cabinets over the bar, and pulled out a glass and a bottle, studying the label. "Is this a coincidence?" he asked.

"Do you like that sort?"

"Anyone who's not a congenital idiot likes this sort."

"I can't take credit," she said. "Cali stocked the bar. And yes, it's possible she studied you and figured out it was a drink you liked."

He poured the drink, then held the glass up against the window without tasting. "All your glassware? Everything safe for the children?"

"What kind of a family would we be if we did not protect them?"

"And yet you're hauling them into this mess."

"I'm not sure I can explain it to an outsider," she said. She took his silence as inquiry. "We give them an environment where they can learn and explore safely. But the galaxy is what it is. We don't tell them otherwise. We take it as our responsibility to help others, even if they're not PSI. To stay out of this fight because of the children . . . we'd be lying to them. Children know when you lie to them, and then they never believe you again."

"That sounds like an excuse."

She felt a pang of disappointment. "I did say I wasn't sure I could explain."

"Are you a good mother, Captain Shiang?"

Children know when you lie to them. "Not always, no."

"Are you a good captain?"

"I have no context with which to answer that question."

"That is a poor excuse."

She shook her head. "I've had six months. They haven't removed me yet. I have not been tested."

"This mission. Will this be your test?"

"Ask me in three days."

He fell silent for a moment, and took a sip from the glass. "Why am I here?"

He would not, she thought, appreciate knowing how protective he was making her feel. "Several reasons," she equivocated. "In part because I thought it would be easier to communicate face-to-face."

He scoffed. "Try again."

She raised her eyebrows at him. "All right, then. I don't trust your Admiralty, and I don't trust your Captain Foster."

"He's not *my* Captain Foster."

"Do *you* trust him, then?"

Çelik was silent for a long time. "I do," he said at last, grudgingly. "At least the way you mean it. If it came down to it, Captain, he'd defend your ship as surely as you defended mine."

"Before or after he drew us into the line of fire?"

At that he looked briefly stricken, but he glanced away too quickly for her to make out anything else in his face. "It works out better this way," he told her, shifting the subject. "I can coordinate with my people on *Galileo,* and we can keep our information in sync."

It was as rubbish a response from him as it had been from her, and she dropped the pretense of subtlety. "Captain Çelik," she asked him quietly, "what is your mission? Not the one you were assigned. *Yours.*"

"I am going to kill them," he said candidly, without anger or passion. "One at a time. With my bare hands, if it is possible. And if MacBride was in on this, in any way at all . . . he can be last. He can watch the others die, one by one, and know it's coming for him. I will tear the heart from him, as he has done to me. I will watch him bleed and bleed and bleed."

"It won't be enough."

"Of course it won't. But it is all there is."

"And then?"

The question seemed to surprise him. "And then what? Then I will be finished."

Guanyin felt suddenly as if she were standing on the edge of a cliff, so high she could see nothing below but fog, concealing land or ocean she could not know. She thought he had been standing with her, but she realized that he had already jumped, probably the moment the raiders had destroyed his ship. She felt exhausted, and sad beyond measure, and utterly useless. She looked away from him and moved toward the door.

"You will forgive me, Captain," she said, "but I must rest. If you need anything, there are guards outside the door. They are not prison guards," she continued, anticipating his objection. "They'll go away if you ask. But they'll also answer any questions you have, or get you anything you need. If you like," she added, "you can meet me in the morning. I generally have breakfast a little after six o'clock, but I usually have at least two children with me at that time."

He looked momentarily disconcerted. "Perhaps after breakfast, then," he suggested.

"As you wish." And she turned and left the room, feeling like a passenger on a ship that no one was flying.

CHAPTER 17

Galileo

The trip to Canberra would take them thirty-one hours, although *Galileo* alone could have done it in twenty. *Orunmila*'s agility was due, in part, to a smaller stellar battery; she could only spend fourteen hours in the field at a stretch, and her recharge took a full seven hours. Even seven hours was an impressive technological feat, given the ship's size. Elena was itching to look at the battery config, see if she could optimize it; but having spent two weeks aboard a PSI ship the year before, she knew better than to offer. Even with Trey—who had been one of their own—vouching for her, it had taken a full week before they trusted her with anything proprietary. Besides, *Orunmila* had its own mechanics, and they had more knowledge of how they might optimize their hardware than she did.

What they did not have was the parts. She suspected *Orunmila* might have some use for some of the surplus she kept in storage, but strictly speaking the equipment was classified. She wondered if, as part of *Orunmila*'s cooperation in this mission, she might be allowed to offer it to them anyway.

She supposed it was worth the question. After all, after last year, she could hardly make her reputation with the Admiralty worse.

Galileo's field was tuned and steady, and they monitored *Orunmila's* wake, six minutes ahead of them. She prowled the engine room as long as she could, hovering over the readouts, until Ted finally threw her out. "Do something else," he insisted. "You are making everyone nervous."

Despite their long personal relationship, Ted was always a professional in the engine room. He wouldn't have said it if it wasn't true. So she left.

She thought of sleeping. She knew she was overdue. To be efficient, she should lie down now and take the opportunity. But she was keyed up, too much adrenaline in her system, and she did not think sleep would come. Ted had it backward—*she* was the one who was nervous. Thirty-one hours of mundane stop and go . . .

And then Canberra.

She almost never remembered her dreams, but she always remembered her nightmares. And so many of her nightmares were about Canberra, and Treharne, and the man she had killed for the sin of trying to steal her ship.

Second-guessing was pointless. She had come to terms with that years ago. Her mission had been to get her people out, and take what civilians would come willingly. He would have been willing to leave, the man she had shot; but he would have left their bodies behind him. He had gone mad. They had all gone mad. And she had found a purpose to her career she had never anticipated: to keep such a disaster from ever happening again.

Eventually her restlessness brought her to the gym. She changed out of her uniform, and started with a meticulous, repetitive dance warm-up, letting the complaints of her muscles distract her. After a year away from ballet, she was discovering picking it up again wasn't so easy. She had stayed in shape, but running and lifting did not work the knees and thighs the way dance did—and neither fed her soul the same way. She had missed the discipline of dance, and the music. There was something about moving to cadence, to melody, that let her tap into the melancholy she so often shoved aside. It made her feel a little less lonely. After the horror and grief of the last day, she thought it might help.

She moved slowly and precisely until her muscles burned, and then she switched to tumbling to work her arms and upper back. She continued until every muscle in her body was as unhappy as her weakened knees.

"You've kept it up, Songbird."

She rolled out of a handstand and saw Dee standing by the locker room door, wearing shorts and a tank top. Dee was a lifter. She used to tease him about his endurance, tell him he ought to do more running . . . but in truth he had always been in extraordinarily good shape.

"You too," she replied. She walked over to the wall and picked up a towel, wiping off her face and arms. Indeed, eight years seemed to have made no material difference in his appearance, and she found herself looking around at anything other than his broad shoulders and bare legs.

"It's the key to immortality," he told her. "Exercise. Sex, too; but you could argue that's just a subset."

"You haven't changed much, have you?"

"You have."

She dropped her smile. "What did you want me to do, Dee?" she asked, walking toward him. "He needed to know."

"So somewhere in the 'us' and 'them' game, you became 'them'?"

"Greg's not 'them,' " she said irritably, passing him to go into the locker room. *For fuck's sake, Dee.*

He followed her. "The hell he's not," he said hotly. "He'd sell you out in a second if he knew what you got up to."

"He *does* know, Dee."

"Bullshit."

"Look." She turned on him. "You stayed behind. You stuck with that son of a bitch Çelik because it was the right thing for your career. I left because I wanted to work for someone I could trust. We both got what we wanted. What the hell is your problem?"

"I trust Çelik with my life!"

"Well, that's looking like a mistake, isn't it?" Her regret was instant, and she swore to herself. "I'm sorry, Dee," she said, holding out a hand. "It's not on him, this attack."

His face had closed at her words, and when he spoke he was calmer. "It's all right, Songbird," he said. "And . . . I don't know that it's not on him, you know? This transport—it was some big-ass secret. He didn't tell us why, though."

"He wouldn't have done it if he had known it was going to cost him ninety-seven people."

"He would have if he thought the mission was important."

She wasn't sure she believed that, but she wasn't going to argue with him. "Did you talk to him at all? MacBride?"

He shook his head. "Between being pissed off and being unconscious, he didn't have much time for chatting. What the hell happened out by that wormhole, Elena? MacBride was pretty clear he got screwed. Is that true?"

"I don't know all the facts," she hedged.

"Fuck that."

He did know her. "Yeah," she admitted, "he got screwed. They needed a fall guy, and for some reason it was him instead of us."

"So Jimmy was right. In a way."

"That all of this is our fault?" The thought made her tired. "I don't know, Dee. I don't know what happened or why. But someone smarter than I am told me once that death is on the murderer. That none of us can look back and decide what we did or didn't do that caused it to happen. And it's the murderer who we're going after."

He shook his head. "You always make it sound so clear."

"You used to find that a comfort."

"Maybe I've grown up."

"So now I *haven't* changed?"

She smiled as she said it, and for an instant her mind was flooded by a sharp tactile memory: his skin, smooth and damp, tasting of salt, the only thing between her and despair. She looked away and took a careful breath. Dee, who knew her too well, took a self-conscious step backward.

"You trust Foster to pursue this," he said.

She nodded. "Even if we don't like what we find." And at this point, she was almost certain that she wouldn't. "He may be the boss, Dee, but he'll toss politics the instant they get in the way. He—"

She broke off, frowning.

"What is it?"

169

She held up a hand to silence him, and waited. After a few moments she heard it again: a subtle, faint harmonic above *Galileo*'s usual mechanical hum. Not distressed, not shrieking, just . . . out of place. She touched the comm behind her ear. "Ted, what have you got down there?"

She heard the irritation in his voice as he replied. "We have green across the board, Chief. Why?"

"I heard something. Check the logs."

Ted made an annoyed sound, but she knew he would comply. When he spoke again, all doubt was gone. "We've got a wobble," he told her. "Negligible. Doesn't even put us past tolerance. How the hell did you hear that?"

She headed back out into the gym and went toward the door, Dee at her heels. "Drop us out, Ted. Now."

She had made it into the hallway when she heard the familiar whine of the field spinning down . . . and then a warped warble, like a sick bird, as the ship returned to speed. Fear closed over her heart. "Ted?"

"She won't spin down," he told her.

The harmonic was getting louder. "*Galileo*, why can't you drop out?"

"The field generator is damaged," the ship told her conversationally. "Any attempt to drop out would result in a field collapse and catastrophic warping."

Catastrophic warping. What had Çelik said about military euphemisms? "How much longer can we stay in the field?"

There was a pause, and she swore under her breath. "Generator overload in six minutes, eighteen seconds."

"Recommendations?"

"Detach the field generator."

"What are our odds of surviving that?"

"Fifty-seven percent likelihood of partial crew survival."

Shit. "Give me something else."

"Repair the generator flaw."

"Why didn't you recommend that one first?"

"Time estimated to repair the generator is twelve minutes, twenty seconds."

This time she swore aloud. She rounded the corner and swept into engineering, followed by Dee. Ted met her by the door. "Ted," she said, "get everybody out of here and into shelter." She turned to Dee; he was not part of *Galileo*'s crew, but he had authority. "Contact Commander Broadmoor and start securing the rest of the ship. If we have to detach, it's going to be a rough landing."

Dee nodded and headed back out the door.

Greg came through on her comm. "Chief?"

"We're hydroplaning," she said tersely. "I'm going to try to fix it. Lock us down."

To his credit, he did not argue, just disconnected. An instant later the general alarm was sounding.

Elena ran to the other end of the room and up the stairs. The generator room was separated from the greater machine floor by a clear polymer door a meter thick, in case of another military euphemism: *incendiary events*. The whole room could be decoupled from the ship and shoved into the field, allowing the ship to fall—with very little grace—back into normal space. No ship had ever done it, as far as she knew, and she'd found *Galileo*'s estimate of their chances of survival surprisingly high. There had been a few generator failures early on in the development of the original design, hundreds of years ago.

Nothing of those ships or their crews had ever been found.

She had *Galileo* open the door and went in, pulling a spanner from her wrist kit and approaching the generator. *Galileo* pulled up a 3D deep scan of the core, and she saw the flaw right away: a crack, no more than a nanometer thick, running right down the center as if it had been drawn with a ruler. Repairing it was not a complex job; all it required was a molecular re-fuse. But while they were in the field, it was active, and she would need to re-fuse it by hand.

By a very steady, very fast hand.

"*Galileo*," she ordered, "when I get this re-fused, drop us out. If I can't re-fuse, detach as late as possible. Understood?"

"Acknowledged."

Sweat dripping behind her ears from her long workout, she shoved panic aside and began the meticulous process of re-fusing the generator. This was a task she had done a thousand times, albeit never in an active field. Never when failure would mean a very swift, very exothermic death. Her hands were steady, but she could not quite silence the timer in the back of her mind: *too slow, too slow,* it kept whispering. When she hit halfway, she couldn't resist. "Time," she said tersely.

"Two minutes, twelve seconds."

No, no, no. She was not working fast enough. This was easy work. Methodical. *Knit, shift, knit, shift.* No reason she couldn't do it faster.

She thought of *Exeter,* and remembered the belly of the ship vaporizing. She thought of Çelik's severed leg, and the way he stomped across a room, refusing help, denying the pain that drained the color from his lips. She thought of Dee, and the infant he had rescued all those years ago. She thought of Greg, who was trusting her, right now, to save them all, and of Trey, and how he had always believed in her, no matter what they were facing. She thought of all the people she had tucked into her heart, one at a time, for all the years of her life.

Knit, shift.

She hit the end of the generator core and dropped her hands, taking a step back. Nothing changed. The harmonic was still there, whining in her ears, louder than before, louder than anything she had ever heard. The last thing she would hear.

Come on, she thought at her ship. *Save me.*

She thought the sound would deafen her . . .

. . . and with a familiar tone, *Galileo* dropped out of the FTL field.

She allowed herself to collapse against the wall, and closed her eyes. She became conscious suddenly of how damp she was, her clothes soaked through by more than the sweat from the gym. Moisture was dripping from her scalp and down her neck, and she could feel her heart thumping rapidly in her chest. Her fingers were still closed around the spanner, her muscles taut; slowly she relaxed them, then slipped the instrument back into her kit without looking.

"Good girl," she whispered to her ship, then she commed Greg. "We're clear," she told him.

"Good work, Chief. When you're free, come to my office."

Free. What a funny word. She chuckled, and realized she was reacting to the adrenaline in her system. After the day she'd had, she should have been used to it. "Five minutes," she said, and disconnected. She laid one hand against the bulkhead and patted it, then opened her eyes and pushed herself to her feet.

When she came out of the generator room, she saw Ted

standing in the center of the empty machine floor, looking up at her. She frowned at him. "I told you to get everybody out."

"I did."

She sighed and climbed down the stairs. "What purpose would have been served by you getting blown to bits along with me?"

"Saving time," he said, falling into step next to her as she headed for the exit. "If you'd been killed without me, he would have shoved me out an airlock."

CHAPTER 18

"I've got Ted doing a sweep," Elena told Greg. "Low-level. Starting with the critical field systems, all the way down to refrigeration and climate."

"How long is that going to take?"

"Six days, give or take."

"That long?"

She met his eyes. "We've got to cover everything, including the weapons systems. They're no less vulnerable than anything else. And I've put everyone on twelve-on, twelve-off. I could make it eight and eight, but I'd rather everyone stay rested and fresh. I don't want anything missed."

Greg, who was fighting so hard to contain his rage that his hands were shaking, couldn't imagine how anyone was going to get any rest for a while. "Is that with *Galileo* to calibrate?"

She stared out the window, face unreadable. "No. Visuals and instruments only."

He had asked, when she first came in, if it could have been missed in their normal maintenance routines. She had told him of course it could have been missed, given the chaos after the battle. But she didn't believe it any more than he did.

She stood by the window next to his desk, arms crossed, elbows in her hands, one foot tapping absently against the floor. Her hair had trailed out of the tight knot at the nape of her neck, and he could see patchy sweat at the armpits of her black leotard and in a wide stripe down the center of her back. There was a hole in the back of the tights she wore, and he thought one of her shoes had lost its strap. That would annoy her—it would take her months to get a replacement pair. Her lips were set and her skin had an undertone of gray, as if she had been sick. He could not remember when he had last seen her so shaken.

He could not remember when he had last been so furious.

"Is Jess looking at the security records?" she asked.

"If anything's been altered, she'll find it. Nobody on *Exeter* could hide anything like that from her."

"Greg—"

"Don't defend them, Elena." He kept his voice low. "You know it wasn't one of us. One of those people tried to kill us, so don't even think about making excuses for them."

"I'm not making excuses. I'm just—" She exhaled. "Maybe it was earlier. Maybe one of the raiders hit us in the right spot. Maybe—"

"That is bullshit and you know it." He took a breath, clenching his fists. Yelling at Elena wasn't going to help anything. She wasn't the one he was angry with. Hell, she had just saved their lives.

He thought about how close she had come to losing her own, and the anger flared again.

"We had most of them on board at one point or another," she said. "But who did it isn't the most important question right now. It's *why*. Why would Shadow Ops sabotage us when the Admiralty ordered us to go after these people?" Easier for her to focus on that, he supposed, than on whether or not someone she knew had sabotaged her ship.

He didn't have that luxury.

She continued. "They could easily have ordered us off, instead of trying to kill us. What kind of agenda could they possibly have?"

"You really think S-O has any agenda we could decode?"

She seemed surprised by the question. "Of course. They're warmongers, Greg, but not irrational ones. I could see—barely—some rationale for kidnapping MacBride, but hitting us? What kind of statement does it make, having two starships destroyed by sabotage in such a short period of time? What do they get out of it?"

"You think, with what we know of them, we can just sit here and work it out?"

"No." She thought for a moment, and then she straightened, her expression clearing. "But how about we ask them?"

It took them several minutes and a handful of comms hiccups to get through to Admiralty Central and make their request. Elena let the vid connection run idle; a shameless waste of bandwidth. Not her style. She must be very, very angry.

After a moment, Admiral Waris's face appeared. "Chief Shaw?" She looked concerned. "Elena, is everything all right?"

Greg had shifted out of his chair and onto the sofa in the corner, out of the line of sight of the comm. He studied Admiral Waris, an officer he had known tangentially for fifteen years. A woman of about sixty, she still had an unlined face, although the skin around her cheekbones was losing definition. Her blond hair was cut to fall perfectly over the pale skin of her forehead and around her ears; it tickled her collar, but grew no longer. He supposed she was attractive, but he had always felt a chill when he looked at her, as if the fixed look in her eyes concealed some kind of machinery.

"No, Admiral," Elena said bluntly. "And I think you know why."

"Is this about the engine failure?" Waris asked. The Admiralty kept track of all Corps starships; telemetry data on the incident, including the in-field repair, would have been transmitted as soon as they dropped out of the field.

Greg had sent a more detailed brief to *Orunmila,* along with an explicit request for help. He was glad Waris couldn't see him; he didn't think he would be able to hide his own blind anger. Sometimes, as counterintuitive as it was, he needed to leave the diplomacy to Elena. "*Cassia*'s turned around," Waris added. "Captain Vassily will be there to assist in a few hours."

"That's not necessary, Admiral," Elena said smoothly. "*Orunmila* will be here in a few minutes."

"It's amazing that no one was hurt. I don't expect half a dozen mechanics in the Corps could have pulled off what you did."

Greg watched Elena closely. It was an effusive compliment, but it was also true. Elena brushed past it as if the Admiral had said nothing. "If I may, Admiral, I'd like to speak candidly," she said. "I'm a bit shaken up after all this, and I'm not sure I'll succeed at being as circumspect as I ought to be right now."

"Of course, Elena," Waris told her. "You know you don't need to ask with me." Warm. Friendly. Almost convincing.

"Thank you," Elena said. She laced her fingers together on the desk. "Admiral, I'm finding it . . . strange that we had our generator core sabotaged not eighteen hours after *Exeter* got blown to hell by a bunch of raiders she should have been able to vaporize with a fraction of the weaponry she had on board."

"I don't follow you."

Elena rubbed her eyes, and Greg recognized, with some surprise, his own habitual gesture. "Can we just stop this, Admiral? Because I've had a bad day. Not as bad a day as some, but a pretty bad one, and I'm not in the mood for coy political fencing. It's never been my best skill, anyway." That was prevarication, Greg knew; she excelled at politics when she saw a reason for them.

"Elena, dear, I know you're upset—"

That was an error. The maternal approach never worked with Elena, whose mother was not maternal in the way most people would recognize. Greg supposed, with Elena brushing off the tactic all these years, Waris would not have realized what a misstep she was making. "Yes, *Ilona dear,* I am upset. I am upset, because someone in your little gang of Shadow Ops friends wants me dead, and instead of doing it cleanly, you throw *two hundred and twenty-five other people* in the path as well."

This was beginning to sound less like diplomacy.

Waris looked convincingly surprised. "You think *we* did this?"

Elena ignored the interruption. "Now, you can tell me what the hell is going on, or I can stream to the whole damn sector everything I know—and everything I have guessed—about what you all have done to Niall MacBride."

And that, Greg realized too late, was Elena's miscalculation.

All of the maternal warmth vanished, and Waris's blue eyes went cold. "If you think you'll be *allowed* to go to the streamers, Commander," she said, "you haven't been paying attention."

Ice crept down Greg's spine, but Elena's expression remained calm and neutral. Watchful. How was it, Greg wondered, that she was such a horrible card player, when she could so comfortably face down a woman he was beginning to believe wanted them both dead? "If you think there's anything more you can do to me after today, Admiral, you're the one who hasn't been paying attention."

Waris's lips thinned. "Wait," she said, and her face disappeared, replaced by a holding pattern. Elena did not move. In theory, the pattern meant nobody on the other side was watching, but he thought she was right not to trust it.

After a moment, Admiral Waris reappeared, and next to her, transmitting from another location, was Admiral Herrod. Greg wasn't sure the relief he felt was rational. "Captain Foster," Herrod asked, "are you there?"

"Yes, Admiral."

"Good. Then I only need to say this once." He leaned forward, a deep frown on his face. "Threats of mutiny are unseemly and unnecessary, and it is only the extreme extenuating circumstances we are all dealing with that's keeping me from disciplining you both. Do you understand?"

"Yes, sir." He and Elena said it together. Greg was not sure Elena meant it.

Herrod sat back. "Shadow Ops is not responsible for what happened to *Galileo,* and we are not responsible for what happened to *Exeter.*"

Elena, who seemed entirely too unintimidated by Herrod's

scowl, said, "But you know who is behind it." It was not a question.

"We have no solid intelligence," Herrod said. "But yes, we know. MacBride contacted—or was contacted by—Ellis Systems. They are the ones who financed the raid to break him out."

Of course, Greg thought, just as Elena frowned. "Ellis works for you."

Waris looked annoyed again, and Herrod spoke. "We have had a . . . parting of the ways with Ellis," he said, and Elena's eyebrows went up.

"Because of last year."

"Yes."

Greg stood, and moved behind Elena so the admirals could see him. "Why?" When Waris's lips tightened again, he amended the question. "Respectfully, Admiral, they've received a great deal of support from you over the years. And Shadow Ops in particular shielded them from the consequences of what happened last year. We're more likely to be able to mount a defense against another attack if we understand why they've decided we're the enemy."

That seemed enough to persuade her. "They wanted compensation for the destruction of their facility. We don't have those kinds of resources."

"Compensation." Elena spat out the word. "They're lucky they weren't prosecuted for war crimes."

"The point, Commander," Herrod said, moving past her commentary, "is that Ellis feels we owe them. In lieu of us actually paying them, they have taken something we need. And as we're all putting our cards on the table here—we need you to take it back."

Greg frowned, suspicious. "Why not just give us an order, sir?"

"We have given you an order," Waris reminded him. "The Admiralty has ordered you to pursue the parties responsible for this attack. All we are doing here is clarifying the details."

Elena met Greg's eyes, and he thought she was thinking the same thing he was: *Is this how you recruited Captain MacBride to do your dirty work last year?* "What is it you need for us to do, Admiral?" Elena asked.

"Officially," Herrod said, "your mission is to find that Syndicate tribe and capture who you can, so they can be charged with what happened to *Exeter*. Unofficially? We need MacBride returned."

"Dead or alive," Waris put in.

Elena's eyebrows went up. "You're telling us to kill him."

"Alive is acceptable," Waris said. "But if you can't capture him, take him out. By any means necessary."

"You're talking about assassination." Elena sounded horrified, and Greg stared at her, willing her to let it go. She looked away from him, shaken, but fell silent.

"Why?" Greg asked. Waris fixed him with her icy stare, and he elaborated. "He was sentenced by court-martial to life in prison."

The admiral gave him a cold smile. "All you need to know, Captain Foster," she said, "is that if you accomplish this task for us, your ship will be permitted to continue serving the Corps with the same distinction she has served for the last eight years. I think that's sufficient. Don't you?"

That, he thought, was as clear a threat as she could have made without actually pulling a gun. "Yes, Admiral," he said.

"So we are all in agreement here." Herrod sounded angry. Greg wished he could be sure who the man was angry with.

Elena was still looking away. Greg replied for them both. "Yes, Admiral."

"Get in touch with us when it's done," Herrod said, and disconnected the comm.

Greg considered swearing, but none of the words he knew seemed sufficient.

"You can't really mean to kill MacBride," Elena said.

She had finally turned back to meet his eyes, and the doubt there stung worse than he would have expected. "We were planning to find MacBride anyway," he pointed out.

"That's not actually an answer."

He moved around the desk, pacing in front of her. "If MacBride comes at us first, I'll do what any of us would do. But shoot first and ask questions later? Hell, no."

He caught relief in her eyes. "We need to find out why they want him back so badly." When he nodded, she said, "Do you think that'll get us leverage?"

"I don't know. But I think we may need it."

"I don't even know who our enemies are anymore." She looked at him, her dark eyes tired, and pushed herself out of the chair. "I don't want to go. Not with *Galileo* like this."

"Neither do I." He wanted to reach out, to take her hands in his, but he wasn't sure what he was hoping to get from it. "I'll talk to Captain Shiang. Somehow," he added dryly, "I don't think our request is going to surprise her much."

····················

CHAPTER 19

I don't care what kind of orders come through the Admiralty," Greg told her again, "you keep this ship right here until we get back."

Jessica leaned against the wall of Greg Foster's quarters, watching as he sorted through his meticulously stacked clothing for items to pack. She had been in his room only once before, back when she was still a lieutenant commander, and she had been astonished at the sterile environment. Her own things were organized, but in a far more personal way, her space decorated with color and small works of art. Greg had very few possessions beyond his Corps-issued clothing. Four physical books stood on his bookshelf, but she was not sure he had ever read them. The frame that had held a picture of his wife was gone, the top of the dresser as bare as the day the room had been completed.

"What about *Cassia*?" she asked.

He stopped and gave her a look. "What do you think?"

He was doing this a lot more lately: testing her. She understood it, but it still annoyed her. She didn't want to train to take his place. She didn't even want the authority she had. But she could not disagree that he had let far too much slide with his previous second-in-command. "I think I find excuses to keep them off," she replied.

He went back to packing. "Exactly. I don't want anybody getting on or off of this ship, especially anyone involved with the Admiralty. They may have good intentions, but until we know for sure what happened, they're contaminating a crime scene."

Jessica tried to picture herself explaining to someone like Admiral Herrod that she was sorry, but she couldn't risk his shuttle destroying evidence. "Permission to speak candidly, sir."

"For fuck's sake, Jess."

It was a standing joke between them; she had never been anything less than candid with him, permission or not. "I'm pissed off at you for running out on me again."

He stilled, and turned around to look at her, half-annoyed, half-apologetic. "I'm not running out on you," he said, but his voice was gentle. "We'll be in constant communication. This will be a quick op: three days out, three days back. I'll be home before Ted finishes his diags, and you'll be in the loop the whole time."

She went on as if he hadn't spoken. "Because I'm not hiding out on my own ship to haul your insubordinate ass out of the fire again."

Something lightened in his eyes. "But you did such a good job of it."

"I'm *serious,* sir."

"Jess." He took a step toward her. "I don't want to be leaving now, either. Some motherfucking bastard tried to destroy my ship, and I'm extremely unhappy about that. I would much rather stay here and dig up evidence with you, and then publicly disembowel the culprit. But I don't have a choice."

"And Elena has to come with you."

At that his eyes slid away from her. "Whose idea do you think this was?"

This was too much. "Jesus Christ, Greg, can't you at least take responsibility for this one? I don't care whose idea it was, you wouldn't be going along with it if you didn't believe she was right. Why would you rather have everyone believe she's dragging you around by your dick than that you don't trust the fucking Admiralty?" He hit her with one of his famous glares, and she lifted her chin. "And you can cut that shit, too. I got about a dozen of those from Çelik earlier, and he makes you look like a fucking *pussycat*."

"You go too far, Commander."

"Fuck you, Greg, you don't go far enough. You spend all this time worrying about everybody else—about me seeing what's really going on here and maybe thinking it's a bad fucking idea—when you need to be thinking about covering your own ass. You think the Admiralty is going to take care of you? You think Herrod is enough to insulate you from all this? Are you even sure he's on our side?" Dammit, there was no time. *I should have pushed this months ago.* "He may have saved your career at the court-martial, but do you really believe he hasn't attached a cost?"

He was quiet for a long time after that. "It's not worrying about you," he said at last, "not really. But the safety of this ship *is* my responsibility. That includes your safety, too, as long as I'm in command. And yes, I get to decide what that means. I understand how you feel," he interrupted when she opened her mouth. "But for now, Jess . . . I'm going to have to ask you to trust me."

She studied his face. He had a way of looking down at her that made her feel that he was somehow not half a meter taller than she was, that he was holding her gaze with those beautiful gray-black eyes face-to-face with her, as an equal. Had he been the sort of man she found attractive—or really, she had to admit, anything other than her superior officer—the look would have been positively seductive. He was the antithesis of Çelik, master of intimidation, bestowing sparse approval at uneven intervals to make his crew constantly reach for more. Greg Foster stood here, steady and constant, asking her to believe in him simply because he believed in her.

Damn, damn, damn. "I hate you, sir," she said, and he smiled, relaxed again.

"Understood, Commander." He turned back to finish packing, and she realized he had conducted the entire exchange with a pair of folded underwear in one hand.

Accepting defeat, she let her gaze sweep around the room. "Did you get rid of the booze, sir?" she asked.

"All of it."

"I wish you still drank, sir."

She was rewarded with a laugh. "So do I, Commander."

The door chime went off, and he turned to her, frowning, just as *Galileo* said, "Commander Keita is at the door."

He gave her a questioning look, and she shrugged. "Well, *I'm* curious," she said.

Greg turned back to his packing. "Let him in."

The door slid open, and Keita stepped through, wide enough

to fill the whole doorway. As she stood between the two men, she realized she hadn't noticed before how much they resembled each other: Keita was built wider, his expression less closed, but both handsome to a fault, with strong jaws and expressive lips, both watchful, observant, taking up space with unconscious confidence. Jessica had been surprised, at first, meeting Keita; he was so unlike the men she had seen with Elena. Seeing Keita and Greg together made her wonder about a lot of things.

Keita opened his mouth to speak, and then caught sight of Jessica. He frowned, looking confused, then regrouped. "Captain Foster, do you have a moment for me?"

Greg had looked over his shoulder only long enough to acknowledge Keita's presence, then had returned to his packing. *Shit,* Jessica thought, *Elena told him about her history with Keita.* "Of course, Commander." His voice had gone flawlessly polite.

Keita stole another look at Jessica, and she thought that open expression could not have done him many favors during his career. "Can we . . . could I speak to you alone, sir?"

Jessica was still, waiting for Greg's reply. "Commander Lockwood hears everything I hear, Commander."

Keita gave her a more measured look and took a resigned step into the room. "I'd like to accompany you to *Orunmila,* sir."

Greg kept arranging the clothes in his bag, but Jessica thought he was just moving things around. "Why?"

Keita shifted, and Jessica wondered if he was this uncomfortable around his own captain. "I am useless here, sir. I belong with Captain Çelik."

"And how does Captain Çelik feel about that?"

"Sir, he—" Keita broke off. "I haven't asked him, sir. But he needs me."

"Why?"

"Captain—permission to speak candidly, sir."

Greg met Jessica's eyes, and she caught a glimpse of sour humor. "Go ahead, Commander."

"I know you don't like me. And I understand why."

"That's quite an assumption, Commander."

"I don't think it is."

They were looking at each other now, and Jessica was reminded of the goats her uncle used to raise, facing off on opposite sides of the field. She did not think Greg was the type who would start this confrontation, but she did not have a good sense of Keita. All she knew was that Elena worried over him like a mother hen, which struck her as a strange vestige of a love affair. Given what he had been through, Jessica could not blame her friend for worrying; but to Jessica, he was just another potential suspect.

And she sure as hell didn't want him to have access to the captain of her ship.

"We shouldn't be transferring anyone else off of *Galileo*," she put in.

Greg looked over at her, and the tense moment dissolved. "I agree," he said. "But I'm interested in Commander Keita's reasoning."

Keita straightened, and Jessica noted he wasn't stupid enough to keep pissing with the man he was trying to convince. "I don't know enough about *Galileo* to help with repairs, or even with everyday operations. I could help sort through evidence"—here he shot a quick glance at Jessica—"but I'm guessing nobody here is interested in letting me do that."

Definitely not stupid, Jessica thought.

"And I know Captain Çelik, sir. Better than you do. Better than Elena—than Chief Shaw does. Whatever you're worried he might do on Canberra, sir, you're probably right. I want a chance to talk him out of it, or at least to protect him as much as I can."

Greg chewed on that for a moment. "What about the mission?"

"Do you mean would I like to be part of it?"

"I mean what's your take on what the mission is?"

Keita looked away. "They murdered my friends, sir. I won't say I'm objective here." He looked back at Greg, calm and steady, and Jessica thought he was telling the truth. "But I want to see them exposed. I want to see them named and tried publicly. There's too big a risk of the whole story getting swept away if everybody disappears."

Jessica thought she saw dawning respect on Greg's face. "Nobody's going to put up with the truth about MacBride coming out," he said, and Keita nodded.

"They can do what they want with him, sir. He's had his day in court. I want the bastards who destroyed my ship."

Which was, Jessica reflected, exactly the right argument to use with Greg Foster. More of her captain's spirit was bound up in this ship than even he realized. After a moment, Greg relented. "I'll approve your addition to the mission," he said, "but only if Captain Çelik clears it. You're his officer, not mine. Your involvement is his call."

Keita looked relieved. "Thank you, Captain. I'll speak with

Captain Çelik right away." At Greg's gesture of dismissal, he turned and left, letting his eyes sweep over Jessica one last time on his way out.

Greg kept his eyes on the door. "What do you make of him, Jess?"

"On or off the record?"

"Off."

"I don't trust him."

"Why not?"

She frowned, trying to articulate it. "I can't get a steady read on him," she admitted. "I think I'm getting him, and then he goes sideways. He's like one of those pictures where the stairs are going up unless you look at them at a different angle, and then they're going down."

"Elena's got a history with him."

"I know, sir. Does she trust him?"

"She says," he told her carefully, "that she doesn't trust her judgment of him."

"That'd be a 'no.' "

"For all practical purposes," he agreed. His next words were more hesitant. "Has she ever talked to you about Canberra, Jessica?"

A shiver of revulsion went through her. "Not in detail, sir. Just cannibals and death."

"She said earlier that *Exeter* changed after that mission."

"Odds are, sir, that *she* changed. Doesn't mean a thing about *Exeter*."

He frowned, and she had to remind herself that he probably wasn't even thinking about the fact that he was still glaring at her. "Ellis tapped into someone with access to *Exeter*," he mused aloud. "One of her own crew. That's still your conclusion?"

"I'll take your word that it was Ellis, sir. Based on what I know, it's extremely unlikely that someone outside of *Exeter*'s crew sabotaged their targeting systems."

"So someone turned on their own family."

The thought was simultaneously sad and disgusting. "It looks that way, sir."

"Okay." He turned away from her again, closing his duffel. "Primarily, Commander, I need you digging up data on Canberra. We've got to figure out how to land on that nightmarish rock, which means extrapolating from eight-year-old intel. But on top of that—I want to know *Exeter*'s vulnerabilities, and that includes personnel."

"That's a lot of people to research, sir."

"You said yourself it wasn't an ordinary grunt. Focus on officers, and anybody in the ranks who shows some aptitude. In particular, Jess? Find out if I just gave that vulnerability access to a PSI ship."

"Now I really want him to stay here," she said glumly.

"I can contain him on *Orunmila*."

I'll bet, she thought.

PART II

CHAPTER 20

Orunmila

Guanyin stood inside the door of Storage Nine, watching Aida frown over the environmental controls. He was scanning the refrigeration units one at a time, examining temperature and pressure readings. That he seemed little more than annoyed comforted her a little, but not enough.

"How was this detected?" she asked.

"We got a warming alert on one of the units," Cali replied. "No error, just a warning, and then the unit compensated and all the readings returned to normal. I called Aida to open a maintenance ticket, and it took him about five minutes to determine that someone had screwed around with it."

Storage Nine contained their long-term food stores. As long as they were within a few weeks of a supply station, they would never need to touch them; indeed, if their own farming thrived the way it did most of the time, they wouldn't need them even then. Storage Nine was nothing but a safety net. As a prank, it was remarkably unimpressive; as attempted sabotage, it was useless.

On its own, at least.

"When did this happen?"

Cali looked pointedly at Aida, who finally looked up from his work, annoyed by the interruption. "I don't know when the system was sabotaged. It was timed to happen today, but it was triggered earlier."

"We have no security here?"

Cali shifted, looking uncomfortable. "Some of our data is gone."

Guanyin's stomach froze. *Such an innocuous phrase.* "Gone?" she repeated. "How does our security data disappear?"

"I don't know."

"What you're saying," Guanyin said, "is that it was not just Storage Nine that was sabotaged, but our security monitoring."

Cali nodded. "This is why I commed you."

"What's the time frame of the lost footage?" *And you should have told me this first.*

"Twenty-four hours," Cali said. "It came back online just this morning."

"Twenty-four hours of lost footage, and no one was alerted?" Guanyin shook her head; that was her second problem. "Aida, what happened in here? What were they trying to do?"

"If I had to guess," Aida said, giving up all pretense of trying to make progress while they were talking, "someone was trying to hack into the storage environmentals."

"What would that have accomplished?"

He threw her a look. "We would have lost several months' worth of prefab soy paste. Frankly, Captain? This is a kid's prank. One of those teens from *Aganju*, maybe. All they do is hang around in the square and talk about how bored they are."

It was plausible. It made the most sense. But Guanyin could hear a whispering voice in the back of her head. Twenty-four hours ago. *Galileo*'s accident—which was almost certainly not an accident—had happened around the same time. But as an act of sabotage, this was a confusing effort. Wasted soy paste would not stop them from pursuing the raiders. Cali had almost left Guanyin out of it entirely.

She did not care for what she was putting together in her head.

"Cali," she asked, "weren't you scheduled to spar with Captain Çelik?"

"I told him I'd be late," Cali said. "I can cancel, if you like."

Guanyin shook her head. "Keep the appointment. I'm going to keep it with you."

Guanyin thought she had never seen a man as stubborn as Raman Çelik.

When he had first asked her for a sparring partner, she had consulted Xiao, certain that he should not be putting that kind of pressure on his very new wound. Xiao had surprised her. "His wound is sealed, and the temporaries are sturdy," she had said. "That Central doctor did a nice job attaching it. Çelik should be careful with it—it's more vulnerable than natural bone, especially at the attachment point—but he's not likely to disconnect the thing, unless he torques it especially badly. Of course," she had added, "it's almost certainly painful as all hell. If I were him I'd be staying off of it as much as I could."

Guanyin was not surprised he was inviting pain. Given what was before him, she suspected he felt he did not have the luxury of avoiding it. That it was also a stark reminder of what he believed was a personal failure was, she suspected, not unwelcome to him.

Cali circled him, wary and focused, waiting for an opening, waiting for him to move. He was slow, graceless; he favored the artificial leg, showing that he at least had some sense about it, but eventually he would forget, shift his weight to it, and stumble to his knees. It would have made a lesser man angry, but he kept his temper, regrouping each time, relaxing his stance, letting Cali come to him. And she did, over and over, with her practiced feline quickness; and despite the fact that she did not attack his weakest point, he stumbled and fell every time.

And always got back up again.

Eventually Cali, drenched in sweat, put up her hands. "I am sorry, Captain Çelik," she said in her broken Standard. "You have worn me out."

It was one of Cali's oldest and most reliable opening lines, and Guanyin was a little surprised when Çelik did not take the bait. Instead he stood tall and straight and bowed slightly from the waist. "Another time then," he said in dialect. Cali frowned, and Guanyin smiled. His dialect was nearly accentless, and a good deal smoother than Cali's Standard. Cali might have won the fight, but Çelik had asserted a different sort of victory.

Çelik waited until Cali had disappeared into the showers before he turned to Guanyin. "Aren't pregnant women supposed to exercise?" he asked.

He was as drenched as Cali had been, but it suited him better—or at least, Guanyin admitted to herself, she was more in the mood to watch him. He had been sparring in nothing but shorts, utterly unself-conscious. He was in good shape for a man of his years—or any years, she had to admit. It was easy for Cali, who was young and active, to maintain her strong and lovely form, but Çelik clearly worked hard for his build. He was as fit as Yunru, who was fanatical about it; but Çelik was taller, broader, his muscles well-defined under his bare skin. His body was hairless, although she had seen him shave his face. Given his vanity she assumed he'd had the hair cosmetically removed, but the look suited him. It was easier to see the subtleties in the color of his skin: darker over his face, lighter brown across his upper back, warm everywhere with undertones of copper, as if his blood ran close to the surface. She wondered how her own skin would look against his, and imagined her hand, paler and cooler, resting against his chest, fingers spreading against the smoothness, feeling his damp sweat under her palm . . .

She turned away. The hormones always hit her around six months, and to Cali's endless irritation they always steered her toward a man. Yunru was generally accommodating at such times, but the girls had not been sleeping, and she knew he was tired. And in truth, she would have felt awkward in his bed, knowing she would not have been thinking of him at all. "I take exercise before breakfast," she told Çelik. "If I wait, the day fills up and I do nothing."

He limped over to where she sat, moving with care, his metal foot slapping the floor. She could see the skin above the graft, red and raw, but nothing in his expression betrayed pain. "What do you do?" he asked her.

"When I am pregnant, I run," she told him. "I don't need balance."

He shook his head. "You get no upper body work running." She watched as he lowered himself onto the bench next to her, using one hand to keep himself from collapsing. It was a grace-less move, but he betrayed no embarrassment.

"I get enough upper body work lifting my children."

"That is not a workout," he said. "Your oldest is not even twenty-five kilos. What do you do when you are not pregnant?"

"I don't remember," she said, and he laughed.

"You must like it," he pointed out, "if you keep doing it."

"What, having children?"

"Getting pregnant."

"There are things I like and things I don't," she confessed. "I get terribly sick at first, and in the last four weeks I am as weak as a newborn puppy. But I seem to be good at it. It's easy for me to become pregnant, and my babies are full-term and healthy."

"Duty, then?"

She felt suddenly shy. "I have always wanted children, even when I was a little girl." Which was strange, given the early childhood she'd had. "It's inborn for me, I think. It feels like . . . an imperative. Something I must do while I can."

"So you will have more."

At that she shook her head. "This will be my last." She rubbed her stomach absently. "I've spent all of my twenties pregnant, and it's not good for the ship to have me out of com-mission when the pregnancies make me sick."

His eyebrows knit. "You should choose a second," he said. "She could look after the ship when you were not feeling well."

A simple solution to a simple problem, although she knew he was not insensible of the politics. But he had heard, somewhere in what she had told him, how sad she was to be bearing her last child.

Çelik shifted, and winced; and Guanyin wished she had

been looking away. "I can tell you what you're doing wrong, you know," she said.

"A pregnant woman is going to lecture me about keeping my balance?"

"You're expecting your body to respond the same way, but it can't. Because it's not the same."

Something in him shuttered, and she wondered how hard-won his equanimity with Cali had been. "If you want to see how my body responds, you only have to ask," he said to her, and this time his grin was predatory and false.

"Does that sort of remark work for you?" A part of her was genuinely curious.

"It doesn't have to. I'm the captain. But you know what that's like."

She shook her head. "It's not my nature to . . . advertise like that."

He looked pointedly at her belly. "Seems to me you don't have to."

"It's not easy when you're captain," she told him. He should know this. "Cali and I have known each other since we were children. I have had Yunru for years, since before I was appointed. Beyond that, it gets too complicated. One needs to be wary of appearing to play favorites."

"I solved that one."

"How?"

"I fuck everyone."

"You must be very busy."

He laughed at that. "Everyone who asks," he amended. "Not everyone does."

"Is that why you are angry with Commander Shaw?"

"Don't be silly. She is hardly alone in not finding me irresistible."

"So why, then?"

"If she'd been working for me, she'd have her own ship by now."

Guanyin thought of Commander Shaw: smart, driven, disinclined to take orders. With what little she knew of Central, she was not at all sure even Çelik could have coached Shaw into command. "Do you feel Captain Foster is holding her back?"

"I think he doesn't want to lose her."

"Apparently neither did you."

"She was the smartest kid I had that year, and he just had to have her."

"You're jealous."

"Of course I'm jealous. Some neophyte captain, ten years younger than me, gets handed a brand-new starship and plucks the best kid I've got right out from under my nose? Who does he think he is?"

"Do you like anyone at all?"

"Not really, no."

"I suppose that simplifies your life."

"What is it you get from liking people?"

He had returned to being genuine, and she resolved to keep the conversation away from his injury. "It's not something I decide to do, you know," she said, wondering if he really had so little experience with friendship. "There are people I must spend time with, and sometimes it's pleasant. It can make a great many things a lot easier."

"Like whatever it is you've come to ask me about."

She had known, throughout her life, people who were both

perceptive and ill-tempered. They were the most dangerous to have around: they could see vulnerabilities, and had no compunction about exploiting them. For reasons she did not understand, Çelik seemed to treat his knowledge of her with more care than she expected. She knew better than to assume that would continue. "I find myself," she said carefully, "in a position where I could use some advice. And I don't know anyone else who might be able to give it to me."

There were a dozen jokes he could have made after the exchange they had just had, but he watched her patiently, no ridicule in his expression. "I will help if I can," he told her.

"There is one problem—" she began.

"You do not know if you can trust me."

She smiled in spite of herself. "If you're going to read my mind, I won't bother telling you any of it."

He leaned on one elbow, shifting slightly closer to her. She could smell his sweat, sweet and musky; *vegetarian,* she thought automatically, and pushed the awareness away.

"You are still not sure when you are talking to me, and when you are talking to Central."

"That's exactly it," she admitted. "When I trust, I risk all of my people. There's more to be considered than my personal judgment."

"Would it help if I told you I have no intention of discussing anything about this mission with the Admiralty?"

"And I'm just supposed to believe you?"

"How important is this advice you need?"

She looked away, frustrated. "That's part of the trouble; I don't know. It might be all in my head, shadows and paranoia after everything that's happened. But I can't shake the conviction that they'll be coming after us. I'm afraid I'm seeing things that aren't there."

"Is that something you do often?"

Guanyin thought back over her life, from the half-remembered indignities of her childhood to her training with Chanyu. "Not since I was small," she said, a little surprised.

"Then I would guess," he told her, "that whatever you believe you are seeing is really there."

He was half a meter away from her, his head lower than her shoulder. She was sitting with her arms folded around her stomach—there was nowhere else to put them these days—turned so she was looking into his eyes. She could not believe, no matter how cautious her mind told her to be, that her heart was wrong about this.

"My question," she told him, "is about refrigeration. Specifically, I'm wondering about the refrigeration on a Central starship. If it's hooked into the ship's larger systems somehow."

He frowned, thinking. "That depends," he said. "We've got independent refrigeration units all over the ship. Those are different from longer-term storage and shipping."

She felt her heart begin to beat faster. "I'm thinking of long-term storage and shipping. Could a ship be damaged beyond the storage unit if someone sabotaged the environmental controls?"

"That seems like an inefficient way to go about it."

"But possible."

"In theory, if we were in the field, an environmental problem could sap our batteries, force an early dropout."

"Like what happened to *Galileo*?"

But he was shaking his head. "No, nothing so catastrophic.

The ship would detect the fast battery drain and execute a controlled dropout. It would be an annoyance, an inconvenience, but the odds that serious damage could be done are slim."

Could that be it? she thought. *Could it all have been to try to slow us down?* "Surely there are better ways of causing a ship to drop out. I could think of a dozen that could work on *Orunmila*, but would involve less subterfuge."

"But I am guessing those systems are more secure," he suggested, and she realized he had figured it out without her telling him anything.

"That suggests this was not planned," she mused, "or at least was not planned well."

"If I am reading you right," he added, "it also suggests it was someone familiar with Corps starship architecture who did it. Someone who did not know that *Orunmila* was different."

"Yes."

"So it would have had to be one of us."

She nodded. "Aida says someone with sufficient skill might have sabotaged the system remotely. As you say, our food storage systems are relatively open. But yes, it does seem logical to conclude that the person responsible was not PSI." She thought tact would be pointless. "I have my own opinion of Commander Keita, although my knowledge of him is slim. But what can you tell me of your Doctor Youda, Captain Çelik?"

"That he's fundamentally a coward," he said candidly, "and that his recent field promotion has left him in a pretty comfortable spot career-wise. I don't like him, Captain, but I don't see him motivated to do something like this. Among other things, it would require far too much effort."

She shook her head. "Aida thinks it's a child's prank. I can't dismiss that, either. We are full of bored children at the moment."

"Guanyin." He had not used her name before; she liked how he pronounced it. "Whatever you are seeing is really there."

She held his gaze for a long moment, grateful for the absence of his habitual brittle sarcasm. "I know," she said at last. Gracelessly she pushed herself to her feet, wishing for a moment she had put a hand on his shoulder to help herself up. "Thank you for the advice, Captain Çelik. You have been very helpful."

And without looking back, she walked out of the gymnasium.

CHAPTER 21

Galileo

"L et me get this straight," Captain Vassily said. "You're turn-ing down assistance because *Galileo* is a *crime scene?*"

They must be taught sarcasm in leadership training, Jessica thought. "Yes, ma'am," she replied, keeping it simple. "I'm not authorized to allow—"

"Where is Captain Foster?"

Shit. "Captain Foster is continuing pursuit of the fugitives," she said truthfully. "He's out of contact."

I'm not available to anyone, he had said. *Not Vassily, not Herrod—nobody. I don't want direct contact from anyone but you.*

Despite Captain Vassily's incredulous expression, Jessica thought the woman was beginning to give in. She hoped so. Captain Vassily was some intimidating hybrid of Greg and Ra-man Çelik: professional and direct, but impatient with what she perceived as foolishness. Jessica didn't think the woman was disputing her use of the term *crime scene,* but clearly she was also considering the possibility that Jessica was an inflexible idiot who had misunderstood orders.

Jessica resolved to ask Greg, when he returned, if it was her job to look stupid just so he could get things done. She was pretty sure she was going to be in the mood to start a fight.

"We can offer you medical help, at least," the captain said at last.

That one was easier to refuse. "That's very kind of you, ma'am, but there were no injuries in this latest incident. You've already taken the worst of *Exeter*'s wounded. Our staff can handle the people we still have."

Captain Vassily kept frowning. Like Greg, she managed to make the expression both deeply threatening and impossible to evade. But although she had the same sort of effortless good looks as Greg Foster, she lacked his articulate eyes. Jessica had seen everything from ire to despair to laughter in Greg's eyes, and she had come to recognize he was far more vulnerable than most people knew. He was too strong for his own good, really; he thought he could handle anything. He thought he could handle all of this. He thought he was riding off to round up the bad guys, and somehow restore justice. Dammit, he was naive.

Captain Vassily's dark eyes gave away nothing.

"I've got to get these soldiers to Aleph Three for treatment," she said at last. "But—if I offered to come back afterward, keep our weapons live, such as they are—would that be welcome, Commander Lockwood?"

She thought of how close Elena had come to being blown out into the FTL field, and Ted's slow and meticulous inventory. "Thank you, Captain," she said. "We'd be most grateful for the backup, as much as I hope we won't need it."

When the comm completed, she sat back in Greg's office chair, exhausted. Jessica had always been good in social situations, the perpetual life of the party; but she was used to being direct. There was far too much subterfuge involved in command-level decisions, and she disliked it intensely. What would have made sense here was for her to tell Captain Vassily the truth: that Captain Foster had run off tilting at windmills— again—though this time with the full faith and authority of the Admiralty behind him. Not the entire Admiralty, of course; just a few of the crazies who belonged to Shadow Ops.

You know about Shadow Ops, don't you, Captain Vassily? They're the gaggle of brass huddled in a poorly lit room planning galactic domination, or interstellar peace, or possibly a solstice picnic, depending on which one of them is blowing sunshine up your ass on any particular day.

Yeah, that was unlikely to be helpful.

She left the captain's office and went back to her own quarters. As the door slid closed behind her, she felt some of the knots in her neck relax. "*Galileo,*" she ordered, kicking off her shoes and shrugging off her uniform jacket, "give me what you've gathered on Canberra."

Galileo had been compiling and analyzing all official mentions of Canberra, crawling Corps history, news reports, unencrypted personal correspondence, and whatever random mentions had flown over the stream. Very little of the data was high-level classified; now that Jessica was a commander, even the Admiralty field reports were open to her.

Which means, most likely, there's fuck-all of interest in the Admiralty field reports.

She had a suspicion she was going to have to resort to less legitimate methods for anything substantive, but that required more care than simply requesting a compilation from *Galileo.*

"Written or verbal?" the ship asked her.

"Written." Jessica dropped onto her couch and put her feet up, leaning back. Text appeared half a meter before her eyes. Before she began scanning it, she added, "Give me a verbal history of *Exeter,* too. From her christening on up."

Galileo's detached voice filled the air. "The CCSS *Exeter* was commissioned on 3356.23.123, an iteration of an earlier model of D8000 engine called . . ."

Jessica tuned out the droning technical details—if she'd wanted that sort of history, she'd have asked Elena, who would have related it with far more enthusiasm—and focused on the history of Canberra Colony. If *Galileo* came up with something at all relevant, she trusted her multitasking mind to tune it all back in.

There were a few images from the colony's early days. Jessica, who had grown up on a lush, tropical world, found Canberra desolate and lonely, dominated by rock, dry earth, and odd scrubby flora. But the longer she looked at it, the more it took on a sort of austere beauty, a serene starkness that was almost soothing. Home was home, she supposed.

Vid throughout the colony's three-hundred-year life span was sparse. They had asserted full autonomy after only sixty years, and after that their contact with Central was almost nonexistent. Still, the Third Sector ships visited several times each year, and Jessica was able to watch the brief but courteous conversations between generations of Corps captains and the Canberran government. About half the time, the colony took the help that was offered; the remainder of the discussions tended to involve cheerfully inviting Central to mind their own damn business.

The collapse was swift and shocking, even given the spotty footage Jessica was able to find. Six months before *Exeter,* the CCSS *Kievan* had dropped a supply of seeds and dried staples, and their captain had surreptitiously recorded her crew's entire mission. The rain was nearly constant, and apart from a glib and expansive local governor, the tempers of the colonists were short. *Kievan* had raised an alert that had put all of the Corps' Third Sector ships on rotation, but nobody had any idea the destruction would happen so quickly.

"*Galileo,*" Jessica interrupted, "if they couldn't plant, how long would it have taken Canberra to burn through the supplies dropped by *Kievan*?"

"Four to six weeks," the ship responded.

The next Central drop on Canberra had been three months later, and there was as yet no sign of mass starvation, much less of the cannibalization that was to come. "They had another source," she mused.

"Hypothesis is consistent with the facts."

She knew PSI traded with them—they'd had the final contact, before *Exeter* had arrived—but she wondered about the raiders currently landing on the planet. The Syndicates never gave anything without some form of payment, and Canberra had nothing to trade; but Jessica wondered what landing privileges would have been worth to them. Despite the alarm raised by *Kievan,* Central hadn't had the resources to monitor what else the colony might have been up to.

Galileo returned to her historical narrative, and Jessica turned to the topographical information. Unsurprisingly, the planet's surface had changed very little. What had not been eroded by eons of acid rain and storms was not easily adaptable by the colonists. But there were a handful of low-lying areas in which the colonists had raised small towns that blossomed into cities. The lack of sprawl resulted in efficient, easily powered spaces, and for a few hundred years, Canberra had looked— from a distance, at least—healthy.

The terraformer configuration, which appeared random in the scans, was explained by the terrain. The old terraformers were small and somewhat overpowered, requiring frequent maintenance and replacement parts; but there had been twenty of them, dropped into sheltered areas all over the planet, and even during *Kievan*'s visit they were reading green. No indication of any kind of equipment failure or overload. Except—

Jessica frowned, and scanned back through the data. Seven power sources, all clustered near one of the planet's poles. No terraformer ident from them; no identifying information at all. When had they shown up? She ran the timeline backward, suddenly more bothered by the gaps in the data, and found they had appeared somewhere between thirty and forty years ago. She scanned forward to the scant contemporary information she had, and found a three-year-old meteorological scan. The storms had been heavy, and too much of the surface had been obscured, but she could still make out three of them, burning silent and steady through the dense atmosphere.

What the hell had they wanted with power sources?

Jessica interrupted *Galileo*'s narrative of *Exeter*'s christening. "*Galileo,* do we have any records of large shipments to Canberra between thirty and forty years ago? Something that would match those power signatures?"

The ship paused, scanning external sources. "Neither Central nor the commercial shipping liners delivered anything to Canberra in that time period."

Shit. Of course not.

Well, she had known it would come to this.

Opening an encrypted interface, Jessica pulled up the stealth data collector she had been working on for a year. She had not tested it sufficiently; indeed, the entire structure of the thing was half theory, based on a set of cryptic message authentication headers she had run into during the incidents on Volhynia. Still, she thought it was solid enough to hide its own tracks, even if it didn't find her what she wanted. And if it did . . . Greg would forgive her transgression.

With some care she entered the parameters of the power sources and the time frame, and set the collector off to worm its way through the Admiralty's classified data. Almost as an afterthought, she set herself an alarm. It wouldn't give her enough time to escape official repercussions, but she would at least have some warning before someone showed up to throw her in prison for spying.

"*Galileo,*" she said, too keyed up to listen to textbook history anymore, "skip forward on *Exeter.* What happened to them after Canberra?"

"Replaced as Corps flagship in the Third Sector on 3378.19.345 by CCSS *Dobrynya,*" *Galileo* said. "Primary mission remained diplomacy and aid. On 3378.27—"

"Stop." Jessica frowned. "How long was *Exeter* Third Sector flagship?"

"Four years, eight months, nineteen days."

"Isn't the typical term five years?"

"Yes."

"Explain the discrepancy."

"No explanation available."

How the hell does Elena talk to this machine without throwing things? "Speculate."

"Conflicting mission parameters," *Galileo* listed. "Inability to fulfill a diplomatic requirement. Complaint or request from Third Sector colonial consortium. Disciplinary action against an officer or officers of the CCSS *Exeter*."

Jessica stood, pacing the room impatiently. "*Galileo,* what's the official resolution of the Canberra mission?"

"Colony distress was reported past the stage where recovery was possible. Colony triaged and abandoned."

What a bloodless epitaph for fifteen thousand people who had torn each other to pieces. "So the official line is we went in as soon as we knew there was a problem, but we were too late?"

"Yes."

"Convenient."

"Clarify."

She rolled her eyes again. "I mean—never mind what I mean." She didn't know how to explain to an artificial intelligence her instinct that *Exeter* had borne the brunt of an Admiralty bureaucratic mistake. She touched the comm behind her ear. "Ted, are you up?"

He picked up immediately. "Still pulling together intel on Keita," he told her. "You want what I have so far?"

She had almost forgotten the captain's personal vendetta. "Not now. I need to bounce some things off of you." She gave him a recap of what *Galileo* had told her about *Exeter*. "Is it just me, Ted? Because this is smelling a lot like bullshit."

"Careful, Jessie. People will think you're a cynic."

"Am I wrong?"

"You think the Corps lied about what happened on Canberra?"

"No, but I think there's more to it than the party line."

"You're starting to sound subversive." His tone had become mildly teasing, and she knew she had him hooked.

"I don't want to be subversive," she insisted. "I want to know who blew the hell out of *Exeter*."

"Which has what to do with Canberra?"

"Probably nothing," she admitted. "But given that it looks like one of her own people is involved in both her destruction and our attack, I find myself interested in what might have happened to make *Exeter* fall out of favor with the Admiralty."

"Explain to me why that's not a stretch, Jess."

She frowned, trying to articulate the thought. "Imagine you're Ellis," she began. "You're pissed off at the Admiralty, or Shadow Ops, or Central as a whole, for whatever reason. Let's take it at face value and say they owe you a big whack of money and you're not going to get it. So you're looking for a way to get back at them. Who do you look at?"

"The Corps is full of cranky soldiers—we've got a few of them here."

"A soldier who's used to being discontented isn't going to feel like he deserves anything different," she said.

"I don't think you've been around enough discontented soldiers to draw that conclusion."

"Maybe," she conceded, "but are you telling me some ensign or sergeant—that Faris kid, or one of Lawson's random med techs—is going to have the knowledge to pull this off? Never mind the reach? Motive, maybe. But what about means?"

"Fair enough."

"So how about someone who was going somewhere, but suddenly had the rug pulled out? Wouldn't you knock on their door, and at least feel them out?"

"So you're saying," Ted repeated, knitting her thoughts into something coherent, "that something happened around Canberra that took *Exeter* from being the up-and-coming darling to an ordinary peace-and-vegetables ship, so when Ellis got pissed off it was *Exeter*'s crew they started with?"

"It doesn't sound like enough, does it?" she asked. He was circling a plausible idea, but it didn't quite unify everything in her head.

But Ted seemed more convinced. "I don't know, Jess. It's not illogical. It's just not the only possibility."

"You're telling me you found something on Keita that might be a match?"

"Not yet," he said, "and I'm not sure I'm going to. He's got a solid record. And he wouldn't be the first second-in-command who did a stellar job while looking like an odd choice on paper."

"I don't know whether to thank you or be insulted."

But Ted didn't laugh. "You think maybe the captain is barking up the wrong soldier?"

She equivocated. "I think he's barking for the wrong reasons. But Keita's a little shifty for my taste, too."

"And neither one of you trusts Elena's impressions of him."

Not you, too, she thought, annoyed. "Give me a break, Ted. You think she's objective about anything right now?"

"What does objectivity have to do with it? Seriously, Jess.

You think Elena would ever have trusted someone who could do something like this?"

"I think," she told him, "someone trusted whoever was behind this. There are no good answers here, Ted. There's just death and blame."

He was quiet for a moment. "Okay, Jess. I'll keep on him. And you—"

"Me what?" The words came out sharper than she intended.

"You remember," he told her, "that you are not in this alone." And he disconnected.

We're all in this alone, she thought. But he had managed, for a moment, to make her feel a little better.

CHAPTER 22

Orunmila

*I*f *the Admiralty had any real idea of the value of PSI's intel on the Syndicates,* Greg thought, *they would have been a hell of a lot more friendly over the years.*

He had walked into Captain Shiang's office knowing there were gaps in his knowledge. Two hours later, he was staggered by his own ignorance—and how much his chain of command had to learn. Shiang had stood, one hand braced against her lower back, lecturing Greg and Çelik in meticulous detail about the Third Sector Syndicate tribes. Her depth of knowledge was impressive, as was the fact that she seemed to have it all at her fingertips, rattling off statistics and dates in response to every question he and Çelik managed to ask. She was forthcoming and self-assured, and if she resented having to share this data with them, she betrayed nothing. He wished he'd had a chance to meet her months ago, before *Galileo* had been dropped on her doorstep, before she had come to see him as a threat; he would have—*could* have—approached her entirely differently.

The Third Sector Syndicates, like most groups in the sector, were far less organized than the Fourth and Fifth Sector Syndicates Greg was used to dealing with. In the Fourth Sector the tribes were exploring a consortium, and looking for ways to tap into legitimate markets; in the Fifth Sector, they had managed to contract with entire colony governments willing to overlook the often questionable sources of their supplies. But in the Third Sector, tribes remained fiercely independent, allying only occasionally for complex operations. Ironically, their recruiting efforts mimicked PSI's: they took in anyone who was willing to swear the oath. Captain Shiang, undoubtedly not insensible to the similarities, clarified the details.

"As a rule," she said, "they recruit adults, but they have a preference for families, siblings, or multigenerational nomads. Often they find people who have had trouble with the law and see no other alternative; but the oath is uncompromising, and is enforced by taking lives, if necessary. The bonds of the tribe are absolute. They die for each other, willingly, all the time."

Greg wondered how many Syndicate raiders had died at *Orunmila*'s hands.

In contrast to Captain Shiang, who paced restlessly throughout the presentation, Çelik sat motionless, attentive, and silent apart from a few pointed questions. He had extended his injured leg, the mechanical toes splayed to keep the artificial limb stable. Greg could not believe the pose was comfortable, but he supposed Çelik would settle for *comfortable enough*. *Exeter*'s captain had lost none of his intelligence or perceptiveness, but Greg could not help but notice the man's lack of sarcastic remarks. Indeed, he treated Captain Shiang with more respect than Greg had seen him treat anyone, and Greg thought if Çelik was manipulating the PSI captain, he was doing it with tremendous subtlety.

"My biggest concern," Captain Shiang said, after she completed their history lesson, "is the nature of the attack on *Exeter*. It matches none of the known patterns of the tribes we are familiar with." She sat at last, lowering herself stiffly into a chair. "As a result, we cannot know for certain which tribe it was, or what further resources they might have."

Or what else Ellis might have given them. "How many are they likely to have holed up on Canberra?" Greg asked.

"*Aganju* saw one ship go in after the raider we were tracking," Shiang replied. *Orunmila*'s sister ship had been watching Canberra since the tracker had reported back. "Captain Abanov is querying our other ships to see if he can establish the size of this tribe, and possibly the identity. In general, Syndicate ships carry no more than six crew, but most often two or four. And we have never seen more than three ships in a raiding party."

Why such small parties? Greg wondered. *Why divide their resources like that? Why not band together for a larger reward?*

"Given the richness of the weapons they had," Çelik asked, his thoughts apparently following Greg's, "would they have joined with another tribe in this?"

She shook her head. "I cannot say it is impossible. But . . . they don't do that for a robbery, as a rule."

"They don't use drones as a rule, either."

"No," she agreed, "they do not."

"*Aganju* can't track them all the way down to the surface, can they?" Çelik asked.

"Not with Canberra's weather."

Which meant they were blind. "Three ships," Greg mused. "So that's eighteen, at the most, but probably fewer."

"You cannot judge them by numbers as you would your own

people, Captain Foster," Shiang warned. "They are guerrilla fighters. They are trained to deal with large defenses, and they will figure out our vulnerabilities. Their strategy is to punch through with as small a hole as possible, and take what they want quickly."

"Yes," Greg agreed. "But how often do they have to play defense themselves?"

The sticking point, in the end, was personnel. Çelik drew a hard line. "Corps only," he told Captain Shiang.

"You do not have enough people," she pointed out.

"For a strike team? Certainly we do." At last, Çelik's arrogance was making an appearance.

"Your people are not all combat soldiers."

"This is our war."

Shiang's teeth clenched shut, and Greg saw the flash of anger in her eyes. "We have fought the Syndicates for twenty generations," she told Çelik, in her own language. "For them to do what they've done, in our territory? It's an act of war against us as much as against you."

"You did not lose ninety-seven people."

"Over five hundred years, we have lost thousands."

"This is not your mission."

"Neither is it your private avenue of revenge."

Çelik's expression darkened sharply, but Captain Shiang did not flinch. Greg found his esteem for her climbing by the moment, but this was not the time for them to go to war with each other. "Captain Çelik is right," he said quietly. "This is our mission. But I agree with you, Captain Shiang. We don't have enough people with combat training." *And some of our people are suspects.*

Çelik turned his glower on Greg. Greg kept his face expressionless. Whatever emotional abyss Çelik was circling, part of him knew that Greg was right, that their resources were meager, that they did not know whom they could trust. After a moment, Çelik's temper palpably receded, and he settled back in his chair. "For a strike ship of six," he said, "we would need three more."

Captain Shiang beat Greg to the question. "There are five of you."

"We don't need a medic," Çelik said, "and we don't need a mechanic."

Greg shook his head. "We need a pilot. I'm not flying into that soup without the Chief."

"She's not a combat officer."

"She was down there before."

"So was Keita."

Greg glanced at Captain Shiang, who met his eyes for an instant; he had the distinct impression she knew exactly what he was thinking. "We need to have as many people who know the territory as possible," he said.

Çelik scoffed. "The territory won't even look the same."

"My first officer is extrapolating topographical data," Greg told him. "We'll have something resembling a map."

"We don't have shit for records on Canberra."

Captain Shiang cleared her throat. "I think you may find, Captain Çelik, that our records are somewhat less sparse than yours. I will have Captain Abanov contact your first officer, Captain Foster."

That was another curiosity. Central had abandoned Canberra. Once every year or so, a group of meteorological scientists dredged up interest in the place, and tried to take some readings. The last time this had happened, the group had lost two expensive unmanned drones to freak storms before giving up. PSI, it turned out, kept a much closer eye on the planet— and seemed to have much more durable equipment.

Captain Shiang had apparently decided that the best way to deal with Çelik's concerns over Elena was to ignore them. "I have two people in mind who have experience fighting one-on-one with the raiders. They will know what to expect. I will have them put teams together so we can cover multiple landing sites."

"Volunteers only," Çelik said at last. "You don't order anyone, is that clear?"

Instead of eviscerating him, Captain Shiang nodded graciously. "Of course."

She stood; they were dismissed. Greg watched as Çelik rose clumsily, yet still without a hint of self-consciousness. Greg should have been impressed with the man's determination, functioning with a substandard prosthetic in an unfamiliar environment; but there was an arrogance to Çelik's complete disregard for what was going on. He was not considering his own injury. He was not thinking of the uncertainty of what they were facing. He was not thinking of the limitations that their entire landing party would have on that crippled, lifeless rock.

He's not thinking like an officer, Greg thought, and that was a problem.

Greg turned to Captain Shiang as Çelik left the room. For an instant, her serene, closed expression slipped, and he caught a glimpse of both fatigue and deep worry in her eyes. *Not for the mission,* he realized, surprised. *For Çelik.*

"Captain," he said, "may I have a word?"

Her expression shuttered again, and the contrast was striking. "As you wish, Captain Foster," she told him. She stayed on her feet, one hand straying to her back again, the other smoothing the fabric over her expansive stomach. He wondered if she was in pain; she had to be uncomfortable, at least, given her small frame.

"I'd like to discuss the security you have on this ship."

Her fine eyebrows shot up. "Do you have specific concerns, Captain?"

Yes, he thought. *I am surrounded by too many people who are trusting based on sentiment.* "You're aware that someone from Central was involved in the attack on *Exeter.*"

There was a flicker of emotion in those eyes; sadness again. "I am, Captain Foster. And may I say I am sorry to hear it. Betrayal by a comrade is far more brutal than betrayal alone."

An interesting sentiment.

"Given that we haven't identified the perpetrator," he said, "I'm concerned about the possibility that we have inadvertently brought some threat to *Orunmila.*"

She looked at him silently for a moment, then lowered herself stiffly back into her chair. "It is possible," she told him, "that I have already considered this possibility."

"What have you done to protect the ship?"

"That is not your concern, Captain." Smooth. Calm. If he had offended her, she was choosing not to let him know.

"Respectfully, Captain," he said, "it is. Just as you understand the Syndicate raiders in ways I don't, I understand the Corps and how our soldiers operate in ways that you can't, not with your lack of exposure."

She leaned on the desk, spreading her fingers on the surface. "So you would like me to outline our security procedures so you can evaluate how effective they might be against your clever soldiers?"

Great—apparently I offended her after all.

"What I want, Captain," he said, his frustration seeping through, "is for us to get where we're going and settle this mission. And I don't like the possibility that I've brought people on board who might jeopardize more lives."

"Is that what you think you've done?"

"I—" There was too much he couldn't tell her. "I can't know that, Captain." It was as much of the truth as he could give her for now. "But part of why I'm talking to you is that it's enough of a possibility that I want to make sure you know about it."

"Who do you suspect, and why?"

"I suspect everyone," he told her, "because I can't eliminate anyone."

"But you have no specifics."

He thought of Keita eight years ago, panicked in the rain, drawing a weapon on Elena. "I don't have enough," he conceded. "We all have weaknesses. I can't know whose weaknesses are relevant."

She settled back in the chair. "Will you vouch for your own people, Captain? For yourself, and Commander Shaw, and your first officer, whom Captain Abanov is taking into his confidence?"

That was easy. "Yes."

"Then I think you must allow Captain Çelik to vouch for his people as well."

"Do you really think he's objective at this point?"

"I think none of us are objective," she told him. "And I think none of us is telling the whole truth. Tell me, Captain Foster: Why is *Galileo* here, now, at this time? Why does Central feel the need for an extra warship in this sector?"

Greg regarded her, sitting rigidly in her chair, hands folded on the desk before her, staring at him with frank dislike. The expression made her look something like her actual age. He thought about telling her *Galileo*'s placement was irrelevant, that it had nothing to do with Central's position on PSI; but that, he was certain, would mark the end of any useful conversation.

"Among other reasons," he said at last, "Central is aware of the heightened Syndicate activity in the area. It's impacting our supply chain."

"This has been true for quite some time, Captain Foster. I am to believe that Central has only recently awakened to this fact?"

"Rebalancing resources takes time, Captain Shiang."

"Everything takes time, Captain Foster. Just as it took time for the Syndicates to find someone to provide them with twenty-six automated drones. I do not believe in coincidence, Captain. Do you?"

The Syndicate was an entirely different scenario. It wasn't relevant to this at all. He had no way to convince her of it. He was fairly certain, in her shoes, he would be mistrustful as well. Resigned, he turned away. "Coincidence is sometimes all we are left with. As for my warning to you . . . I'll assume it has already been heeded." He left the room, feeling her eyes on his back.

"Would it be bad form," Jessica began, "to start yelling at you now? Or should I save it all for when you get back?"

Greg had found *Orunmila*'s gymnasium, and was running laps on their track. The gym was largely abandoned, with a few people in one corner lifting weights, and one other runner pacing Greg a polite half lap behind. Apart from the odd color scheme and the occasionally anachronistic equipment, it might have been any Corps athletic facility. Captain Shiang might think him an alien, but in some ways their people were not so different.

He let Jessica rant about feeling like a fool in front of Andriya Vassily, the circular nature of her status reports simultaneously annoying and comforting. "You'd be short-tempered, too, if you had to deal with civilian scientists all day," he told her at last. "It's bark more than bite."

"I don't like having them so far away," Jessica confessed. "I'll tell you, sir, I don't mind the thought of having more firepower than we've got. My shoulder blades have been itchy ever since we nearly blew up in the field."

"Mine too. Have you received the data from *Aganju* yet?"

"This would be the massive, disorganized dump from some pissed-off-looking PSI captain called Abanov? Yes. *Galileo* is chewing on it."

Despite her word choice, there was something energetic in her voice, and his own pulse sped up. "What's up?"

"Maybe nothing, but . . . I've found something odd."

He listened while she explained the appearance of the seven power sources three decades earlier. "You can't narrow it down more than that?"

"There's nothing in the official record," she told him. "*Galileo*'s looking for more from the PSI records, and I'm seeing if I can correlate supply and manufacturing around that time period." She paused. "I'm wondering, sir, if they're part of what allows the raiders to take off and land in the storms."

"You think they're beacons?"

"I think the Syndicates might be *using* them as beacons."

Which meant Greg might, as well. "That might suggest a specific set of landing sites," he mused out loud. "Check on that, too, Jess. Use that data from *Aganju,* and find out where the raiders are holing up. I'd like a shot at surprising them, instead of flying right into their defenses."

"Pretty sure surprise is out, sir, as they already know you're coming."

"You've found the big flaw in our plan, Commander." Greg found himself catching up to the other runner, and he realized that he'd been speeding up. With some effort, he steadied his breathing and dropped back to a sustainable pace. "Find out what those damn things are while you're at it. They could be decoys as easily as beacons. I want to know if they had enough foresight to set a trap." There was a brief dropout in the comm signal, and he frowned. "Jess?"

She had heard it as well. "We've been getting comms hiccups, sir. I've got Samaras looking into it."

He opened his mouth to chastise her for giving the task to someone new, then reminded himself of Samaras's background. New or not, the man was capable of handling a comms repair. "All right, then. What else have you got?"

He listened to her summary of *Exeter*'s history, and frowned when she told him about the ship's premature loss of flagship status. "I don't remember any gossip about that," he told her.

"Would you have been in on it, sir?"

He thought back. *Galileo* would have been less than a year

old. He would still have been intoxicated by the beauty and possibility of his ship and his crew. He would have thought of *Exeter* only in passing. "It's possible I was," he admitted, "and I just don't remember." He cursed. "I'll ask Çelik, but given his state of mind, I'm not sure he'll tell me a damn thing."

"What's his state of mind?"

"Pissed off," Greg said, "and not thinking beyond getting down to Canberra and kicking someone's ass."

"Sounds charming."

"As long as I don't need him for strategizing beyond that, he's fine."

"What about everyone else?"

He knew what she was getting at. "Elena is jumpy as a cat."

"Over what?"

It was curiously comforting that Jessica didn't know. "She's been uncomfortable around me since all this started."

"So leave her alone."

"Not so easy. We got stuck in the same room."

Jessica was silent.

"Don't start, Jess."

"I'm not saying anything," she told him. "Except this one thing."

"Jess—"

"Be careful, sir."

That caught him off guard. "I'm fine. Why me?"

Jessica chose her words carefully. "Because she's bleeding over this, sir," she said. "And you'd do anything to stop her bleeding."

"You make that sound bad."

"The first rule in any triage situation," she reminded him,

"is to stop your own hemorrhaging before you look after any-one else."

"I'm not bleeding."

She was quiet for a moment. "Just be careful, Greg. It was bad enough before when you guys were fighting. Nobody needs that again, least of all you."

Maybe not, he thought, *but in some ways it was easier.* "I want topographical projections for Canberra in six hours, Jess. As detailed as you can get. That'll give us enough time to lay out a flight plan before we get there."

"What I really wish," Jessica said, the grumbling in her voice familiar and comforting, "is that we were there with you, and we could just light up that damn planet with nobody going down at all."

"Don't you think that lacks subtlety?"

"Fuck subtlety. You have to admit it'd work."

He kept running after she disconnected, rolling her words over and over in his head. She was not without a point. Nuking the planet would take care of the raiders and MacBride all at once. But they would never know what really happened, and he and Elena would forever be half-informed agents of Shadow Ops.

He wasn't sure which outcome would be worse.

CHAPTER 23

....

E lena spent the morning exploring the ship.

Strictly speaking, she should have found Dee—or even Jimmy—to talk about their forthcoming mission. But flying here with Greg and Dee, the atmosphere tense and quiet, had left her raw and out of sorts, and she found she did not want to speak with anyone for a while.

Easy to blame Dee's presence, and what she had told Greg about Canberra; but she knew Dee wasn't the problem. The problem was everything Greg had said to her the year before—and, if she was honest with herself, her own need to wish all of it away. What he had confessed, she wasn't sure—love? lust? distraction?—but she knew she didn't want it. Over the years they had built, she thought, a friendship in which she was safe and secure and valued, and it hurt to think that it had all been pretense. Ever since he had been officially divorced she had held her breath, waiting for some kind of declaration from him, and every day that went by without it she had relaxed a little more. Perhaps his confession really had just been a product of the turmoil around his failing marriage. Perhaps she really had been right about their friendship after all.

And then he had attacked her over Dee, and she had lashed out instinctively, and she knew nothing was changed or healed or resolved. And she had no idea what to do next.

She wandered *Orunmila*'s corridors, learning her way around. The year before, after they had unraveled MacBride's crimes, Elena had spent two weeks on *Penumbra*, a Fifth Sector PSI ship. There she'd had a guide: Trey, who already knew the ship, who could introduce her to the inhabitants, could vouch for her trustworthiness. She felt at home there, because he was their family, and she was his.

Orunmila was both familiar and utterly alien.

Among other things, the architecture was substantively different, despite being similarly built from bits and pieces of other ships. As she wandered down side corridors and narrow passages, she realized that parts of *Orunmila* were far older than anything in the Fifth Sector. She passed a corrugated metal wall that she could swear she had seen in a vid re-creating the first post-disaster launches. But there were other, less subtle differences: where *Penumbra* had been laid out in grids, *Orunmila* was made up of winding curves, and despite trying to discern order from the twists and turns, she quickly found herself disoriented. Were it not for a series of horizontal stripes in various colors that ran at the level of her knees, each leading to a different area of the ship, she would have become hopelessly lost.

It was not until she was overtaken by a crowd of running children, all under the age of ten, that she realized why the stripes were so low on the wall.

Children everywhere.

There had been children on *Penumbra*. Trey had been remarkable with them: patient, indulgent, answering the same questions over and over again. Just as he had for her, indulging her curiosity until she reached the limits of his knowledge. *No wonder you are an engineer,* he said to her once, laughing. *You must know everything, even when there is no end to it.*

All her life, her curiosity had made her an anomaly, something peculiar. Somehow, with him, she felt valued for all the things that made her different. He had loved her for all the reasons she had always felt unlovable. And when she told him she was leaving him, unable to face living on a stationary world, needing to live among the stars more than she needed him, he loved her still.

Even as she missed him, she carried in her heart that core of strength.

Eventually hunger drove her back to the square, where she discovered that Central currency was as welcome on *Orunmila* as it was on any colony. Elena bought an enormous bowl of yogurt and white strawberries, and a large glass of juice made from an orange and two cantaloupes. She carried her purchases toward the center of the square, and found a small table on the perimeter. She tackled her food with more enthusiasm than she thought was in her. Her last meal had been a hasty breakfast on *Galileo* before they left, made up of some reconstituted powdered protein that was orders of magnitude less appetizing.

"Mind if I join you?"

The voice was familiar, and she stifled a flash of irritation at the intrusion. "Sure," she told Jimmy, and resigned herself to being grateful he had decided he didn't hate her anymore. He sat down, a tall mug of coffee in his hand. "You're not eating?" she asked.

"Already ate." He frowned at her plate. "How do they get fruit?"

"How do *we* get fruit?" She had wondered herself, but the question annoyed her coming from Jimmy. "They have the same friends we've got." She finished the rest of it with less relish, then sat back, her fingers circling her juice cup. "You've been here a while," she began, searching for conversation starters. "What do you think of the place?"

He looked around, frowning, and it struck her then that where she was comfortable, he felt unsettled and out of place. "None of it makes sense," he replied irritably. "Trying to isolate everything like this. Trying to do it all in one place. And bringing children along." He shook his head. "How can they do that, when it's not safe?"

Elena did not know how Third Sector PSI felt about children. She only knew how Trey felt about children, and how he had raised the children who had come to his ship when he was captain. "I believe," she said, "the argument is that the galaxy is not safe, and to tell them it is would be a lie."

"One thin metal wall between them and vacuum." His disapproval was palpable. "Naive."

So much she had forgotten about this man. "If you're trying to be risk-averse you're in the wrong business," she told him.

"I'm not risk-averse," he said. "I'm trying to get *other* people to be risk-averse. Speaking of which," he added, shifting in his chair and leaning toward her, "what do you think about Captain Çelik leading the charge down to Canberra?"

Elena kept her face neutral. Greg was working with Shiang and Çelik on their attack strategy, and she was fairly certain who was to lead it was very much up in the air. "I think he's a man who knows his own mind," she said carefully. "Why do you ask?"

He arranged his features earnestly, and she had to fight to keep from snapping at him. Jimmy had always been a manipulator, using charm and sincerity to elicit specific emotions. It had worked on her—more effectively than she liked to remember—before Canberra, before the reality of the galaxy she lived in crashed down on her head. Afterward he had seemed so transparent she did not understand how she could have been so deceived.

"I'm worried for him, Elena," he said. She thought that part was probably true; given how ambitious he had always been, he would take his duty toward Çelik seriously. "What happened to *Exeter*—it's hit him hard. And you know Çelik; he doesn't process anything. Everything he feels gets chewed up and spat out as sarcasm and off-color jokes."

"I'd be more worried if he was behaving the way he always has."

"His reaction is normal, sure," Jimmy countered. *Backpedaling*, she thought. "But he's not ready for duty. Never mind his injury, which is catastrophic. If he damages that prosthetic, do you know they'll have to take his leg up to the hip? Full-limb leg grafts are almost never completely stable. He'll be crippled for good. And all because he's too angry to think straight."

I imagine he knows that, she wanted to say; but she didn't think that was Jimmy's point. "What do you want me to do about it?" she asked. "I haven't been near him in almost eight years, and we weren't exactly best friends back then."

"He respects you."

She laughed out loud. "Come on, Jimmy, you can do better

than that. Why don't you give him a medical order? You're chief of medicine now, aren't you?"

It was an unforgivably callous thing to say, at least as awful as what she had said to Dee back on *Galileo*. She should have felt guiltier, but Jimmy didn't rise to the remark. Instead he looked away, his jaw stiffening, and she caught irritation in his eyes. "I may have the rank," he said, "but he's not giving me the respect. He's brushed me off at every turn. He makes me consult with Doctor Xiao. We don't even know that she's had real medical training, and he listens to her over me." He turned back to Elena, all sincere concern again. "I'm afraid it's because she tells him what he wants to hear. But if you and I went to him, presented a united front, he might listen."

Regardless of his disparagement of Doctor Xiao, his worry seemed genuine. Elena leaned back, choosing her words carefully. "The thing is," she told him, "I'm not so sure we would be presenting a united front."

Another flash of irritation. She was beginning to find it familiar. "You really think he's prepared for this mission."

"I think," she corrected, "that I don't have a right to tell him he needs to stay behind, just because he's wounded."

"How the hell is he going to move around down there?" he demanded. "Are you going to carry him?"

She thought back to Canberra as she remembered it, to the cold air and the acid rain and the gravity just a little stronger than what she was used to, making her slow and clumsy. Jimmy had carried Niree through all of that. Elena had carried her pulse rifle, and the life of a girl she wasn't sure deserved saving. "If I have to."

He choked out a laugh. "Come on, Lanie. You're going to

jeopardize this mission by bringing a cripple down with you? By being hamstrung looking after him, instead of finding those raiders? You're really going to let him do this?"

"Yes. I am."

"This asshole bothering you, Songbird?"

She recognized Dee's voice behind her, but she kept her eyes on Jimmy, who sank back in his chair and looked away. Still annoyed, but all the defiance was gone. He kept his lips set as Dee pulled out the chair next to her and sat down.

"Jimmy's just worried, that's all," she told him.

"Uh-huh." Dee sounded derisive. "Is she blowing you off, too, Jimmy?"

Jimmy shot a glare at Dee, full of a much less veiled dislike than the one he had given Elena. *Good heavens*, she thought, *it may be more awkward in their quarters than in mine.* "I don't understand why you two can't see this," he told them. "He is not up to this mission. He can't do it. He's going to get himself killed, and he may take the whole landing party with him. You two are going to let it happen, just because he's Raman Çelik and nobody says no to him."

Elena could have tried to explain it to Jimmy, to tell him that she shared his worries, but not his conclusions. Instead, she and Dee said "Yes" at exactly the same moment. She bit down on a smile.

Jimmy's eyes flicked between the two of them, and his face darkened. For a moment the heat in his eyes turned into something icy, and then he straightened. "You're wrong," he told them quietly. "This is a fucking disaster, beginning to end, and you two don't even care enough to stop it." He stood, turned, and stalked off into the crowded square.

Elena frowned after him. "How long has he been like that?" she asked Dee.

Dee let out a laugh. She turned to look at him, and he swallowed it at her look. "Seriously? He's always been like that. You're telling me you didn't notice?"

"I—" She hadn't. She had noticed, after Canberra, that Jimmy was sharp and unpleasant with her, passive-aggressive and angry. Not unlike Çelik, she had thought at the time, and had remembered that ships tended to take on the personalities of their captains. But before Canberra . . . she had liked Jimmy. He had told her about life on *Exeter,* had given her guidance, had even flirted with her a little bit. She thought Canberra had changed him. Now she wondered if all that had changed was her perspective.

Dee's face had arranged itself into sympathy. "It's not just you," he said gently. "He's always been a manipulative son of a bitch. He'd much rather make other people do his dirty work."

Elena looked back out over the crowd where Jimmy had disappeared. "It doesn't make sense, though," she said, inexplicably sad. "He's got the power to make Çelik's decision for him. Why does he need us?"

Dee was quiet, and she turned to look at him again. His expression had sobered, and she saw deep uncertainty in his eyes. "What do you think Captain Çelik would do if someone tried to pull rank on him right now?"

Elena had never known Çelik well enough to answer that question, but she knew what she would do. "You're saying he'd defy the order."

"I don't know," Dee said, "but I think it's likely. And then . . . if he does that, Elena, he has nothing left. Nothing. I don't want to do that to Çelik; do you?"

Dee's face was full of anxiety and exhaustion. Everything in her longed to ease his worry, to take all his responsibilities onto herself and tell him it would all work out. He had always pro- voked protectiveness in her. "What are you going to do, Dee?" she asked on impulse. "When all of this is done? Will you stay with him, or will you find another ship?"

His lips tightened, and he looked away. "It's criminal, that they'd ground him," he said.

"I agree. But that's not what I asked."

Grief spread over his face then, along with that strange, naive incomprehension that was as familiar to her as Jimmy's hostil- ity. "I don't know," he confessed. "I was— I know you think he's an asshole, Songbird, and in most ways you're right. But he's a good captain. He was a good man to serve. The thought of stepping out there and taking on the job of second to some stranger—it makes no sense to me."

It did not even cross his mind, she noticed, to go for a cap- taincy of his own. "He'll need someone to look after him at whatever desk he gets stuck at," she observed.

He shook himself, looking back at her, a hesitant half smile on his face. "That might be all right. I'm not like you, horrified at the thought of living under the light of some star. Planets aren't so bad. And you're right; he'll need someone."

Oh, Dee. Her heart turned over as she watched him play it out in his head. He had always needed a purpose. That was what had torn him to pieces on Canberra: his purpose was to save people, and they had saved almost no one. "So all we need to do between now and then," she concluded, telling herself to feel happy for him, "is to keep him from killing himself on this mission." She shook her head. "Jimmy is not without a point, you know."

"So why didn't you agree with him?"

"It didn't happen to me, Dee. It wasn't my ship, my friends. But I *do* want them," she said with conviction. "I want to catch them. I want to see them suffer, although I'll settle for a court of law. If I'm Çelik—or you—no way some doctor is going to keep me away from the action. I'd lie, cheat, steal, and tell the Admiralty to go fuck itself, and I wouldn't think twice."

"You always did know your own mind, Songbird."

He said it with kindness, and a little envy, and she let her eyes rest on his for a long moment. She had always been a little bemused by the image he seemed to have of her. She had always thought of certainty as something of a character flaw, making her inflexible, causing her to say things that were what most of her senior officers termed "career-limiting." When she had learned that Dee actually admired her for it, she had felt like someone had turned the world on its head.

She looked away from him, conscious of the smell of the soap he used. She could remember, far too clearly, the comfort she had taken in his arms, the feeling of looking after someone who needed her, of allowing herself to be soothed by his surprisingly gentle hands. *Six months alone,* she thought. Dee was a known quantity. He wasn't someone new, would not expect anything beyond the moment, would not need her to fall in love. Was it such an awful thought, taking some comfort from an old, dear friend?

The thing about love, Trey had said to her once, *is that it spoils you for anything less.*

"Back on *Galileo*," he was saying, "when that converter went bad. You were amazing."

That snapped her out of it. "I wasn't," she told him, vaguely embarrassed. "I was doing my job."

"Do you ever just fall apart? Over anything?"

More than you can possibly know. She thought about falling apart quite frequently, she reflected. Despite the sense of wholeness she had been left with after Trey, she still found herself blindsided now and then by the fact that she would never see him again, that their paths had irrevocably diverged. Adding *Exeter* on top of that had been more than enough; but the nudge she felt every time she saw Captain Shiang and the child she was carrying—the shadow of what might have been—sometimes made her wonder how long she would be able to cope at all. "I'm saving my collapse for a rainy day," she said. "It's just that sometimes bits of it come out sideways."

"Yeah." He was silent a moment. "You do have friends, you know. You don't have to do all the collapsing alone."

Yes I do, she thought. *I hurt my friends too much if I collapse in front of them.* "About what I said to you back on *Galileo,* Dee. About Çelik. I'm sorry, truly. I was just—prickly and defensive, I guess."

"If that's you prickly and defensive, I'd hate to see you in a genuinely foul mood." He laughed at her look. "That's me trying to tell you it's okay, Songbird. I'm pretty much constantly pissed off, myself, now. I can't quite absorb it, you know? All of them, just . . . gone." His face fell. "We see a lot of places where people have died, but we don't see that much dying, you know? I keep thinking, there they were, one moment, just like we are now, breathing, thinking, doing their jobs—and then they were nothing. Gone. In a hundred years—less, probably—nobody will even remember their names."

"Nobody will remember our names, either." But she reached out and put a hand on his arm to soften her words. "Not that it's worth a damn thing, Dee, but I agree with you. It all seems so meaningless, like it's all left to chance. But . . . *we* can remember their names. It's not enough, it doesn't change anything, but we can remember them. We'll find those raiders, Dee," she assured him. "And they'll be brought to justice like all the rest."

"You really believe that? That there will be justice?"

"Always."

"How in the hell do you stay such an optimist?"

"Because the alternative," she told him, "is becoming a brooding bore in the middle of a community square."

He laughed at that, and smiled.

"You know," he said, and she realized she had been staring too long, "I meant what I said on *Galileo*. About you keeping it up. You look good, Elena."

Her real name. It had been a code between them once. She dropped her eyes, more tempted than she was willing to admit. "Oh, Dee." She shook her head. "You are sweet. But I can't."

"Foster?"

Oh Lord, Dee, not you too. "No. Greg and I, we're . . . not that." *What we are, I don't know, but we're definitely not* that. "It's— I had someone, and I'm still kind of stuck."

"No harm in holding on to someone else while you're getting unstuck," he suggested.

His eyes were so kind. "I know, Dee. But it would pull me apart, I think, and there's no time for that."

He nodded, accepting. "Okay. But if you change your mind, you find me, yeah?"

I am insane, turning him down. "Yeah." Ignoring the physical tug, she got to her feet, taking her juice. "Don't brood too much," she told him. "It doesn't help. You can trust me on this."

And she turned and fled while she still could.

CHAPTER 24

Raman worked methodically through his weight routine, and thought about prisons.

He was still sore from his sparring session with Cali, but after the interminable meeting with Captain Shiang and Foster, during which he had to listen to strategizing around issues he had no intention of addressing, he needed privacy. At his request, Captain Shiang had provided him with a weight bench, and he was able to lie down on it in front of the room's wide window and lift to his heart's content. The sweat and the strain quieted the drumbeat of pain in his leg, and for a few minutes, increasing the weight little by little, he was able to feel almost whole.

His body annoyed him. For most of his life, it had served him well, allowing him to do whatever he needed—or wanted—often under less-than-ideal circumstances. But it did not seem to be coping with his injury. Just when he felt he had found a rhythm, the foot would land at a slight angle, and the joint would howl in protest. He was careful, walking down the halls where everyone could see him; but in these rooms, on his own, he found himself stumbling a lot, even falling. He was not a man to get enraged over futility, but he had to admit his temper was fraying. He had so little left to ask of this body; surely one bad leg wasn't enough to incapacitate him.

You're expecting your body to respond the same way, but it can't.

Damn woman. She was in the state she was in by choice. He had not chosen any of this. He knew he was hurt. He knew he was not the same.

Never the same. Never again.

She was too young to know so much about campaigning, to understand about loss, to watch silently, with kindness, and let him do what he needed to do. For her sake, he wished Chanyu had not retired. For his own . . . he was glad not to be dealing with that blinkered old man. Captain Shiang saw more than he wanted her to, yes . . . but she saw what he needed her to see as well. He was not sure anyone else did.

He pushed the lifting far past the point where he should have stopped, then lurched to his feet to head for the bathroom. The pain tore through him like flame through paper, and he had to close his eyes for a moment to avoid passing out. Perhaps staying off of the leg had been a mistake.

Instead of taking a shower, he filled the bathtub, making the water as hot as he could stand it. It was the pain, he was sure, that had made him rebuff Cali's advances, offered repeatedly and with varying levels of subtlety since he had come on board the day before. She was a lovely woman, and had been pleasantly blunt about her interest. Under other circumstances he would have taken her up on her offer, probably more than once. But if the pain had not destroyed his libido, it had certainly tempered it; and although Cali seemed to have a strange attraction for his prosthetic, he could not muster up the kind of enthusiasm he thought she merited.

Besides, seduction for entertainment was a last resort, something to turn to when he had nothing else. In a strange way, it felt like giving up, and he had too much to do to give up just yet.

The door chimed while he was soaking, eyes closed, feeling his muscles loosening. The sound was more melodic than the standard Central chime, and it made him feel even more like he was staying in some sort of elite resort. He made a mental note to ask *Orunmila* if she could change it. "Who is it?" he asked the ship.

"Captain Foster," she told him in Standard.

Well, what the hell is this? "You should have an accent, *Orunmila,*" he said.

"Specify."

He thought, for a moment, it might be nice to have the ship sound like Captain Shiang.

With some regret he opened his eyes and hauled himself out of the bathtub using the multiple handrails. It crossed his mind to stay naked and dripping, a towel around his neck, just to annoy the man; but in the end he dried off rapidly and pulled on the loose black trousers he had found in a drawer. "Come in," he called, and stepped out of the bathroom just as Foster came through the door.

Raman watched Foster's eyes sweep the elegant room. His face betrayed no surprise, but Raman suspected Foster had noticed its unusual opulence. "Nice, isn't it?" Raman said by way of greeting. "You'd think I'd told them I was royalty. Perhaps they just assumed."

Foster's lips pressed together, and Raman wondered if the man would ever develop any kind of a sense of humor. "I need to talk to you," he said.

"Always nice to get a courtesy visit," Raman said, "especially only five short hours after you've come on board." He made his way—carefully; damned if he was going to fall in front of Foster—across the room to the bar, ignoring the shooting pain that hit with each step. "You're a scotch drinker, as I recall."

"I quit," Foster told him.

Oh, Lord. "So she's made you a puritan, too, has she?" he asked, pouring himself a drink.

Again Foster was silent. *He's not nearly as much fun as Shaw,* Raman thought. She would take the bait, at least sometimes. "I need to ask you about your crew," Foster said.

Without thinking, Raman downed half the glass of scotch in one gulp. "Now why would my crew be any of your business?"

"Because one of them is behind the sabotage," Foster replied. "And you know it."

He took a moment to regret that Foster's first officer was so good at her work. "I have a lot of officers," he said. "Should I go alphabetically?"

"Why don't we start with Keita?"

Raman had seen enough to know that Foster's initial choice of suspect was not objective at all. "He's a good soldier," Raman said. "Consistent. Loyal. Lacks a bit of imagination, but most people do, don't you find? Or perhaps you don't notice."

Foster had looked away, his impatience barely contained. "What I've noticed is that he's not command material."

"Given your own history with first officers," he said, "I'm not at all sure you should be lecturing me about Keita." Foster did not answer, and he shrugged. "I keep him around for the same reason I keep anyone around. Because he's loyal, and because I can keep an eye on him."

"So you don't trust him."

"I don't trust anyone," Raman explained. "But I don't think people change that much, do you?"

"Is it the same for Jimmy Youda, then? Keep your enemies closer?"

Raman allowed his eyebrows to go up. "Youda's a tolerable medic," he said, "with no sense of humor. Not as bad with patients as with real people, though. Lawson likes him. Liked him." He took another drink. "He's hardly the sabotage type, though. More the type who stands on the sidelines and complains about how it's being done."

"So who on your crew *is* the sabotage type?"

"All of them. None of them." He shrugged and turned away; it was an irritatingly irrelevant question. "Your first officer has efficiently exonerated most of my enlisted personnel. What you really need to know is why any of the others would have sold out their crewmates for a pack of raiders."

Foster would find no satisfying answers. Raman had done background checks on his people himself, during his hours of forced inactivity in *Galileo*'s infirmary. Money and family troubles abounded, but there was no one in such dire straits that they would risk their lives for whatever payoff a Syndicate tribe might have been able to provide.

Which meant a different motive, and that bothered Raman far more.

"Have you considered," Foster asked, "connections to Canberra itself?"

"Without motive, look for means?" He shook his head. "There aren't any connections to Canberra. Central hasn't been near that poisonous rock for nearly nine years."

"Leaving it for the raiders to use as a temporary hiding place. Maybe with the assistance of some Corps sympathizers."

Raman swirled the liquor in the glass and sipped again. She had a fine cellar, Captain Shiang. "Spinning conspiracy theories?"

"Always."

"She really has rubbed off on you."

"I don't think she's thought much beyond having to deal with going back."

"You've always underestimated her, you know."

"You don't know a damn thing about her."

That had managed to shove Foster off the subject of *Exeter*'s crew. Raman laughed at him. "I know whatever theory you're putting together, she's put it together ahead of you."

"Like whoever is behind this was part of *Exeter* when the original Canberra mission happened?"

Well. Perhaps Foster wasn't entirely without imagination after all.

"Did you know anything about the place that the landing party didn't?" Foster asked. "You can't tell me the vid you had was the most up-to-date information."

That had been Raman's first question to his command once the landing party had returned without Treharne. "That was all we had until it was too damn late. But I didn't have to spend too much time shouting at the Admiralty before the whole mess started to unravel. There was another vid, showing the place in the state more or less as we found it. It got buried, lost because they had so many vids from colonies that were actually asking for help."

"Canberra never asked?"

"They shouldn't have had to." He felt a flash of that old anger. "We shouldn't have left that vid to languish for so long. Every person on that damn colony dead, because the Corps doesn't have enough people slogging through the mail."

Foster, apparently, had no heart. "Was that all?" he prompted. "Just the newer vid?"

"There were also the terraformers." Foster frowned, and Raman sighed, taking another sip. So tempting to finish the glass, to fill it up again. "The story was terraformer failure. But even if the things had shut down, it should have taken the natural climate another ten years to reassert. Three months should have been more than enough warning. There was no scientific reason for that planet to begin eating the colonists when it did. Everyone spins the story as a failure of communication, like we all should have known the place was going to hell. But in reality? One way or another, it was the weather, and to this day nobody knows why."

"Has anyone studied the planet? Figured out how it could hit so fast?"

Raman laughed again. "With what resources? We can't even get them food in time to keep them from eating each other. We're not going to waste meteorologists on a planet nobody should have bothered to settle to begin with."

"But surely it's important," Foster pressed. "The equipment failure happened there, and nobody knows what caused it. Who's to say it won't happen somewhere else?"

"Who's to say it hasn't?"

Foster was silent, and Raman saw his mind working. Despite his limited imagination, he wasn't a stupid man. "You're saying there have been others."

"I'm saying Canberra isn't the only weird climate crisis we've hit. Triomphe. Nova Akropola. Liriel."

Foster had served at Liriel, Raman recalled. Decorated for bravery. Credited, along with his team, for rescuing nearly thirty thousand people. Not yet a captain then; just a lieutenant commander, a boy. He had done a good job there, but Raman wondered if he had really never wondered how Liriel had deteriorated so quickly.

"Liriel went sulfurous," Foster said. "Terraformer failure doesn't do that, and that one they've studied."

"Fair enough," Raman said. He'd had the same arguments with himself; Foster, being who he was, would take longer to accept the unsettling possibilities. "Catastrophic climate change, then. Random. Bad luck. It's not impossible, of course, but the key is to figure out when it's going to happen, and how fast, so we can get the proper equipment in place to prevent it."

"Was that the kind of thinking that got *Exeter* demoted from flagship?"

"You've been investigating my ship." Raman felt his detachment slipping.

"You're saying there was another reason?"

Raman drained the glass, reaching for the bottle. "It's the usual bargain we make," he said. "We shame the Admiralty into doing what they should have done all along, and they punish us for it." Dammit, Foster knew this.

"They were explicit about that, then?"

Raman scoffed. "Of course not. But you know how it goes. As long as you're useful, you can do anything. The second you call them on their bureaucratic bullshit, they'll get you for it. You think that isn't exactly what's been happening to you this year?"

Foster considered. "I think," he said, "that the left hand doesn't always know what the right hand is doing."

"You're going to be coy about this."

"Consequences of my own actions don't need to be shared."

"Ah. A *martyr*." Raman shook his head. "Tell me. When you were a boy, did your mother slap you every time you laughed?"

"Is it absolutely necessary for you to be so consistently abrasive?"

"I think so, yes."

"Why?"

"You stole from me."

"*Stole?*" Foster laughed, but Raman did not think he was actually amused. "You're still talking about Elena. Nearly eight goddamned years later. What is wrong with you?"

Foster was much more interesting angry. Raman drained his glass. "You could have had anyone for *Galileo*," he accused. "The whole damn Corps was applying for your little ship. But you had to come after *my mechanic*. Every dumbass spanner jock I had, she had more brains than all of them put together. She was doing damn good work for me—hell, for all of us. Keita would have been institutionalized if she hadn't intervened."

"You know what Keita did down on Canberra. That he drew on her."

Raman nodded. "He told me. Years ago."

"And you *still* promoted him?"

At that, he felt himself growing genuinely angry. "You're going to judge a soldier in the field? After where you've been, what you've seen?"

"I don't judge *him*," Foster snapped. "I judge *you*. Drawing on a civilian that you suspect got one of your people killed is one thing. Drawing on one of your own is something else. It's not just a discipline problem, Çelik. Keita has a crack in him, running right down the middle. You think you're doing him a favor, protecting him from that?"

"I think your girl did a pretty good job of patching him up."

At long last Foster lost his temper, and Raman watched, gratified, as the man strode up to him, squaring off centimeters from his face, his jaw set. "She is not '*my girl*,' " he said. His voice was low and dangerous; Raman supposed a lot of people found him intimidating when he was angry.

Foster continued. "She is not a *thing* that can be stolen. She made a choice. If she hadn't come to *Galileo,* Reid would have had her on *Constellation,* and you know it. And she is just as wrong about Keita as you are. You're both clouded by sentiment, by the shadow of this hellish mission that failed when it shouldn't have."

Raman stared at him for a long time. "Keita didn't sabotage your ship," he said evenly.

"You'd better hope he didn't," Foster said, his face still close. "Because whatever you're planning to do to those raiders—that's what I'll do to Keita."

"She won't forgive you for that."

At that Foster's face twitched into a brief, humorless grin, and he took a step back. "Here's the difference between you and me, Çelik," Foster said. "All these years later, you're still waiting for her to tell you she was wrong. That you told her so, that she should have stayed with you, at least until you could shove her into a captaincy. That she should have become just like you, arrogant and cynical, always knowing every goddamned thing, one step ahead of everyone she meets. Successful. Cold. Alone. Me?"

He looked suddenly deflated. "I have a job to do. I'm not sure it's the one the Admiralty thinks I should be doing, but I know what it is. And if she won't forgive me—whatever else she is, Çelik, she's an officer. Not some reflection of my ego, or some justification of a scrap of faith I put in her eight years ago when I interviewed her for a job."

He turned to the door. "We're not all extensions of you, Çelik. Not put here to make your life more trying, or to impress you. Even Shiang sees you as a conduit, an intermediary. I wonder, sometimes, what the hell you'd do if you ever had to live your life without being reflected by someone else."

"Nice speech," Raman said after him. "But even you know you should be reporting to her, not the other way around."

Foster turned, fire in his eyes, but abruptly the lights dimmed and turned blue. A low klaxon sounded. "Emergency, Level Three," *Orunmila* said calmly. "Lockdown initiated."

Without thinking, Raman headed for the door, Foster in step with him. "Closest stairwell is around the corner," he said as the door slid open. *Damn* this prosthetic; he was getting better at not falling over, but he still couldn't move fast enough. "Don't wait for me; I'll meet you down there."

Foster lengthened his stride. "What's a Level Three emergency?" he asked over his shoulder.

"It's a breach," Raman shouted after him. He gave up the

pretense of grace and leaned one hand against the wall, using it for balance, the prosthetic propelling him forward at odd angles. Every step brought the now-familiar jarring pain, but he kept moving. A breach could mean they had been hit, and were taking on vacuum, but he didn't think that was it. Sitting here, in the middle of nowhere, charging their batteries?

No—the enemy had come to them.

CHAPTER 25

G reg commed Elena while he ran.

"Where are you?" she said in his ear before he could speak.

"Outside Çelik's quarters," he told her; "I'm headed for the stairwell under the square. Where are you?"

"Just left the gym," she replied. He could hear her feet hitting the floor, the slight acceleration of her breathing. "I'm following a pack of security people. Gotta say, Greg, they don't seem surprised by this."

"I don't think this tactic is new to them." Greg had heard tales from Valeria of Syndicate hits. When the number of raiders was small, they would look for a vulnerable spot near a ship's storage area, and try for a quick punch-and-grab. Over the centuries they had developed a reasonably wide repertoire of attack patterns, and PSI had developed a corresponding set of defenses. He thought, though, that this hit was unlikely to be about cargo. *There's no way this is a coincidence.*

He wondered what PSI protocols were for an attacker that was trying to bring down the ship.

He emerged from the stairwell to a group of a dozen people in black PSI uniforms, all gripping high-energy pulse rifles before them as they ran in rough formation down the hallway. At the front of the crowd he recognized Calista Annenkov, Shiang's security chief. When he fell into step with them, she spoke to him.

"Central. Are you armed?"

Weapons had not been part of the deal when Captain Shiang had agreed to allow them on board. "No, ma'am," he said.

"Stay behind us, then," she said tersely, and he nodded.

Behind him, he heard a familiar footfall; he turned to see Elena joining the group. They exchanged a look. It was insanity, running toward a gunfight without a gun; but he knew she couldn't stay away any more than he could.

They approached a reinforced double door, and Annenkov held up a hand. The soldiers split, spreading to either side of the door. Elena ended up opposite him; he caught her eye briefly, and she gave him a nod of acknowledgment—and then, absurdly, she winked at him. He almost laughed. She always felt better when the other shoe dropped.

Annenkov listened at the door for a moment, then spoke in a low voice, querying *Orunmila* for data. After a moment she looked up, her eyes sweeping over each of them in turn. "There's air and gravity," she said, "but their seal isn't complete. We're leaking, but slowly. Do not let them leave."

Before he could wonder how much of that Elena had understood, the door slid open, and Annenkov led them all in firing.

Greg slid in against the wall, staying low, eyes adjusting to the dark room. It was a small storeroom with a high ceiling, and would have been ordinary had the rear wall not been punctured by a tube a meter in diameter. He had an instant to register the hull damage—a rough, ragged edge sealed by some kind of expanding foam—before he caught movement in the back of the room. A flash from behind a gray crate, nearly two meters high, and the wall just above him exploded in flame and heat. He crouched lower to the floor and squinted through the gaps in the room's stacked contents: three raiders, two shooting, the third bent over something on the floor. Two raiders shooting should have been easy, but they were clearly experienced, firing rapidly along the walls, pinning down Annenkov and her people. As Greg watched, one of the PSI soldiers caught a blast in the arm.

He took his eyes off of them for an instant, seeking out Elena. She was in the middle of the floor, crouching behind a storage lockbox. As Greg watched, Annenkov pushed away from the wall, running the length of the room. At the same time, Elena moved, still close to the floor, to dash to another box closer to the raiders' line of defense. When she was safe at her next destination, she looked up at him; he nodded at her, and made his own move closer to the room's punctured wall. He had a hunch what that third raider was doing. If Annenkov and her people could handle the two who were shooting, he thought he and Elena could deal with the last.

Elena hunched behind the crate, wondering how long it would take the raiders to figure out what Greg was up to. The unarmed raider was almost certainly setting a bomb; there was no other explanation for their persistence in the face of superior numbers and firepower. They wouldn't have to hold off the PSI guards much longer to be able to set their trap and escape.

She wondered how powerful the explosive was, and what they thought they were blowing up.

She saw Greg move, and she ran again, this time making it within a meter of their location. One of them had seen her, and was firing at her cover; the other was shooting over her head toward the storeroom door. She could see the barrel of a pulse rifle when she craned her neck over the edge of her hiding place, and as she watched, it swung around toward Greg.

There was no time to wait for Annenkov to distract them again. She ran out from behind the box and confronted the raider, arms tensed. Startled, the man swung his rifle toward her, knocking her off balance as she punched ineffectively in his direction. Before he could recover his equilibrium she grabbed the barrel of his rifle, jerking it sharply toward her; he let go with one hand, but her fist caught him sharply under his chin. His head snapped back, and she yanked on the gun again, bringing her knee into his gut. He made a sound, but his grip on the rifle did not loosen.

Across from her, she saw Greg behind the unarmed raider, and she hit her raider again, drawing the attention of the other gunner. Leaving off his targeting of the PSI guards, he aimed at Elena. She thought briefly of those vids she had seen where people used the bodies of their enemies as shields; the man she was wrestling with was not nearly so under her control. She braced her feet, ready to pull at the rifle again; but this time he was ready for her, shoving the rifle past her and shaking himself loose. She tripped, dropped to the ground, and as he aimed at her again she saw the other raider turning toward

Greg. In desperation she hooked one foot around her raider's ankle and pulled him down with her. He rolled as she did, and they recovered together; he gripped his rifle and aimed toward her this time, and she swept her leg against the rifle, knocking it aside. A shot went wide, and she started scrambling to her feet . . .

. . . and then the gravity went off.

Raman braced himself against the wall with his good leg, edging slowly toward the raiders. Entering late, after the shooting had started, was working in his favor; although he made a fine target, creeping spider-like along the wall, his lack of weapon and general slowness rendered him uninteresting to the invaders. These could not, he thought, be the same people who had masterminded the hit on his ship. These people were clearly idiots. Two guns and one bomber, against half a dozen PSI guards and three Central soldiers? Did they really think they would have a chance at escape?

He saw Foster creep closer, saw Shaw, bare-handed, try to wrestle the gun away from the raider who had targeted him. He used the distraction to move closer, pushing away from the wall and using the prosthetic as a walking stick. He could see clearly, then, the bomb being attached to the floor. Nothing that small would have a sophisticated timer, he suspected. All they needed to plan for was getting away.

Cali had stopped shooting for a moment, and had one hand behind her ear. An instant later, the pressure on his injured knee lifted, and the artificially generated pressure impulses from the prosthetic lightened. Cali had shut off the gravity. He glanced at the raiders; the one who had been about to shoot Shaw had stumbled, unsettled. The other was spinning toward the ceiling, his body limp, caught by a stray shot from his comrade, and his estimation of their intelligence dropped again.

His zero-grav training had been decades ago, but he found his body remembered it. He pushed off across the room, discovering that the spidery foot of the prosthetic allowed him to control his trajectory with some subtlety. He was level with Shaw's head when he reached her; grabbing the edge of the crate that the raiders had hidden behind, he pulled himself down and kicked Shaw's attacker with his flesh foot. He braced himself against the recoil, but the raider spun sideways, firing wildly as his body floated toward the back wall. A moment later, one of Cali's guards fired, and they were down to one.

A pity, Raman thought. The man might have known something.

The bomber, who had ignored all of this, had finally finished his work, and had launched himself toward the opening in the wall. He seemed better prepared than the others, gripping the corrugated sides of the tube; but Foster grabbed his elbow, delivering some well-placed kidney punches. Explosives, it seemed, were a better motivator than rifle fire, at least for this man; he fought fiercely, and his elbow caught Foster in the face more than once.

Below him, Shaw had climbed hand-over-hand to the bomb, and with one foot hooked under another lockbox, her fingers scrambled at the floor. A moment later she had the device in her hands. "Let him go!" she shouted to Foster, and the captain released his prize. The raider shoved himself down the tube and vanished. An instant later, Shaw threw the device after him.

"Everyone out!" she shouted.

To their credit, Cali's people did not wait for an explanation. Raman grabbed Shaw's arm, tossing her toward the door, then pushed off the crate after her. Cali waited on the other side of the doorway, catching her people one by one as they went through into the normal gravity of the hallway. As soon as they were on their feet, they headed down the stairs.

He stumbled when he hit gravity again, feeling briefly disappointed. "Get down the stairs, Captain Çelik," Cali said tersely; but he ignored her, reaching his hand through the doorway. Foster caught it, and Raman hauled him through, steadying him as he stumbled against the wall. The three of them headed away from the door.

"Seal Storage Twelve," Cali said as they started running down the stairs. The door slid shut behind him, and Raman heard a secondary lock. Cali gave them all a look. "At least one level away, everyone. And keep your damn heads covered."

In fact, they'd only made it halfway down the flight of stairs when the door blew open and the blast flung them all into the air.

CHAPTER 26
....

Galileo

PSI, Jessica thought, operated with a significantly different
definition of *organization* than the Corps.

Aganju kept chronological records on Canberra, but they had
not separated any of the information into categories. Streams
of meteorological data were cluttered with radiation readings,
seismic disturbances, and occasionally measurements from an
automated probe. It took her nearly twenty minutes to figure
out that their prioritization changed daily: any statistically significant variation in data caused that parameter to be tracked
more closely.

And one of the parameters it was tracking was the visibility
of the power sources.

Like Central's data, the PSI data revealed nothing that might
identify those seven points on the map, but it did demonstrate
a clear correlation between specific weather patterns and landing of Syndicate ships. The larger storms that formed over the
oceans had a tendency to spin up, blow inland, and cling furiously to the northern mountains, spreading rain and fog and

acid across most of Canberra's single major landmass. Smaller storms and rain squalls were individually of little consequence, but they tended to arrive in clusters and interact unpredictably. The mountain storms were stronger and longer-lived; but they were also far more stable. *Aganju*'s records showed that the raiders had a clear preference for landing during the stable storms, but even then, Jessica reasoned, they would still have had to run into some luck. Many of the storms hung over the northern hemisphere for weeks or even months, some of the power sources winking into visibility for an hour or so, often less. Facing a twenty-two-minute descent time, a pilot would find them chancy beacons at best.

She frowned at the data, the indicator from her stealth collector blinking silently in the corner of her eye. *What the hell are those damn things?*

As she stared at the storm patterns, Jessica's collector light went bright red, and died.

For an instant her mind went blank; and then she began swearing loudly, pulling up her interface and firing off tracer after tracer, looking for some vestige of the collector. There was nothing: no backtrace, no echo, no gap anywhere suggesting it had ever existed. Which might mean it had done its job and self-destructed on discovery; but it might also mean she had blithely transmitted proof of her own lawlessness into the hands of her enemies.

Whoever they were.

Her comm beeped politely, and she froze.

"Who is it?" she asked *Galileo*.

"The message carries no ident," the ship told her calmly.

"What about auth headers?"

"Auth headers are valid but not readable."

Fucking gibberish, she thought desperately. *Just like those messages last year. That'll teach me to code to a base I don't understand.* "Can you decode it?" she asked.

"Message is already coded for Jessica Lockwood, self-destruct on separate contact."

That piqued her curiosity. "Self-destruct? Really? How—" *Fuck, Jess, what are you thinking?* "Put it through," she said. "Audio only."

She heard the faint digital echo of the signal being completed, and for a moment there was only silence. Then:

"Commander Lockwood, I wonder if you could offer me a defensible reason why I have just been awakened by an illegal data collector rummaging through my classified records."

It was Admiral Herrod.

"Sir," she began, with no idea how she was going to finish her sentence. "I'm—"

"Relax, Commander," the admiral interrupted, and Jessica thought he sounded vaguely amused. "If I was going to have you busted, you'd be in the brig already."

"We don't have a brig, sir." It was a reflexively foolish response.

"Be that as it may," Herrod said dryly, "I thought it was worth finding out the answer to my question first, given that you're querying data on a mission that happened nearly nine years ago. What are you looking for?"

But something different had occurred to her. *Don't be an idiot, Lockwood,* she told herself; but she had to ask anyway. "Sir, how did you detect my collector?"

"You think you're that good, Commander?"

She took the question seriously. "Yes, sir, I do. I'll admit the collector is something of a work in progress, but I'd hold it up against the best work I've done, or I wouldn't have released it into the wild." He was silent, and she tried again. "Consider it a professional courtesy, sir."

Jessica had spoken to Admiral Herrod a handful of times since her promotion. What struck her about him was not his manner, but his inconsistencies. There were times when she was certain he was the official voice of the Admiralty, and that if she saluted incorrectly or her hair fell into her eyes, she'd find a note about it in her next official eval. But sometimes—and she was hoping now was one of those times—his observations were more nuanced. More *human*. She liked him better at times like that, but she had no better sense of whether or not she should trust him.

"Your collector is based on other work with which I am familiar," he told her.

Her spine was tingling again. "Your work, sir?"

"I'd hardly identify the creator to you, would I, Commander? Can we return to the point?"

She wanted to press him, to make him clarify his cryptic remarks, but she was surprised he had given her the information he had. And . . . he was right. He had her. He had traced her own work right back to her doorstep, and she had as much as admitted to him it was hers.

So why is he even talking to me?

She could think of no reason not to tell him the truth. "I've been compiling topographical data on Canberra, sir, and I've run into something I can't explain." She told him about the power sources.

Herrod was quiet for so long she began to wonder if the connection had dropped. When he spoke again, all of the humor and sarcasm was gone from his voice. "Under the circumstances, Commander, I'd advise you to avoid running searches on Canberra. Even with a stealth data collector."

"Due respect, sir." Jessica's shoulder blades were itching again, but she was too annoyed to keep silent. "Our people are going to head down to that planet, and I don't want them going down blind."

"You want to discuss strategy, Commander? Because topographical map or not, your people are going to have, at best, a very vague notion of what they're going to be dealing with."

"Understood, sir. But given the nature of this mission, I'm going to get them whatever I can."

More silence. Jessica was beginning to recognize when Herrod was stopping to think. "Commander Lockwood," he said at last, "I believe you understand enough of this situation to know I'm . . . disinclined to take you to task for your investigation methods under these particular circumstances. So why don't you tell me, specifically, what you need?"

Trust, or not? She took a breath. "We're speculating the Syndicates have been using the power sources to triangulate takeoff and landing, although they'd still be close to useless in most of the storms. I'm trying to figure out when and why they appeared, and what the hell they are."

"What will that get you?"

She closed her eyes, suddenly exhausted. "I don't know, sir. Maybe nothing. But I'd like to know more about them than I do, especially if we can use them like the raiders have been using them."

There was a long pause. "Okay, Commander," Herrod said

at last, "here's what we'll do: I'll do some investigation from here, and I'll let you know what I find."

Jessica shifted uncomfortably. "You know, sir," she said, suddenly concerned, "you could just let my collector go, and—"

"I'm aware you don't trust me, Commander," the admiral said. "Would you feel better if I said I didn't trust you, either?"

"No, sir."

"Then let me rephrase." His voice hardened. "You are out there on your own with half your systems offline. I am here on Earth, where we are defended by enough firepower to take out the entire Third Sector and still have ammunition left over. Stop taking risks, Commander. I'll contact you when I have data." And he cut her off.

She paced the floor of Ted's office in engineering, aware of his worried eyes on her. "*Galileo*," she asked, "what's Herrod's academic background?"

"Admiral Herrod has four advanced degrees in mathematics and intelligence engineering."

"Cryptography?"

"No official training in cryptography."

"What branches of mathematics?"

"Number theory. Differential calculus. Linear algebra."

Might as well be cryptography. "What's he done with his career?" Before *Galileo* could begin to recite Herrod's complete professional record, she clarified. "Has he done anything at all related to cryptographic work?"

"No records to indicate official cryptographic work for Central Corps."

She frowned. There had to be a way to get at this. "*Galileo*, has he sent or received any encrypted messages recently?"

"Admiral Herrod's professional correspondence is classified."

Of course. "What about stream activity?"

There was a long pause. "One hundred seventy-seven thousand eight hundred and nine messages on stream with a greater than fifty percent likelihood of being related to Admiral Herrod."

"How about in the last two years?"

"Four thousand, five hundred and forty-seven."

Ted had begun to catch on. "You think he's your crypto designer?"

"If he's not, he has to know who it is," she said reasonably. "He was waiting for that collector to show up."

"But he couldn't have known it would come from you." He shook his head. "Why does this matter?"

"Because if it's him, I think we may be able to trust him."

"I can't agree," he told her. "None of us can trust him. He's not just part of this, Jess. He's one of the people who told Elena and the captain that killing MacBride was a perfectly acceptable solution to this problem."

"You think he believes they'll do that?"

"No. I think he believes Çelik will do it." Jessica looked up at him; he was frowning, but his dark eyes were worried. "If this wasn't a kidnapping—if this was some premeditated escape plan set up by MacBride—you know where Çelik grew up, Jess. Tethys is an eye-for-an-eye place. Literally. On Tethys, killing MacBride would be perfectly legal. The only problem would be figuring out how to do it ninety-seven times."

"If it comes out that MacBride's involved in these attacks," she pointed out, "there's a good chance the Corps will execute him anyway. Elena and the captain won't let Çelik do it first."

"You think they can stop him?"

"Ted, he's *crippled*."

"He's got a serious injury for which he has been treated. He's mobile, he's still got his rank, and he's on a PSI starship. Tethys may be eye-for-an-eye, but if PSI even suspects MacBride has associated with raiders, they'll hand the pistol to Çelik themselves."

"Now you're stereotyping," she said angrily. "You can't think that all of them—"

"It doesn't have to be all of them, Jess. It only needs to be one."

She closed her eyes, trying and failing to remember the last time she'd slept for more than three hours uninterrupted. "Okay," she conceded at last. "I can see it that way. Herrod helping us so Çelik will make sure MacBride's execution goes smoothly." She opened her eyes. "But if that's what he wants, Ted—I can trust him to help me with this, if nothing else. He wants to make sure we have the best picture we can get of that planet, so the attack is successful."

"Or," Ted countered, "he's setting you up, so when PSI kills MacBride he can make it look like you were aiding and abetting them."

"I can take care of myself, Ted."

"No, you can't. None of us can. Shut up and let me help."

She opened her mouth to argue with him again, when she caught yet another flash from her comm. *I wasn't this popular in high school*, she thought briefly; but it was *Galileo*'s comms officer, Samaras. "What is it, Lieutenant?" she asked.

"We just received a signal from *Orunmila*, ma'am," he replied, somewhat breathlessly. "She's been attacked."

CHAPTER 27

Orunmila

They came out of the field not a thousand meters from our hull," Cali said, sitting patiently on an examining table as Pilau, one of Xiao's nurses, spread disinfectant sealant over her injured arm. "Bored straight through. If we hadn't been on the same level, they would have breached into the stairwell before we reached them."

Guanyin stood close to her, eyes on her friend's face, avoiding the sight of Cali's wound. It was not deep, Pilau had said; a little skin sealant, and she'd be fit in a few hours. The more serious injuries had been to Captain Foster, who had caught the brunt of the blast; but even he was expected to be back to normal by the next morning. Guanyin let her eyes shift briefly to Commander Shaw, leaning against the wall next to the table where Xiao was treating Foster's wounds. She was looking around restlessly, as if she was not sure she belonged there. Guanyin felt a wave of irritation. Why couldn't the woman be worried like a normal person? Why all this strange standoffishness? Was it such a crime, to be concerned for someone you cared about?

Çelik stood next to the table where Foster was stretched out. His bare back was scattered with abrasions, already treated and beginning to heal. The two men were conversing in low voices, and Guanyin found it something of a shock, having them not fighting with each other. Battle, she had observed, often made friends from enemies, at least for a time. And at this point it might make her life a lot easier if they were talking.

"They shouldn't have been able to come out of the field so close." Cali was voicing Guanyin's own worries. "Is this something new they've got? A new weapon, a new FTL field? Because if it is—"

"—we will need preparation," Guanyin agreed. She studied Cali's anxious features, carefully hiding her own emotions. "When you have recovered, Commander, I will require a report of the battle readiness of all of our Guards, and a proposed strategy for training for this kind of breach." She reached out and took Cali's hand, allowing herself a moment's vulnerability. "I'm glad you're all right," she said.

Cali gave her a wan smile. "They didn't stand a chance," she replied, a little of her usual twinkle returning. "And I have to admit—they didn't do too badly, those Corps people. Even Çelik—in zero-grav, he was as good as any of us. Give me a few weeks to train him, and he'll be adequate for our Guard."

Which was about the most complimentary thing Cali could say about a person.

Guanyin caught Pilau's eye. "Make sure she is looked after," she said, and patted Cali's arm before turning away.

"Don't hurt anybody," Cali said to her back.

I cannot promise, Guanyin thought, and approached Captain Foster's bedside.

When she had arrived on *Orunmila* at the age of five, she had never spoken in her life. Chanyu had told her that the woman who gave her to him—mother, sister, aunt, stranger; she never knew—had said she was an idiot. "She said inbreeding, or possibly chemicals in the food," he had said. "Some rubbish. I could tell within minutes there was nothing wrong with you." Apart, of course, from her temper. Everything enraged her: food that touched on the plate, blankets that would not stay properly folded, rules about naps and mealtimes and where she could and could not go. That, Chanyu said, was how he knew she could make noise, because she would shriek like a furious peacock for half an hour at a time. It was only the dog, given to Chanyu along with Guanyin, who could calm her down, licking her face with businesslike regularity until she quieted.

She had started talking quickly, but it had taken her nearly ten years to master her temper. And there were still days when she wanted to shriek and shriek until the universe fell properly in line.

"Captain Foster," she said as she approached. Speaking Standard would help; she would have to think, and she would be less likely to say something she would later regret. "How are you feeling?"

"Fine," he said; and she looked over at Commander Shaw. The woman shifted against the wall and looked away, still useless. Guanyin briefly considered slapping her, just to see what she would do.

Instead she turned to Xiao. "How is he?" she asked, in dialect.

"Bruised," Xiao told her. "Probably in some pain, although he won't admit it. That seems to be an epidemic with the Corps." She shot a disapproving look at Çelik. "Dislocated shoulder was the worst of it. I want to finish looking at his knee, and then I was going to discharge him."

Foster pushed gingerly up on one elbow. "You understand us, Captain Foster." Guanyin figured there was no point in anything but directness at this point.

"I understand enough," he said in Standard. When she raised her eyebrows, he shrugged. "I'd just butcher it if I tried to speak it," he told her.

"Are you one of those people who obeys doctor's orders, Captain Foster?"

He said "yes" just as Shaw said "no."

Guanyin pinned the woman to the wall with a look. "I will trust you to look after him, Commander Shaw," she said. "We do not have much time between now and Canberra. I will not have you impaired before the fight has even begun." Then she shifted, drawing herself taller, so she could take in all three of them with a single sweep of her gaze. "Except that the fight began long before today, didn't it?"

Next to her, Çelik shot Foster a look. "I told you she'd figure it out," he said.

And that was enough. "Do not *ever* speak of me as if I am not here before you," she snapped, hanging on to the last frayed bits of her temper. Behind her she heard Xiao's feet retreating. "You look at me as if you know everything and I know nothing, and you are pleased when I figure something out as if I were a *performing dog*." She took a step toward him, and was gratified when Çelik instinctively pulled back. "The only reason I must piece together any of this is because you are withholding information from me, and that is neither charming nor entertaining. I am helping you with this mission because you cannot do it without me. You would have no idea where the raiders were had we not been able to track them. The only ship you had to pursue them has been disabled. And you, Raman Çelik, would not be here *at all* if we had not come to your aid."

She stepped back, addressing all of them. "Shortly after you arrived, one of my storage systems was sabotaged. Had *Orunmila* been architected like a Corps starship, we would have been without reserve battery power when those raiders attacked, and they would have been able to destroy our propulsion systems. They would have crippled us. This suggests the saboteur was familiar with Corps architecture, and made the assumption that *Orunmila* was the same. Which leads me to conclude that someone from Central Corps has conspired with a Syndicate tribe in an attempt to cripple my ship." She addressed her final comment to Captain Foster. "I have eight hundred and twelve people here. Soon to be eight hundred and thirteen. Whatever my personal feelings, I will not have them pay for my sentimentality. Explain yourselves, explain this situation, or I will drop you on Wuhan and you may find your own way home."

Foster looked chagrined, and somewhat annoyed, but she didn't think he was annoyed with her. She wanted Çelik to look chastened, but although he was no longer grinning at her, neither did he seem abashed. He looked, for the first time since she had seen him buried in rubble on his own ship, entirely serious.

But it was Commander Shaw who spoke.

"It's too late for that," she said softly. "It was too late as soon as you answered *Exeter*'s distress call. You're involved now, all of you."

All of you.

Hell.

For a moment Guanyin wanted to let loose that childhood fury, to howl at them until they told her the universe was not what it was. Everything they had worked for, everything Chanyu had taught her. Her family. Her children. All in danger, in the line of fire. All because she had cared enough to help. All the times she had felt frustrated by Chanyu's old prejudices, by his insistence that the Corps soldiers were too different from them to be trusted. All the times she had insisted that he was wrong, that people were the same no matter where they lived.

But Chanyu was gone, and it was too late for caution, and she had no other choice.

"Tell me the rest of it."

"As part of what happened last year," Shaw began, "we became aware that a subset of Central Gov—a bureaucratic organization called Shadow Ops—was involved in weapons research."

At that, Çelik became alert. "You have proof of this?"

"Not anymore," Foster said.

"What we saw was destroyed in the explosion by the wormhole," Shaw explained. "One of the things was a hardware cloak. Crude, and ultimately not sufficiently effective, but a decade ahead of where I thought we were."

Guanyin wove that into her understanding of the story. "So the drive that got the raider to Canberra so quickly? That is part of your advanced research?"

"That's what we thought, at first. But all of those drones on top of it—Central Gov doesn't have that kind of money."

"Every government has money for weapons," Guanyin said.

"Not enough to be able to throw away that many drones,"

Shaw asserted. "On top of that, we couldn't figure why they'd attack *Exeter*. It seemed like overkill, if all they wanted to do was get rid of MacBride. But when *Galileo* was attacked, we assumed they had to be behind it."

"Why?"

Foster answered this time. "It became clear, during and after our court-martial, that there were some people in Shadow Ops who would have found all of this much easier if we just vanished."

" 'Some'?"

"They're not united," Shaw told her tiredly. "Some favor violence as a way to justify unifying the colony worlds, giving Central a stronger alliance. Some advocate for longer-term, more peaceful solutions. We're . . . not sure who's who."

"They would sabotage one of their own ships for *politics*?"

"They would. In this case, though, they claim they didn't. They're telling us it was their former corporate contractor Ellis Systems. We're pretty sure they manufactured the cloak we found last year." Her eyes fixed on Çelik, and Guanyin thought she looked resigned. "They have reason to believe MacBride coordinated with them willingly."

"So it was Ellis Systems who financed this kidnapping?" she asked. Next to her, Çelik had grown still. "Why would they destroy a starship for him?"

"He knows something." This was Çelik, and there was a menacing growl in his voice. *So this is news to him as well.* "MacBride must know something, and that cowardly, murderous rat-bastard sold it to them."

"That's not all of it," Foster said. He was looking at Shaw when he spoke, and for a moment Guanyin caught between the two of them a look of complete understanding. "We promised Shadow Ops we'd either bring them MacBride, or kill him."

"You're *dealing* with them now?" Çelik asked incredulously.

"Not so much dealing," Shaw explained. "They were quite clear that it wasn't an optional request."

"The problem is," Foster said, "that the only hope we have of figuring out S-O's motivation in all this is if we find out why MacBride is so valuable to both them and Ellis. If we don't fuck it up by murdering everyone on sight"—here he gave Çelik a pointed look—"we might be able to find out exactly what it is they don't want MacBride telling anyone else."

"Stop." Guanyin kept her eyes on Foster, but wasn't really seeing him. She felt dizzy, nauseated, like she had night and day for the first four months of this pregnancy. "You are telling me that my ship, my crew—we are all expendable to your Shadow Ops. That all that is important here are secrets held by one man." She needed to unravel all of this in her head, and she could not do this with three Corps soldiers staring at her, waiting for her pronouncement.

She regrouped. "We are not interested in Central's internal politics," she said firmly. Ten minutes ago, that statement would not have been a lie. "The raiders are a clear and present danger to my ship, to your ship, to all ships in this sector. Central's wishes for your Captain MacBride are not relevant to us. Is that clear?"

"Yes, Captain," said Shaw.

Guanyin turned to Foster, who nodded, and then to Çelik, who said, "Perfectly clear, Captain."

"You are all being monitored," she told them. "Not only by electronic security, but by my guards. Any suggestion that any of you are passing secrets to your government or in any way acting in bad faith toward us will result in all of you being thrown in the brig, and the mission completed without you, regardless of what consequences that may bring." Her stomach was rebelling; she needed to lie down. "We will speak of this again later," she told them, "when I have had time to think it through."

She turned and fled the room. As she passed the others in the main infirmary, she caught Cali staring at her; she just shook her head and sped up. Out in the hallway her stomach lurched, and she ran for the nearest bathroom. Locking the door behind her, she threw up, over and over; and even when there was nothing left, her body kept heaving, trying to expel the poison in her soul.

I am sorry, she whispered to her unborn daughter. *I am sorry that we have built this world into which you will be born.*

CHAPTER 28

Twenty minutes later, having been excused by Dr. Xiao, Raman rang the chime at Guanyin's quarters.

The door was answered by a guard Raman didn't know: a graying man of about forty, barrel-chested and short, who glared up at Raman, singularly unintimidated. "Wait here," he growled when Raman asked to see his captain. Raman stood obligingly by the door, his eyes taking in the room. It was different from her office, furnished with couches and soft chairs rather than tables and counters. There were a few pictures on the walls—mostly drawings of dogs done with various levels of skill—and there were plants scattered everywhere, from a tall, palm-like tree in one corner, to a small flat of herbs on a side table. In one corner was a box filled with children's toys, overflowing with stuffed animals and soft-edged developmental puzzles. He recognized one iconic game that had been popular since his own distant childhood. His mother had told him it was designed to build his deductive reasoning skills.

I just thought it was fun.

He had sat in silence through Xiao's ministrations, wanting to rage at Foster and Shaw for keeping MacBride's culpability secret. But he realized that he was not sure with whom he was angry. That MacBride would have arranged his own kidnapping had always been one of Raman's theories. He had already been prepared to kill the man when they found him. But the Admiralty—or Shadow Ops, to the extent that they were different—had not given him his rightful opportunity for revenge. Instead they had shoved him aside. Already, even before he had been officially stripped of command.

He thought he was most angry with himself.

Guanyin kept him waiting a long time. A few days ago, he would have considered it spite, or some kind of power play, now that he was here on her turf. Now he considered the very real possibility that she was struggling with whether or not she wanted to speak to him at all.

No matter—I can wait. Until they reached Canberra, he had nothing else to do.

Nearly twenty minutes passed before she appeared through a door on the other side of the room. He heard the brief sound of voices—a child asking a question and laughing—before the door closed behind her. She was still in her uniform, but she had unpinned her braids from their intricate knot, and they hung down her back to her waist. He had never known anyone whose hair grew that long. She looked considerably less green than she had in the infirmary, but no less furious.

"Thank you for seeing me, Captain," he said. Sometimes the trappings of rank were not such a waste of time.

"Why are you here?"

She spoke in Standard. Emphasizing the distance between

them. She was more than angry, then: she was hurt. Mistrustful. He had worked so hard to make her relax around him, and their sin of omission had destroyed all of that progress.

One of the first things he had noticed about her, ten years ago when they had first met, was how extraordinarily her face changed when she was angry. She was the sort of woman he had always liked to look at: tall, despite her slim build, with a regal elegance to her, and a stillness that implied watchfulness. But when she was angry, and her eyes flashed? She became abruptly otherworldly, some fire goddess an instant away from striking down her enemies with one flip of her graceful fingers. He had tried, whenever he ran into her, to spark just a little of that fire in her, but he had never made her this angry before. "I have come to offer my help, Captain," he told her.

"And why would you believe I need your help?"

"Because I also need help," he replied. "This is new to me as well, and it should not have been."

"Why not?"

"I knew about Shadow Ops," he confessed. "I suspected they were not the ineffective bureaucratic research committee we have been told they are. I truly did not realize their work was dangerous, and sometimes counter to the stated goals of the Admiralty. And I did not know this was a secret they would choose to keep from me."

"How is this a thing you could have missed?"

He clenched his teeth briefly. "There were some . . . events I misinterpreted."

Her eyebrows shot up. "You are saying you were wrong?"

"Of course not. I made guesses. They were incorrect, but they were only guesses."

"Then you need no one." Her look was dismissive. "I do not need your *wise counsel,* Captain Çelik. I am not the naive child you saw when you first met me." She turned to leave.

"Well, you certainly have *that* wrong," he said mildly to her back.

She stopped.

"I remember that day." There was a throw rug in the middle of the floor; he stepped around it, wary of its oddly textured surface. "Chanyu was always accompanied by the same entourage. I had assumed one of them was his second, but they seemed such a drab group. A few children, a few Chanyu's own age. One or two terribly old. They all stared at me politely, bland as soy paste, and they never moved without Chanyu's approval. None of them spoke. But in my mind, they were a monolith: Chanyu's Idiots.

"But you." He switched to dialect. He would get the subtleties wrong, but he wanted to make sure she was listening. "You did not listen to him. You did not keep quiet. You seemed a little overwhelmed by everything: by me, by the freighter crew, by Chanyu's Idiots; but you did not let that stop you. You asked questions. You made inferences. You were curious, and adventurous. And smart. So much smarter than Chanyu. I did not see a naive child that day, Guanyin. I never saw a naive child. I saw a captain in training. He chose well. I knew that from the start."

She had not moved, and he risked continuing. "You are feeling like I lied to protect you, the way you feel Central lies to protect its children. The problem with that is that I do not lie to children. They always know it, and then you have lost the moral high ground that you must have with someone you are trying to teach."

"You think you had moral high ground?"

She had switched to dialect as well, and he felt something in his stomach loosen. "Never," he said. "I was not trying to protect you because I thought you were a child, Guanyin. I was trying to protect PSI from the stupid moves Central has been making in this sector since before I was given a command."

"It's not your place—nor is it Central's place—to protect PSI." But her tone had softened, and he thought her spine looked a little less stiff.

"No, it is not. But neither is it our place to haul you into our internal politics."

Silence. He waited the span of heartbeats. Then: "Is there any value in understanding how we came to be where we are today?"

"Eventually, perhaps. But I think that is a more complicated question than where we must go from here."

She turned to face him. The flash was gone, and with it the fire goddess. Instead she was Captain Shiang Guanyin, a woman of grace and intellect and no goddamned bullshit. "Would you have me sit obediently while you explain what our strategy would be?"

"Captain Shiang, if you were about to enter into a situation where you needed to understand something you did not—the nature of neurosurgery, for example, or some kind of legal dispute—would you walk in blind? Or would you find someone who knew about the law, or about neurosurgery, and use their knowledge to inform your decisions?"

Her chin lifted. "You are saying you'll act as my expert on Central Gov?"

"As much as I can," he said, with a half bow. "Although as I discovered, I do not have the scope of knowledge I had thought."

At that her face relaxed entirely, and she moved fully into the room. She walked over to a cabinet and opened it, revealing a familiar bottle. "Would you like a drink?"

He thought he might like the whole bottle. "Thank you, no," he said. "I prefer not to drink alone."

She closed the cabinet, and they both moved to the sofa to sit down. She leaned heavily on the arm of the couch as she lowered herself, a strategy he remembered his own mother using when she was carrying each of his younger siblings. He sat himself, still clumsy, and shifted so that the couch took all of the weight of his damaged leg. The pain of the prosthetic eased with the pressure, and he felt a relief that was almost sensual. "Do you drink much?" he asked her, curious.

She shook her head. "I do not drink on duty, or in front of the children. That doesn't leave me a lot of hours to work with. And I can never sleep after liquor. I think the last time I had a drink was . . . goodness. Before Lin was born. Three years."

His mind composed a picture of her, loose-limbed and tipsy, and he hauled himself back to the matter at hand. "Tell me, Captain: What is it you need to know about Central Gov?"

She closed her eyes. She looked older with her eyes closed; he could see shadows below her lashes, and lines around her lips that would deepen as she aged. One hand rested on her stomach; a thinking gesture for her, he had noticed. "If I say 'everything,' " she replied, "will you laugh at me?"

He did not laugh. "I think we can begin there, Captain Shiang." And he started to talk.

CHAPTER 29

Y ou don't have to stay."

"I told her I'd look after you."

"Elena, it's my knee. This is not some major life-threatening injury."

"I promised."

She still would not look at him. Greg studied her profile: her nose, the fine line of her lips, her determined jaw. Her eyes, resolutely staring at the opposite wall, avoiding his. He remembered what Jessica had said: *Be careful.*

Pointless advice. He had no idea how to be careful with Elena.

He tried again. "This wasn't plasma fire, either."

At that she shot him a look, hot and hostile. Six months ago he had been hit nearly point-blank with a plasma rifle. Had they been five minutes farther from help, he would not have survived. She had been worried for him then, too, but it had taken him nearly two weeks to recognize the concern in her brittle body language.

"Elena." He kept the tension out of his voice. "I'm all right. I'm sure all I need is one night's break from the gym."

She relented, dropping her eyes. "I'll stay, for now, if you don't mind," she told him, more subdued. "You know how I am after a fight."

He did. So many of their colleagues vented adrenaline after a battle with drinking and dancing, among other things. She had always lingered in the crowd for a few minutes, inventorying her friends, and then retreated to someplace less populated. After their first few years serving together, he would often join her, sitting by one of *Galileo*'s massive windows, looking out into the stars, or the FTL field, or the surface of a planet they had just left, companionably silent, letting the tension of the battle drain away.

"It's been a long time, hasn't it?" he said, and was rewarded with a smile.

"I suppose it's not nice to get nostalgic for firefights, is it?"

"In the grand scheme of things," he said, "we've been lucky." She said nothing, and he risked asking a more pointed question. "Was it bad, after Canberra?"

She shrugged. "It was . . . ugly. Allegations flying around about PSI, Çelik brutally pissed off about Treharne. And Niree. I didn't really have anyone to talk to."

"What about Dee?"

She glanced at him, then looked away again. "I couldn't really talk to him about my own feelings. He was all caught up in 'how could this happen?' I kept thinking that all those years, when I was a kid and working toward getting into the Corps, I never thought I'd be shooting a starving man in the chest."

"Makes the dream feel different, doesn't it?"

"Killed the dream, really. Reality, right in the face. I miss it," she added softly. "Being that naive. Is that stupid?"

He remembered his own childhood, before his mother died. All of the colors in his world had been so much brighter. "No," he told her. "It's not stupid at all."

He managed to doze for nearly an hour—Elena next to him the whole time—before Jessica commed him, full of obscenities and worry. He let her go on for a while, exchanging amused glances with Elena throughout, before she settled down enough to send him the topographical map she had put together. The three of them pored over it, speculating about flight patterns and landing areas, and eventually put together what seemed to be a reasonable set of recommendations to take to the others. It was the most normal interaction he'd had with Elena in more than a year, and he caught himself trying to dissect it. If he could figure out how he had put her at ease, he might be able to do it again, might be able to guide them back to where they had been.

He tried to ignore the voice far in the back of his mind that asked, *Is that really what you want? To go back to the way it was?*

He was relieved when Cali appeared to summon them to Captain Shiang's office. She called it a *mission briefing,* but Greg wondered how much of it was going to be symbolic. He suspected, at the very least, that Shiang would make sure they understood just how much they were depending on her for success. But success with what—he couldn't know.

They followed Cali down the corridor. His knee still ached, but walking did not seem to worsen it, and he was acutely conscious of the relative insignificance of the injury. Elena strode at his side, her step unconsciously even with his; if she was surreptitiously watching his gait, she hid it well. Sometimes, he reflected, she looked very much a soldier. Amazing how well she could hide what went on in her head.

Cali led them not to Shiang's office, but to a comfortable sitting room. Youda and Keita sat on opposite ends of a long sofa, one of Captain Shiang's guards, a short, gray, stoic man introduced as Hoelun, seated in between them. Next to Youda there were three empty chairs in a row. Elena took the center chair, and Greg placed himself between her and the doctor.

Çelik was standing in the front of the room, talking with Captain Shiang in a low voice. Cali left Greg and Elena to approach them, and when Shiang looked up, Cali fell into place standing behind her. Greg was a little startled when Çelik did the same thing. He resisted the urge to glance at Elena, but he would have to remember to discuss it with her later.

"I have asked you all here," Captain Shiang began, "because before we arrive, we must have a candid discussion about the objectives of this mission."

He felt Elena tense.

"It seems there are a number of agendas in this room," she said. "I would be lying if I told you I felt they were all equally valid. But validity is not the issue here. What we must do is come to a consensus. If you are all in disagreement, it doesn't matter how many of my guards I send down with you. If you are not fighting in the same direction, you will fail."

Greg thought of Jessica's suggestion to blast the planet from orbit.

Keita spoke first. "With respect, Captain Shiang," he said,

"we do have some common ground. We want to find the raiders who did this, and if possible, Captain MacBride along with them. After that—"

"— is the sticking point." This from Çelik, who admitted it without rancor. "My preferences are not a secret to any of you." He took a breath, and Greg thought his next words came with some effort. "I will consent, here in front of all of you, to the transport of the guilty parties back to *Orunmila* for judicial disposition."

Next to Greg, Elena shifted. It occurred to Greg, with all the conversations they'd had, that he didn't know what *her* preference was. "What if that's not an option?" she asked aloud. "What if there's no way to take them alive?"

"Nobody risks their lives for those people," Greg said flatly. "If they come in shooting, we shoot back."

"We are agreed, then, correct?" Captain Shiang looked at each of them—one after another—before stopping at Captain Çelik, who nodded.

It was shoving the problem downstream, but for now, it would do.

Greg brought up Jessica's map, and reviewed their conclusions. "There are half a dozen viable landing spots," he said, "but this one"—he gestured on the map to the former location of Canberra's capital city—"was the most accessible during the storm system that was active after *Exeter* was attacked. Assuming those power sources really are being used as beacons, that's the site the raiders will have used. That's where we'll land. These other two are possible but less likely. They'll be taken by Cali's and Hoelun's teams."

Cali went over the usual fighting tactics used by the Syndicates, going back to the battle they had just been through as a point of reference. Greg began to see the wisdom of the raiders' strategy: if your primary goal was theft, even over your own survival, defense was less important. Two of the raiders who had attacked *Orunmila* were there to protect just one person with just one task. They had an escape plan, but not a robust one; that, it seemed, was unlikely to have been an oversight.

Based on what Captain Shiang had told him before, he wondered what these three had done to earn their death sentence.

The PSI captain watched the discussion in silence. She looked, Greg thought, tired but composed. He also thought she was not listening as much as thinking, her expression turned inward, that hand absently rubbing her stomach. He caught Çelik glancing at her once or twice and wondered what the man had said to her. Or perhaps the key was what *she* had said to Çelik. Greg wasn't sure he had ever seen anyone yell at Çelik the way Shiang had.

"So we are agreed," Hoelun said, when they had been over the plan repeatedly. "We will take the islands. You Corps people take the capital. We fly in high, see what we see. If there's nothing, a quick land-and-recon, and then we head back here. And radio silence unless we have contact."

Greg and Elena nodded. Keita kept his eyes on Captain Çelik, waiting for orders; but it was Captain Shiang who spoke.

"Under ordinary circumstances," she said, "I would strongly suggest we abort this mission, document what we have, and await reinforcements." She met Çelik's eyes. "I understand, of course, that none of you would agree to this."

"I would." They all turned to stare at Youda, and he stared back, defiant. "She's right. This is insanity. This Syndicate tribe hasn't shown anything resembling real intelligence; hell, if we wait a week, they'll have probably blown themselves up, or suffocated on that rock. Pursuing them down to Canberra is not just petty vengeance. It's suicide."

"I think," Çelik said quietly, "that *petty* isn't precisely the word you were looking for, Doctor."

It was interesting to note, Greg thought, that while Youda had not reacted to either Cali or Captain Shiang chastising him, he colored deeply at Çelik's words and looked away.

"Why do you suppose she didn't tell them about Ellis and MacBride?"

He and Elena were walking back to their quarters. Somewhere behind them, half-hidden, were the guards Captain Shiang had assigned to watch them. Greg suspected, if he turned and looked, that he would see the man who had been running with him that morning.

"She's pretty good at leaving things out," Elena continued. "She didn't even tip off Dee and Jimmy."

Because she's worried one of them already knows, he thought; but he did not say it aloud. He felt her eyes on him, but he would not look at her. Keita's behavior had been calm, businesslike, professional, showing none of the rawness he had betrayed back on *Galileo* in Greg's office. Jimmy Youda had been more emotional, radiating dislike and mistrust. Greg could not be sure if his problem was xenophobia, or genuine concern with their battle plans. Even being aware of his own biases, he had to admit Keita had said nothing Greg himself would not have said, and Youda's reservations, despite Çelik's harsh response, were not out of line, either.

He wished, for a moment, that it was Jessica with him, offering him her assessment, blunt and subjective but free of any kind of emotional baggage. A year ago he would have asked Elena flat-out how she felt about the implication that one of her old friends was guilty; now, he was not sure he wanted to know the answer.

"I suppose," he replied, "she didn't think it was relevant."

"It seems more likely she was trying to catch someone out." She sounded irritable. "Not that I want them to know. It's bad enough as it is. But if we can't trust each other—"

He stopped at that, turning to look at her. "We *can't* trust each other, Elena. You know that. Do you think, at this point, that it even matters?"

"Well *of course* it matters," she said reasonably. "When we get to Canberra—"

"What the hell are we going to do when we get there?" He lowered his voice, conscious of the people passing them in the hall. "We've got Çelik, who makes a promise out of one side of his mouth, but doesn't give a shit about anything beyond revenge; we've got Shadow Ops, who doesn't give a shit about the people who actually did this; and we may have a saboteur who may or may not get every one of us killed down there. How the hell is any of that a plan of action?"

Her lips set. "You can't know—"

"No, you're right, I can't," he said sharply. "But I can tell you this: you told me from day one of this nightmare that you were not objective about these people. You're spinning a fairy tale based not on fact—not even on observation, not even on your instincts, Elena—but on your own emotional need to believe that people you haven't seen *in eight years* are exactly as you remember them. Has it ever occurred to you that they *are* exactly the same, but you didn't see them clearly back then?"

"Dee wouldn't do this, Greg."

"Just like he wouldn't pull a gun on you? And what about your friend Jimmy? A mediocre medic idly climbing the promotion ladder, waiting for senior officers to die off before he gets anywhere?"

"He's not mediocre, Greg. And he sure as hell wouldn't know how to hack into a security system."

"So you admit Keita is a more likely suspect."

"*No.*" But she turned away from him. "Even"—she swallowed—"even if he was somehow involved in what happened to *Exeter,* he would never have gone on to hurt *Galileo.*"

"You want to connect those dots for me, Chief?"

"If he had anything to do with *Exeter,*" she insisted, meeting his eyes again, "those deaths were a mistake. He wouldn't have known anyone was going to get hurt, and he wouldn't have risked it happening to anyone else. Dee is a lot of things, Greg, and not all of them are terribly nice or professional. But he would lay down his life before he'd even consider harming one of his own."

"Are you *completely forgetting* everything that happened the last time you were on that planet?" He supposed he ought to be grateful she was at least considering the possibility Keita might be guilty, but her constant dismissal of Keita's old crime was more than he could take.

"I explained to you about that! He—"

He shook his head. "No, Elena. Not again. It was bullshit the first time you spun it, and it's not going to get any more palatable."

She scowled, and he knew before she said it what was coming. "You're going to accuse me of not being objective because I *fucked* him? Am I getting that replay as well?"

"I don't give a shit if you did or didn't!" he shouted. "I don't care if you fucked him, and Çelik, and Youda three in a row every second Thursday! I care that you are not seeing any of this clearly, and *yes*, goddammit, it's because you are personally involved, and you can't haul your head out of whatever part of yourself that's doing the thinking right now."

"Oh, and you're so much better?" she returned. "You are *obsessed* with the fact that Dee and I were lovers. You don't understand it, because you swallow fucking *everything*. You don't need *anyone*. Who did you turn to when your life went to hell after Liriel? Did you get on the comm to your wife, give her a chance to support you, give her *anything* but stoicism and distance? Jesus, no wonder she started screwing other men; she must have been starved for someone to feel *something* for her."

That knife hit true, right into his heart, right between his ribs into the soft tissue. It was the truth of his marriage, or at least *a* truth. It was a truth of all of his relationships, and he would have thought she would know him well enough to understand why. She was slapping at him with whatever she had, tearing at him to stop him from seeing what he was seeing, and he was finished with putting up with it.

"What right do you have?" he snapped. "We are on a *mission,* Elena, with stakes that we don't even understand, that we can't even discuss with the people we should be able to trust. I am trying to talk to you about a man that you have *told* me you don't know anymore, and all you do is claw at me like some pissed-off mountain lion—like you've been doing since this started. What the hell did I do to deserve that?"

She shifted away from him. "Last year—"

"*Fuck* last year, Chief. I have apologized to you every way there is. I am sorry for what happened. I am sorry about the things I said when my head was completely fucked to hell. I am sorry you feel lied to, and I am sorry that everything else we were to each other means so *fucking little* to you that all you can think about is *one thing* I left out. I don't even know what to say to you anymore. I'll apologize again, would that help? I'm sorry, Elena. Does that make a difference? No? I didn't think so."

Her eyes had grown wide and vulnerable, and he steeled himself against the familiar urge to protect her. "Well, how the hell am I supposed to know what to say to you? You won't talk to me. You talk *at* me, and *around* me, and you doubt what I'm thinking, and you know nothing, Greg, nothing about what happened to me last year, never mind that nonsense you spouted—"

Nonsense. That's what she took from it all? Knowing she was baiting him didn't help anymore. "I know what happened last year. I was there."

"You weren't there for all of it, Greg."

"Okay, *fine*." He took a step toward her. "You went through some other big tragedy, some other horrible thing that you didn't fucking tell me about because you couldn't trust me because of whatever goddamn reason you decide to use this time. So what was it, Elena? Was it bad enough? Does it excuse you ripping my guts out every time I'm trying to talk to you?"

She opened her mouth, and he thought she would speak; but then she stilled, and her mouth closed, and for an instant he thought he saw her lovely eyes grow damp. Then her expression went blank, and she straightened, no longer shrinking away from him. "No," she replied, and her voice was unemotional—shutting him out, as she did more and more these days. "It doesn't. You're right. I've been completely unfair, and I'm sorry."

He had thought, somehow, that if she ever said those words he would feel grateful, even relieved. But hearing them now, as he looked into her hollow, distant eyes, he felt they were one step away from lurching off a cliff. "I—" He looked away. "It's been hard on both of us," he said, which was as close as he could get to giving her forgiveness.

"Do you ever think," she asked softly, "that we're no good for each other anymore?"

No. But he *had* thought it—frequently. He had thought it just moments ago, on the other end of one of her sharp remarks, before he thought she might think so, too. Now, he felt her slipping, as if he should have tightened his fingers just an instant sooner. "It's the stress," he told her. "Everything that's going on."

"I don't want to tear into you," she said. "I have no right. This needs to stop, Greg. You and me—this needs to stop."

He took a step toward her, but she backed away. He relented, frustrated, wishing she would yell at him again. "We can stop without losing each other, Elena."

"Can we? Really? After all of this?"

And before he could answer, she turned away, heading off down the hall, away from their quarters. As he watched, she broke into a run.

CHAPTER 30

After the meeting, Guanyin immersed herself in her own family for a while, tucking in the girls herself for the first time in days. Lin held on to her for a long time, and Guanyin took the time to sit, holding the child, feeling the little girl's heart fluttering against her chest. Lin made her feel powerful and helpless, knowing what she needed to do, utterly unable to do it. Tomorrow at this time it would be finished, one way or another, and Guanyin could do nothing.

Once the girls were asleep, she went for a walk. She had tried, throughout the meeting, to sit still, to conceal how often she had to shift just to remain comfortable. Now, despite being mentally and physically exhausted, she could not bear the thought of lying down. She took the long loop through the civilian side of the ship, smiling and chatting and catching up with the people she knew. By the time she reached the square she felt thoroughly refreshed, and the screaming pain over her kidneys had faded to a tolerable throb.

She was trying to talk herself out of a huge cup of coffee

when she caught sight of a familiar figure seated alone at a table in the center of the square: Commander Shaw, eyes studying the contents of her own cup, oblivious to the world around her.

The hard chairs at those tables were far more comfortable for Guanyin these days than the sofas in her own quarters. *And coffee really would be nice . . .*

She bought a cup and made her way over to the table.

"Commander Shaw," she asked, "may I join you?"

The woman started, looking up. Guanyin saw her expression flash with surprise before she arranged it into its usual professional angles. "Of course, Captain," she said formally.

Guanyin pulled the chair out, and lowered herself in carefully, wondering at the woman's spectacularly bad poker face. "I am sorry to disturb you," she tried. "I can't stay in one place for very long these days. I get very uncomfortable."

She wondered if Commander Shaw would make a remark about her ill-advised coffee, but instead the woman gave her a tight, worried smile. "I can imagine."

Shaw's eyes had flicked to Guanyin's stomach. She always did that, Guanyin realized. When they had met, Guanyin had thought it was simply a lack of exposure to pregnant women, but it had happened every time since.

Can you imagine? Have you imagined? It would, Guanyin realized, explain a great deal.

"I am quite lucky, you know," she said. "I have a dear friend who tried when I did. We planned, since we were girls, to have our children together. But she could not carry. Xiao told her there was no reason, that she should just keep trying; but after she lost three, she could not face losing more. There are people here who are angry with her, who believe she should keep trying

298

if there is a chance, because they do not have the option themselves. I do not really understand that," she confessed. "That there should be some hierarchy of loss, that someone's pain should be dismissed simply because it is not the only pain there is. We all know there is no fairness in this life, but I do not think it is wrong to be angry because of that."

She sipped the coffee. It was rich and strong, and she knew the baby would kick her all night for it.

"How did you know I had a miscarriage?" Commander Shaw asked her.

"Some of your colleagues seem to disapprove of the fact that I am pregnant. You, on the other hand, are worried about it. I made a guess."

"It was a long time ago. I should be finished with it."

"Why would you think that?"

That brought the woman up short. Guanyin thought she understood why Çelik had been so sorry to lose her: they were not dissimilar. Both of them seemed to think they ought to be immune to their own humanity. "I'm a mechanic," Shaw said at last. "I understand that things go wrong sometimes."

"Do they teach you this, in your Corps training? That everything that happens to you can be deconstructed and analyzed like a piece of hardware? Are you the sort of person who considers yourself above emotional responses?"

"I suppose I think I ought to be," she said honestly. "Because I work with machines, and they make sense to me, far more than most people do. And because I'm an officer, and people depend on me."

This was surer ground. "And yet leadership involves emotion at every step." It had been one of Chanyu's earliest lessons, and one reinforced by years of watching him. "You must be aware of your own emotional reactions, and you must have a sense of theirs. And you must be able to change tactics based on human interplay. It is largely intuition. If you ignore emotion, you will be a useless and tone-deaf leader, and you will have no authority."

Commander Shaw smiled. "You sound like an Academy lecturer."

"So they *do* teach you this." *Well, maybe the Corps is not a lost cause after all.* "Did you study leadership, then?"

"I had to, if I was going to get a good deployment. You can get through CMA—the Academy—without it, but you get more control over your deployment choices if you take it."

"So it was only a means to an end?"

"At the time, yes." Her smile turned sad. "I had no idea, really, what was ahead of me. I knew what I wanted, and the Corps had requirements I had to fulfill to get it."

"Are you a good leader, then?"

A shrug; Shaw was embarrassed. "Sometimes. I am better leading than following, I suppose." She did not make it sound like an accomplishment.

Guanyin thought of Çelik's question to her: *Are you a good mother?* "Then you must know yourself better than you think."

"If I knew myself . . ." Shaw trailed off. "Do you ever look back on your life and see, so clearly, the moments where you screwed up? Where everything would have been different if you had, in one small instant, done something else?"

"You sound very much like my friend," Guanyin told her. "The truth of it, Commander Shaw, is that there are very few such moments, that life is a continuum, that we are all riding currents, and turns are inexorable. The only value in looking back is to learn. If the past has nothing to teach us, we must learn to leave it behind."

At that, Shaw gave her a curious look. "Do you know, that's the kind of thing Captain Çelik used to tell us. He wouldn't put it quite so nicely, of course."

Shaw seemed surprised to find a pleasant memory associated with Çelik. "Why did you choose *Exeter*?" Guanyin asked, curious. "After all of your preparation and checklists."

"You mean why, when I dislike Captain Çelik so much?"

"Exactly."

The woman leaned forward, fingers around her coffee cup. "I wasn't really worrying about someone four ranks over my head. *Exeter* had an early model D8000 engine, and I was itching to work on one of those. And on top of it—she had a good reputation. No matter where my career went, having *Exeter* on my record was going to look good." The smile drained out of her face, and the sadness took over again. "She will be missed."

Guanyin was always forgetting that Çelik was not the only one grieving his ship. "You knew some of the dead, didn't you?"

"I hadn't been in touch with any of them in years. It's not like I lost family."

"There it is again," Guanyin said. "The hierarchy of loss." But she found she couldn't be irritated with the Corps people anymore. Never mind their odd, rigid, emotionless culture—no one should have to become accustomed to tragedy.

"I don't really see myself as having lost much," Commander Shaw told her. "I've been fortunate in my life, and in the people I've had around me. I didn't even understand, really, until Canberra, and then . . . it's funny. What happened there gave me the energy to do something about how unhappy I was on *Exeter*. Suddenly I wasn't interested in wasting time being miserable anymore."

"So you did gain something from your experience there."

"I suppose I did." She seemed surprised. "Before that . . . I joined the Corps because I didn't want to be stuck in Alaska for the rest of my life. I stayed because I didn't want anything like Canberra to happen again."

"You stayed," Guanyin summarized, "because you wanted to help."

The woman shrugged, and Guanyin thought she was embarrassed again. "As ideals of service go, it's a bit backward."

"I don't think it matters how one comes to it," Guanyin said. "Here we are raised with it. By some lights, your conscious choice makes your claim to an ideal the stronger one." In spite of herself, she smiled. "Chanyu believed we needed to stay segregated from the Corps. He knew Captain Çelik, and would work with him, but he never trusted him, not really. But when I would talk to Captain Çelik, never mind how persistently boorish he could be, I would think all the time how much like us he was." She looked Commander Shaw in the eye. "You are as well, I think."

The woman's eyes lit for the first time during their conversation, and Guanyin thought she was pleased. "It's not enough, though, is it?"

"No," Guanyin admitted readily. "I do not dislike your people, Commander Shaw, but there is something to mistrust, and whether it is someone here or not, I cannot take the risk simply because I like you. Do you understand?"

"I do." Commander Shaw looked tired again. "We can't even trust each other, really."

Guanyin thought it was worth the question. "Who *do* you trust here, Commander Shaw?"

The woman smiled, but this time it did not reach her eyes. "You are the second person to ask me that tonight, Captain Shiang." And the smile faded. "Greg."

"And Captain Çelik?"

"Captain Çelik I trust not to be a part of any sabotage, but given his state of mind, I won't speculate past that."

"Do you really trust your captain?"

"As you are a fairly observant person," Commander Shaw allowed, "I can understand why you'd be surprised by that. But . . . yes. With my life. Which doesn't mean he doesn't drive me to madness sometimes."

"All good captains drive their people mad."

Commander Shaw let out a surprised laugh. "Well," she said, finishing off her coffee, "I can't argue with that."

CHAPTER 31

In her dreams Elena could smell him: vanilla and sweat, a little bit sweet, entirely human and male. She could not see his face—she saw his face less and less often in her dreams—but she could hear his voice, deep and gentle, and feel his heartbeat against her ear. He was whispering to her, and sometimes laughing, and she felt safe and whole and loved.

She dreamed of one of their last conversations, after they had agreed to part, after they had acknowledged they each needed more than the other could give. *How can I do this?* she asked him. *How can I be strong without you?*

And he put his mouth against her ear, and she felt his warm breath as he said: *You have always been strong without me, m'laya.*

She awoke with a start in her strange bed, his voice echoing in her mind. A moment passed before she remembered none of it was real, and she rolled over to look out the window. The polarizer dimmed the bright light of the field, and she queried the time. Another eight hours and they would be at Canberra.

As quietly as she could she pushed off the sheet and swung her legs over the edge, sliding off the bed and dropping gently to the floor. She glanced briefly at Greg, lying in the lower bunk. If he was awake, he was not letting on. He had been asleep when she came in, and she had felt a strange mix of relief and irritation. Her conversation with Captain Shiang had left her thoughtful and unsettled, and she was wondering, for the first time in months, if she ought to just tell Greg everything. She had told Captain Shiang the truth: she trusted him, above anyone else she knew, and none of their pointless squabbling had changed that.

You have always been strong without me.

She missed Trey, viscerally, despite her certainty that they had made the right decision to separate. She had told Dee the truth when she had said she was not ready to take a lover. But someone to talk to? It had been a long time since she had been able to talk to Greg, and she had laid that completely at his feet. Tonight, though, she wondered if they were both too reticent, both afraid of shattering the fragile connection they were trying to rebuild.

If it was so fragile, was it worth saving?

She slipped into the bathroom and shut the door, keeping the lights dim and taking a long drink of water. Pulling the tie from her hair, she stretched it around her wrist, unraveling her braid. She picked up her comb and tugged it through her thick curls, then redid the plait, tightly, as if she were about to go on duty. When she finished, she pulled the elastic off of her wrist, and stopped. Trey had given her this tie, when they had first met. Before she had loved him, when he was just a kind stranger. Before she had even known his name.

There was a knock on the door and she jumped. "Elena?" Greg asked hesitantly. "Are you okay?"

"Yes," she answered, rushing to fasten off the braid. "Just a minute."

She opened the door to find him standing less than a meter away, bleary-eyed and concerned, their fight apparently forgotten. He slept shirtless, and her dream came back to her in a flash. Heat flooded her face. *Dammit,* she thought, *it's not like I've never seen his chest before.* They had worked out in the same gymnasium on *Galileo* for eight years. She had seen him running, lifting, showering, wearing nothing at all, and it had never meant anything, not really.

Not that she hadn't noticed. He had been unavailable as long as she had known him, but she had noticed. He was fit and toned, like Dee, only slim and streamlined where Dee was thick and broad. When she had first joined *Galileo* she had watched Greg running in the gym, lap after lap, sleek muscles moving underneath the dark skin of his back, effortlessly powerful. She had never considered anything other than friendship, but it had never been possible to ignore how beautiful he was.

Oh, stop it, she scolded herself. *It's a damn good thing he's sleepy, or he'd see you blushing like a damn teenager.*

"Just a dream," she said, and gave him a hesitant smile.

He did not smile back. His eyes—those strange gray-and-black eyes—held hers, reflecting nothing of their earlier argument, no anger, no hurt, just simple concern. "Do you need anything?" he asked.

"I—" She stopped. It was the middle of the night, they were both exhausted, and tomorrow they were heading down to a dead planet to face an unknown enemy. She might never have another chance. "Would you—can I talk to you?"

He looked briefly startled, but nodded. Turning away from her, he took one step across the room to his bunk; she watched his back for a moment before shaking herself and moving to the wall opposite the door. She crossed her arms and leaned back; he sat on the bunk, feet on the floor, elbows on his knees, waiting.

He looked so guarded.

She took a breath. "Earlier, Greg, when you asked about last year. Something else did happen. And it wasn't about you, or your fault, or any of that, but it's tangled in my head with everything else, because it was all at the same time. And being here—" She was rambling; she needed to focus. "I can't get away from it. But it's not on you, none of it, and I am sorry. Truly. Because you're right. Being angry with you is not fair."

"What happened, Elena?"

All this time, nearly a year now, and she had told only one person, never mind Captain Shiang's guess. She had no idea what he would say. Before she could lose her nerve, she put the words together: "I had a miscarriage."

She forced herself to watch his face. Shock, at first. She didn't know what he had thought she would say, but she had clearly surprised him. "You—" He broke off, and looked away, and she couldn't see what he was thinking. "Is that why you left him? Why you came back to *Galileo* with me?"

Oh, hell. Of course. He'd have no reason to assume otherwise. "It wasn't Trey's, Greg. It was Danny's." Danny Lancaster, a man she had dated for two years, whose death on Volhynia had triggered everything else that had happened in the Fifth Sector. "It's why I broke it off with him last year."

Slowly he turned back to her, and this time his face was easy to read. "You were going to have a *family* with him?" he demanded, incredulous. He stood, pacing the tiny room, one hand running over his short hair. "That simpleminded, over-possessive *jarhead*?"

Her jaw tightened. "Don't speak ill of the dead."

"What the *hell* were you thinking, Elena?"

"*This* is why I don't tell you things," she retorted, stung. She pushed to her feet. The room was too small; there was nowhere to go but toward him. "I'm trying to tell you something important, and the first thing you do is assume I'm a *congenital fucking idiot*. It wasn't *planned,* Greg. Danny scored a drug while he was on Cygnus that neutralized the infertility shot."

"You're saying he drugged you."

These were not the details she needed him to know. "He said not, that he just took it himself. But the way the stuff works . . . I think he must have."

He kept scowling, and she knew what was coming. Greg was a captain, before anything else, no matter what. *Dammit, I should have kept my mouth shut.* "There was an officer on my crew *drugging* you without your knowledge, and you didn't tell me?" he shouted. "What the hell is wrong with you?"

All the agony of the last few days hit her at once, and restraint deserted her. "It wasn't about the Corps, Greg!" That would make no sense to him at all, she knew. For Greg, everything was about the Corps. "It wasn't about Danny, and it wasn't about you. This happened to *me,* and if I'd told you at the time I'd have had to deal with your anger on top of everything else, and I *couldn't,* and now you stand there and shout at me like I've let the side down, and *I'm the one who has to live with this.*"

She felt tears on her face, but she wasn't sobbing. "He's *dead,* Greg. He's paid as much as anybody could pay. And I tell you this awful thing, and all you can think about is which fucking *regulations* he broke and every time I see Captain Shiang, with that baby inside her and all of those children around I can't breathe because I fucking *panic* and it is all tangled in my head and it is *not about you*!"

She turned away from him. This had not helped at all, and all of her rage was still focused on Greg. Of course she could trust him. She could trust him to be her captain, and to prosecute a soldier who had done something illegal to her. Hell, he would have punished Danny with no evidence beyond her word, and he would have believed he had done it for her. Her world was full of crewmates, of people who knew the regs and were military and loyal and always did the right thing. And none of them were who she needed.

She needed someone who didn't need her to be so fucking strong all the time.

She heard him shift behind her, moving closer. She braced herself, waiting for the patient, rational, military explanation that she wouldn't be able to argue away, that would bury the last part of her that hoped against hope she wasn't really all alone.

"I'm sorry," he said.

She blinked. There would be more, she was sure, and it would undo the tiny flare of comfort she felt at the words.

"Elena." Something brushed her bare arm: a fingertip, gentle, hesitant. It fell away again. "I'm sorry that happened to you. I'm sorry I couldn't help you at the time. I'm sorry I said the wrong thing just now."

"It's not on you," she told him again. She could feel him behind her, his warmth radiating over her back. "It's not your fault. It's not yours to fix."

"Maybe not," he said, "but I'm sorry all the same."

She tried to inhale, but her breath hitched.

"Elena," he said again, and this time his fingers stayed on her arm, and she turned around and let herself lean against him. His arms went around her waist and she wrapped hers around his neck, and for a long time she just stood, awkward and still. And then she began to cry, slowly at first, then in an unrelenting flood, wondering why there were tears when most of what she felt was overwhelming relief.

After a while she became aware of the room again, of the quiet, familiar thrum of *Orunmila*'s engines, of the faint movement of the ventilated air against her back. And . . . other things. The warmth of Greg's arms around her, strong and safe; his collarbone against her cheek; the smell of his skin, no vanilla, but musky and familiar. Animal. *Lovely*. She had a moment of utter clarity, realizing her arms were around a man who had wanted her for years, who had been alone for a long time, longer than she had been alone, and desire snaked through her, bright and sharp. She heard her own breath quicken, felt her heart begin to race.

Don't move, she told herself. If she didn't move, it would pass, and she could let him go.

"Elena?"

Oh. His face was close to hers, and she could feel his warm breath when he spoke. *Don't move,* she thought again, but she inhaled, felt his skin against her cheek, his shoulders under her hands, those lovely muscles that she would watch when he ran. He was so beautiful, and she wasn't alone, and maybe she didn't have to be so strong, not just now.

"Greg." She lifted her head, and met his eyes, and kissed him.

However long it had been for him, he had not forgotten what to do. His lips were firm and soft as he nudged her mouth open, and he tasted her tongue with his own, inviting her to taste him back. For a long moment she was dizzy, pressing her lips to his, falling into his rhythm as he devoured her, slowly, deliberately, with growing insistence, and she thought she would fly to pieces if she did not keep kissing him, if she did not get closer to him, if she did not . . .

What the hell am I doing?

She pulled away, stumbling, looking at the floor, the walls, anywhere but at him. His hands were on her waist, and she looked up to find her own against his chest; she dropped them abruptly as if he were on fire. "I'm sorry," she stammered, and took another step back. His hands fell away from her, and she thought she had never been so cold.

"Are you?"

She met his eyes then, and all of the heat and hunger she was feeling was reflected in their gray-black depths. Such beautiful eyes. All these years, and she had never understood how hypnotic those eyes could be, how they could pour out warmth and want and kindness all at once. "I—" What had he asked her? "I didn't mean—"

"It's all right," he said, taking a half step toward her again. "You don't have to be alone."

"I do," she protested, but her voice sounded weak, and he shook his head.

"It doesn't matter," he said. "What happened earlier. What

happened before. None of it matters. You don't have to be alone."

You don't understand. She wrenched her eyes away and moved past him; her arm brushed his, and she thought her skin would turn to flame. She clenched a fist, her fingernails biting into her palm. "*No*," she said, and her voice sounded much stronger this time. "Don't lie to me, Greg. Not after all this." She opened the wardrobe, rummaging for something to wear, and her hands found a pair of trousers. "Tell me it doesn't matter to you, that I don't feel what you feel. That I'll never be where you are."

He turned away from her, and she hated herself for saying it, but it had to be said.

"Enough is enough, Greg. I will not hurt you anymore. You are—" Her voice broke, and she squeezed her eyes shut for a moment. "Of everyone in my life, you are the person I want to hurt the least, and that's all I do. Maybe that's all I've ever done. And I *will not* do it anymore, do you hear me?" She could not find socks—*fuck the socks*—and shoved her feet into her shoes, heading for the door.

"You don't have to leave," he told her. "I won't—"

"I know you won't, Greg." She stopped for a moment, and took a breath, and made herself speak more calmly. "This isn't you. None of this is you. None of this has ever been you. You are not who is weak here." All the time he had spent apologizing to her, and it had never felt like enough. God, how selfish she was. "I am sorry. I am sorry. I am finished."

And without looking at him, she punched the door open and ran from him, again, for what she had to make certain was the last time.

Orunmila's convoluted corridors would have defeated her if she had not thought to pull up the map overlay. She knew they weren't far—none of the infantry quarters were far—but they were two levels down, and any random wandering she might have attempted would have made her hopelessly lost. As it was she nearly missed the door, all the way at the end of a dead-end corridor, tucked in a corner of the ship. They would have windows on two walls, she realized. Luxury.

The door opened as soon as she hit the chime. They were both awake—Dee in a chair by the back wall, a book projected in the air in front of him; Jimmy lying on the bottom bunk scrolling through a game. At least she hadn't woken anyone up.

She caught Dee's eye. "I'm sorry to bother you," she said, "but do you have a minute?"

She saw inquiry first in those dark eyes, but after a moment he lifted his chin, and she knew he understood. "Jimmy," Dee said, "can you give us some time?"

Jimmy didn't look up from his game. "For what?"

"Just mission prep." When Jimmy didn't move, Dee glared down at him. "Give me a break, will you?"

Jimmy rolled his eyes and slapped his feet to the floor, glaring from Dee to Elena. "Mission prep my ass," he said. But he slid his feet into his shoes and stood. "This ship is too goddamned small," he grumbled, and shoved past her out the door.

She almost flinched when she heard the door slide shut behind her. She had no idea what to say. She had no idea what he would think.

"Help me," she said, and she had no strength left at all.

CHAPTER 32

You can't go, sir," Youda insisted, for the third time. "Given your injuries, it's not safe."

Raman pulled off the narrow boot he had been trying to fit over his spidery foot. "Wider and shorter," he said briefly to Cali, who took the boot back and frowned at the collection she had brought with her.

Across the room at the bar, Commander Keita was assembling his pulse rifle, carefully checking the functionality of each part as he went, focused on his work. He was already in an environmental suit, the fabric helmet and gloves heaped on the countertop next to the remains of a bottle of particularly fine scotch. Raman had intended to finish it the night before, but in a fit of superstition he had left a few millimeters swimming around the bottom. Someone would drink it, surely.

Guanyin stood against the wall, arms crossed over her massive stomach, standing in that regal way she had, half at attention, half utterly relaxed. She was watching the scene, her face unreadable. He had wondered, when she had shown up with

Cali, if she was going to try to talk him out of going. He realized, as she watched Youda's growing agitation with absolute tranquility, that she had already said what she was going to say to him. She really was going to trust him to choose.

It annoyed him.

He would have said something to her, but Youda was not finished yet. "Your environmental suit won't seal properly around that prosthetic," he was saying. "We don't know how the atmosphere will affect the signals to your brain. We don't know how it'll affect the graft area. It could cause an infection, sir. It could damage the unit.

"You could die," the medic finished bluntly.

Cali held out another boot. It appeared to have been manufactured for some sort of misshapen child. With some focus, he narrowed the toes of his metal foot and pushed it into the rubber shoe. When he hit the bottom he uncurled the joints, feeling carefully in all directions. He pushed himself to his feet and took a few experimental steps across the room, surprised by how stable it felt. Against the bare floor the prosthetic felt slow and clumsy; in the boot, responding mostly to pressure rather than touch, it felt much closer to a real foot. He knew better now than to rely on it completely, but only in zero-grav had he felt steadier.

He caught Guanyin's eye, waiting for some variant of "I told you so." She said nothing, just looked back at him. Youda was still ranting, and after a moment her lips twitched, almost imperceptibly, and he caught a glimmer of amusement in her eyes.

Youda was winding down. "You're too important, Captain," he said decisively. "With everything we've already lost, we can't risk you as well. I'm going to have to override your decision, sir, and insist you stay on board *Orunmila*."

At that Guanyin had to drop her eyes. She used the excuse of addressing Cali. "I think we have a fit, Lieutenant," she said. "Thank you." Cali gathered the rejects and left the room, shooting her captain a disrespectful glare on her way out. Guanyin brushed the comm behind her ear. "Mr. Aida," she asked, "how close are we?"

"We'll be in planetfall distance in twenty-two minutes," Aida said, "but we'll have to stagger to hit all the landing sites."

Raman caught her eye and nodded. "That's fine, Aida," she told him. "Please have the shuttles ready to go."

Youda was staring, beginning to look genuinely angry. The man never had liked being ignored. "Captain Çelik, as the ranking medical officer on board—"

"I think Doctor Xiao might disagree with you on that," he said. He stepped into his environmental suit, carefully tucking the trouser legs into his mismatched boots, brushing the seal closed with his fingers. He and Keita would double-check each other's seals before they landed. Youda might be right about the boot, but he suspected both it and his artificial appendage would last long enough for him to do what he needed to do. He would not need them after that.

"Doctor Xiao isn't Corps," Youda insisted. "I'd be surprised if she even has a real medical degree."

God, what a petty little man he was. Raman pinned him to the wall with a glare. "Doctor Youda, in order to complete this mission, it is necessary for me to be part of the force heading down to the surface. It is not necessary for you to accompany me. Your objection to the mission parameters is noted. You should feel free to file a formal report with the Admiralty back on Earth. I'll even sign the paperwork for you if you like."

"I'm authorized to have you arrested, sir."

At that, Guanyin spoke up. "Not on my ship, Doctor Youda." Her voice was flawlessly polite, as always. He thought most people would not notice the edge of ice to it.

In a last-ditch effort, Youda turned to his old friend. "Keita, come on. You know he can't do this. He'll only slow you down."

Keita's expression was far less guarded than Guanyin's. Anger flashed, and Çelik saw one of his hands clench into a fist. The man had always defended him, sometimes blindly. He never could draw the right lines between duty and friendship. "It's his orders I'm taking," Keita said, his voice calmer than Çelik would have expected, "not yours, Jimmy. He has a right."

Guanyin was looking at Keita, a little line casting a faint shadow between her eyebrows. She missed very little. Raman found he enjoyed it as long as she was dissecting someone else. "Gentlemen," he said, "if you would excuse us. Keita, I will see you at the shuttle in a few minutes."

Keita nodded, holstered his rifle, and headed for the door. When Youda showed no signs of accompanying him, he grabbed the smaller man by the elbow and hauled him bodily from the room, ignoring the swears and protests.

Raman waited until their voices had faded down the hall. "Do you agree with him?" he asked Guanyin.

She kept her hands folded over her stomach. "Medically? Of course. But I do not understand why he feels he is permitted to do more than advise."

He wondered, then, if any of her own people would try to stop her if she decided to join his mission. He thought, not for

317

the first time, that she would be a formidable warrior, despite her slimness. "A quirk of regulations," he told her. "Officially, the ranking medical officer can overrule my orders if he believes I'm unfit for command." He tucked his gloves in his pockets. They would go on last, to be checked by at least two other people.

"Why do you have this rule?"

He raised his eyebrows, then decided she really didn't know. "Because sometimes captains go insane," he told her, "and the crew needs a protocol that doesn't involve them individually deciding whether or not to risk their careers."

She looked interested. "Is it so difficult to tell, for a layperson, if a commander has gone mad?"

"You tell me," he said to her. "Do you think I've gone mad?"

She tilted her head, and he felt a twinge of annoyance again. He was leaving this place behind, dammit. "I do not think I am a layperson, Captain Çelik," she said coolly. "And no, I do not think you are mad. But I understand why your doctor does. He does not understand. Doctors think about life, not death."

"You think Youda thinks about life?"

She equivocated. "I think he thinks less of us who do not believe it is the only consideration." She let one palm slide over her belly. "I think he would lock me in a soft room until my child was born, and keep that child wrapped in cotton until it was old enough to speak."

A fair assessment of Youda, he thought. "How would it have anything to say?"

At that she gave him a genuine smile. "It is a philosophy I understand, of course. I find I have a strong instinct to protect my children from everything negative. But I also understand how counterproductive that is."

"And there is Yunru."

She nodded. "He is pragmatic where the children are concerned. He is better with them than I am."

"He would not object to your putting yourself in danger."

"He would not understand your Doctor Youda at all."

Çelik thought the father of Guanyin's children, whom he had spoken to a few times, a bland, unimpressive little man. "That's more discernment than I would expect from him," he said. "It's possible I've misjudged him."

"I don't think you have misjudged him," she said. "I think you just don't like him."

"He's not very bright, you know."

At that she laughed out loud. "He is perfectly intelligent. Just because you are more so does not take anything from him. And he is a remarkable parent. Your approval of that is not required."

Her laughter poured into him, like molten metal in his veins, and he felt taller and stronger and paradoxically lighter than before. He was not the sort to feel incapable, not ever; but there was a particular intoxication that happened when he knew a mission would go well. He felt hopeful, and nearly buoyant. He would find these raiders, he would find MacBride, and he would avenge his crew. He had power again. He had control.

He took a step toward her, taking in the line of her jaw, the smile still playing over her lips. "Can you make me a promise, Guanyin?" he asked.

Her eyes danced. "That depends on the promise, Captain Çelik," she replied.

"Watch everyone," he said seriously.

"Given that there are more than eight hundred people on this ship," she pointed out, "I cannot promise that."

"Watch the ones you don't know," he insisted. "Anyone you have not known for years. Even if you think you can trust them. Even if someone you know trusts them. This . . . I don't understand it all," he confessed, bothered by his own ignorance. "But MacBride is only a piece of it. They destroyed my ship. They very nearly destroyed *Galileo*. They sabotaged and attacked yours. I don't believe the poison stops there."

Drained of their humor, her dark eyes looked fierce and impenetrable. "Do not fear for my ship," she told him firmly. "You must get beyond this idea that I am naive simply because I am young. I have seen more than you think. I may have spent most of my life here, in this place, but I remember enough. I remember that the woman who brought me to PSI, the woman who saved my life, was the same woman who sold my brother to slavers. One act of kindness can be redemptive, but very often it is not."

To his astonishment, she lifted a hand to his face and brushed his chin. He needed a shave, he realized suddenly, feeling her fingernails skip across the stubble. He would have thought her fingers would be cool, but in fact they were warm, and the touch radiated throughout his body. This was unfortunate. He had no time for this. He lifted a hand to shove hers away, but instead he caught her fingers and very gently pushed her hand back down to her stomach.

"You trust too much," he said.

"You are afraid for me."

"Yes."

"Like your Doctor Youda is afraid for you. Protect the mad captain."

"No. Youda is a fool. I am—" He could not complete the sentence. "Promise me," he said, finding himself pleading. "Promise me you will not trust."

She nodded. "I promise, Raman. And you must promise that you will not let your own fears keep you from your mission."

He would do it, and he would be done. "I fear nothing."

"Then neither do I."

And before he could move, she shifted forward and pressed her lips to his, balanced on her toes, her hands still on her belly. Alarmed, he kissed her back, aware he was doing a bad job of it; but before he could correct the problem, she had settled back onto her heels again.

"I would like it," she said, as if nothing had happened, "if you could manage to return." And she turned around and left him standing there, his fabric helmet crushed in his hand.

CHAPTER 33

Galileo

Jessica leaned back in Greg's chair, her mind annoyingly uncooperative. She usually turned to work when she felt helpless, but today she was finding focus elusive. The year before, when Elena was lost and she had thought Greg was dead, she had set herself to unraveling a mystery a quarter of a century old, and the task had held her together. Now, it seemed, her old coping mechanism had deserted her.

"Shiang's sending you with weapons, right?" Jessica had asked Greg when he commed before his descent to Canberra.

"I've got a handgun and a pulse rifle," he assured her.

"And a decent env suit? That planet is a fucking mess, sir. It'll eat up an old suit in twenty minutes."

"We've got all the right equipment, Commander. Stop worrying."

She had frowned. There was something in his voice, something he wasn't telling her, but she knew better than to make him cough it up now. "I'll stop worrying when you comm me, sir, and tell me you've got MacBride in custody on *Orunmila*."

At that he had sighed. "Not sure that one's going to be in my power, Jess."

She understood why he wanted MacBride back alive, but she couldn't bring herself to be too sorry at the thought that MacBride might die on that inhospitable rock.

Admiral Herrod had sent her, over a meticulously encoded comm signal, ten years' worth of ultra-classified Corps data on Canberra. Most of it seemed irrelevant—dry governmental reports, supply projections, terraformer maintenance schedules— but she did find a vid that had been inadvertently buried, una-vailable to Captain Çelik and *Exeter* before their fateful mission eight years before. It was from a PSI crew, as the last one had been; they had stayed less than three minutes on the surface, leaving behind a handful of containers of raw grains and bread, fleeing from colonists who were clearly starving. Jessica felt sick watching it. Those were the people Elena had faced: desperate, starving, weeks—perhaps months—past hoping for rescue.

No wonder Çelik had ranted at the Admiralty.

"*Galileo,*" she asked, squeezing her eyes shut, "did anybody speak for Niall MacBride during his trial?"

"No."

She frowned, thinking, and opened her eyes. "How did MacBride end up on *Exeter*? Why was she used for the transfer? She's not a prison ship."

"No official records on MacBride's transfer."

Of course. It had all been a big secret. She scanned Herrod's data, and in a few moments found the sealed order placing MacBride on *Exeter:* signed by three admirals—including Herrod—Captain Çelik, and Exeter's chief of medicine, Derek Lawson.

Lawson.

He had been killed in the attack. Keita had said the doctor had been uncomfortable with MacBride's treatment . . . but he had drugged the man again when he woke up.

She filtered the data for any mention of Lawson or *Exeter*'s medical staff. Most of what she found were the details of the drugs MacBride was being given, and the intravenous diet he was being force-fed. Jimmy Youda, she noted, had logged an official objection to that, and she amended, a little, her bad opinion of him. She moved back to the earliest reference she could find: audio of a meeting of an unnamed group of people. When she played it back, she was almost certain the speaker was Admiral Waris—less because she knew the woman's voice than because she was arguing.

"—*have a ship that can do this,*" the woman said impatiently. "*Her medical chief volunteered her services to me directly. There's no reason to pull* Cassia *into this.*"

Jessica checked the date of the conversation: three months ago. Before *Galileo* had arrived back on Earth. Before MacBride's conviction. They had already been setting the man up.

And Lawson had approached them of his own accord.

Before the events of the last year, Jessica had viewed Shadow Ops the same as most of her colleagues: retirement without retirement, a place where old, Earthbound admirals could keep their rank without having to actually do anything. For some, it was a coveted position. "*Galileo,*" she asked, "did Doctor Lawson ever ask to be transferred off of *Exeter*?"

"Sixteen transfer requests in the last eight years."

"To where?"

"Earth."

"Refused?"

"Approved by Captain Çelik. No transfer slots available."

Every six months since Canberra he had tried to get back to Earth. "Who's he survived by?" she asked.

"Four children, seventeen grandchildren."

"Corps?"

"All of Derek Lawson's next of kin are civilians in residence on Earth."

It was not implausible, she thought, that he would have volunteered his assistance in hopes of finding a home with Shadow Ops. She wondered if Çelik would have helped him.

She wondered if she would get the chance to ask him.

"Did Lawson have money troubles?" she asked.

"Insufficient information to respond definitively," *Galileo* replied.

Which meant nothing commonly viewed as money troubles. "How about his health?"

"Last records on Derek Lawson show moderate osteoporosis consistent with age. Superior muscle tone. No cardiovascular anomalies. Mild rhinovirus."

"When was this?"

"Five days ago."

Discovering that Lawson had died with a cold nearly undid her. "There's got to be something," she mused. "Either this is a coincidence, or he didn't care about dying in the attack." *Or,* she realized suddenly, remembering the drunken trajectory of the drone that had struck *Exeter, he didn't think the attack would be so bad.*

Was it really possible it was all a mistake?

She rubbed her eyes again. She was wheel-spinning, killing time, because she had nothing to do until Greg got back.

A quiet, ident-free chime sounded in her ear, and she tensed. She had set it up before Greg and Elena had left for *Orunmila:* a signal trap on Greg's off-grid, a simple instruction that made *Galileo* whisper *Someone is looking for you.*

She slipped into Greg's quarters and assembled the off-grid, pacing next to his bunk as the connection completed. When she'd set the trap, she had thought Greg would be the only one she was hearing from. This time, she had a hunch it wasn't him.

"Commander Lockwood, are you signaling unauthorized ships in your area?"

At Admiral Herrod's words, she froze. "Sir?"

"If you think you can code around me, Commander, you haven't been paying much attention."

She bristled at his tone. "Sir. Regardless of whether or not I *could* do that, I haven't. What are you talking about?"

"There are five unauthorized ships in the field, and they're chatting. Encoded. In a Fibonacci knot."

She felt a moment's relief. "That's hardly suspicious, sir. People use a coded knot for all kinds of things. When I was a kid, we used to use it to send cheat codes for games. At any point in time in the stream, you'll see hundreds of chains like that."

"You may want to pay some attention to this one, Commander. Because none of the ships in this little cheat code circle are sporting idents, and they're all closing on your location."

Her relief vanished. "Coordinates, sir?"

He rattled off the numbers as she brought up the comms grid. She frowned at the pattern. Five ships in the field, all headed in different directions, all scheduled to emerge at differ-ent times—but all ringed around *Galileo*. She swore thoroughly, then thought to say "Sorry, sir."

"I take it," Herrod said dryly, "these aren't your signals."

"No, sir," she said decisively. "We've been comms locked since the attack. Everything is going through Admiralty channels."

"And yet here we are."

Well, hell. "I don't know that it matters at this point, sir," she said. "I've got to comm *Cassia* for backup."

"I'll send you *Eritrea* as well," Herrod told her. "Do not tell Captain Hollett anything about this, or what you're doing there. She won't ask questions, but she'll defend your ship. Un-derstood?"

"What's her ETA?"

Herrod paused. "Nineteen hours."

"That's a little late, don't you think, sir?"

"*Cassia* should be enough, if it's only five ships."

If.

Bastard.

"According to my readings, even the closest ship is five hours off," he told her. "Let me know if *Cassia* is delayed."

And what good will that do? "Yes, Admiral."

She waited for Herrod to disconnect, then signaled *Galileo*'s comm center. "Samaras, get me Captain Vassily on *Cassia*."

"Yes, ma'am."

She heard that digital hiccup again, and frowned. "What's the status of the comms diags, Lieutenant?"

"Still looping, ma'am, but so far we haven't—" He stopped, and Jessica was instantly alert. "Commander, I can't get through to *Cassia*."

"What do you mean, 'can't get through'?"

"I mean we're not getting the signal out. All I'm getting from the system are loopbacks. We're talking to ourselves."

Shit. "What about the stream?"

Another pause. This time, when he responded, he did not hide the tension in his voice. "Nothing, ma'am. We're isolated."

Jessica cut him off. "*Galileo,* why aren't you receiving?"

There was a pause, and her stomach lurched. *Galileo*'s automated mind worked faster than anything Jessica could perceive. A pause meant missing data, or a malfunction. "No data to receive," the ship said calmly.

"You're telling me the stream has just disappeared?"

"Hypothesis is consistent with the facts."

"Don't you think it's more likely that something is wrong with us?"

Another pause. "Hypothesis is consistent with the facts."

She swore again.

As far as *Galileo* was concerned, the comm system was functioning, and indeed was connected to the outside world.

And yet there was nobody there.

Jessica opened her comm to the whole ship. "All hands, this is Commander Lockwood. We've got unknown incoming, unknown arrival time. Battle stations, sidearms ready, no exceptions."

Greg and Elena, it seemed, were not the only ones about to engage the enemy.

CHAPTER 34

Canberra

G reg felt a skewed déjà vu as their shuttle dove through Canberra's clouded atmosphere. The last time he had flown in weather had been six months ago, on Earth, taking a shuttle into Missinipe to visit his father after the court-martial. Thanks to the commercial ship's intertial compensation system, he had been able to practically ignore the lightning storm he had descended through, watching the show from the sedate safety of the cabin. Atmospheric disruption fascinated him—wind, tides, cloud cover—but Canberra's weather was different. This was storms and rain and an oxygen-thin atmosphere, wild weather patterns with little predictability. Elena had plotted some possible takeoff routes that might be available over the next twelve hours, but even those, she said, could not be counted on.

"We can predict the macro weather just fine," she had told him. "But the storms change too quickly on the ground. We're going to need to be awfully careful flying in this stuff."

She had not returned by morning, but showed up ten minutes early to *Orunmila*'s shuttle bay, greeting him formally and withdrawing to perform her usual preflight check on all three ships. She had been dressed, he noticed, not in her uniform, but in a plain black turtleneck and trousers. PSI clothes, likely borrowed from the common wardrobe they kept in their gym. He had not been surprised—he had noticed she had left in a pair of his pants instead of her own—but then Keita had arrived. She had met the other man's eyes just once, given him a brief smile, and gone back to her task; but there was no mistaking the telltale blush that crept over her cheekbones.

And didn't that bring the point home.

I'll never be where you are, she had said. That he had been married for most of their acquaintance wasn't the issue. That she had fallen in love with someone else while his marriage was falling apart wasn't the issue. The issue was him, and what she would never feel for him.

Eight years they had known each other. He had watched her with more men than he could count, and it had never bothered him, not seriously. He'd had her companionship. Her heart. Everything that mattered.

Almost everything.

Keita wasn't good enough for her, but that wasn't the point. The point was she didn't love him, she wasn't going to love him, and less than that wasn't enough for him. Having her body without her heart would have dismantled every last real thing that still existed between them.

And even now, in the clear-eyed morning before battle, he was quite certain he would have taken the risk. He thought he might give up years of his life just to kiss her again.

They hit the upper stratosphere and he felt the familiar tug of natural gravity against the shuttle's artificial field. He looked over to see Elena frowning at the readout; she was trying to compensate, but with this much turbulence he didn't think she would get very far. He stared across the aisle at Captain Çelik, who had his eyes closed, whether against boredom or nausea Greg could not tell. He swallowed, and tried to breathe evenly.

"We've lost contact with the others," Elena said. Greg checked the time; right on schedule, suggesting their weather forecast had been accurate enough. He wished he found that thought more comforting.

Moments later he was bouncing around in his seat, body slamming against his shoulder restraint. Through the shuttle's windshield he watched them fly through clouds, gray and black. "Sorry, folks," Elena said to the room in general, her eyes grimly on the controls. "No point in trying to fight gravity here. Hold on; I'm going to try to drop lower and see if we can get a smoother weather pattern closer to the surface."

Next to her, in the copilot's seat, Keita sat, jaw set, eyes out the window. He was the only one of them, Greg reflected, who seemed to recognize the seriousness of what they might be walking into. Elena was focused on the flying, her typical single-mindedness reacting only to her recalcitrant instruments. Çelik appeared indifferent, although Greg knew better. Greg thought he would at least have some time before *Exeter*'s captain became actively suicidal; if he knew anything about Raman Çelik at all, he knew he wouldn't leave a job half done. As long as any of the raiders were alive, Çelik was not a danger to himself.

The clouds disappeared, replaced by driving sheets of icy rain and the sight of a distant, pale horizon. The shuttle projected a 3D scan over the front window, and Greg looked it over, frowning, as Elena kept her eyes on the instruments. "Anything?" he asked.

"We can see one of Jessica's power sources from here," she told him, "but nothing else. No engine residue, no ship signatures, nothing."

Damn. He tried not to let his frustration get the better of him. Despite the fact that this was the most obvious landing site, it was still possible the others were having better luck.

"Wait," Elena said. She reached in to the projection and zoomed in on an area ahead of them. "Look."

There was a faint glow on the ground, pale enough to be phosphorescent stone; but the shape was perfectly round, and almost certainly artificial. "What is it?" Greg asked.

The shuttle had no answers. "Could be exhaust residue," Elena speculated. "Something with a vertical takeoff."

"Set us down a few hundred meters away," he told her. "If you can."

They came to a flat plain, and even in the dim, predawn light Greg could make out the remains of some building foundations around what might have once been a town square. A lot of it looked blasted and burned, but in places there were beams and walls that seemed oddly melted. The rain, he thought, corroding the materials used for building. An ordinary planet would have reclaimed the residue and enriched its own soil, even if it was disinclined to make itself comfortable for humans. This one seemed to spit poison at everything.

Elena would tell him he anthropomorphized too much.

She set the shuttle down in the center of the open space, with maximum visibility all around. Of course, even maximum visibility was dreadful; through the window he could not see more than a hundred meters away. Lighting would do them no good; it would only reflect off of the freezing rain and diminish their sight further. Every part of his training told him this situation was untenable: an unknown number of an unknown enemy on unknown terrain that would surely kill them if they stayed too long.

Well, he thought, *at least we know* that *much.*

Çelik, across from him, was grinning, unbuckling and hauling himself to his feet with alacrity. *Easy,* Greg thought, *when you don't care about getting home again.* He caught Keita's eye, and he thought the other man was thinking the same thing.

They took a moment to pull on their hoods and check each other's seals, and then they all four drew their pulse rifles and pressed their backs against the wall. Elena hit the door control, and the whistle of the wind blew cold air into the shuttle's cabin. He went first, Keita following a moment afterward, the soldier peering into the dark, rifle in his hand. Elena dropped out third, and Çelik last. He would not be agile with that foot, Greg thought; but he was surprisingly quick, and Greg decided to leave the worrying to Keita. *If Elena really trusts him,* Greg thought grudgingly, *maybe I can trust him a little as well.*

"Which way?" He spoke through his comm; they might have been able to hear each other over the howling wind, but shouting was pointless.

Elena gestured into the darkness, and they set out.

The lights from the shuttle went out a moment later, and he moved forward slowly, waiting for his eyes to adjust. After a few minutes the shadows grew more distinct, and he could tell that the sky was growing lighter; but with the density of the clouds, he did not think it would ever be full daylight.

They fanned out slowly, keeping each other in sight, Keita on Greg's left, Elena and Çelik to his right. Keita stopped at one point, staring at something on the ground, and Greg moved to join him.

"Bone?" Keita asked, nudging the object with his foot.

Greg frowned. Bone would be his guess, but it was too stunted and warped to be human. The rain again? Or were there wild animals here? If the Syndicates had found a herd they could keep, that might have explained their choice of this forsaken place.

He crouched down to take a closer look, and then froze. "Keita," he whispered, letting his comm carry the sound. "Did you hear that?"

"Six o'clock," Keita breathed. Greg saw Keita's hand close on his pulse rifle, ready to confront whatever was coming up behind them.

Greg was halfway up when he was hit in his midsection by something swift and hard: someone had run into him headfirst, and bounced off of him when he landed on his back with a jarring thud. He rolled to his feet, turning to his attacker, who was already rushing him again, ducking in close where Greg could not hit him with the rifle. Slinging the useless weapon over his shoulder, Greg feinted and punched as the figure passed, catching his attacker on the jaw. He had a fleeting impression of wide eyes through the clear flexible cover of the dark hood—an older version of his own environmental suit—and had to lift one arm to block the return punch that was thrown. He moved in close to apply an elbow to the chin; the figure staggered backward, reaching behind its back. *If you were armed,* Greg thought, confused, *why didn't you just fire from a distance?* He knocked the weapon from the unprepared fighter's hand; a short-range rifle, and quite old, by the look of it. These could not be the raiders with the technology to fly a three-day distance in fourteen hours.

Looking too long at the gun proved to be an error, though. His attacker was still shaking his head—or hers, he realized; the agility and accuracy required more coordination than muscle density—when he was struck from behind, low on his back. He felt an alarming tingle radiate down his left leg, and then a shooting pain; he pivoted in an attempt to fight back and found the leg wouldn't carry his weight. He dropped, kicking with his better leg, but he had given his first attacker time to recover, and now they were both on top of him. He threw punches where he could, but few of them landed. They were trying to pin his arms, and he struggled to keep them free, jabbing with fists and elbows. He managed to get his knee under one attacker and throw him off, but another body replaced the first. He could feel himself tiring, could feel the pain in his leg sapping his energy, and he realized he needed to do something, and fast. In a rush of adrenaline he rolled onto his knees, only to catch a foot in his stomach, and another to his jaw. Spots of light appeared before his eyes, and his vision blurred. *Dammit,* he thought, rolling over and kicking someone in the face, *I'm going to lose.*

He heard the telltale sound of a pulse rifle firing, and one of his attackers went down. The other two were hauled off of him bodily. He tried to push himself up on his elbows, but something was wrong with his arms; they could not support him. He blinked and saw Keita, who reached down and hauled him up by his collar. Greg tried to shuffle his feet under him, but he could not stand. He shook his head, and his vision tunneled alarmingly. He squinted into the rain, only to see Çelik and Elena, ten yards away, fighting their own battle. She was wielding her rifle like a club, the strap looped around her arm so the attackers could not take it away; Çelik was swinging at every attacker, connecting with most of them; but he, like Greg, was down a limb, and there were too many of the enemy.

Greg tried to move toward them, and his leg gave way entirely. He dropped to his knees, waiting to be overwhelmed again; but the attackers, it seemed, had abandoned him in favor of an easier target. "Keita!" he shouted. Next to him Keita ran forward, just as Greg saw Elena take a hit to the head. She staggered and ducked, but came up swinging. One of the attackers got a grip on her rifle and used it to pull her closer where he could connect more easily with her jaw.

"Captain Çelik." Greg heard Elena's voice over his comm, calm and quiet, as if she was not holding off six men. But instead of Elena continuing, it was Çelik who spoke.

"Commander Keita, get Foster out of here," Çelik snapped, out of breath. Greg saw one of the attackers kick at Çelik's bad leg, and the man lost his balance entirely, dropping onto his back with a quick, harsh gasp of pain.

"Captain—" Keita began, but Çelik broke in.

"That is an order, Commander," he said severely.

"Countermanded!" Greg tried to shout, but the word came out garbled. Keita had stopped, and was turning to him. Greg felt Keita's arms slide under his shoulders. He struggled, feeble and dizzy; but it was useless. He tried to reach down, to grab the ground, to slow Keita down. He saw the swarm cover Çelik, kicking and punching; saw Elena swinging furiously with the pulse rifle; saw it yanked from her grasp; saw its hilt swinging toward her head. He gave one furious wrench of his shoulders. "Let me go!" he said, as clearly as he could, and eventually fell back on swearing. He knew he should have refused to let Keita come.

Keita dragged him through the mud and rock. He could not focus at all anymore, and he kept slipping in and out of consciousness; he traveled city blocks in the blink of an eye, was back at the shuttle before he had had a chance to breathe. "Direct order. We go back."

"I have my orders, sir." Keita's voice was tight and unhappy.

Greg opened his mouth to argue. They had to go back. He could not leave her here. Not here, not defenseless.

Not where she had been torn apart all those years ago.

"We go back," he demanded; and then the darkness swallowed him.

PART III

CHAPTER 35

Canberra

Every time I come here I end up staring down a gun.

Elena kept her eyes on the woman who had taken her pulse rifle. She could see little through the rain-streaked hood of the raider's env suit, but she made out deep-set eyes, dark skin, hollow cheekbones. The woman was a few centimeters shorter than Elena, narrow through the shoulders, but solid— her punches had established how strong she was. Now she held the rifle high, aiming at Elena's head.

Elena counted the others: eleven—no, twelve people, and not all of them armed. Their env suits varied as well, she noticed: some of them were made from older materials, or had gloves and hoods that did not match. Some were worn through in places, patched with industrial tape. Suits like that couldn't last in this weather. Suits like that would disintegrate in less than an hour.

Where did they come from?

"Who are you?" the woman asked Elena.

Elena stared silently, keeping Çelik in her peripheral vision. Two of the armed raiders were trying to haul him to his feet.

In one swift move, the woman reached out and jerked Elena's hood off, taking a few strands of hair with it. Rain, cold, and noise hit her simultaneously, and she squinted against the howling wind, resisting the urge to try to snatch the hood back. Her eyes began to water, but she knew any feeling of burning on her skin was in her imagination; the atmosphere would allow her five, perhaps ten minutes before it tore open her throat.

At least it doesn't smell like charred flesh this time.

The woman had noticed the neckline of her borrowed shirt. "PSI," she spat, betraying emotion for the first time. "Kill her."

"She's not."

He had been standing behind the woman, unarmed, his face obscured by rain; but Elena did not need to see him to recognize him. The last time she had seen Niall MacBride—on Earth, as he was being led to his own court-martial—she'd had ample opportunity to become acquainted with his voice. He had been protesting his treatment with a long stream of creative profanity, and she had not blamed him a bit.

MacBride took a step forward, and Elena caught the glint of his blue eyes beneath the clear hood. "She's a Corps mechanic," he said. "Shaw. Off of *Galileo*."

The woman studied her, then nodded down at Çelik. "And him?"

Çelik answered for himself. "Keita," he said. "I'm second-in-command of the CCSS *Exeter*."

All Corps captains knew each other by sight. Elena waited for MacBride to identify Çelik, but he said nothing.

"Can you think of a reason," the woman asked, "why we shouldn't kill you both?"

"A mechanic could be useful," MacBride suggested. His tone was disinterested.

"I thought *you* were a mechanic, MacBride." The woman sounded vaguely annoyed.

He shrugged. "There's a lot to be fixed, Tsagaan. And there's something to be said for redundancy."

Behind her, Çelik was still struggling, and the raiders trying to pull him up began to grumble.

"What's the problem?" Tsagaan asked.

"He won't stand."

Tsagaan gestured with her rifle. "Then shoot him."

"If you kill him," Elena said, "I won't help you."

Another step closer, and Tsagaan dropped the nose of the pulse to press it against Elena's stomach. "If you don't help us," the woman said, "I'll kill you, too."

Elena's eyebrows shot up. "Then I definitely won't help you," she said, and waited. She should have been terrified; but she was wet and breathless and cold, skin down into her bones, and she was too angry to play games.

She could see Tsagaan's narrowed, intelligent eyes studying her face. In the semi-dawn darkness she could not discern their color, but there was a speculative shrewdness about them. Elena thought the woman would understand she wasn't bluffing. "Very well," she said at last, taking a step backward. "Bring him."

"We *can't,*" one of Çelik's captors said, and Elena thought it sounded like whining.

Those intelligent eyes grew briefly annoyed. She took in Elena again. "You bring him. If he can't walk, we leave him out here. Understood?" Almost as an afterthought, she tossed Elena her hood.

Elena pulled it on as she moved to Çelik's side, then tugged his arm across her shoulders, lifting him up as well as she could. To her surprise, another figure—slim, and no taller than Jessica—took a few steps toward them.

"I'll help," she said. She moved to Çelik's other side and slid an arm around his waist—or tried to; her arm barely reached across his back. He braced his hand on her shoulder, and Elena saw her shift to take his weight.

Following Tsagaan, they struck out into the dim daylight.

All of Elena's focus was taken by trying to keep Çelik on his feet. If some of his injuries were faked, it was not all of them; although his artificial leg would take weight, he seemed to be having trouble balancing on it, and she wondered how badly damaged it was. He leaned on her heavily, using their shorter companion only for balance, in one of those strange chivalrous gestures of his. She wanted to ask him what he had noticed about their captors.

The most obvious oddity was that most of them were unarmed. In addition to Elena's rifle, Tsagaan had a hand pistol at her waist, as did the two men who had halfheartedly tried to get Çelik to his feet. But the rest of them, including MacBride and the woman helping Çelik walk, were empty-handed. Nine combatants unarmed. It was a curious omission.

As was the fact that they hadn't been killed outright.

At length they rounded a ruined wall, and in the center of the debris, Elena saw a sunken circle among the rubble, three meters across. As they approached, the circle split down the middle, exposing a dim ray of artificial light to the dreary morning. With a faint mechanical hum, the two halves of the circle folded into themselves, exposing a passage into the ground.

Tsagaan stepped forward and disappeared into the hole, all
the unarmed raiders following. Elena helped Çelik shuffle forward, and discovered the hole opened on a flimsy metal stair-
case that descended into a spiral. There was no visible handrail,
and without asking she moved in front of Çelik and took one
step down. He put one hand on her shoulder for balance, and
she cautiously began to descend, step by glacial step, waiting
for Çelik to squeeze her shoulder before she moved again. The
other woman dropped behind them, one hand under Çelik's elbow to help him balance.

The last two armed attackers came after them.

The stairs opened into a small room, filled nearly to capacity
with the dozen people who had gone before them. Elena's eyes
swept the walls—flimsy, temporary dividers, suggesting the low
ceiling was dropped—before her attention was caught by their
captors. Most of them had pulled off their hoods, and were
stripping off their environmental suits. To Elena's surprise, very
few of them were in uniform. Instead, they were dressed in a va-
riety of clothes: soft shirts in blues and greens; trousers in black
and brown and white, made of everything from cheap no-wash
fabric to sleek, fitted bioengineered silks. *Civilians*. That might
explain the lack of weapons.

Tsagaan was dressed all in dark brown, a utility vest shrugged
over her practical, close-fitting clothing—the same uniform as
the dead raiders on *Exeter*. She was somewhere between ten and
twenty years older than Elena, with short-cropped dark hair and
unlined brown skin, but with a set to her full lips that spoke of
both authority and annoyance. Elena knew better than to judge
someone by their appearance, but she saw nothing that made her
doubt the woman would kill them in a heartbeat if she wanted to.

"Bring her," Tsagaan said.

Reflexively Elena gripped Çelik harder, and turned to see one of the civilians moving toward her, reaching for her arm.

"Do not touch me," she snapped. Something in her voice must have made an impression, because the civilian stopped, and looked back at Tsagaan. Elena met the woman's dark eyes.

Tsagaan frowned, but she looked more annoyed than angry. "Your friend needs medical attention," she said. "He won't be harmed." When Elena didn't look away, she added, "You have my word."

And what's that worth? Elena thought; but when she looked back at Çelik, his eyes on hers were clear and alert. Reluctantly she let him go.

Tsagaan turned away again. "Badenhorst," she said, moving toward the door, "take him with you, and find out how badly he's hurt. And MacBride, find out who he really is, will you?"

"I'll go with them," a familiar voice said; and Elena turned. The small woman had finally removed her environmental suit, and Elena took in her white-pale skin and her wide, deep blue eyes. A flutter of recognition went through her, and she frowned. She had to be wrong.

Who would choose to return to this place?

It was Tsagaan who removed Elena's uncertainty. "Fine, Ruby. But evaluate him and leave them, you understand?"

Ruby. Good Lord, it *was* her. Taking orders from a Syndicate raider, but otherwise entirely comfortable in her surroundings. *What could have brought her back here?*

Ruby herself seemed to find nothing unusual in their reunion. She waited for Elena to finish studying her, and then she gave her a quiet nod: *Trust me.*

Elena had no choice. She let Çelik go, and Ruby took her place at his side. The pair began lurching slowly out of the room, MacBride a step ahead of them.

The civilian moved toward her again, but Elena just shot him a look. "I'll come with you," she said when he opened his mouth to object. "You don't have to haul me."

Elena fell into step behind Tsagaan, aware of her escort following too closely. She let her eyes stray over the people they passed: more civilians, still divesting themselves of environmental suits, watching her with a sort of detached hostility. As they passed through the doorway she realized she had counted more than had attacked them: nearly three dozen. And when they passed through the doorway, she realized this wasn't a small group of raiders.

They had been brought to a settlement.

The room they entered was deep and tall, walls made of an unfinished gray building compound of the sort used for decades to build temporary shelters. Elena's eyes went to the structural reinforcements, placed at precise three-meter intervals along the walls. It was unattractive, but clearly solid work. She could hear the hum of mechanical systems: air filtration, atmospheric recycling. There was a chemical odor in the air that suggested mineral reclamation as well, but she wasn't certain. She had enough structural training to know how to build a temporary shelter, but this place seemed designed for more than that. She counted eight levels, some with scaffolding and catwalks allowing direct access, and at least a dozen doors.

Not temporary at all.

They passed more people. There were another five uniformed raiders, all armed, but far more civilians walking without weapons—at least thirty. She saw no hierarchy; raiders acknowledged civilians, even chatted with them. As far as she could tell, this was voluntary cohabitation.

Where did they all come from?

They went through another door and down a long, non-descript hallway. The ceiling was low, nearly touching Elena's head; Çelik, she suspected, would have to bend over, which wasn't going to be easy given his impairment. As it was she felt intensely claustrophobic. Starships were small and confined, but they were surrounded by space, by emptiness, and here she was too aware of the tons of earth pressing above her head. Still, the engineering appeared sound, and she recognized something important:

They could not have built this in this weather.

"How old is this place?" she asked.

Her captor did not acknowledge her.

Tsagaan stopped at a door that was fitted, to Elena's surprise, with a physical numeric lock. Tsagaan kept her body between Elena and the keypad, but Elena counted the presses: nineteen. She'd be unlikely to stumble on the combination by luck. The keypad suggested a nod to energy efficiency—or possibly a fluctuating power grid.

Tsagaan stepped into the room, and Elena was crowded through the door by her escort. The place was slightly larger than her tiny room with Greg on *Orunmila,* but the lack of windows made it feel much smaller. Still, it was furnished with two beds and a dresser, along with a separate bathroom, and there were pictures on the walls. Comfortable. Not a cell at all, she realized: quarters. Living space.

Tsagaan watched in silence as the civilian searched Elena,

stripping off the jacket of her env suit and pulling her toolkit from her arm. He patted down her legs, then pulled off her boots one at a time, leaving her standing in her borrowed socks. All in all, it was a perfunctory search, but he seemed satisfied enough when he finished.

He moved back to the door and slouched against it to watch. Tsagaan turned to face her. "Who else are you sending down after us?" she asked.

Elena did not answer her question. "How old is this place?" she asked again.

Tsagaan's eyebrows quirked up. "You think that's how this will work? I give, then you give?"

"I think you're a murderer," Elena said coolly, "and I'm not giving you anything."

"You have already given me a great deal," Tsagaan said. "For instance, I know that if I threaten your friend, you'll talk to me."

"And I know," Elena returned, "that we have something you want, or you would have killed us already."

They stared at each other, and Elena watched the emotions play over the raider's face. Elena had the sense that she was usually far more circumspect, and it occurred to her that this woman had known for days they were coming after her. She had even sent her people to die in a poorly thought-out attempt to stop them.

She's tired. More tired than I am. Maybe more desperate.

"This place," Tsagaan told her, "is thirty Central years old, give or take. It was originally built as a storage facility."

"For smuggling?"

"That is a charged word, Mechanic Shaw."

"Be that as it may."

"Initially for materials storage, yes," Tsagaan said. "The adaptation to a living space happened later, when it became clear such a thing might be needed. The residents here are generous with their facilities. Our relationship with them has always been cordial."

Elena replayed the tense in her head three times before she realized what Tsagaan had said. "These people. You're telling me—" She turned to the civilian, who kept slouching, looking at her through hooded eyelids. "You're *colonists*?"

"You should have checked more closely when you abandoned us," the man said. She couldn't miss the taut thread of anger in his voice.

But she wasn't interested in arguing with him. She turned back to Tsagaan. "How many are here? Why haven't you told anyone?" *Why didn't Ruby tell anyone?* "You can come and go from this place—how can you let them stay here, underground, with nothing?"

"What makes you think that's what we're doing?" Tsagaan looked genuinely surprised.

"This is our home," the man said again. "Why would we tell you we're here? So you can take it from us?"

There was no point in trying to unravel his conflicting arguments. "So all this time," she said, "when we've been thinking you've been flying two or three ships in and out of here—all this time, you've had living space. Allies." All the plans they'd made, all the battle briefings—it was all irrelevant, all wrong.

"Now that you know my defenses," Tsagaan said evenly, "why don't you tell me about yours? What has Central sent after us?"

Which was a desperately stupid question. Elena began to wonder exactly how many pieces she had been missing. "After what you did? What do you think? You murdered ninety-seven soldiers with automated drones. Above and beyond anything else, Central can't let that stand, politically or otherwise. All of this here"—she let her hand sweep the room—"is immaterial. They'll dig you out and burn you up."

"Us too?"

This was from the man standing behind her. She looked at him more carefully this time. He was nominally her age, too thin, with a narrow nose and wide-set eyes shrouded in heavy lids. The slouch, she decided, was calculated; despite leaning a casual shoulder against the wall, every muscle in his body was tense.

"As they don't know you're here," she told him honestly, "I expect so."

His eyes left hers to look at Tsagaan. "I told you," he said.

She frowned at him. "And I told you. We're not doing anything stupid, not now."

"What are you planning?" Elena asked. "If you were going to send more drones after us, you should have done it instead of sending that pathetic tactical team."

And that, of all things, made Tsagaan lose her temper. "Those people gave their lives for this tribe," she snapped. "You will speak of them with respect, or I'll kill you anyway, *fuck* what you can tell me."

"Honor among thieves, is it? Is that why you killed your own man back on *Exeter*?"

"You don't know anything about honor." Tsagaan stepped up to her, fists clenched. "He paid the price for what he did. He paid it willingly, and he did that for all of us."

Elena tried to parse that. "What did he do? Did he try to steal something you weren't sent to steal?" *No—he had been outside the ship.* She tried again. "Did he attack the wrong target? Or—" She remembered the strike drone, lurching drunkenly en route to *Exeter*'s hull. *Oh.* "The drone hit. That wasn't supposed to happen, was it?"

"He had been taught how to operate them," Tsagaan admitted. "He made an error."

An error. Ninety-seven soldiers. "He's murdered all of you, you know," she said calmly. "If it had just been a simple strike— even if you'd killed a few people, you'd have had a chance. But this? The whole Corps will be after you, forever. Every ship in this sector will be on you. And I'm betting PSI will be happy enough to do the same." She looked up at the low ceiling. "Not much of a place to live out your days," she remarked.

Tsagaan stared at her silently, and Elena thought she was shaking. At length, the raider leader looked back at the civilian. "Lock her in," she said, her voice tight. She turned back to Elena.

"If we're all going to die here, you'll be dying along with us."

CHAPTER 36

Raman leaned heavily on Badenhorst, deliberately stumbling at regular intervals. The raider, like most people, was smaller than Raman, but he had no trouble supporting Raman's bulk, and he kept one hand on the barrel of his rifle as he walked. If Shaw had still been there, Raman thought the two of them might have overwhelmed Badenhorst; but on his own, he was going to have to wait for a better opportunity.

And then there was Ruby to consider. He had no way of knowing how long she had been back. Until he could determine how much she was involved, he needed to keep her out of the line of fire.

MacBride, of course, was a different matter. Raman had no idea why the disgraced captain hadn't outed him to the Syndicate leader. He had to know Raman was there to kill him, and he probably could have had Tsagaan eliminate Raman without a second thought. If he were suicidal, his behavior might make sense; but *Demeter*'s former captain did not seem suicidal. If Raman was reading him properly, he was confident of his welcome here, but not entirely happy about it.

Under other circumstances, Raman would have been curious about what MacBride had to say about this place.

They followed a short hallway to a room without a door. The room contained a row of bunks, a tall cabinet, and a familiar medicinal odor; Raman took the space for a temporary infirmary. Badenhorst helped him lower himself onto one of the bunks, but it was Ruby who spoke to him.

"Lie down," she said. "You're safe here."

He turned to look at her, ready to remark on her deep naiveté; but when he met her eyes, he saw nothing but concern and compassion. Ruby, the girl they had saved all those years ago, the girl who had fled this place. Why was she back here?

Why was she helping him?

"I need to search him first," Badenhorst said, and damned if the big raider didn't sound apologetic. Raman studied the man: sturdy and strong, he would have fit in with any Corps infantry platoon. Beyond that, he had behaved throughout with unwavering calm and caution, and now he was looking at Ruby with something like gentleness on his face. Her esteem mattered to him—probably not enough to keep him from following orders, but still. It was a vulnerability, and that was a start.

Beyond the raider, MacBride leaned against the wall, arms folded, stiff and unreadable. He looked far less military than Badenhorst. On some level, Raman supposed he was.

Badenhorst removed Raman's env suit, allowing him to balance against the door frame, and patted him down thoroughly. Before removing his boots, the raider gestured at one of the bunks. "I expect this'll be easier if you're sitting," he said.

Compassion for his prisoner as well. Another vulnerability.

Raman sat on the edge of the bunk, his knee throbbing. About halfway through the fight on the surface, he had stopped receiving signals from the prosthetic, and based on how it was taking his weight, he suspected the thing had snapped. He gripped the sides of the bunk as Badenhorst pulled, and he heard both the raider and Ruby hiss as the prosthetic was exposed.

It was broken, snapped in the center, held together by a handful of tiny filaments. It was dark and unresponsive, but worse, the connection to his knee was raw and swollen. He glanced up at Ruby, who had stepped forward. "I don't suppose you can repair it?" he asked.

She shook her head, eyes on the connection to the stump. "We don't have the technology," she said apologetically. "I can bind it, though, and get you an analgesic for the pain."

"Are you a doctor, then?"

She shook her head. "We haven't had a doctor here in five years."

He wondered how many they had lost in this environment to the lack of medical knowledge. "Skip the painkiller," he said shortly. He looked back at Badenhorst. "If you don't find any lurking incendiaries in my boot," he said, "I wouldn't mind having it back. The leg is much more stable with it."

Badenhorst was either unaware of being baited or professional enough to ignore it. He ran his hands inside Raman's boot, carefully probing the sole and the heel, then handed it back. Ruby opened the infirmary cabinet and returned with a roll of medical tape, and began winding it around the split in the leg. She was taking some care, but every time she wound it around, the connection rubbed against his knee, and the pain jolted up his spine and into the back of his head.

Not that he needed anything to worsen his mood.

She finished in short order, and Badenhorst stood over him as he tugged the boot back on. He settled his foot on the floor. Apart from the pain, the leg seemed to be holding his weight well enough. Without sensory feedback, though, he was going to have to be careful. He stood, slowly, one hand against the wall, and tested it; it held. He looked up, his eyes meeting MacBride's, and the pain was suddenly unimportant.

"Badenhorst," MacBride said, his impassive eyes on Raman, "can you leave us alone?"

Oh, yes, Raman thought. *Leave us, Badenhorst. I will be quick, I promise.*

But Badenhorst was apparently not a fool. "Sorry, MacBride," he said, and Raman thought he was genuinely regretful. "You know Tsagaan's conditions. I can't leave you with him."

"She could stay." MacBride nodded at Ruby.

Raman wondered if she would stay out of the way if he asked her, or if he would have to subdue her first.

"I can't," Badenhorst insisted. "It's too risky."

"What's risky?" Raman asked. "Is your boss out there going to kill you for fucking up, like that fellow she spaced when she attacked my ship?"

It had been a guess, but Badenhorst blushed deeply. "I don't expect you to understand our traditions," he said, and after a moment Raman realized his color was due not to anger, but to sadness. "Tsagaan had no choice. When one of us makes a mistake—"

"What mistake did he make?" Raman asked. "Not blowing my ship up in a single shot?"

"Nobody was supposed to get hurt," MacBride put in brusquely.

At that, Raman laughed out loud. "Is that what you told yourself when you sold out your government? The people who worked beside you and saved your ass every day for your entire fucking career? 'Nobody will get hurt'? My God, the Admiralty must have beaten you in the head, because you never used to be so stupid."

"It's the truth," Ruby insisted, her huge eyes apologetic. He remembered that expression. He remembered thinking she had to know how disarming it was. "It was meant to be bloodless, the whole thing. It was meant—"

"To be what? A taxi service?" What they had meant was irrelevant. "What's your part in all of this?" he asked her.

She fell immediately silent, and looked up at Badenhorst, who shook his head at her. Not a threat, Raman recognized. A warning. *He's protecting her.*

"I have a better question," Raman added. "Why am I not dead?"

"Because Tsagaan hasn't ordered you killed." This fact came from MacBride.

Raman's eyes swept the room. "Recycled air, unfinished walls, aging environmental suits? And this, I'm guessing, passes for some kind of hospital? More people are a liability in this place. She's keeping us alive for a reason, and not just because you outed Shaw as a mechanic." That puzzled him, more than MacBride concealing Raman's identity: Why would MacBride protect Shaw, of all people, after her part in what had happened to him?

"There are circumstances here you don't understand," MacBride told him.

You couldn't possibly believe I care. "And while I'm wondering these things," Raman went on, ignoring MacBride's last statement, "why are *you* still alive? I got the story of who's behind liberating you, such as it is, but I find it hard to believe those fucked-up traitors in Shadow Ops would let you know anything important enough for Ellis to be willing to spend the kind of money they've spent to snatch you."

MacBride bristled. "You have no idea what I know."

"Well, that's true." He took a step, and the prosthetic held; Badenhorst stiffened, but apparently did not consider his mobility a danger. "I had no idea you'd have the sense to disobey an illegal fucking order, although I'm still trying to figure out how you were dense enough to let yourself get court-martialed over it. You should have walked away from it, like Foster did. Instead you get yourself—" He stopped, and realized he didn't know. "What was your sentence, anyway?"

"Life," MacBride said, his jaw tight. "No comms, no stream. Just four walls, and anything they decided to give me."

Raman couldn't keep his eyebrows from shooting up. It was an impressively awful sentence. "You really did piss off the wrong people, didn't you?"

"You can't blame me for wanting to get out, then."

"No, I can't. But if you had any honor, you'd have done it by killing yourself, not my crew."

Badenhorst frowned. "Your crew? I heard—" His eyes flicked briefly to MacBride. "We were told your captain survived."

"Oh, yes," Raman said, belatedly remembering his subterfuge. "Captain Çelik. Angry little man. Good thing he's not here, because I'm pretty sure he's not in the mood for anything beyond snapping a few necks."

"Çelik's not that stupid," MacBride said dismissively. *Dismissively*. "He knows his people understand the risks of battle. Losing a few soldiers—"

MacBride's eyes had the chance to widen before Raman's forearm connected with his throat and slammed him against the wall of the small room. Badenhorst's rifle was out, leveled at Raman's midsection; but for now, at least, he was choosing not to fire. "*A few soldiers?*" He pressed his arm against MacBride's neck, staring into the man's wide, alarmed eyes. "Ninety-seven people, MacBride! Ninety-seven people who trusted me, who did as I said, who believed until the moment you murdered them that I was going to get them out of it!" It wasn't until the words were out that he realized he had given away his identity.

"Let him go, Commander," Badenhorst said levelly, missing Raman's revelation.

"Fuck off, Badenhorst," Raman snapped, his eyes not leaving MacBride's. "I already know she's told you not to kill me, and you strike me as a company man. Unlike Captain MacBride here, who killed innocent people because he was afraid of being alone."

"I didn't—"

Raman shoved him again, cutting off his words. "And this would be the part of the routine when you give me the 'I had no idea' line and pass the buck. Someone else's fault, is it? Just like what happened last year? 'I was just following orders. I didn't know what they were going to do.' Except you did then, and you did now. How in the hell did you think a pack of chicken-shit guerrilla fighters were going to bust you out of the brig of a Central Corps patrol starship? With a bouquet of flowers and a friendly smile?"

"Let him go!" Ruby shouted. She reached up and grabbed Raman's arm, tugging ineffectually.

MacBride coughed, and Raman allowed him a little air. "We were a Fifth Sector ship, Çelik. Raiders never tried to hit us in the Fifth Sector. I assumed that here—"

"What did you call him?" Badenhorst asked.

He was paying attention to that.

Raman tilted his head at the raider. "Less stupid than you, MacBride. A little slow, but he catches up eventually."

"Help me, Badenhorst!" Ruby was weak, but persistent.

But Badenhorst was still. "They'll come after him," he said. "A lot of them will come after him. He's the ship's captain. They won't leave him here helpless."

"My rank has nothing to do with it," Raman said, still fixed on MacBride. "What you do with us doesn't matter. You can't kill ninety-seven soldiers and wipe out a starship and expect to walk away."

MacBride's eyes had widened in horror, and Raman leaned against him, slowly. One good shove and he could break MacBride's neck . . .

Ruby let him go.

An instant later, her foot connected with his knee, and he found she wasn't so weak after all.

The impact of the kick shot daggers through his whole body, and he convulsed, releasing MacBride as he curled up, collapsing to the floor. His eyesight filled with flashes and auras. The room vanished; all sensation of the floor, the temperature of the room, even gravity disappeared in the face of the agonizing wave of pain.

When he came back to himself, Ruby was wringing her

hands anxiously. *Never apologize for taking down your enemy*, he thought at her. Badenhorst had hooked him under one arm and was pulling him toward the cot. Raman reached out with his free arm and pushed himself on top of the bed.

MacBride was leaning against the wall, still staring at Raman. "You said *wipe out a starship*. Are you telling me *Exeter* was destroyed?" he asked.

"In that respect, I didn't lie about my identity. I don't have a ship anymore."

MacBride shook his head. "I never meant for it to go like this."

"But it would have been all right with you if it had just been one or two fatalities," Raman said. He felt drained, exhausted. "The guard. Maybe the doctor; he kept you drugged, after all. No great loss there. Speaking of which, did you know he had four children? All grown, long since moved out of the house; but he was pretty fond of them. Kind of a boor about them, now that you mention it. He'd get this look on his face when he spoke of them—real pride, real affection. Love. I'm betting they loved him, too, and now they have nothing but dust. If it had been just him, Niall, would that have been all right?"

Ruby had moved toward him. "You should lie down," she said. "Let me look at the stump."

"Thank you," he said, "but I think you've done enough for now."

Ruby hung back, stricken and unhappy. MacBride stared down at Raman. The horror of it was apparently still sinking in; he had that look on his face that Raman would often see in the families of the dead. "If I were a merciful man," Raman said, "I'd say what you have to live with is justice enough. But I've never been a merciful man." He met Badenhorst's eyes; the raider still had his hands on his rifle, wary. "You'll tell your Tsagaan who I am, of course."

Ruby said, "We can't—"

"I must," Badenhorst said.

Raman nodded. "I would welcome the chance to talk to her." And with more effort than he thought was still in him, he hauled himself once more to his feet. "For now? I want to see my engineer." He thought, under the circumstances, even Shaw might forgive his possessiveness.

CHAPTER 37

Orunmila

For a slight woman, Doctor Xiao had a prodigious grip.

Greg had come to in *Orunmila*'s infirmary, his memory crystal-clear, adrenaline flooding his system and bringing him instantly, head-poundingly awake. He had attempted first to push himself into a sitting position. When that had turned out to be an ill-conceived idea, he had given the doctor his most brutal *you better answer now, soldier* stare and demanded to know where Keita was.

"Mr. Keita," Xiao had replied, entirely unintimidated, "is making his report to Captain Shiang. You will have your own opportunity to report to her, when you're better."

"I'm fine now."

"You took a hit to the spine," she corrected, "and multiple blows to the head. You have a concussion, and some nerve damage I am still repairing. You are extremely lucky you are young and fit, or you would be stuck here for days instead of hours."

At that, he had struggled again to sit up, and this time she had grabbed his bicep and shoved him firmly back on the bed, jolting his head uncomfortably. "Stop doing that," she commanded, "or I will knock you out again. I am not finished with you, and you will not leave until I tell you that you may."

She was not, he recognized, completely out of line. After all, her job had nothing to do with his mission on Canberra. Greg was just someone she was supposed to heal. She could not understand how urgently he needed to get back down to that planet.

If they have killed her I will vaporize the whole place, and Keita with it.

With what felt like a superhuman act of will, Greg relaxed back onto the examining table, and after a moment Xiao released his arm. She fussed over his knee and his battered ribs, muttering to herself in a combination of Standard and dialect. He caught the word *stubborn* in both languages, and something he thought was slang for *stupid kid*. That, he thought, was unfair; she could not be much older than he was. He wondered if she talked to Captain Shiang like that.

He was pretty sure she did.

Thirty-five interminable minutes later he was following the gold stripe down the corridor as rapidly as he could, his head still pounding hideously, his injured knee bound tightly and anesthetized. He must have looked much how he felt, because the same people who had been nodding politely at him that morning gave him a wide berth, moving to the other side of the corridor or ducking through a doorway as he approached. Maybe, if he was inhospitable enough, they'd let him leave the ship.

Maybe they'll demand it.

His plan was momentarily thwarted by the two guards at the door of Captain Shiang's office, but just as he was evaluating what it would take to knock them down, they stood aside. "You're expected, Captain," one of them said, with nothing but polite disinterest on his face.

The door slid open, and Greg absorbed the scene: Captain Shiang, standing behind a chair at the head of the table, Cali seated at her right, Hoelun at her left. They seemed unhurt, and he concluded they had found nothing. *Just us, then*, he thought, clenching his fists. *The lucky ones.* Another man, vaguely familiar, sat next to Cali. There were four guards inside the room, one at each corner, but Greg did not think they could reach him in time. Standing at attention opposite Captain Shiang was Dmitri Keita.

Greg took two steps toward him, and punched him in the jaw.

Keita went down, his arms coming up in defense. Greg dropped himself on top of the man, ignoring the objections of his leg. Keita made a sharp, clipped gasp of sound as Greg's knees dug into his ribs. Greg hit him again, aiming for Keita's chin but delivering instead a blow between lower jaw and cheekbone. He'd get only teeth for that, no real injury. He needed to focus to do this properly, but all he could see was the hilt of the rifle swinging toward Elena's head as Keita yanked him away like a helpless doll.

He never got a chance to land another punch. His arm was caught at the elbow, and a wide, sinewy forearm slid around his neck, pulling him bodily off of Keita. He resisted for an instant, but he knew when he was beaten. Hitting wasn't going to get him what he wanted anyway.

But for a moment, it had been mightily satisfying.

"You insubordinate son of a bitch!" he shouted. Keita was shaking his head, pushing himself to his elbows. "I'll have your commission for this! I'll see you rotting in prison for the rest of your life!"

Keita's left hand went to his jaw, and he gently pressed against his cheekbone. His eyes held Greg's; he looked angry, but not out of control. "I was following Captain Çelik's order," he said.

"And the second he was in the hands of the enemy, *I* was the ranking officer on that rock!"

"I don't work for you, sir."

Utterly specious. "Is that how you justify your actions?" Greg asked. "You don't serve on my ship, so my rank doesn't matter? Is that how you justified trying to kill Elena all those years ago—you weren't on *Exeter,* so you didn't have to obey the rule of law?"

That one connected as well as his punches had. Keita pushed himself to his feet. "If she told you that much, *sir,*" he said tightly, "you also know her feelings on the matter."

Her feelings. "I know she's a sentimental fucking *idiot,* and she shouldn't have trusted you for a second."

"There were eighteen people down there, Captain! If we'd gone after them—"

"It was our *duty* to go after them, *fuck* the odds!"

"THAT IS QUITE ENOUGH."

The words, bellowed in Shiang's melodic alto, broke through Greg's rage, and he straightened, turning to look at her. She seemed a head or two taller, her rigid spine radiating anger and disapproval. The flash in her dark eyes seemed to envelop the entire room. Stiffly she stalked around the table until she was standing before Greg and a still-shaky Keita; but it was Greg she focused on.

"You both seem so concerned about jurisdiction here, but you forget that *this is not your ship*. For you to have stormed in here, Captain Foster, and thrown punches in my presence is an offense for which I am quite prepared to put you in prison. And you, Commander Keita." She turned on the other man, whose eyes widened a little in surprise. "If this charge of insubordination is factual, I would like to know why I should not take you into custody as well until your own people can investigate the incident. You are not my officer, but I have no tolerance for the sort of semantic hair-splitting you seem prone to." Her eyes swept back to Greg. "I will give you one chance, Captain Foster, to explain to me why I should not lock both of you up and throw away the key."

"I have to go back," he said.

Her eyebrows shot up, but before she could respond, he got backing from an unexpected source.

"Agreed," Keita said. "We can't leave them there."

Her gaze nailed Keita again, but the man stood his ground. When she looked back at Greg, he saw in her eyes the beginning of something that might have been understanding.

Damn, he thought, *I should have punched Keita days ago.*

She turned away from them and moved gracefully back to the head of table. Greg noticed, for the first time, Cali's expression: the woman was gaping, mouth wide open, at her captain. Next to her the blandly handsome young man was smiling a little, looking pleased. Shiang, he suspected, had not done much shouting in front of these people. Perhaps now she would consider doing more.

"Very well, gentlemen," she said evenly. "What is your plan?"

Greg glanced at Keita. "We go back down. We get them back."

She looked irked. "That's not a plan, Captain Foster. That is panic. Try again."

He felt frustration rising. "Due respect, Captain, but we don't have time—"

" 'Due respect'? My goodness, Captain Foster, I am beginning to wonder if you are not a comedian of some sort rather than an officer. You have not shown me due respect since the day we first met." She gestured to the empty chairs. "Sit down, gentlemen."

Greg felt Keita stiffen beside him. Neither of them moved.

"I have no intention of abandoning your people," she clarified. "But I will not toss objects at that planet like a child pitching toys from a crib just because you are both upset. Now *sit down,* and we will formulate a plan that has a chance of getting us all what we want."

She waited, and after a moment Keita moved toward the end of the table. Greg glanced over his shoulder at the guard who still had an arm around his neck; the man let him go, and he sat down at Shiang's left. He could not bring himself, yet, to look at Keita, but he was willing to accept the man as an ally if it would get them back down on that rock.

Once Elena's home, I'll have the time to hit him again.

When they had both settled, Shiang lowered herself down into the chair at the head of the table, her right hand absently running over her stomach. "Yunru," she asked, "what is the weather situation?"

The bland young man replied. "The storm systems are erratic," he said. "We can model what is happening, but no more than twenty minutes ahead of time, and what's happening under the cloud cover is anybody's guess. Any ship we try to land is going to be playing probabilities."

"When is the next probable window?"

"Twenty-six hours," he said.

Greg put an arm on the table, reflexively tapping his fingers. "That's too long."

Shiang shot him a look, but he thought it was not without sympathy. "You are not thinking, Captain Foster."

Of course I'm not thinking, he thought. He struggled to haul his mind to the problem at hand. What would Elena say to him now, if she were here? Probably something like *"Who's being sentimental now, Greg? You're supposed to be a strategist."* And she'd be laughing at him, at least a little, no matter how dire the circumstances.

He nodded. "Okay." His fingers kept tapping, as if they belonged to someone else. "Eighteen people down there, at least. Are you sure?" Reluctantly he made himself look at Keita, who nodded.

"Twelve on them, six on us."

Greg frowned. He had not, since they left, thought back over the short, uneven battle. He remembered the horde swarming Elena and Çelik. Only a few had been doing the actual fighting. The others—not all fighters—had hung back, staying out of the fray. Their own six attackers had been more thorough. "Why only six on us? And why didn't they shoot us?"

"They were carrying crap. And they weren't all armed."

Captain Shiang's head came up at that. "That is wrong," she said decisively. "Raiders never travel unarmed."

Greg frowned. "Even with limited weaponry?"

"There is never limited weaponry in this sector, Captain. There is only old and obsolete weaponry."

"So—two groups? Two tribes?" He shook his head. "It still doesn't make sense. Even with old and obsolete guns, why didn't they shoot?" He remembered now: six men launching themselves at him, being torn off by Keita, turning and fighting again; one of them pulling a gun but not firing it. Even the hit to his spine had been something solid: someone's boot, or the hilt of a rifle. Rationing battery power and ammunition? That would mean their resources had gone into the drones, and not their day-to-day weapons. Even so . . . "They didn't want to kill us," he said.

"How does it help to know that?" Keita asked.

"It suggests," Greg told him, finally catching up, "that maybe taking us alive—or at least some of us—was the point in the first place."

Keita shook his head. "What difference does it make? Even if they keep everyone on their ships, they can't stay down there for long. Not even those expensive drones had enough shielding to stand up against the atmosphere and the rain."

"If *Aganju*'s intelligence is correct," Greg reasoned, "they don't have enough shelter for their own people, never mind ours. Captain," he said, "do you have the records from our shuttle?"

Captain Shiang gave her ship a command in dialect, and the vid from their front window began to replay. He reached out to flick his fingers through the image, speeding up playback; when the surface glow appeared, he stopped it. "There," he said. "So faint we couldn't pick it up until we were almost on top of it."

"Radioactive rock," Keita said dismissively. "Or fallout. Toward the end they spent a lot of time blowing each other up."

"*Orunmila*," Greg asked, "what are the dimensions of that power signature?"

"Power signature is spheroid, long diameter 3.67721 meters, oblateness .037."

"Natural phenomenon?"

"Odds of signature being artificially constructed: 88.3 percent."

Keita still looked puzzled, but Greg saw Captain Shiang sink back in her chair. "You think it is a shelter," she said.

"That would explain why they've been able to use the place so effectively as a hiding place," he reasoned. "It would also explain why our estimate on how many people we were going to meet was so far off."

"You think they may have taken your people there?" she asked.

"It's a reasonable conclusion," Greg said, "if we assume they could have killed us but didn't."

"Wait." Next to him, Keita leaned forward, frowning at the stilled vid. "Have we still got Commander Lockwood's map, Captain? Can we overlay it here?"

Captain Shiang spoke to *Orunmila* again, and Jessica's intricate schematic appeared over the dim gray vid image. Keita studied it for a moment, then looked at Greg. "I think that's where I found her," he said.

The infant? "Are you sure?"

"Found who?" Captain Shiang asked.

Keita looked over at her. "When we came down here eight years ago, I found a baby as we were leaving. She'd been left on the ground, laid out on some old shirt in the rain. I took her with us. But—she'd been left right there, ma'am. By this power signature. I thought she was abandoned. But what if they were trying to get her to safety?"

"You think this shelter predates the disaster." Her eyes met Greg's. "Captain, did Central ever account for all of the colonists lost on Canberra?"

"With the weather and the accessibility issues? I doubt it." He hit his comm to ask Jessica.

"But it doesn't make sense," Keita said, arguing with his own conclusion. "If they were alive, and the raiders knew it—why all the secrecy?"

"Raiders do not measure the lives of others as they do their own," Captain Shiang said. "They may have their own reasons for keeping any survivors a secret."

"If we assume the unarmed people we encountered were survivors—they didn't behave as if they were coerced."

"Given that they had no weapons, you cannot draw conclusions from their behavior."

Greg's comm flashed orange: *Comm blocked by receiver. Try again later.* "Captain Shiang, is my comm open?"

She glanced at him, distracted. "We've done nothing to lock it down, Captain." Then the import of the question struck her. "You're not receiving an answer?"

He shook his head. "They've blocked incoming." He could think of a handful of reasons Jessica may have done that, and none of them pleased him. "Have we received any Maydays?"

She tapped the comm behind her ear. "Aida, what is the current sector status?"

There was a brief pause, and Aida responded, his voice relaxed. "There are still pro forma warnings at the *Exeter* site, ma'am, but there's nothing else pending."

"Can you see if there are any ships in *Galileo*'s vicinity?"

"Nothing, Captain. All in-field traffic is hours away." Another pause. "Do you want to divert?"

She looked at Greg, and he realized, in that moment, that if he asked for her help she would give it, never mind leaving Çelik—and Elena—on the surface. So much had changed in just a few short days.

Reluctantly, he shook his head. "My crew will look after her," he said. It was the truth, although it did nothing to ease his own worries.

Captain Shiang nodded, her eyes still on his, and he thought, despite her inexperience, she knew what he was thinking. "As you wish, Captain." She leaned back. "Then I think our problem has become how we manage to land on that planet while escaping the detection of an unknown number of people who know it far better than we do."

CHAPTER 38

Galileo

We've got sixty-two percent of our weapons back online," Ted told Jessica. "The rest are still isolated and dormant."

"How long?"

"Seven hours."

Jessica stopped herself before rubbing her eyes. "Is that a real estimate, or a bullshit engineering estimate?"

Sitting in Greg's chair, watching Ted seated across from her, Jessica reflected that Elena would have glared at her for that remark. Ted just rolled with it. "No bullshit, Commander. We can bring them up in stages, have some thin coverage in the next, say, ninety minutes. But anything more than that? Without automated checks, it just takes time."

Leaving *Galileo*'s automated diagnostic systems out of the loop had seemed madness to Jessica at the time, especially when it came to their weapons systems. Now that their comm system was dead, though, she was suddenly grateful for Elena's paranoia. "Any way you can increase coverage? Even if it slows down the overall restore?"

"I'll look into it," he said. "When is *Cassia* due back?"

"Five hours." *Four hours, fifty-six minutes, and a bunch of seconds,* she thought. *Too damn long.*

"Didn't Herrod say those ships were five hours out?"

Three hours now. "But with everything we've seen, from those drones to that long-range raider to the one that dropped out right on top of *Orunmila,* I'm not counting on any of those readings being accurate."

Part of her hoped it was *all* inaccurate, that there weren't any ships circling at all, that this had been done as some kind of fear-generating experiment. Maybe even a Corps drill. *Wouldn't that be nice,* she thought, *to be able to think vengeful and poisonous thoughts about my own command chain, instead of whatever random deadly tech is out there waiting for us.*

"We could try just reenabling them, Jess."

She looked at him. "They got into our generator core, and into our comm system. You really think that's a good idea?"

He shook his head. "Just one to hold in reserve, in case it becomes a choice between 'what if they sabotaged our weapons' and 'let them blow us to bits.' " He stood. "I'll rearrange the repair schedule, Commander, and get us as much coverage as I can. Beats nothing at all." He saluted, and turned to leave, and she was struck by the unfamiliar sidearm at his waist. Ted always called himself a pacifist, but she knew he wouldn't be shy about defending his own.

Uncomfortable sitting in Greg's place, she stood and walked around the desk. She wore her own weapon, her faithful short-range shooter designed to be light and quick in close confrontations. When the comms had first gone down, she had resisted the urge to sling a pulse rifle over her shoulder. She might have felt personally safer, but she didn't think panic from the acting captain was likely to inspire the crew. She had briefed them on what she knew—which was almost nothing—and set Mosqueda and Samaras to rooting out whatever was confusing *Galileo*. She had interrupted them only once for an update.

"It's spaghetti," Mosqueda had said irritably. "A big tangled mess, right in our comms center. *Galileo* is working to unravel it as well, but it's going to take some time."

No permanent damage was good news, but it wasn't enough.

Emily Broadmoor had been more encouraging. "Don't worry about keeping them on alert, Commander," she had said. "We train like this all the time. Six-hour shifts, overlapping by an hour, light prep training while we wait. You can count on the infantry, ma'am."

Trust your people, Jess. She knew now why he'd reminded her of that: because sometimes, that was the only choice.

"*Galileo*," she said, "how are we doing with the shipping data?"

After the first hour on alert, Jessica had realized that there was no way she could sustain her sense of urgency. She had reviewed Emily's brigades, paying them the same compliments she had heard Greg give them, feeling like an utter impostor; but when she had walked through engineering, reassuring everyone that they were prepared for whatever would come, Ted had leaned over and whispered "Nicely done" as she was leaving. And indeed, as she toured the rest of the halls of the ship, she saw crew members straighten at her presence, answer her with confidence, return to their tasks just a little more relaxed. Apparently, she really was doing something right.

She wondered if Greg, with his easygoing confidence, was sometimes faking it as well.

Without access to the stream or the Admiralty records, all she had was the data sent from *Aganju,* her own limited research, and the scattered information Admiral Herrod had found. Somewhat to her surprise, the problem was not finding enough stolen goods reports to account for the systems on Canberra. The Third Sector had distinguished itself for nearly a century as a pirating and contraband center. The problem was associating what had been taken with a possible destination. Never mind figuring out what it might have been assembled into.

The most useful thing she had found was a lost shipment of wind generators, written off by the freight company when their shipping vessel had gone missing in the Third Sector thirty-seven years earlier. Wind generators would have been perfect for a planet like Canberra. Even when its climate had been stabilized, it was prone to sudden storms and prolonged cloud cover. Stellar batteries would have done as well, but they were far more expensive, and they couldn't have counted on a steady charge. Wind generators were low-tech, durable, and cheap—cheap enough that the freight company had not even bothered to replace the shipment.

Jessica took a moment to wonder what had happened to the freighter crew.

Once she had established a time frame, she was able to narrow her search, but there was nothing that jumped out at her: no chemical converters, no logic cores, no odd bits of weatherproofed technology. *So maybe they are just batteries,* she thought; but that idea always led her to the same place. Canberra hadn't needed that much extra power. Why would they have built generators?

The door chimed, and she looked up—she had left it open,

intending for visitors to enter unimpeded, but there stood Lieutenant Samaras, hesitant even at attention. Some of that, she suspected, was his size: he was the tallest man she had ever seen—raised on Aomori, where the gravity was nearly as low as the gravity on Mars—and broadly built, obscuring the entire doorway. He was also by nature shy, and she expected he tried to minimize his own size when he spoke to people. She was aware that her own small stature probably aggravated his worries on that front, and she stood as tall as she could, gesturing him inside. "Do you have something for me, Lieutenant?" she asked.

"I— " He straightened, and saluted her. "Yes, ma'am. I have an idea how we might work around the comms problem."

He had, she recalled, a substantial background in comms tech. "Can you get us listening, Lieutenant?"

"No, ma'am, not that. I—it's just a theory."

"Go ahead, Lieutenant."

He leaned forward. "Commander Mosqueda and I have been looking at how this thing has entangled itself. *Galileo* is making some inroads in getting rid of it, but basically, it's because *Galileo* is as sophisticated as she is that it's as . . . well, rooted, ma'am, for lack of a better word. So I was thinking," he said, warming to his subject, "what if we gave it less to work with?"

"How do we do that? Lobotomize *Galileo*?"

She had been kidding, but he took the question seriously. "That'd take longer than letting *Galileo* unravel it. But what we can do is isolate one of our shuttles, and let the shuttle shake it off."

"Run that by me again?"

"The shuttles are all tied to *Galileo,* right? So they're all infected as well. But we can sever them. It doesn't require an external comms connection to disconnect a shuttle from *Galileo*'s comm system. That's part of the loopback mechanism. We sever the shuttle's connection, then help out its AI as it unravels the virus."

"And that'll happen more quickly than *Galileo* untangling this thing?"

"In theory, ma'am, if Commander Mosqueda and I work along with it," he said. "It's still going to take a few hours, but if we can do that, we can—theoretically—set our personal comms to route through the shuttle instead of *Galileo*'s mains."

Jessica tried and failed to come up with a fatal flaw in that idea. "Excellent, Lieutenant," she said, and meant it. "You and Commander Mosqueda get that started, and let me know as soon as we have a line to the outside world."

"Yes, ma'am." He snapped back to attention and saluted her, and he seemed straighter this time. He turned, and left the room.

Jessica began to pace, restless again. Ordinarily she would have talked to Ted, bouncing her convoluted thoughts off of his unflappable mind, but he was busy shoring up *Galileo*'s defenses, preparing for the undefined attack she was still certain was before them. She did not dare imagine talking to Greg or Elena. She felt an entirely different sort of panic, knowing they were dealing with the issues on Canberra without having her as backup.

She turned back to Greg's desk and picked up the pulse rifle she had left on the shelf against the wall. It had been too long since she had done any real battle drills. Slinging it over her shoulder, she went to find Emily Broadmoor and her infantry.

CHAPTER 39

Canberra

E lena kept going back to the paintings on the walls.

There were three of them, all done with some skill, in a mix of ink and watercolor: old traditions. Two were dark—bleak landscapes, all stone and sterile soil, almost monochromatic— but one was bright, a sunrise over lush cropland, done in warm oranges and swaths of green. The planet wouldn't have seen cropland like that for hundreds of years. She wondered if the painting was that old.

The colonists had remained. By choice. That much Elena understood. *Galileo* could be on fire, collapsing around her, and she would still fight to cling to her home. Despite her dislike of life on land, she could empathize.

But why had Ruby never told anyone they were there? Why, if they had help and resources, were they still silent?

Central would have been reluctant to intervene, she knew. There had been evacs, even in Elena's lifetime, that had been involuntary; but the standing order was that people who didn't want to be evacuated were to be left alone, even if it was to die.

The trouble was, it was rarely such a clear-cut situation. Liriel had been classic: the government had asked for evac, but the population had not been united, and the soldiers who had been sent to help had encountered opposition. It had been tangled and messy, and something of a miracle that the Corps had managed to extract most of the colonists without igniting a full-on civil war.

Even if Central had known there was still a stable settlement on Canberra, they would not have wasted resources on people who did not want to leave. And now, of course, those same people were harboring fugitives. Elena was not entirely sure the Admiralty would automatically see that as an act of war, but it would not incline them to helpfulness.

She paced, because sitting was infuriating, and tried to piece it together. Tsagaan had all but admitted to being hired by Ellis, but something had gone wrong. One of the raiders had made a mistake, and the incident had attracted far more attention than it should have. *That might explain why Ellis isn't here already,* she realized. If they wanted distance from the incident, the best thing they could do would be to stand back and let Central vaporize Tsagaan's people. Whether they would or not, she suspected, depended entirely on what they needed from MacBride.

Without warning the door slid open, and she started, squaring her back against the wall. When she saw Çelik, alive and glowering, half-carried by Badenhorst, she let her eyes close for a moment in relief. He was all right. *And I'm not on my own after all.*

She stepped forward to take his other arm, and he leaned on her heavily. Her relief disappeared. "What happened?" she asked, helping him toward one of the bunks.

"Ruby kicked me," Çelik told her. He shrugged off both her and the big raider to lower himself to the cot.

Badenhorst scowled at him. "You tried to murder MacBride," he said.

Çelik had been unarmed and injured, in the custody of an armed Syndicate raider. *Of course he did.* "Did you succeed?" she asked him.

He was settling himself down on the bunk, placing his injured leg with care. "I told you," he repeated, as if it should have meant something to her, "Ruby kicked me."

Elena wanted to kick him herself; his timing was horrible. She looked back at Badenhorst, but he had turned away and was heading for the door. "What happens now?" she asked him, and he stopped.

"I don't know," he said. He would not turn to look at her. "But you need to stay here for a while." He went out the door, and she heard the lock engage as it closed.

She turned back to Çelik, reminding herself he still outranked her. "Sir," she began.

"This is probably not the time for one of your self-righteous rants, Chief," he said.

She had been hoping he was all right, hoping he would help her find a way out of here. Instead, he had turned into one more problem she needed to work around. "Are you all right, sir?" she asked.

But it seemed he had no intention of discussing his injuries. "MacBride claims he didn't know what happened."

So much for pleasantries. "Do you believe him?"

"I do." He sat up, swinging his legs to the floor, placing his right foot with care. "Which makes him both a mass murderer *and* an idiot. Did you get anything out of Tsagaan?"

"She says the drone attack was an error," she told him. "And she got very unhappy when I told her Central would retaliate no matter what she did to us."

"Of course," he said, his voice all acid. "I got the same thing from Ruby and Badenhorst. This was all apparently some big misunderstanding. MacBride was supposed to be picked up in a horse-drawn carriage and spirited away to some fancy resort. I wonder if he's disappointed?"

Elena began to wonder how he had failed to kill the man. "Respectfully, sir," she said, "we need to figure out how to get out of here. We need to get a message back to *Orunmila* and let them know they're not fighting one Syndicate tribe."

"You have any brilliant ideas on that front, Chief?"

She sat down on the bunk opposite his. He might be focused on the wrong mission, but he hadn't lost his analytical mind. "I didn't get much from Tsagaan, sir, except that this facility has been here for decades, and their alliance with the colonists goes back at least that far. And the colonists . . . they see us as the enemy."

"So we're low on friends here, is that what you're telling me?"

Well, that sounded better than saying *it's hopeless*. "What I'm telling you is that I don't understand why we're still alive."

His eyes narrowed. "That's the real question, isn't it? Before she became MacBride's knight in shining armor, Ruby actually looked after me. She stabilized the prosthetic and gave me my boot back. She's probably regretting it," he allowed, "but there was real kindness there. So the *colony* might see us as the enemy, but she might not be the only colonist who's willing to see things a little less starkly."

"Which might help us, if we can get out of here before the Corps decides to just nuke this place."

He shook his head. "Captain Shiang won't allow indiscriminate bombing."

"It's not going to be up to her, is it?" He looked aggravated, impatient, and she realized she was distracting him from his vendetta. "We have a duty to these colonists, sir," she said. "We need to get word out, if nothing else."

The door slid open again, and before Elena had a chance to react, Tsagaan and Badenhorst were inside. Badenhorst stood between her and the raider leader—an odd choice, she thought, since Çelik was the one who had shown a tendency toward violence—and Tsagaan stared down at Çelik, her expression grim.

"Badenhorst tells me you are *Exeter*'s captain."

Elena tensed, waiting for some form of outburst, but all Çelik said was "Yes."

"You lost ninety-seven people. Out of how many?"

Çelik's eyebrows shot up. "Are we playing percentages now?"

"Do not misunderstand me, Captain," Tsagaan said, and began to pace before him. "I am not interested in diminishing your loss. But before this mission, I had seventeen people. I now have twelve."

"There are a lot more than twelve people in this shelter," he pointed out.

"The colonists," she said to Çelik, "are not raiders. They're not even fighters. None of this is their responsibility. Do you understand?"

There was an undercurrent of emotion to Tsagaan's measured words that Elena took a moment to identify: *worry*. The woman was worried, and whether that was more about the colonists or Central's reaction, Elena could not be sure.

Çelik leaned forward, settling his elbows on his knees. The move caught Badenhorst's attention, and the raider shifted away from Elena, his hand on the barrel of his rifle. Çelik ignored him. "I understand what you're trying to make me believe," he said. "But I disagree with you. They may not be raiders, but they are absolutely fighters. And given how long they've been hosting you here—before the fall, wasn't it? maybe decades?—they *are* responsible. They are protecting you from justice."

Tsagaan's lips tightened again. "Justice." She spat the word. "This is a thing you believe you understand? When there are people in this sector who must steal to survive? Who must—"

"This colony has no need to steal," he told her. "If they had asked us for help—"

"And what did the Corps do for them last time? Nothing!"

"How about we knock off the politics for a minute?" He waited for Tsagaan to nod, and Elena reflected that despite his disdain for Greg's diplomacy, Çelik was a solid negotiator himself. "Here's the reality, Tsagaan. It doesn't matter how long you hide here. This isn't a place you can leave undetected. Neither is it a place you can perpetually defend. I can't say what Central will say about the colonists, but you and your tribe? They will have to prosecute you."

"Because you lost a few members of your crew."

She had to be provoking him deliberately. "You can deflect all you want," he said. "You know I'm telling you the truth."

Tsagaan turned her back to Raman and paced across the

small room. "What will Central do," she asked after a moment, "if I tell them that not all of my people knew what was going to happen?"

"You're asking for mercy."

"I'm asking for justice. The mistake was mine. I will not have my people suffer for it."

"So you would prefer that we, perhaps, pretend that nobody died? That you didn't destroy a Central starship in full view of the entire sector? That we decide on a punishment based on—what, kidnapping? Jailbreak?"

"Our goals have been the same for centuries. It is not unreasonable to expect you to recognize that we have not changed."

"What about your patron?"

Her face closed. "What of them?"

"If you could give us something we could use—"

"They would never hire us again!"

"After what happened, Tsagaan, would you really take more work from them?"

"Look around you, Central. This is what we are doing with their money. We are helping these people. What did *you* do for them?"

Elena couldn't keep silent at that. "Everything they asked," she said.

Çelik shot her a glare, and with a small shock she realized that, in this conversation, *he* saw *her* as the problem. He turned back to the raider. "I expect, Tsagaan, that you're smart enough to recognize our dilemma. Beyond politics, we have only your word that these colonists didn't know what would happen. But they do now, and no one has signaled us, despite the fact that you can come and go from this place." He paused, and in that moment, Elena knew what he was going to ask. "But there may be a way Central would be willing to listen to you."

Tsagaan looked over at him, frowning. "What would that be?"

"Give us MacBride."

Elena felt her temper flare at him again, but her annoyance didn't prepare her for the raider's response: Tsagaan laughed out loud. "Absolutely not."

"He's the one who consented to the jailbreak. He's the one who can tie all this to Ellis. If you give us MacBride, we might be inclined to assume the scale of the attack was just stupidity."

Tsagaan shook her head. "You don't know who you're dealing with," she told him; but she didn't sound angry. She sounded resigned.

Çelik frowned. "He's that valuable to you?"

"He is everything to us."

"Why?"

But that was all they were going to get from her. "If Ruby is unacceptable to you," she said, her expression closed, "we have others who serve as adequate medics. You should allow them to help you. If you do not threaten us, we will not kill you. You have my word."

She walked out, Badenhorst at her heels, and they were left staring after her. Elena met Çelik's eyes; he looked as puzzled as she did.

They were left alone for a while after that. Çelik stretched out and closed his eyes; Elena, never assuming he was asleep, left him to his thinking.

I don't want him to kill anybody, Dee had said to her the night before. *It's not who he is. It would destroy him.*

Don't you think that's what he wants? Elena had asked.

She had taken up nearly an hour ranting at him, furious with herself, disoriented and frustrated, unable to see a way out of the mess she had made. Dee had done what he always did: listened, always with kindness, always with the assumption she would figure it out. And then they had talked at length about their respective captains, and how they were going to see them through this mission. Dee had looked after Greg for her; she had a duty to look after Çelik in return.

When the door opened again, she jumped to her feet, instinctively moving in front of Çelik; but this time it was only Ruby, standing in the door frame, hands open before her. "I'm sorry," she said, "I didn't mean to startle you."

Leisurely, the picture of unconcern, Çelik sat up, swinging his legs to the floor. "You'll have to forgive Commander Shaw," he said. "She's a little jumpy, what with all these people threatening to kill us."

"It seems to me," Ruby said quietly, "that you were the one trying to kill."

"Can you blame me?"

"He didn't realize how bad the attack was, you know."

Well, isn't that convenient, Elena thought. "What about you?" she asked, too annoyed to pursue the subject of MacBride. "I assume these people know you've been outside this place. Don't they care what you've been doing?"

Ruby looked less exhausted than Tsagaan, Elena decided. Those huge eyes of hers were calm, but the set of her lips suggested resignation and sadness. Elena wondered why she wasn't angry. "Of course they care," Ruby said simply. "They're family."

"Why didn't you tell anyone they were here?"

"I swore not to." Ruby took a step into the room, letting the door slide closed behind her. She had not, Elena realized, grown much since she had left Canberra: she was smaller even than Jessica. "What happened back then was unfortunate. But I had no choice."

"No choice but to trap Treharne, you mean." Elena wanted to hear her admit it.

At that, Ruby looked away. "They were going to kill me."

"Surely they would have eventually anyway."

"Would you die," Ruby asked her, "for a stranger?"

"That's actually part of my job description."

"Would you die for us?"

Elena considered. "That depends on how much you knew about the Syndicate attacking *Exeter*."

To that, Ruby had no response.

"Why did you leave this place?" Çelik asked her, trying another tack. "Why were you on the surface that day?"

Ruby seemed far more comfortable with Çelik's questions than Elena's. "I had a fight with my father," she said simply, "and I ran away, and I got captured."

"You said nothing to us about that," Elena said. Ruby had seen all of it, had heard all of their conversations. She had to have known they were looking for survivors.

"I wasn't allowed to tell."

Well, that lacks perspective. "People were *eating each other,* and you weren't allowed?"

"No one off-planet could know about the shelter," Ruby told her. "We couldn't risk letting anyone in, even strangers. We knew what was happening, and how easy it was for people to go mad. Even if I'd tried to go back—they wouldn't have let me in."

Elena digested the implications of that. "You left those people on the surface to die *on purpose?*"

Ruby shot her a hostile look. "It was a lottery. We all agreed to it."

"You abandoned them. Your own people. To become—" She couldn't say it. "What they became."

"We think it was the atmosphere," Ruby said, more subdued. "Something in the malfunctioning terraformer, maybe. Something that caused hallucinations, or maybe brain damage. If you hadn't found me, it would have been me, too."

"Why did you come down here in the first place?"

"We knew what was happening. We could see it. And we knew nobody would help us."

"How could you know that? You *never once* called for help."

"You don't understand. We—"

"Stop." This came from Çelik. "You're right, Ruby, she doesn't understand. Commander Shaw lives in a different universe." He was staring at Elena, and this time she took the hint and kept her mouth shut. "So maybe we can get back to Tsagaan, and what's going on here."

Ruby looked nervously between them, her eyes settling on Çelik as she spoke. "I don't know all of it," she said. "She's been careful about who she talks to, but I overhear things."

"And Badenhorst shares information with you."

Ruby nodded. "He's not part of the inner circle, but he gets more than I do. Ellis sent her those drones as prepayment, and gave Usovicz the data on how to use them. When he failed—when they tore the ship apart—he did what was right."

"Allowed her to kill him?"

"He left the tribe open to retaliation by a major organized power. He committed suicide. It was his job. She—" Ruby swallowed. "She's angry about that. Not at him, but because it happened."

"She's not just angry because we're coming after her," Elena said. "She's had time to leave, but she's waiting here."

"Well." Ruby shuffled her feet. "I'm not completely sure about this part, but—I don't think she's been paid, and she doesn't want to leave until she gets the money."

"What profit is there in staying?" Elena asked.

"Even if Ellis has the tech to get in here where we don't," Çelik pointed out, "they can't zap themselves through that atmosphere with no warning. Assuming they need MacBride alive, she's got some leverage, as long as she's willing to kill him." He looked up at Ruby. "Is she?"

Ruby nodded.

"And her tribe, these raiders. These are the people you have all trusted for decades," Elena said.

"It's not like she's happy about killing people," Ruby said, defensive. "She only does what's necessary."

And isn't that a familiar argument? "Do you know why Ellis wants MacBride?"

Ruby's head shake was confident. "I don't think Tsagaan does, either."

"So she just wanted the money, then?"

"It's not like we don't need it."

"You think she did this for *you*?" Elena was incredulous. "Never mind the fact that the Syndicates have never done anything for anyone but themselves—you *don't* need the money. All you need to do is tell people you're here."

Ruby drew herself up and glared. "And Central would help us? With the surface the way it is? They'd pull us out of here like digging moles out of a garden."

"Ruby." Çelik's voice was quiet, almost gentle. "You're right. Central isn't going to help you. But if you help us, it's possible they won't kill you outright. Because what they'll do, if they can't detain the people responsible for what happened, is they'll drop enough nuclear ordnance to turn this planet into radioactive glass, and they won't waste time sorting the colonists out from the fugitives first. "

Ruby turned to him, unmoved. "Those people you lost, Captain. Would you sell them out just because they made mistakes?"

"No," he said readily. "But I wouldn't hide them from the law, either."

"*Your* law."

"I'm betting you weren't raised to think murder was acceptable, no matter how close you were to those raiders."

But Elena wasn't interested in convincing Ruby of anything. "I still don't understand why Tsagaan didn't just kill us," she said.

"She needed information," Ruby tried.

But Elena shook her head. "MacBride saved my life by telling her I was a mechanic. Tell me, Ruby: Why does it matter to Tsagaan that I'm a mechanic? Granted, your ventilation system sounds in desperate need, but you can't tell me nobody else can fix it."

Ruby's fingers knit together anxiously, and it seemed the most honest gesture she had made so far. "We have something that we'd like you to look at. To examine for us. To repair, if you can; but mostly we want to know what's wrong with it."

" 'It'?"

"My father," Ruby elaborated, "was the expert. He spent seven years with it, and couldn't find anything. When he died last year, they asked me to come back; but I'm nothing like the mechanic he was."

"What do you mean," Elena said, "that he couldn't find anything?"

"We know it broke," Ruby went on. "We know they all went bad. But after all this time, we haven't been able to figure out why. You're right, Commander Shaw, we don't want to be stuck down here. That thing is our best chance at a future, at some real autonomy again."

Elena thought of the storms and the toxic rain, the atmosphere waiting to shrivel the lungs of whatever tried to breathe it. "You can't be serious."

And once again, it was Çelik who filled in the blanks. "Connect the dots, Shaw. She's talking about a terraformer. They've preserved one of the terraformers that tore this place down, and Ruby wants you to fix it for her."

CHAPTER 40

Orunmila

D o you have a minute, Captain Foster?"

"No."

Greg kept his back to Keita, his eyes never leaving his drink. Back on *Galileo* he found he could always clear his head in the pub, even after he had given up alcohol, but retreating to *Orunmila*'s bar had been a mistake. He had ordered soda water, which he did not want, and had spent the last twenty minutes watching bubbles creep up the sides of the glass and vanish. Liquor had never made him stop thinking, but it had been very good at blunting the ragged edges of the worst of his thoughts. Now, completely sober, he kept thinking of Elena and Keita and *Galileo*'s silence, all in turns.

When the meeting had broken up, he had taken a moment to comm Andriya Vassily, who eased his fears a little. *Cassia,* she told him, had just finished offloading the wounded at Aleph Three, which had taken longer than she had hoped; but she expected to be able to rendezvous with *Galileo* in a few hours. In addition, she told him that the readings at *Galileo*'s location were normal. "No other ships, no debris or radiation, and exactly the heat reading you'd expect from an idled starship. I talked to Commander Lockwood earlier, Captain, and I don't think you need to worry." Captain Vassily wasn't one for casual compliments; he would have to remember to tell Jess what she had said.

Once he could speak with Jess again. Until then, he would have to find a way to quiet that amorphous unease creeping under his skin, aggravating his existing agitation.

He kept seeing Elena, the raider swinging a rifle at her head, her profile growing smaller as Keita hauled him away from her. It would be so easy to let the anger overwhelm him again. Keita knew nothing. Whatever she had taken from Keita the night before, whatever she thought she saw in him, Keita didn't know her, didn't know what she needed, didn't know how little she understood her own vulnerabilities. Greg's need to get back to her was uncomfortably physical, his muscles tense, adrenaline needling every nerve ending. He had to remind himself over and over again that they needed to wait.

Five minutes talking with Abanov, the captain of *Aganju*, was enough to convince him that their speculation about colony survivors was likely correct. *Aganju* had made frequent visits to Canberra as the fall of the colony neared. The population had been thinning rapidly, and becoming increasingly hostile; but the colonists had repeatedly refused even temporary evacuation. They had, of course, gone mad in the end; but they had not begun that way, and Abanov reported that their refusal had appeared unanimous.

The possibility of an existing colony meant a lot of things, including that Central's intelligence system had failed.

Surprise, surprise.

Keita interrupted his brooding. "I'm still a part of this mission, sir."

Dammit, the man wasn't going to take the hint. "I'm not sure what you are, Mr. Keita," he said levelly, "but I am certain you are interrupting."

Apparently after working for Çelik for his entire career, Keita wasn't going to be put off by one of Greg's icy moods. "If we're going to go back down there," he said, "you need to tell me where we stand."

"I don't need to tell you a damn thing, Mr. Keita." Greg kept his eyes on his glass, but he wasn't seeing it anymore.

He heard Keita shift. "Do you want to hit me again, sir?"

"Of course." His arm still ached; he had not returned to Doctor Xiao's disapproving ministrations.

A small sound; it might have been laughter. "You and Captain Çelik aren't so different, you know. Neither one of you understands her at all."

Greg's hands closed into fists. *Oh, please,* he thought. *Keep this up, and I will hit you again, and you won't get up this time.* "I trust, Commander, that you're not feeling the need to dictate to me how I deal with my officers."

Keita was silent for a moment. "I take it back," he said at last. "He's not nearly as blind as you are."

Greg stood and turned; Keita, standing a meter behind him, stiffened, his posture wary. "You do not get to say one word about her, do you understand?" Keeping his arms at his sides was almost impossible. "I do not care what you were to each other. I do not care what you *are* to each other." He thought, if he said it often enough, it might become true. "The way I see it, you have tried to kill her twice, and if she's hurt, so help me, I will disconnect your head from your body with my bare hands."

Keita didn't even have the sense to look afraid. "Does that help? Thinking about killing me?"

"Yes." It didn't. Not at all.

"Then do it." Keita spread his arms. "You stand there and talk about it, you punch me in front of Captain Shiang, you think it'll solve all your problems. I want them back, too, Captain, and yes, I would give my life for them. Just like you would."

For one moment, Greg indulged the thought: in his mind, his hands closed around Keita's neck, and twisted. His imagination stopped there, though. He had seen people die. He had killed in combat. But he had never killed anyone in the heat of rage. Rage had always driven him, since he was a child, and it had never driven him toward anything good.

He swore, and turned away. He wanted to roll back the clock and trade places with Elena, to be the one who fought with Çelik, to be the prisoner instead. He wanted to have said something different to her the night before, something that would have made her stay, something that would have helped instead of driven her to Keita. Something that would have made this whole day play out differently. Keita was not the one at fault.

There was nothing he could like about having a clear head.

Eventually Keita cleared his throat. "Is that the only stuff they sell in here?" he asked.

Greg looked down at his glass. "I don't think so."

"Mind if I join you?"

Greg shook his head.

"She stood out from the beginning," Keita said, his fingers curled lightly around a crystal glass holding a splash of dark liquid. "Usually the new ensigns, they're kind of like a litter of puppies, you know? All barking at each other, jumping up and down panting over the same bullshit you know they'll be sick of in a month. I had trouble remembering names most of the time; I'm lousy with faces until I've known someone a few days."

"Nicknames," Greg guessed. "Is that why you call her Songbird?"

Keita smiled, looking vaguely embarrassed. "We—me and some of my friends—came up with that one back at CMA. Someone pretty and entertaining, but not too bright."

"Did she know what it meant?"

"Wouldn't have annoyed her so much if she didn't."

So from the start, Greg realized, he had wanted to get under her skin. He wondered if Keita had recognized it as flirtation.

"She was never a puppy like the others, though. She always hung back a little. Watching everyone. And she always remembered what you said, sometimes word for word."

Ah, yes. That one I know.

"You meet people in this business sometimes," Keita continued, "and you know they're going somewhere. Not like the folks who are always going to be grunts, doing security or crypto or mechanics or something and maybe make lieutenant, or LC if they kiss the right ass. Those people are never going to be in charge of anything, never going to set the pace."

Greg had to raise an objection to his characterization. "They're just as critical as the leadership. Maybe more so."

"I know that, sir," Keita said, and his eyes were clear and full of self-knowledge. "You know what Captain Çelik said to me once? He said that people with too much imagination had no place in the ranks. He said if they weren't in command, they were dangerous, because they could never just shut up and follow orders."

And wasn't that Elena down to her socks? "So tell me, Commander Keita," Greg asked, "how did you get to be Çelik's second-in-command?"

If Keita was bothered by the implied insult, he did not show it. "That's what I asked him when he offered me the job. He said, 'Because you're loyal to me.' I said, 'Everybody's loyal to you, Captain.' And he laughed."

"How'd you take that?"

"That he's pretty sure I'm stupid, but he thinks I might be useful."

"And this doesn't bother you at all?"

Keita sipped the liquid, and Greg felt a sympathetic, aching echo of warmth down his own throat. "I know myself pretty well, Captain Foster. I know I'm not made for command. But I trust Çelik, and if he thinks this is the best place for me, I'll do the best job I can."

There it was, Greg thought: that chasm of blindness that informed everything he had learned about Keita. He had a fleeting thought—*she does like them broken*—before he returned to the subject. "You must be wondering why Elena isn't my second on *Galileo*," he said.

Keita laughed again. "No, sir," he said firmly. "You forget: I know her. Captain Çelik, on the other hand, doesn't understand why she doesn't have her own ship. It pissed him off from day one that she didn't care about anything other than the engines."

Which wasn't true, either, but Greg did not want to interrupt anymore.

"I guess what I'm trying to tell you, Captain, is that Çelik sees a piece of her, but he doesn't really understand her strengths. You see a different piece of her. Maybe you see more of her. Maybe all of her, I don't know, but I don't think so. Because if you saw all of her, you would not be panicked at the idea of her down there without you."

Greg took a sip of his own drink. God, he hated sobriety. "You don't know shit, Mr. Keita."

Keita looked at him for a long time, while Greg studied what was left in his glass. "Last night," Keita said at last, "she talked to me. For an hour. Talked, sir. That was it."

It wasn't relevant. It made no difference. But some of the vibration crawling up Greg's spine subsided and he thought he might after all get through this without hitting Keita again. "That's not my business, Commander."

For a moment he thought Keita would add something, but it seemed he had the good sense to let it go at that. "Look, I know what you're thinking: maybe she's dead already. But I don't think so. They didn't shoot us, and there's a reason for that. And if she's alive? She's going to stay that way. So you and me, we need to do our part of it and get back down there to get her out."

Greg regarded the younger man, trying to figure out how much of his speech was performance. Part of his curiosity, he knew, had to do with how different Keita was than the other men Greg had seen Elena choose over the years. Apart from her PSI captain, she had gravitated toward men who were not quite as bright as she was; who were handsome, and good-hearted, and unlikely to demand much from her. She had used the word *love* now and then, but he did not believe she had loved any of them. As far as he knew, she had not been in love until last year, and then with a man that he found he could not help but like himself. And that, he knew, was at the root of his jealousy: Keita didn't fit either mold. He didn't understand Elena's choosing Keita at all.

"Post-traumatic stress," she had called the relationship. He wondered what Keita would call it.

"So what do you see as 'our part,' Mr. Keita?"

Keita drank again, then put his glass down on the table, his expression intense. "I'm no brilliant military strategist, Captain. But we don't know how many people they've got down there, and we don't know the terrain. We could send twenty soldiers or two hundred, and we might still get our asses kicked."

Which had been exactly Greg's argument to Captain Shiang. *We need to surprise them,* he had insisted. *We need to figure out how to get down through the weather. The Syndicates do it.*

To which Shiang had snapped, *For all you know, Ellis Systems has given them new nav systems along with all the other toys they have used to make fools of you.* But he could not resent the insult. Her worry was too similar to his own.

"We'll have to head down through a storm, or they'll just be waiting for us again," Greg said to Keita. "We need some kind of stabilizing signal up here, in orbit. Even so—as you say, they know the terrain. They'll see us a hundred kilometers off."

Keita leaned forward. "I was thinking about that. At the levels those power sources are radiating, they could camouflage our signal, if we came in close enough."

"These guys had twenty-odd automated fighter drones," Greg pointed out, "and a field generator that let them drop right on top of us. You think they've got ordinary sensor equipment?"

"If they had any more drones, they would have sent *them* after *Orunmila* instead of an understaffed suicide mission," Keita insisted. "And you saw the firearms they had. Whoever supplied them didn't give them everything."

It was, Greg had to admit, not a terrible argument; but he knew he wasn't trying too hard to poke holes in it. He doubted Keita had much objectivity, either. "There's only one problem," he said, and downed the rest of his soda water. "I don't know if I can trust you."

"That's all right, sir," Keita said, unoffended. "I trust you." Greg just looked at him, and he continued. "You want to send me down there unarmed, or with half your firepower, or with a suit that's set to disintegrate in twenty minutes, that's your call. I'm not in this to make you like me. I'm in this to get them home."

"What about justice?"

"We get them home," Keita reasoned, "other methods are back on the table."

Like nuking the planet. "We may need to be more subtle," Greg said. And he told him about Captain Shiang's theory.

Knowing what he did of the man, Greg half expected Keita to throw in the towel at that. Instead, Keita frowned, considering. "You know, sir, there's someone who would know what resources they have. Or at least what they had eight years ago."

I am a goddamned fool. "Ruby," Greg said.

Keita nodded. "Lanie lost track of her years ago, I know. But I don't think anyone has really tried to find her. If we can track her down, maybe we can talk to her."

"You think she'll talk to us if we tell her we're planning to attack her people?"

"She's the one who left," Keita pointed out. "Maybe she'll be happy to help."

It was far from a perfect plan. It was a patchwork of speculation and crossed fingers. But it gave him something to hope for, something to do besides pace and prowl until he could go after Elena. He nodded to Keita. "Then let's go find her."

CHAPTER 41

Canberra

Elena caught Ruby's eye. "What did your father say about this?"

The terraformer was housed in a room nearly as large as the common area, but located far away from the central hub. It was a spire-like machine, two and a half levels tall, its exterior an old-fashioned matte steel gray. Elena had studied very little meteorological engineering, but she knew the basic components of the device: analytical circuitry, power generation, waste disposal, conversion and fuel chambers. The best terraformers, given sufficient fuel, were nearly self-driving—breaking down an atmosphere's unusable elements into components it could reassemble for a number of uses. The older units, like this one, tended to be more complicated and less intelligent, producing a fair amount of waste product that required disposal. This unit was powered down, and appeared to have at least been cleaned.

"He said it was too complicated for him," Ruby replied. "His expertise was more in artificial environments. He spent a fair amount of time pulling it apart, running diags, but never found anything."

"He didn't try turning it on?"

Ruby shook her head. "It poisoned the atmosphere up there in three months. Down here, with our old ventilation system, he figured it'd take it maybe twenty minutes."

"Couldn't he just turn it off?"

"Failsafe," she said. "It's got a timer. Turn it on, and it's on for at least an hour. It was intended to prevent inadvertent over-mixing of the atmosphere."

Lots of good reasons for a deeply precarious system, Elena thought. Everything she had been taught from childhood told her it was a bad design; but she knew enough about the terra-former industry to recognize that robustness was sometimes sacrificed for utility, often for desperately good reasons.

"Is this why you didn't kill us?" she had asked Ruby as they headed through the shelter's curved hallways.

Ruby shook her head. "It's why she didn't kill *you,*" she clarified. "We wanted intelligence about what Central was up to. When she thought you were PSI, you were expendable, but as a mechanic . . . Niall had said he'd look at the terraformer for us, but even with some mechanical experience, he wasn't sure he could find out much about it. Tsagaan figured you'd help in exchange for Keita's—Captain Çelik's—safety."

"She could have just asked for my help, like you did."

And Ruby had given her a look. "Would you have helped a Syndicate raider who had just attacked a starship?"

Elena couldn't figure out her honest answer to that question.

She walked around the unit, looking it up and down, noting the access panel that was still open. "I can't promise you anything," she cautioned. "Terraformers are not my area. I understand the principles, and I can take it apart and understand how the components talk to each other; but I can't tell you I can fix it."

"That's all right," Ruby said. "If you can figure out what's wrong, that's a start."

Elena wondered what Ruby would do if she could produce that information. Even if she could fix the unit, it wouldn't mean reclaiming the surface. One terraformer would service a small, domed city on a planet like this, but it couldn't fight back the atmosphere for any reasonable area. She could not imagine Tsagaan would want a small, domed city on the surface, somewhere they could be scanned, discovered, attacked. This underground setting was perfect for a Syndicate tribe: a base of operations, invisible to their enemies, where they could hide indefinitely. Unless they intended on maintaining this shelter in addition to a city, which presented a different challenge: batteries.

"The other problem," she continued, "is a power source. Unless that ceiling opens out onto a clear sky, the battery is unlikely to have much of a charge left."

Ruby looked surprised. "If you can hook up a line, we can charge the battery," she said. "We've got plenty of power down here."

Elena stopped. Of course they did, and she should have noticed it sooner. Ventilation for this entire space—and this distant chamber suggested it was far larger than she had estimated—plus food, waste disposal, and any internal luxury systems they might have. She supposed the raiders could have brought in batteries . . . but no. They'd had decades to prepare this living space. "Is that what's on the surface, then?" she asked. "Power generators? Batteries? How are they protected from the weather?"

"I don't know what's protecting them," Ruby said. "My father mentioned some kind of reflective setup, I think, but to be honest I never paid much attention."

"How long have they been here?" she asked.

Çelik, who had been leaning against the door frame, his weight surreptitiously off of his bad leg, looked up sharply. "Why?"

Elena met his eyes. "They're dynamic," she told him. "They've been reading as constant output all this time. With reflective shielding, that means they've been adapting as the atmosphere has become more volatile." She looked back at Ruby. "When did they get here? How long have you had them?"

"Why does it matter?"

"It matters," Çelik explained, with more gentleness than Elena would have, "because they were apparently designed to power a large, permanent underground installation. If you picked them up a year before the collapse, then someone had some foresight. Twenty years? I'd be inclined to ask who was planning ahead that much."

"I—" Ruby looked thrown. She kept her eyes on Çelik. "I don't know. If they work, what difference does it make?"

Elena turned back to the terraformer. "Why didn't anyone call for help, Ruby?" Elena asked again. "They didn't even call your Syndicate friends. Did you never ask that question, either?" Elena backed away from the terraformer, her eyes scanning the walls up to the ceiling, then down close to the floor. Despite the depth of the shelter, they would have kept access to the power as low as they could. Stepping away from the terraformer, she crouched before one of the small charging stations embedded in the wall and pried it loose.

Without a power meter she was limited in what she could discover; but the exposed electronics told her a great deal. Simple enough architecture: inputs, outputs, buffers, surge protection. More sophisticated EMP shielding work than she was used to seeing in temporary setups; someone had indeed been thinking long-term. She took a closer look at each of the components, and found the materials looked clean and well-maintained.

"Have you been cleaning these?" she asked.

Ruby nodded. "It's routine."

"Are they like this throughout the shelter? How many?"

"A hundred and forty," Ruby told her. "All identical. I still don't understand why this matters."

Elena ignored her. Now wasn't the time to convince Ruby that someone on this colony had known for decades they would need to get off the surface. Despite the surface batteries, there had to be a backup system. An underground shelter dependent on active ventilation had to have a battery somewhere, regardless of the power source. If she could find the battery, she might be able to figure out how much power the place was using. Because if they were siphoning off only a fraction of what those surface batteries were producing, the batteries had been installed for a different reason.

Atmospheric reflectors made flashy shielding, but why would anyone go to that kind of trouble? They had already been excavating; they must have had the equipment to bury the things. On Jessica's map, they had been powerful, but not large. Why would they need seven of them for a few hundred people? Had they been planning more shelters? Were there others, on other parts of the planet?

Why, if they could build an atmospheric reflector, wouldn't they have put their energy into a better terraformer network?

She rubbed her eyes, and replaced the cover on the power panel. She was thinking in circles, and it was pointless. She needed more information than she was going to get as a prisoner in an underground rabbit warren. Wearily she turned back to the terraformer, and under Ruby's resentful glare, she began to pull it apart.

She found nothing.

She had worked as carefully as she could, aware of her own fatigue. The unit was easy enough to dismantle, its parts uniform for simple construction and replacement. One by one she had removed each smooth, fitted component, and dumped the logs to her comm. They all showed the same thing: normal, no errors. Some of the parts were newer than others—the mix filter had been replaced ten years ago, while some of the waste converters were more than forty years old—but it didn't take much time to scan the logs for nothing. It had been a comfortable, uninteresting, stable piece of hardware throughout its life, and yet something it had done—or its networked siblings had done—had killed people.

Or maybe, she thought, exhausted, *it just couldn't keep up.* The unit was old and unsophisticated. The simplest answer was beginning to look like the right one.

At one point both Ruby and Çelik stepped up to help her. She set Ruby to sorting the parts as she pulled them out, Çelik reading the logs alongside her. He worked more slowly than she did, and after initially putting it down to inexperience, she realized that he was growing more and more ill. He had blinked over a backup battery unit three times longer than he should have before it became apparent she would need to recheck his work. In his condition, nothing he was telling her was reliable.

The next step would be to find and disable the one-hour failsafe, but one look at Çelik changed her mind. He had gone gray, and his skin was moist, his bright eyes rheumy. She slid her spanner back into her toolkit and approached him, placing a presumptuous hand on his forehead. He twitched away irritably.

"You're feverish," she told him.

"Well, that's a huge fucking surprise," he snapped.

"If you're ill, you will make mistakes, and I can't have that." *When did he last sleep? Hell—when did I?* She turned to Ruby. "He needs to rest." *What he really needs is a doctor and a new leg.* She doubted they had that kind of equipment.

Ruby stared at Çelik, and she seemed to at last recognize the seriousness of his condition. She nodded, and helped Elena set the pieces of the terraformer aside before they left it behind.

When they got back to their makeshift cell, Ruby locked the door behind them and turned to Çelik. He ignored her, stretching out on the bunk in exhaustion, and Elena, as carefully as she could, tugged off his short boot. The prosthetic was still held together by the fraying tape Ruby had used to bind the break, but the connection to his knee, the hasty but clean graft that Bob had made, was now torn and bloody, muscle and bone exposed. Worse still were the bruised and swollen areas, some of them sickly green. The wound was infected.

"I'm going for drugs," Ruby said decisively, and left Elena alone with him.

Elena headed into the small bathroom and found a single towel and no antiseptics at all—not even soap. She soaked the towel, hoping their water purifiers were as sturdy as those fancy power outlets, and returned to Çelik. With as light a touch as she could manage, she began carefully cleaning the stump.

God, I hope this is enough. It would have to be enough.

Because she was certain, now, that getting him out of here was the most important mission she had.

CHAPTER 42

Galileo

"The weirdest thing about them," Jessica said to Lieutenant Bristol, "is that they're just sitting there. Like, I don't know, phosphorescent rocks."

They were on the bleachers in the gym, taking a break from the light battle drills Emily Broadmoor had given the infantry. Jessica had joined in, her red head coming up no higher than anyone else's shoulder, as they stretched, jogged, slung and unslung their weapons, working up enough of a sweat to stay alert but not exhaust themselves. As promised, Emily would keep them going no longer than six hours, and then they would be traded for the next shift, where the drills would start all over again.

Lieutenant Bristol nodded at her over his glass of vegetable juice. At least Jessica assumed it was vegetable juice: some green, over-nutritious concoction that tasted a bit like paste. He had, she suspected, no idea what she was talking about. But Bristol, although he would never have the mind of a cryptographer, was a soldier down to his marrow, and he would listen to his commanding officer as long as she cared to talk.

"They weren't, were they?" he asked. "Phosphorescent rocks."

It was a stupid question, but the image made her smile. "That'd be something, wouldn't it?" she said. "Big-ass glowing mountains." She shook her head. "Too powerful, and too concentrated. There aren't any rocks that give off that much of a glow, not without irradiating the whole system."

"So what could they be?"

"Without any kind of ident? Big dumb machines of some kind. Any kind, really." She shook her head in frustration. "So how do I narrow that down? How do I figure out what the hell they are? I could guess from now until doomsday."

"From what I hear," Bristol said, "that might be any minute now." But he was grinning at her when he said it, and she laughed again. *Black humor,* she thought. *Maybe morale isn't all that bad.*

She left him as the drills started up again, heading back to Greg's office and her research. The most logical conclusion, of course, was that the colonists had built more terraformers. It was possible, she supposed, even without a terraformer ident; she wasn't completely up on the tech, but she knew slave units could be produced easily with fairly common parts. What that wouldn't explain, though, was the utter failure of the climate. She'd had *Galileo* interpolate the sort of climate that would require that much power to correct, and how long it would take for the natural environment to take over if the terraformers failed. The answer was in years, even decades, depending on a number of variables. Nothing like sixty days.

It was like the old jigsaw puzzles her aunts used to dredge out of the basement when she was little: the pieces in the box didn't match the picture.

She looked longingly at Greg's chair, but elected instead to pace in front of the desk. The adrenaline was beginning to wear on her, and she needed to be careful. Battle drills and vegetable paste were not going to work forever. *Keep thinking.* "*Galileo,*" she asked, "what do we know about Canberra's registered terraformers?"

Galileo retrieved her local data. "Canberra Colony ran twelve terraformers, four each in three equidistant locations on the planet's surface. Energy transfer capacities ranged from sixteen thousand to forty-seven thousand gigajoules per second."

"Standard?"

"Current suggested terraformer standards are one hundred thousand to four hundred fifty thousand gigajoules per second."

"So old stuff."

"Canberra's terraformers had been continually adapted from the original units."

Two-hundred-year-old tech. *They sure knew how to build stuff that lasts,* she thought. "How did they keep them going?" she asked.

"Base terraformer building blocks are still manufactured for minimal transfer capacity units."

She stopped pacing. "So they just ordered up parts for these things? Officially?"

"Purchase records on Canberra show annual expenditures averaging forty-six million dec units."

"Forty-six mil—where the hell did they get that kind of money?" *Galileo* paused, reaching out for its absent connection to the network, and she interrupted it. "Never mind. What kind of income did the colony have?"

"Canberra leased temporary landing and docking privileges."

Given their location, that made some sense. "Which made them how much?"

"Five million dec units annually from commercial freighter stops."

"So that doesn't include anything they might have taken from the Syndicates."

"No."

It wasn't a bad income, but it suggested they'd had much more interaction with the Syndicates than she had thought. "Give me a list of the parts they bought over the colony's last five years, ordered by quantity," she said.

A parts list flashed before her eyes. Some of the specifics were unfamiliar, but they were the sort of things she would have expected: chemical manipulators, plain filters, sophisticated logic cores. She thought to glance at the manufacturers: Canberra hadn't skimped there. They'd gone right to the experts, bought top-of-the-line parts. Still cheaper than new terraformers, she supposed; but at the rate they'd been going through parts, they'd—

She stopped, blinking at one line.

Ellis Systems.

Not surprising, of course. Despite what Jessica knew of Ellis Systems' dark secrets, most of the galaxy knew them as a manufacturer of sophisticated and cutting-edge terraformers. Fully half the colonies in all five sectors were dependent on Ellis equipment. They had a reputation for durable, clean-running machinery. That they also enjoyed manufacturing weapons and infiltration tech behind their legitimate façade didn't change the quality of what they produced for the commercial market.

There was no reason Canberra wouldn't have bought replacement parts from Ellis, just like anyone else.

There were only three listed. "*Galileo,* what's the function of a terraformer mix stabilizer?"

"The mix stabilizer is designed to compensate for detected atmosphere when adapting gaseous environment for human habitation."

"What happens if it's broken?"

"All currently deployed models of terraformers are designed to alarm and shut down on stabilizer failure."

"Including the old ones on Canberra?"

"Yes."

The theory growing in her head was beginning to make her feel sick. "How does the stabilizer detect the proper environment?"

"The stabilizer interprets inputs from the system's impurity detectors."

"So it decides what's right and wrong based on what it's fed."

"Yes."

She began to taste green vegetable paste in the back of her throat. "*Galileo,*" she asked, "what if —"

Beneath her feet she felt an arrhythmic shudder, and the ship's warm white light was cast briefly with red. "Aft impact," *Galileo* told her calmly. "No penetration. Hull damage: eight percent."

Shit!

Canberra would have to wait. Jessica swallowed bile, and opened her comm to the rest of the ship. "All hands, we are under attack. Battle stations. Prepare to engage the enemy."

Three hours. Herrod's estimate had been off by nearly half.

CHAPTER 43

Orunmila

Ruby, Greg found, was far less difficult to trace than he had feared.

The key was learning that she had apparently, even before she left Canberra, been a trained mechanic, taking an apprenticeship with an Icelandic freighter company just a month after her arrival in Reykjavik. Her foster family had, by all accounts, been proud and supportive of her, even as she grew into adolescence and her initially good performance in school began to falter. They had continued providing her with a home and a stipend, in addition to her salary, even when she began disappearing for days at a time, even when she eventually stopped attending school entirely.

Throughout all of this adolescent rebellion, Ruby kept up her work at the freighter company with the regularity of a seasoned professional.

Greg would never have said so to Elena, but mechanics, in general, had a dodgy reputation. In part, that was due to demand: so much of how the galactic economy functioned these days was dependent on machinery, and there were an awful lot of people who didn't have the faintest idea how the necessities of their everyday lives functioned. When something went wrong, it was often an emergency, and people would pay anyone with even the slightest mechanical ability to fix the problem. Even in the Corps, good mechanics were always in short supply, in part because they rigidly filtered for ethical behavior. He was fairly certain one of the reasons Elena had made it through the Academy without excessive demerits for being outspoken was because she, like Ruby, worked like a seasoned professional at all times. Whatever her politics, whatever her personal situation, Elena knew her job and did it well. Ruby, it seemed, was cut from the same cloth.

And isn't that curious?

Ruby had saved fourteen thousand dec units by the time she turned eighteen, and the day of her birthday she had converted all of it into untraceable currency and vanished. But a good mechanic, he had learned, never really disappeared. He was able to follow a chain of faithful customers, from an aging Academy lecturer to a First Sector senator, until she surfaced again on Aleph Six.

And there he found a connection he did not expect.

A year ago, after *Galileo* had left Earth but before they had run into trouble in the Fifth Sector, *Exeter* had stopped at Aleph Six. They had stayed for two weeks: an extended liberty for a crew that had been overworked and exhausted. Corps records showed that Çelik had bankrolled the whole thing; Corps rumors suggested he had refused to write anyone up for any kind of regulatory infraction in that time. If he had been trying to buy goodwill, Greg suspected he had been successful.

Someone must have seen her.

He asked Keita first. "What did you do on that break?"

"I stayed on board," he said. "I don't like Alephs in general."

Without any way to confirm the truth of that, Greg kept searching. Shortly after *Exeter* left Aleph Six, Ruby's regular customers disappeared, and she was gone again.

He frowned. There had to be some way to trace her. "*Orunmila,*" he said, "can you search the stream for comms matching her ident?"

"Seven hundred and forty matches."

Not many for eight years. "When was the last one?"

"Eight months ago."

Right when we blew the hell out of the Fifth Sector. "Was it encoded?"

"No."

"What did it say?"

There was a brief pause, and *Orunmila* played a short audio clip of a woman's voice, high but pleasantly musical. " 'Please do not contact me again,' " she said.

"Was that sent in the clear?"

"Yes."

"From where?"

"The freighter *Sandoza.*"

Greg remembered *Sandoza,* a freelance freighter with a solid reputation. They would have been happy to hire a good mechanic. "Where were they?"

"En route to Shixin, two million kilometers from the Fourth Sector border."

En route to Shixin. Just like *Galileo* had been. Earth, Aleph Six, Shixin . . . the colony where she had grown up.

It made sense. He just had no idea why she would do it.

"Who did she send the comm to?"

Orunmila told him.

And he should have already known.

CHAPTER 44

Canberra

On some level, Raman knew he was ill, possibly dying. The fever dreams were familiar enough, flashing images from the cell where he lay, to his opulent room on Guanyin's ship, to his mother's house, spartan and clean, the tiny windows keeping out the heat of the day. He was so hot, and everything that touched his flesh made him ache; he shifted constantly, wanting to strip off his clothes, wishing for a lake to bathe in, or at least his familiar shower on *Exeter*. He felt pain, too, throbbing with his heartbeat, radiating up from his knee in great waves. Someone was moaning; someone kept touching his forehead, whispering to him. Cool fingers. Those fingers reminded him of the light touch of Guanyin's lips as she told him she wanted him to return.

Foolish woman. What was wrong with her?

He was not sure how much time had passed when he opened his eyes. The sheet beneath him was cool and dry; he had a fuzzy memory of someone changing it. There was a blanket over him, thin but warm, and someone had washed the stickiness off of his face. He turned to look across the room; Shaw lay on the other bunk on her side, facing him, eyes closed.

Ruby was seated by the end of the bed, watching him. "How do you feel?" she said softly.

Wrung out. "Better," he told her. "Whatever you put on it has helped."

"It needs irrigation," she told him. "And probably some debridement. You shouldn't put weight on it."

"You haven't taken the thing off, have you?"

Reluctantly, she shook her head. "I don't have the knowledge."

"For a tribe that's supposed to take care of you," he observed, "Tsagaan's people have fucked up a lot. But that's what happens when you put yourself at the mercy of people running on self-interest. Or selfishness."

"What's the difference?"

She was not foolish, this young woman. He thought if she had been given better choices, she might have led a very different life. "Self-interest recognizes that we're all in this together, and that I help myself when I help you. Selfishness believes that you exist only to help me. It's not a viable long-term strategy."

"Yet she's done rather well."

"Do you think? I came here to kill her."

"You came here to kill Captain MacBride as well, and he's still alive."

"Only because you kicked me."

She turned away. "I didn't know how badly you were hurt."

"You shouldn't feel guilty. You were looking after him." He could admire the impulse, if not the object of it. "And it was an effective tactic."

"I tried to stop them, you know." Her voice was so quiet he

almost didn't hear her. "I tried to get a message out. But the weather . . . it's been more unstable lately. I couldn't get a signal through, and when the storms cleared, nobody answered me."

"Who did you contact?"

This came from Shaw. She still lay on her side, but her dark eyes were open, studying Ruby's face. Raman wanted to tell her to shut up. Hostility was not going to get them anywhere. "Chief," he said mildly, "this is probably not the time."

"Whoever she contacted is responsible for the destruction of your ship."

"No!" Ruby insisted. "He said he'd tried, but he couldn't stop it. That someone had sabotaged *Exeter*'s targeting systems, removed the logic core."

Shaw sat up, looking abruptly exhausted. "The only people who know it was the logic core that was dismantled," she told Ruby, "are Captain Çelik, Captain Foster, Commander Lockwood, and Commander Shimada, my second."

"Whoever he is, he lied to you."

"He wouldn't lie to me," Ruby said stubbornly. "Central's always lied to us. They abandoned us decades ago. We had to make our own way."

"And look where it's got you."

"That's enough, Commander," he said. "Ruby, listen to me. Central never abandoned this place. Canberra pushed for full autonomy. What were we supposed to do, force ourselves on you? There was no territory in dispute, no ideological bullshit to argue over. Canberra wanted to be left to itself, and it was. We traded with you. I came here a dozen times myself early in my career. But you ultimately trusted the Syndicates to become your liaison to the outside world."

"They saved our lives."

"And at what cost? What are they doing for you now, besides bringing destruction to your door?"

Ruby was quiet, and this time Shaw let her think. Shaw, it seemed, was taking the opportunity to study him instead, and he wanted to snap at her to stop hovering. It crossed his mind that it might have been her and not Ruby who had been touching his forehead, and it brought him up short. He had to acknowledge the possibility that she was worried about him. Dislike, perhaps, only went so far.

"If I help you," Ruby said after a long silence, "will you help us?"

"We'll help you anyway," he told her. "But, Ruby, that means the colony needs to be exposed. To everyone."

She was looking at Shaw, her eyes wide, and the chasm of years between them seemed massive. "When I was a little girl," she said, "it was so pretty here. In the winter . . . it would snow for a few hours every day. They'd let us out of school for it, and we'd run around and make snowballs and dig tunnels. In the afternoons the sun would come out, and warm the snow enough to give it this hard shell of ice. We had a tunnel one year that lasted nearly until spring. Is it strange," she asked, "that I still think of it that way, even though all that's left is a claustrophobic little nest of caves?"

"It's not strange at all," Shaw said. *She has, it seems, acquired some sense.*

As Raman watched, Ruby's expression turned to grief, and all of her vulnerability became resignation. "It was Jimmy Youda who told me about the logic core," she told them.

And I defended him to Guanyin. Cold anger filled him, and

he looked over at Shaw, catching the same rage on her face. But he saw something else there as well: relief.

God, she really had thought it might have been Keita.

"He's still there," Shaw said to him, her voice tight. "On *Orunmila*. With our people."

Guanyin, he knew, was smarter than he had been. She would be watching Youda, as she had promised she would, and Keita and Foster as well. "He's contained on *Orunmila*," he told Shaw, and held her eyes long enough for her to understand the truth of it. Eventually she nodded, just a little, looking no happier, and turned back to Ruby.

"We need to go back," she said, "so we can be sure he's punished."

"I can get you out," Ruby told them. "There's a tunnel in the back, an old maintenance access port that my father put in. It's only used when ships are coming in, and there's nobody scheduled for days. I can get you in there, and you can wait out the weather until you can call your ship."

But Çelik shook his head. "I already told you. I came here to kill the ones responsible."

"Ruby," Shaw put in, "will you excuse us for a moment?"

Ruby stood, her eyes moving from Raman to Shaw and back again. He gave her an encouraging nod, and she slipped out the door.

"She was duped, you know," he said, as soon as she was gone.

"Conveniently. Always conveniently." She shifted. "Captain, we need to leave."

"You go," he told her. "I have a mission down here."

"Which you are not going to be able to fulfill in your current condition."

"Don't count me out so easily, Chief. Just because I let him go before doesn't mean I won't do it properly this time."

Her eyebrows twitched together. She telegraphed less than she used to, he realized; perhaps she had changed, a little, since he had known her before. "So you've reduced it to that," she said. "After everything they did, you snap a couple of necks and we're even?"

Anger bloomed in his heart. "We can never be even. But they will be satisfying snaps."

"Above and beyond the fact that revenge is bullshit, who are you to say that's enough?"

"I am the fucking captain of the CCSS *Exeter*, that's who."

"So you're the only one who lost anything? The only one who gets to choose?"

"I'm *in charge*, Shaw. You want me to take a poll?"

"I want you to grow the fuck up!" She stood. "Good God, you're fixated on revenge like some slighted teenager. You want to know about revenge? I've had revenge. I got to kill a man who had murdered someone I loved. I saved the fucking day taking his life. And do you know how much it felt like justice? *Not one iota.* He died, and I'm not sorry, and it changed absolutely nothing. It brought no one back to life. It returned nothing to anyone. You kill them here, with no backup, and you're not even saving the day. You are committing fucking suicide, and I wouldn't even care except you're taking justice from people who deserve it."

"You think I care if they kill me?"

"You think it *matters* if you care? *This is not about you* and your need to throw yourself off a fucking cliff! There is so much more going on here than one rogue Syndicate leader. We could make so much more of this than revenge."

He lurched to his feet at that. Forgetting, he tried to stand on the prosthetic, and had to reach out to the dresser to keep from stumbling to his knees. "And who's 'we,' Shaw? You and me? Central?" He scoffed. "This is all there is now. There is my dead ship, and there is revenge. You really think you can change me? You always were arrogant as hell. I've done this job for almost thirty years, and I know when it's finished. I know what the end-game is. I am not here for you, or for the colonists. I am here for myself, and *fuck you* for telling me what you think that means."

Surely that would shut her up. Foster may not have been able to smooth-talk her into bed, but he was sure the man had never yelled at her like this.

But she did not back down. She marched up to him until her face was half a meter from his and stared him in the eye. "You've always been a selfish prick, Çelik," she said. "Poisoning everyone who comes in contact with you. But I always respected your leadership. I always believed you knew the job."

"Is this where you tell me how disappointed you are in me? Because I'll spare you the crocodile tears."

"You exhausted my capacity for disappointment forty-eight hours after I climbed on board your ship. I don't give a shit about you and your character, Çelik. I have a duty here, too, and it doesn't involve letting you destroy any kind of case we have against Tsagaan and her people—never mind sweet little Ruby—because you can't let go of the idea that an eye for an eye sets it all straight."

He didn't care about an eye for an eye. That was not what it was about. He thought she understood that.

"My rage let me kill last year, and I don't lose a moment's sleep over it. But you know what happened to my rage?" She leaned forward, her eyes icy. "*Nothing*. It's still there. I'll be angry for the rest of my life about what happened. And my own part in it, and everything I should have done and said. You think nobody understands how you feel?"

And at that his own rage, piercing hot and raging, flooded his entire body. "Nobody *does* understand how I feel!" He pounded his fist into the dresser; the surface buckled. "Ninety-seven people, Shaw, that I was responsible for. Who looked to me for guidance and safety. They died because I *didn't see it coming*."

"You couldn't have anticipated the attack."

"*I don't mean the attack*." She had to understand. She had enough of the bureaucrat in her to know what he meant. "Why did they hand me MacBride to transport? Why all the secrecy? Why send *Galileo* into my sector when nothing was going on? They set me up, and I missed it, and because I was a goddamned fucking fool there are ninety-seven dead soldiers and my ship is gone."

It hit him, then: everything he had built, all of his ambitions, everything he leaned on, valued, loved—parted out for salvage, and destroyed.

"Do not tell me why I need to live, Commander Shaw. I do not need to live. I very desperately need to die, because what this is, what has happened—it is wrong, and you're damned fucking straight revenge won't work. I need to die, because if I don't, I will kill and kill and kill until it swallows anything about myself I ever valued. And *fuck you* if you think I'm going out alone."

And maybe now she would shut up.

But she kept staring at him, and no amount of glaring seemed to shake her. At least he wasn't reading pity from her; an advantage of being so universally disliked, he supposed.

"And what is it, sir, that you value about yourself?"

Dammit, he wished she'd stop calling him *sir*. He had no command anymore. "You think because I'm a son of a bitch there is nothing of value to me?"

"I'm not asking what you think *I* value, sir."

He wondered, though. He thought there must be something, or she wouldn't be working so hard to get under his skin. "I have always believed in the rule of law. I have always fought for what I believe to be the good of all humanity, fuck regulations when it comes down to it. Now? I do not fucking care, do you understand me?"

"You didn't kill MacBride." Her voice was steady and even. Conversational. He was aware of being manipulated.

"Ruby stopped me from killing MacBride."

"Speaking of whom," Shaw said, taking an easy step toward him, "you didn't kill her, either. Even though she admitted being in on killing Treharne."

Her eyes were so steady, so heartless. "She was a kid," he reminded her. "You can't hold her to those choices."

He expected she would argue with him, point out that Ruby had been older than he was when he had left his home, traveling alone to Earth, a planet he had only seen in vid, because the Ugandan pre-Academy program was the best in the known galaxy. But she was not thinking that way. "So your sympathy for Ruby is stronger than your need to kill."

Damned fool. "You think my warm, parental side is still somehow fighting to get out? A sweet, helpless child is enough to keep me from my revenge? If you think I'm vulnerable to sentiment, Chief, you don't pay much attention."

Still she did not shrink from him. "I think," she said, "that you are the same man you were before this disaster, before *Exeter* was lost. I think you still believe in the rule of law, and fighting for the greater good. I think you still believe Central can go fuck itself over half the orders you get, and I do not think you are a cold-blooded killer, no matter how much you want to be one."

"You are a stupid, sentimental idiot."

"About *you*?" She actually laughed at that. "Captain Çelik, I do not like you. I have never liked you. For a year I dealt with you every day, and every day I dreaded it. But I respect you, sir. Not because of your rank or your experience, but because over and over again I have seen you make the right choices." She took another step closer, close enough that she could have touched him if she chose; she smelled of machines and sweat and industrial soap, and all of the odors were comfortingly familiar. "You and I both know you can do more if we get out of here and tell the rest of the sector what is going on. You are the captain of the CCSS *Exeter*, sir. You are a decorated hero. And *everyone*—Admiralty, PSI, even those fucking raiders—will pay attention to what you say."

He did not want to listen to her. It was only his bitterness keeping him alive, only the promise of his hands around the throats of everyone behind this horror. "They took my ship," he said, shoving the words out through a tight throat.

"I know that, sir," she said, and there was genuine sadness in her face. "They will pay. I promise you."

And he took in her mercilessly compassionate eyes, and he believed her.

CHAPTER 45

Orunmila

I t's thin evidence," Foster said to Guanyin.

Guanyin paced her sitting room, fingers to her temples. She had surprised herself by managing to doze for a few minutes, but apparently the baby had sensed her anxiety. She had kicked and kicked, and Samedi had whined at the disruption until Guanyin had given up and climbed to her feet again. The puppy had patiently paced at her heels until Captain Foster had shown up to disrupt her gloomy thoughts, and he was now seated in the corner, alert, his eyes never leaving the man he did not know.

"No one on the *Exeter* crew knew of this."

"I don't know," he said. "But they wouldn't have thought much of it if they did."

She squeezed her eyes shut. "There is no reason anyone should have thought it significant."

"No."

"Why do you?" *Why do I?*

Foster's voice was quiet, drained of energy. "Why else

would she head this way?" he asked. "Never mind one bad relationship—she was a damn good mechanic. She could have found work out here, even if she'd stayed on a station. She could have had a normal life. Why would she disappear, if she wasn't going home?"

"This is very loose logic."

"I know." He waited.

She met his eyes. He should have looked triumphant; this was as close as they had come to discovering something useful. But he looked like she felt: bleak and sad and worried, and older than Chanyu.

Wearily, she commed Cali.

Cali delivered Jimmy Youda in less than five minutes. The doctor entered the room comfortably enough, his handsome face arranged in an expression of vague concern. Guanyin could detect no unease in him at all, and she wondered if he knew he was making a mistake. Cali outweighed him by ten kilos; he should, at the very least, have looked mildly intimidated. Guanyin retreated to the wall, watchful, to let Captain Foster lead the interrogation.

He might shift more easily if you question him, Foster had suggested.

Youda sees me as a child, she reminded him. *Use that, if you can.*

"Make yourself comfortable, Doctor," Foster said. He, too, acted unconcerned, but Guanyin thought anyone who didn't hear the hard edge to his casual tone would have to be entirely deaf.

Youda glanced at Keita, who stood stoically against one wall, and sat in one of her padded armchairs. Another mistake,

Guanyin thought; Youda was nearly as tall as Foster when he was standing, but with him sitting the wiry Corps captain towered over him like a giant. He was thinking, she supposed, that volunteering to put himself in a subordinate position suggested innocence.

She wondered how many years he had spent suggesting innocence.

"Is there news of Captain Çelik?" Youda asked, just the right amount of concern in his voice.

Don't you say his name. She caught Keita's eye and ran a hand over her stomach, resisting the urge to react. Rage was premature.

"Not yet," Foster replied smoothly. Guanyin suddenly felt a wave of gratitude for his unflappable glibness. "Actually, we wanted to ask you about something else."

Youda's eyes met hers briefly; he was evaluating the *we*. "Anything I can do to help," he said earnestly.

Foster crossed his arms. It should have made him look relaxed; instead, it made him look taller, and broader. "Have you had contact with anyone from Canberra over the years?"

Youda looked mildly surprised. "Why would I, Captain?"

Foster shrugged, still easygoing. "Curiosity. They were kids, both of them. The girl and the baby. Maybe you wanted to know what happened."

Youda shot Keita a quick glance. "I—" He looked back at Foster. "I wouldn't want to rat anyone out, sir."

"Rat anyone out? For what?" Foster turned to Keita and pinned him with a sharp look. "Keita?"

"It wasn't important," Keita said defensively. "I just wanted to make sure she was all right."

His shoulders had hunched, and he had curled himself away from them. *What is this?* Guanyin thought. "Did she remember you?" she asked.

At that, he met her eyes, and she did not think he could fake his surprise. "How could she remember me?"

Foster cleared up the mystery. "You're talking about the infant."

Keita looked at the Corps captain. "Of course. It was a closed adoption, and she didn't know who I was, but her parents did. I contacted them first, and they arranged for me to meet her one day when they picked her up at school."

"How did you find them?" Foster asked.

"I'd rather not say, sir," he replied.

Guanyin guessed. "Did our people help you, Mr. Keita?"

"I'd rather not answer that, either, ma'am," he said, but he looked relieved.

She glanced at Foster, who was maintaining his benign posture. "What about you, Doctor Youda?" Foster asked. "Did you ever introduce yourself to that child?"

Youda blinked up at Foster, all innocence. "Of course not, sir. And I would have discouraged Commander Keita, if he'd asked me." He managed to shoot the other man a disapproving look.

"Of course," Foster continued, "there were two survivors. What was the other child's name?"

"Ruby," Youda said. His skin began to go blotchy. "I—I'm not sure how this is relevant, sir."

Behind him, Keita was frowning. He was beginning to lose his equanimity.

"It would not be so unnatural, I would imagine," Guanyin put in, making herself sound hesitant, "to seek out someone with common experiences. Someone who had shared trauma."

Youda managed to look sheepish. "I did run into Ruby, yes," he admitted. "About a year ago. We—it was difficult, remembering. We stayed together for a little while, and then we lost touch."

"Just like that." This from Foster, icy and unforgiving. Guanyin was not sure he was performing anymore.

Youda looked mildly incredulous. "Well, you know how it is, sir," he said. "In the Corps, we move around so much. These things have a natural progression. They never last."

At that, Keita exploded. "Christ, Jimmy, that's low even for you. After what that kid went through? And what is she now, eighteen?"

"Twenty-two," Youda said, defensive. "And don't tell me it was any different than you fucking Shaw last night after eight fucking years, Keita."

Guanyin watched Foster from under her eyelashes. The revelation had clearly been designed to throw him, but she had the distinct impression it wasn't a surprise. She began to wonder how often she herself had underestimated him.

"Where did you meet Ruby?" Foster asked, as if Youda's exchange with Keita had not happened.

"Aleph Six, I think," Youda said, easily enough. "She was working as a mechanic. Piecework. Kind of aimless, poor girl. She'd flunked out of school. I can't imagine how she must have grown up, can you?"

This one Guanyin chose to answer. "Yes," she said smoothly, her voice soft but no longer hesitant. "I can." She pushed away from the wall. "Tell me, Doctor Youda, why didn't you want Captain Çelik going on this mission?"

"I told you," he said, nonplussed. "I didn't think he was fit, physically or mentally."

"And yet you did not volunteer to accompany him."

"I'm not a combat soldier." Keita scoffed; Youda ignored him. "I would have been a liability. You heard him," he reminded her. "What could I do? He was a stubborn man."

"Please do not speak of him in the past tense."

And that, of all things, made Youda finally wary.

"The thing is, Doctor Youda," Foster said conversationally, "you *are* a combat soldier. A damn good one, based on your record. Elena credits you for Lieutenant Niree's survival."

"That's nice of her, sir. But you can't help someone who doesn't want to be helped. Elena must have told you what Çelik was like."

"I have warned you, Doctor Youda," Guanyin told him. She saw his complexion go gray. Behind him, she saw Keita's hands close into fists, his knuckles turning white.

"As a matter of fact," Foster went on, "Elena's told me all about Çelik. Whatever else she thinks of him, she respects him. She did then as well. And you know what else she told me about?" He leaned forward, his height shadowing Youda from the light. "She told me about you."

"Come on," Youda said. "She doesn't know anything about me. She never paid any attention to what I thought, not then and not now."

This time it was Keita who reacted, his hands unclenching, his weight shifting forward. Guanyin shot him a look, and he stilled; yes, he was the one with the brains. "Is that why you dislike her so much?" Guanyin asked Youda. "Because she showed you insufficient respect?"

Youda held up his hands. "Look. I don't know what you two are getting at. I ran into Ruby a year ago, yes. We saw each other for a while. What does she have to do with all of this?"

"Did she tell you," Foster asked, "that she was coming back here?"

Youda's eyes widened, and his face abruptly flushed. "I—no. How could she be back here? Why would anyone come back here? How could they survive?"

"But you know the answer to that, don't you, Doctor Youda?" Guanyin asked, still soft. "You at least knew that someone was here."

"I—" He stopped, his eyes moving from hers to Foster's. He looked uneasy at last; but mostly he looked confused, and she thought he was genuinely ignorant of the details. "No. Look, she said some things. When she was falling asleep. At other times. But I didn't take them seriously."

"I don't believe you," Foster told him. "I think you took everything she said seriously. I think you just didn't know then what they'd do with it."

"They?" An awkward laugh. *An artificial laugh.* "Who's they?"

"Ellis Systems." Foster leaned back, walking behind him. Over his shoulder, Keita looked stricken, but not surprised. *Because he's put it together, too.* "Do you know my first officer, Doctor Youda? They threw her off Tengri when she was fourteen because she'd hacked into the financial data of every single government official they had. She's good. She's better than anything Ellis has done to protect you. And I'm going to have her dissect your finances." He leaned forward, his voice growing icily quiet. "So if you don't want to get thrown to Shadow Ops with nothing but that stupid grin on your face, you'll start talking, and you'll do it quickly."

No, no, no. That will not work. "If I may, Captain Foster," she interrupted. Foster turned to meet her eyes, shrugged eloquently, and nodded. "Doctor Youda, your friends at Ellis Systems precipitated an attack on my ship, and an attempt at sabotage that, although stupid and ham-fisted"—and damned if he didn't glower when she said that—"was still a direct attempt to kill my people. Captain Foster would give you to your Shadow Ops organization. I cannot say that such a solution would be my first choice. And we are, as it happens, on *my ship*."

"What are you going to do," he said, his laugh still sounding incredulous, "space me without a trial?"

Guanyin let her hand circle her belly. She did not drop his eyes. After a moment his good humor faded entirely.

"Captain Foster—" he began.

"My jurisdiction here is limited," Foster said. "So if you've got something to say, say it now and say it fast, and I'll do my best to negotiate a trial for you."

"Back home."

Guanyin wondered where home was for this rootless creature. She met Foster's eyes, and returned his eloquent shrug.

"On Earth," Foster agreed. "I'll even try to get you a nonmilitary trial. It might be possible, since your allies aren't military."

"They're not my allies," Youda said.

She had not known—not really—until he said those words, that he was guilty. She thought of *Exeter,* floating dead in space, waiting to be stripped into components. She thought of Çelik, somewhere down on that rotting world, with nothing in his heart but a whirlpool of revenge and death. She was no longer certain her threat to space Youda had been a bluff.

Her hand stilled on her stomach, and she turned away.

Foster pulled up a chair and sat across from Youda. Eye level now; no more intimidation. "From the beginning, Doctor," he said, and he took the man's confession.

CHAPTER 46

Canberra

Less than an hour later, Ruby had them settled in a utility tunnel two meters from the surface.

"If Tsagaan comes looking for you before the weather window opens," Ruby told them, "there's a ventilation tunnel about ten meters ahead. I don't know if you both would fit, but if you can, there's a good chance they won't look for you in there."

"What is this place?" Elena asked.

"They watch for ships flying in storms and signal them," Ruby explained, as if they should have figured it out themselves. "That way they don't have to triangulate with the power sources for landing."

Elena had given Ruby instructions for continuing their work on the terraformer. "You must be methodical," she had emphasized. "Make no assumptions. Ignore documentation and manufacturer's specs. Something in that machine is not where it should be, but if you start assuming you know what you're seeing, you'll miss it. Start with the pieces Captain Çelik was looking at. Verify everything, and for God's sake, take your time."

Not that it matters.

The terraformer was inert, the cause of its failure hidden for eight years. Whatever their dreams of rebuilding, the colonists would need to abandon this place one way or another. Central might have ignored them before, but now . . . the Admiralty would assign culpability, would insist on arrests, would try to remove anyone left. The wave of frustration she felt toward her own government surprised her. For Ruby, she felt no sympathy; but for the others—this was their home, and they were trying to figure out how to keep it. She could not deny she would have done the same.

"Do you think," she asked Çelik, "this has to descend into bloodshed?"

"That's right, I forgot." Sarcasm had crept back into his voice; he must have been feeling better, and she felt some of her anxiety recede. "You always were one of those love-one-another idealists."

Even in the dim light, she could see the lines on Çelik's face, the tightness in his lips. He was sitting on the floor opposite her, his injured leg extended before him. She'd had to help him through the labyrinthine hallways, but he had said nothing, accepting her assistance without protest. Pride and stubbornness were not always impediments.

Now she just had to get them off the planet.

"I'm not an idealist at all," she told him.

"You still believe in the fundamental decency of human nature. You can't get more idealistic than that."

"You always think you know every fucking thing about everyone."

"I don't know every fucking thing about everyone," he said, "but I understand you."

"Then why did you always push me toward command?" It was an old question, and she had never heard a satisfactory answer.

"If you wanted it you wouldn't have needed me to push you. And you wouldn't have left *Exeter* for some captain who was going to let you skate."

She would not get drawn into another argument about Greg. "So what I want from my own career—that doesn't matter to you?"

"You think the Corps is rolling in competent officers?" He shook his head. "Look at MacBride. Got handed an illegal directive to kill a thousand people. Didn't have the good sense to refuse that fucking order when he got it. Waited until he was on the other side of the sector instead, then fucked it up." He paused, and gave her a curious look. "Is it really that important to you?"

"Is what?"

"You *like* Foster." He said it with puzzlement. "Why does that matter?"

"According to you, I left because he'd go easy on me."

"You said you weren't thinking of your career at all."

She mulled it over, trying to give him an honest answer. "I suppose," she said, "that I need to be comfortable in my work. With the people I work with. People emulate the captain, especially down the chain of command. He—it's not so much that I like him, although I do. It's that he's familiar."

"You do know he's in love with you."

"You shouldn't talk about things you know nothing about."

"Rank doesn't have to be a problem, you know," he told her. "It never was for me. He may be a little on the emotional side, but he'd be professional about it."

God, he's trying to be helpful. She thought she preferred him as an asshole. "He's not you," she said bluntly, "and I'm not a wounded soldier."

"Ah, deflection. You're still pissed off about Niree."

"She was scared and hurt, and you took advantage of her."

"What happened with Niree was no different than what you did with Keita."

"That was completely different." Dee wasn't the only one who had been scared and hurt. She wasn't sure anyone else had ever understood that.

"Don't be an idiot. Do you really think I'd take advantage of someone in her condition?"

"I know her."

"You *knew* her, a little, for a few months before the Canberra mission. The two of you bonded over your mutual dislike for me."

She was always forgetting how little he missed. "Nobody changes that much," she insisted.

The sound he made this time was less humor than incredulity. "Do you *remember* the mission, Chief?"

"Every second of it."

"It changed *all* of you. Do you really not see that?" He was shaking his head. "Jimmy Youda may have never been full of charm, but that mission focused his rage into a deadly weapon. Savin went pacifist on me, and the bottom dropped right out of Keita. You think Niree didn't change?"

"So the affair was some altruistic healing thing you did."

"Hell, no. I enjoyed every moment of it. And I'm the first one who got to see her smile again."

Elena thought back. She had been shocked when she had realized Niree was sleeping with Çelik, and she had been unable to hide her disapproval. She had the uncomfortable realization that her childish reaction had made a bad situation worse. *Maybe I should have stuck with arguing about Greg.* "So how did *I* change?" she asked, intent on shifting the subject.

"You recognized that there were more important things than machines."

She kept silent at that. He was not wrong. She had to concede the possibility he might not be wrong about the others, either. "You said the bottom dropped out of Dee. What did you mean?" she asked. She wasn't sure she wanted to know the answer.

"Well," he replied, "to be fair, I think he never had much of a foundation to begin with. He'd just never had it tested before. A man like that needs to believe in justice, the rule of law, the cavalry arriving before the massacre. This hellish place upended all of that. His eyes were opened, just like yours. He just couldn't take it."

"And yet he's your second-in-command."

"It was either that, or shove him out of the Corps. What the fuck would Keita do if he wasn't in the Corps?" He studied her for a moment. "You saved him, you know."

"I didn't." Her reply was reflexive. Everyone made the same assumption about her relationship with Dee, and everyone was wrong. "You didn't ever think it was Dee, did you?"

For a moment his face looked old and tired. "Of course not. But I didn't see Youda, not even when he was right in front of me. The fuck-ups go back further than last week. Central fucked up when they let Canberra tell them to butt out. PSI fucked up when they didn't raise more of an alarm. I fucked up by sending a fucking survey team to a city that had gone canni-bal. Hell, I made Jimmy Youda, one step at a time."

"I can't agree, sir," she said. She had been thinking of Dee, and of herself, of all the dreams she'd had as a child, everything she had built around her vision of the Corps. "You tell me Ni-ree changed. That Dee changed. That *I* changed. And you're wrong. You are not Zeus, birthing us all out of your head. We are what we're made to be. It's just circumstances that trigger our behavior."

And as she said the words, a sequence of images coalesced in her head:

Exeter, a Central starship, the best security available: sabo-taged by a medical officer.

Galileo, her home, where she knew every access point and every vulnerability: sabotaged under her nose, in the very place that no one should have been able to penetrate.

Orunmila, attacked via an infrastructure oddity that, on a different ship, would have allowed access to centralized systems by design.

By design.

"Oh, hell," she breathed. "It's not broken at all."

To his credit, he picked up her mood instantly. "What is it, Chief?"

She scrambled to her feet, her weather watch forgotten. "The terraformer. It's not broken, Captain. It's doing exactly what it's supposed to do."

At that, he shook his head. "It's a terraformer, Shaw. It's not supposed to spew CO_2 and methane."

"This one is." It was so clear in her head, and she struggled to explain it. "And Canberra would have been the perfect testing ground: isolationist, dependent on a third-party supplier, hostile to both Central and PSI—God, they couldn't have worked it out better if they'd seeded the colony with their own people."

"Testing ground for what? You're telling me someone destroyed this planet *on purpose*?"

"Destroyed? Maybe not. But sabotaged? Hell, yes." Her mind was racing. "If you're doing stealth weapons design, sir, how long would it take you to think of using a piece of hardware that sits on more than half the colonies we have out here? You wouldn't even have to build it into the original unit. Send it an update, or a new part, on some established maintenance schedule, and it just starts doing something else. No errors, no alarms, just normal operations. Maybe even sporadically at first, so people figure the unit is just being fussy. But when nobody's watching, it's flooding the atmosphere, undoing everything that was converted a century ago. And by the time Canberra figures out what's going on—"

"—it's too late to run." Çelik was hauling himself awkwardly to his feet. "Why would they do it, though? What's the endgame?"

"I think we worry about that later," she said, moving toward the exit, watching his careful progress. "Right now, I'm worried about how this happened with a single terraformer."

"Meaning what?"

"They're networked, remember? They talk to each other. What if this one was a trigger? For seven others?"

"Chief, those surface units are *batteries*. Ruby already said so. You're telling me there are terraformers up there?"

"I was wondering why those batteries were built to generate more power than this shelter—or another dozen like it—needs for normal operations." She was making a guess, but it fit. "They were built to support something else. And if I'm right— Jess got no ident from those things, which means, if they're ter- raformers, they're dumb receivers. They'll do exactly as they're told."

He swore.

"Exactly," she said. "We've got to stop them. We have to pull the thing apart before Ruby manages to start it again."

Çelik pointed to his right. "This way. Stay well back."

They had slipped back unnoticed through the utility door and into the corridor. She let him turn the corner before her, then followed the sound of his prosthetic against the floor. She winced involuntarily every time she heard the impact. At this point, he was probably acclimated to the pain, if such a thing was possible. She wondered what he would do when she got him back. A graft would take weeks to grow, months to heal, and in his shoes she wasn't sure she would want to face the amputation that would be necessary. Still, moving the way he was moving had to be frustrating, never mind that he had never betrayed frustration.

She thought back. He hadn't, had he? Not once. She had never caught so much as passing annoyance on his handsome face. Bravery? No, she didn't think that was it. He behaved as if the injury had been there all along, as if his awkwardness and dif- ficulty were no less remarkable than stubbing a toe. Arrogance was part of it, certainly—why should the loss of a leg trouble a man like him?—but she decided ultimately it was pragmatism.

After a far longer walk than made her comfortable, they came around a corner and found the terraformer.

And Elena realized they were too late.

Ruby and MacBride stood back from the machine, looking up at its power indicators, which were one at a time turning green. All of the parts Elena had removed and sorted had been replaced. Brushing past Çelik, she rushed up to them. "You need to turn it off."

They turned to her simultaneously, Ruby looking surprised, MacBride worried. "We can't," Ruby said. "The cycle has started. Even if we interrupt it, it'll be on for an hour."

"Then interrupt it," she insisted. "There's something wrong with it."

MacBride was still frowning. "We went over it, Commander," he told her. "All of the parts were operational, just like you said. Nothing reported any errors at all. I may not have done much terraformer work in the past, but based on my experience—"

"It's not broken," Elena said. "It's *programmed* to destroy the environment."

Ruby choked out a quick laugh. "That's insane," she declared. "What kind of a machine would be programmed to do that?" And then she caught sight of MacBride's face. His expression held horror on top of a dreadful resignation. "Niall?" she said faintly.

He did not look at Ruby, but held Elena's gaze. "That would explain it, wouldn't it?" he asked. "Everything that happened here. If they planted it, if it fed bad data into the network."

But Ruby wasn't convinced. "If they'd all been spewing CO_2 or sulfur, we would have noticed. One wouldn't have been strong enough."

Çelik had limped underneath the terraformer. "Come on, MacBride," he said, "help me shut it down. The sooner the better."

"But it doesn't have enough power!" Ruby called after MacBride, who had moved to help Çelik.

"You have plenty of power, remember?" Elena reminded her. "Those power sources—did you ever go and see one yourself?"

Ruby shook her head. "They were fire-and-forget. We administered everything remotely."

"They weren't built by robots," Çelik reasoned. "Someone saw them go up. Someone knew what they were." Next to him, MacBride was busily removing modules from the unit.

"I—it would have been before I was born, I think," she said doubtfully. "But why does it matter?"

"Because they're not just batteries," Elena told her. "They're terraformers, probably dumb, designed to take orders from the master network. Possibly from this one, which—instead of terraforming the planet to accommodate humans—is amplifying the toxicity in the air. And with this one going live . . . we don't know how the ones on the surface are programmed to react. We don't know if we'll get another weather window ever again."

CHAPTER 47

Orunmila

T he key," Aida told them, "is to have a referent in orbit that'll register—at least partially—through those storm systems. The field generator provides a steady signal, at least until it starts initiating the fold."

"What'll that do to your generator?" Greg asked.

"That's the downside," Aida said, as if Greg had extracted a secret. "Initiation starts at twelve seconds, and spin-down takes another five. We can cycle like that five, maybe six times before the coolant system starts to protest."

Keita was shaking his head. "We can't strand you over this."

At that, Aida looked surprised. "Who said anything about stranding?" He looked at Captain Shiang, who had been watching the exchange in silence, her expression guarded. "Once you've triangulated, you can drop pretty quickly, even if the storm takes out your orientation sensors. Six cycles should be more than enough to get you below the storm line."

Captain Shiang turned to Yunru, who had been watching Aida's presentation intently. He met her eyes and shrugged. "It's plausible," he told her. "But it's risky. The meteorological data we've been gathering over the last several hours has been all over the map. It's an extraordinarily volatile atmosphere, and just when you think it's settling, it kicks up again. The micro-patterns in the nitrogen mix are—" He broke off. "A minute and a half leaves almost no margin for error," he summarized. "Under ordinary circumstances, I would strongly encourage us to wait for the storm break."

"And how reliable is the storm break?" This question came from Captain Shiang, and she clearly did not expect an answer. She sat up straighter, and the room's attention turned to her. "What we have here are a set of dreadful options. Aida, how quickly can you set this up?"

"It's set up now, ma'am," he said, looking vaguely insulted that she would ask.

Greg was ready to jump to his feet, but Captain Shiang held up a hand. "Even when the weather clears," she reminded him, "comms will be unreliable. We will give you your six cycles, Captain, but after that, we have no way of helping you until you contact us. Do you understand?"

Greg was aware of Yunru watching her with his worried eyes, and of Aida shifting restlessly in his chair, as eager as Greg to get started, albeit for different reasons. Keita, seated next to him, was unnervingly still, as he had been ever since they had taken Jimmy Youda's statement. He had said very little to Greg after that, and Greg knew enough to be worried. He was not sensing anger from the man, not yet; but he seemed to be bracing himself against intense loss. Under other circumstances, he would have left Keita behind, but going down alone would have been absurdly foolish.

"We understand, Captain," he said, choosing to speak for Keita as well.

"I want to make one other thing clear," she said, taking them both in with a glance. "This is a rescue mission. This is not a raid, or an attack, or an excuse to vent your spleens. Your purpose there is to retrieve our people. The remainder of this mission can be reevaluated when Captain Çelik and Commander Shaw are home safely."

Our people. Impossible, even under the circumstances, not to feel heartened by that.

Greg had wanted to take his own shuttle back down, but Captain Shiang had convinced him to take one of *Orunmila's* small skirmish ships. "She has greater firepower and more supplies," she had said, and he recognized she was thinking of contingencies. Regardless of her admonishment to focus on bringing back their captured people, she was enough of a realist to know that such a mission, even managed stealthily, was unlikely to be quite so simple. She might be nine years his junior, but he was realizing her experience with guerrilla fighters was far greater than his own.

The skirmish ship was of a type he had not seen before. He thought the shell was an old Eko, but the interior and all of the visible mechanicals were newer than anything that had been on the Eko's specs. Elena would have been able to tell him which pieces were bulk manufactured, and which would have been commissioned specifically for the model—he supposed there was no reason PSI wouldn't order their parts the same way Central did—but he was grateful that the ship had modern controls. He had flown an Eko once, when he was a kid; but that had been under his mother's watchful eye, and he had not even broken the stratosphere in it.

He would have to remember to ask Elena if she'd ever flown one. When he had her back safe, he would have to remember to ask her a lot of things.

They had briefly considered light weapons, but given the size of their ship, Greg elected to take all the firepower Captain Shiang was willing to spare. In addition to a hand weapon for each of them—two of the short-range powerhouses her people had carried into the fight with the raiders—there were four out-sized pulse rifles, and a long-distance gun secured against one of the shuttle walls. They could fire from the air if they had to, and probably take out most of a city block. He could not imagine needing such a weapon, but somehow it made him feel better to have it.

He let Keita complete the preflight while he spoke with Captain Shiang.

"There are four hours until the weather breaks," she told him. "We will give you five minutes beyond that to contact us before we send our own people down."

With the planet's atmosphere, he had no way of knowing that he would be able to signal her successfully in that time frame, even if they were safe. He nodded. "If it comes to that," he said, "let Commander Lockwood know. She'll get you some backup that you can trust." He wasn't sure who that might be apart from *Galileo* herself, but Jess would find someone.

"Between that and *Aganju,* we'll be able to complete the mission," she assured him.

Cold comfort to think that if they all died, Shadow Ops would still have its revenge.

Catching something in his expression, she smiled a little. "Do not have such little faith, Captain. You are not fighting this alone anymore. We have resources your Shadow Ops cannot touch. They lost their battle when they brought us in."

He took her in, this lean, coolly beautiful, very pregnant woman, and decided she was entirely right about that. Remembering his etiquette, he held out a hand to her; but instead of taking it, she drew herself up tall, and saluted him, as cleanly as any seasoned admiral.

"May you have the best of the battle, Captain Foster."

He straightened, and saluted back.

CHAPTER 48

Canberra

Çelik pulled his hands out of the terraformer. "I've triggered the shutoff cycle," he said, "but it's going to finish powering up first. Full shutdown will take an hour."

"Nothing's happening," Ruby said.

"We need to get out of here anyway," Elena said. "If we're right about this thing, it's not going to be detoxifying the air. It—"

She was interrupted by a klaxon, and a dimming of the lights to dark red. "*Emergency*," said a voice over the public comm. "*Atmospheric degradation detected. Evacuation required. Twenty-seven minutes to terminal concentration.*"

Shit. "Come on!" she shouted over the alarm. She rushed to Çelik and grabbed his arm, pulling him toward the exit. He stumbled, and MacBride reflexively caught him. She met the disgraced captain's gaze briefly, and together they supported Çelik toward the door.

Ruby rushed after them, still protesting. "But why would they do this?"

A good goddamned question, Elena thought. They left the terraformer as far behind them as they could go, moving toward the hub of the shelter and the exit to the surface. As they moved closer, they encountered other colonists, and even a few raiders in their brown uniforms. Everyone was headed in the same direction they were. No one tried to stop them. They were all trapped, and they were all vulnerable.

In the large central room, someone was handing out env suits. There seemed to be no real system beyond first-come, first-served, and the deteriorating env suits were handed out in tandem with the new ones. Elena caught Ruby's eye. "Are there enough for everyone?" she asked, keeping her voice low.

Ruby silently shook her head.

"Which one of you did this?"

Elena turned at the sound of that familiar voice and found Tsagaan, rifle raised, glaring at her. Elena held up her hands, palms out, placating. "It's the terraformer," she said. "We've switched it off, but it'll take time to shut down, and the ventilators—"

"I'm not worried about the ventilators," Tsagaan said shortly. "I'm worried about the power. As soon as that thing went on, our power started to fluctuate. Which shouldn't have happened, if the surface systems were engaging normally."

So she knows what they are. "That's the point," Elena told her. "They're not engaging normally, because this terraformer isn't engaging normally."

"The master unit was sabotaged," MacBride told her, "back when the colony was still on the surface. It's directing them to make the climate worse."

For an instant Tsagaan looked furious. Elena watched the

tip of her rifle nervously. She wouldn't be able to stop the raider from firing, but maybe, if she jumped her in time, she could keep her from killing all of them. She tensed, preparing—and Tsagaan dropped the nose of her rifle.

"How do we stop them?" she asked. Looking straight at MacBride.

Elena turned to him. "Why is she asking you?"

"I'll need to issue the shutdown," he told Tsagaan, ignoring Elena's question. "But if I was added to the key after the unit was sabotaged, it might make no difference."

The key? "What are you talking about?" Elena asked.

MacBride met her eyes. "It's why Ellis wants me," he explained. "When they originally contracted with Shadow Ops to do our research, S-O insisted on a binary bio key on anything they developed. That means any future development that happens, we get notified. It was meant to be a failsafe to make sure Ellis didn't sell the tech to anyone else, but I can remove it. That would free them up to use their tech however they like."

"Are you telling me S-O was part of sabotaging this colony?"

He shook his head. "No, Commander. That's a line even S-O wouldn't cross. But they did pay for weapons development, and this would absolutely qualify."

"Come on," Tsagaan told them. Pushing to the head of the crowd, she held up three fingers to the people handing out env suits. She took the bundled fabric, then turned back to the others. "Ruby, stay here, and do what you can for the ventilators. MacBride, come with me. You two—" Her eyes took in Elena. "Do you know terraformers?"

"Well enough," Elena told her.

"Then you as well." She moved to leave.

"Wait," MacBride said. "Çelik. He needs to come with us."

Tsagaan stopped, looking annoyed. "He'll slow us down. There's no time for this."

MacBride stared at her for a long moment, and to Elena's surprise, the raider relented. "Fine," she said. "But nobody waits for him, understood?"

Elena pulled on her gloves, then turned to help Çelik with his seals. She felt nauseated, and she didn't think it was the increasing concentration of CO_2 in the shelter's thin atmosphere. Terraformers had been a part of human life for centuries. Without them, most of the first colonies would have been impossible. Without them, fully a third of the existing established colonies would disintegrate, just as Canberra had, and another third would end up domed with artificial ventilation. Terraformers saved lives, built homes. They did not destroy. This was more than murder, it was perversion.

And it happened right under our nose.

Tsagaan's little ship flew rough, buffeted by the increasing winds on the surface. The raider kept it low to the ground, negotiating ruins and terrain with assured familiarity. Elena, perched on a shallow bench, gripped a handhold in the wall and tried not to think about the likelihood of this being the ship that had blasted through *Exeter*'s hull and taken MacBride.

On the bench next to her, Çelik was holding on with both hands, jaw set, complexion decidedly gray. The narrow seat offered almost no support for a man of his size, and he was forced to brace himself with his legs. He bore most of the weight on his one good foot, but the prosthetic was wedged against the wall, the angle awkward, undoubtedly torqueing the stump of his leg. She hoped whatever Ruby had given him was slow-release. All of this activity was risking aggravating his infection.

Only MacBride sat quietly, expression thoughtful, tuning out everything around him.

"These terraformers would have been built before my time," the raider leader told Elena, her hands steady at the controls. "But yes, probably by my tribe. We have built and sold them now and then. Dumb terraformers are not only more efficient; we can more easily get the parts we need. Try to get your hands on a logic core and you'll have Corps all over you in five minutes, but nobody cares if a few reclamation filters go missing."

The extra terraformers, Elena realized, had been an attempt to build a firebreak. The colonists wouldn't have known they were building it from explosives.

They crested a rocky ridge, and came upon the nearest terraformer. It was a massive duplicate of the unit the colonists had kept in the shelter: a squat, four-legged insect, legs a full level high, round body built in tiers and topped with a narrow minaret designed to deploy chemical changes into the sky. The rain made it impossible to make out more than its silhouette. Elena wondered how easy it would be for MacBride to access the controls. Despite the amount of power it was putting out, the unit itself was not lit.

Tsagaan kept the shuttle flying at full speed until they were almost on top of the terraformer. She broke hard, sending them all lurching, and dropped the ship to the ground. To Elena's surprise it hit with some delicacy, and she realized Tsagaan knew her ship very well.

She helped Çelik to his feet, and he managed to stabilize himself while she double-checked the seals on his env suit.

Tsagaan, ignoring her own suit check, slid the door open and stepped outside. Elena might have been imagining things, but she thought the sound of the wind was growing louder.

MacBride followed Tsagaan out, leaving Elena with Çelik. She waited until the others were out of earshot. "Did Central know what was going on here, sir?"

His pause was too long. "I don't know."

They left the little ship, Elena steadying Çelik as he clambered awkwardly through the doorway and onto the ground. There was no ruined city here, just rough terrain; but it was mostly metamorphic and unlikely to shift underneath him. The wind was quieter in the lee of the terraformer, but the rain was still dense, and she had to squint to make out Tsagaan and MacBride. They seemed to be arguing about something, and she tuned in her comm.

"—only thing standing between my people and death!" Tsagaan was shouting, sounding very close to frantic.

"You need me," MacBride said flatly. "None of the choices are good, Tsagaan. And this needs to be done."

"Don't be stupid. Anybody can send a broadcast signal from this thing. It doesn't need to be you."

"What's the argument?" Elena put in.

They both started speaking at once, but Tsagaan quickly fell silent. "We need to broadcast a signal to the other terraformers," MacBride said.

"I thought all we had to do was turn them off."

MacBride glanced warily at Tsagaan before he explained. "The underground terraformer won't broadcast a shutdown signal, and we don't have time to turn them off one at a time.

They're networked, but they're dumb, and they need to be synced. We need to forward the signal by hand."

Elena looked up at the massive terraformer. There was a bubble of air captured around it—similar to the artificial gravity fields back on *Galileo,* this would be the reflective perimeter designed to keep the radiation generated by the unit from flooding the surrounding landscape. "I take it the comm system is inside the safety zone," she concluded.

"Why not let him go?" Çelik asked.

"Exactly," MacBride said.

Good Lord, they've both got death wishes, Elena thought. "Tsagaan, what's your problem with MacBride's solution?"

"Ellis hired us to bring them MacBride," she said. "If we don't do it, they'll retaliate."

"More than just not paying you?"

"He's valuable to them."

But MacBride was shaking his head. "I *was* valuable to them. For the key to work, my actions have to be voluntary. I won't volunteer to help them anymore."

Tsagaan looked annoyed. "They don't know that."

"But as soon as they do, Tsagaan, they'll kill me anyway."

"You know what'll be left of you if you go into that radiation field?" She gestured up at the massive machine. "They won't even be able to identify you. If I don't have a body to hand them, they will blast the hell out of this planet without any concern about who lives or dies. You need a pulse, MacBride, or this colony really will be dead."

Elena wanted to tell them both to shut up. "Let's turn it off first," she said, "before we start wrangling over who gets to die today."

Elizabeth Bonesteel

MacBride stepped over to the terraformer, and began climbing one of its spindly legs. There was an odd sound coming from the unit, almost musical, and she realized it was the sound of the wind through the structure itself. *Wind powered.* The perfect generator for a lousy climate. That explained how the batteries held their charge. Elena waited until he had gone partway up, then scaled the reverse of the latticed leg until she was facing him. He had opened a panel and was peering into the dimly lit interior. "Do you have a number seven?" he asked her.

Wordlessly, she handed him the spanner from her kit, her eyes never leaving his.

He narrowed the spanner and inserted it carefully into the interior. "The thing about a bio key," he told her, "is that the unit needs to store all of the key data locally. It's not a lot, in terms of storage; but there's always the possibility—especially in this environment—that the decoder will be corrupted."

"Then what do we do?"

"Then you call *Orunmila,* and have her blow these things up from orbit."

And again, we run off and leave everyone behind to die. Tsagaan's shuttle had barely held the four of them. With two other ships—they might save twenty. She remembered a long-ago mission when she had told Greg *A few is better than none.* If she survived this, she would try to remember to apologize to him. "How long will it take to read your DNA?" she asked.

"If it's working, it'll be instantaneous."

He handed back the spanner, then tugged off a glove. She took that from him as well, and watched as he extended the back of his hand into the small lighted chamber. She had stopped breathing.

The terraformer made no sound, but the light dimmed from green to red. *Anticlimactic,* she thought, even as she closed her eyes, relieved.

They climbed down, MacBride tugging his glove back on, and joined Çelik and Tsagaan. Elena could see Tsagaan frowning through her hood. "Nothing's changed," she accused.

"They operate as a unit," MacBride explained. "Nothing gets triggered until we broadcast."

Elena walked over to Çelik. He stood straight, but she had learned to tell when he was favoring his leg.

Tsagaan was arguing again. "I can't have you die, MacBride. My people need you."

"Your people need their leader," he insisted. "Central fucked this planet up. You shouldn't be the one to pay for that."

"My people have already lost their leader!" she shouted. "I brought this on them, do you understand? This is my responsibility. If I take you from them, I leave them with nothing."

"If I'm dead, Tsagaan, Ellis will leave your people alone," MacBride insisted. "They're not going to make a move if there's no profit in it. And you can't do it alone. Between triangulating the signals and triggering the forward—one person won't last long enough to do it all."

"You don't—"

Before she could finish, there was a bright explosion off to Çelik's right. *Rifle fire.* "Get down!" Elena shouted to the others. Tsagaan and MacBride crouched reflexively; Çelik didn't move at all. Elena reached for her nonexistent weapon, then scanned the rocks in the direction of the shooter. They were out in the open; even with the abysmal weather, either the shooter was incompetent, or he had not wanted them dead. She looked down at Tsagaan, who shook her head. "Not one of mine," she said.

Elena moved in front of Çelik and squinted toward a low cliff. Was that the nose of a pulse rifle she saw among the rocks?

Who the hell is out here?

"Don't move!" a voice shouted.

Two figures emerged from behind the rocks and raced toward the terraformer. As they reached the base of the machine, their guns were trained on Tsagaan. "Who are you?" the voice demanded.

A wave of relief washed over her. It was Greg. Whole, healthy, and jumping to conclusions as usual.

Elena maneuvered in front of Tsagaan, blocking their fire. It was becoming a habit, she thought, standing in front of her crewmate's guns. "Greg," she said, "wait. Let her speak."

"Who is she?" he asked. She wasn't sure if his voice held more confusion or fury.

"She's Tsagaan," Elena told him, "the leader of this Syndicate tribe. And if you let her, she'll save our lives."

CHAPTER 49
....

Galileo

W eapons status."

"Low-grade close-range cannons are all up, but we've only got ten percent of our energy shooters," Ted told her.

Jessica swore and opened the comm ship-wide. "All hands, we've got incoming raiders. Weapons live, everyone. They'll likely start with our storage levels. Do not let them breach the ship." She commed Commander Broadmoor. "Emily, what's the status of our shuttles?"

"Ready to launch, Commander," Emily said briskly.

"Go," Jessica told her. "We'll cover you as best we can. If you're in trouble, get them in close and we'll take them out with cannons."

"Acknowledged."

It was a pointless admonition. The transport shuttles wouldn't be as agile as the raiders, but they carried far more weapons, and unlike *Galileo* they were small and maneuverable enough to dodge incoming fire. Emily and her other three pilots would be safer on those shuttles than the rest of the crew left behind on *Galileo*.

"*Galileo,* give me a schematic." Jessica rounded into Greg's office just as the ship projected the sensor-generated three-dimensional map of the ship and the activity around it. She saw the raider, coming about to target *Galileo's* storage levels, and she watched as two others materialized next to it.

"Targeting warning, starboard side," *Galileo* told her calmly.

None of *Galileo's* weapons discharged toward the raiders. "Ted?" She watched the three ships coalesce into close formation and speed toward their hull.

From his position in engineering, Ted said, "Wait."

"Raiders are preparing to fire harpoons," *Galileo* told her.

The raiders grew closer, and she wanted to yell at Ted, to tell him to fire, to do *something,* and in her head Greg Foster said once more: *Trust your people, Jess.*

And just before the raiders were within range, one of *Galileo's* engine vents opened, and a days' worth of heat ballast was vented toward the three small ships. They vanished in a puff of light, hot component atoms dissipating in the vacuum.

Too soon to celebrate, she thought, even as she heard cheers from the engine room over her comm. "*Galileo,* what's the status of those other—"

"Proximity detection," *Galileo* said. "Twelve emerging ships."

Well, she thought, *at least it's not twenty-seven.* "Emily, where are you?"

"Clear of the landing bay," Emily commed. "We see them, Commander." She gave a quick set of commands to the others, and Jessica saw three of them split off as the raiders scattered, circling *Galileo* like hungry cats.

One raider stayed behind, dogging the remaining shuttle, firing a focused burst. As the shuttle dodged and fired in return, one of the raider's errant shots hit the landing bay door, and Jessica watched as a piece of it shattered and spun off into space.

"Landing Bay Seven damaged," *Galileo* said. "Cannot close the outer bulkhead."

Shit. Whether or not the raiders took advantage of that would depend on whether they were in it for theft, or to take the whole ship. "Lieutenant Bristol? Are you down there?"

"Yes, ma'am." Bristol was shouting over alarms; she could hear voices behind him. "We've got fire down here. We're—"

"Get everyone out," she told him, "seal it, vent it, and stand your ground. Don't let them in through there."

"Acknowledged," he said, and she heard him begin shouting to his people before he disconnected.

She tried to remember what they kept in that landing bay. They had been repairing a shuttle there just that morning—was it still there? Well, whatever it was, they could take it out of her pay.

If I survive.

One of the shuttles took out two raiders with a pair of neat, efficient shots, flying through the wreckage to skim *Galileo*'s hull. The raiders regrouped into two groups of five, and *Galileo*'s shuttles followed them. Another three raiders were hit, and they broke off, folding themselves into the FTL field as Jessica watched. *There's too many of them,* she thought, remembering what Greg had told her. *They don't fly in groups this big. They don't work with each other. There's too many of them . . .*

One of the shuttles took a hard hit to the nose and began spinning, end over end, out of control, drifting rapidly away from *Galileo* and out of their crippled comm range. The raiders let it go, two of them splitting off toward the storage levels again, the remaining five turning back toward the landing bay. "Bristol?" she shouted. "You're getting company. You're—"

Another shudder went through the ship, harder this time, and her schematic disappeared.

Shit.

"*Galileo?*"

The ship was silent.

Jessica grabbed the heavy pulse rifle and dashed out of the room. Five raiders, heading for their open landing bay. The two harpooning their storage levels she felt certain the infantry could handle with little trouble, but five ships—especially when the raiders were willing to take losses—had the potential to do far more damage. They could shoot through the bulkheads and get into the ship's main access corridors. They could fly into *Galileo*'s side as they had *Exeter*'s, and take her to pieces.

If you think I'm sitting at a desk while you tear up my home, she thought furiously, *you fuckers can kiss my cryptographic ass.*

Another shudder went through the ship as she ran toward the landing bay. She inhaled; they still had air and lights and gravity. It was possible the shot had only taken out their external comm boosters; close comms might still be possible. If *Galileo*'s self-repair system was still working, they might have it back online in a few minutes.

Which they didn't have.

She rounded the corner and saw two platoons lined up, one behind the other, pulse rifles at their shoulders, aiming through the gravity field into the shattered shuttle bay and out into space. Internally she quailed—she had never seen her own home like that, ragged edges, pieces missing, floors where she had wandered idly on her way home from shore leave shattered and drifting in the weightless vacuum—but all she did was take her place next to Bristol, slinging Greg's heavy artillery onto her shoulder.

"Can we blow them before they hit us?" she asked.

Bristol's lips were set in a thin line. "Damn straight we can, Commander," he said.

He was not a brilliant thinker, Bristol, but in that moment she thought she was in love with him. "Let's knock them out, people!" she shouted.

The small ships were closing, and they fired en masse, some of the shots hitting the edges of the ruined landing bay. Jessica aimed as best she could, hearing the whine of the rifle's machinery in her ear, and there may have been shouting around her, and possibly fire, because the raiders were shooting as well. Something hit the wall behind her, and she was suddenly deaf, and she saw one of the raiders fly to pieces, and then a second; and the third was coming closer and closer, soon it would be too close even if they destroyed it first. "Retreat!" she shouted, but she couldn't hear herself, couldn't hear anything, and she kept firing, wondering why she wasn't running, as she had ordered the others to do. Except that maybe, maybe she could hit it, just one hit in the right place, it was already looking battered, they were so close . . .

Something flared outside, and the raider took a blast on one side and flew to pieces. Jessica was gaping at it, wondering why someone was pulling at her arm; and then she saw it: a piece of the raider, a wing or an aileron, small at first, but getting bigger, its edges all flame, and someone pulled her sharply and something hit her hard and the silence in her mind went black.

CHAPTER 50

Canberra

"Foster," Raman said, "give me your other rifle."

Foster still had his gun leveled in Tsagaan's direction, unmoved by Shaw placing herself between him and his target. Raman would have put money on Foster making some kind of emotional display at finding her alive; yet here he was, covering the enemy, refusing to budge until he understood the situation. The man might make a soldier after all.

Someday. When he grew up.

"Shaw." She caught on immediately, stepping forward—still in the damn line of fire—to put her hand under his elbow. Leaning on her heavily, he hobbled over next to Foster. He reached out and hit the release on the strap of the extra rifle, then slung it easily under his arm.

Foster let the nose of his rifle drop. Raman thought he was glaring at his engineer. *In his shoes,* Raman thought, *I'd be glaring at her, too.*

"Keita? You okay, son?" Raman asked.

"Yes, sir." Keita was also aiming at Tsagaan, his angle avoiding Shaw, but his stance was far less tense than Foster's had been. Keita always was solid in a shootout.

"You know about Youda?"

At that, Foster turned toward him, but Raman did not take his eyes off the Syndicate leader. "Yes, sir," Keita replied. He sounded miserable. Raman wished he might have spared Keita the betrayal of his friend.

"Youda's under arrest," Foster said. His voice had softened, and Raman knew he was talking to Shaw. "Captain Shiang has got him."

"Is she going to space him?" Shaw, unlike Keita, spoke with real bitterness. Well, she knew so much better what it was.

"We do not have time for this," MacBride said.

"You do, MacBride," Raman told him. "You're going back with them. I'm staying with Tsagaan."

He had thought, when MacBride had insisted he accompany them on this expedition, that Tsagaan understood. Shaw had promised him justice; he trusted her to deliver. By bringing him to the terraformer, Tsagaan had given him a chance to make up for the mistake that had lost so many people their lives. His last chance.

Tsagaan scoffed at him, and he thought she was genuinely annoyed. "And how are you going to climb, crippled man? You couldn't even get to that rifle without help."

"I'll do it." It was the last thing he would do, but he would do it.

"You will slip and fall and die, and I'll be dying for nothing."

"Then go back with MacBride. You'll get a fair trial, for what it's worth."

At that, MacBride interrupted. "Come on, Çelik. If you ever

believed that, you have to know now it's not true. None of this was fair, and none of it was just. But you were right. I threw your people into the line of fire, and I need to pay for that."

"I never should have agreed to take you on board in the first place."

"You think I don't know they gave you a direct order?" MacBride shook his head. "You had no reason to anticipate any of this. Hell, Shadow Ops didn't think of it, either. They figured they were tossing me in a hole, where I'd never bother them again. It never occurred to them Ellis might find a way to use me." He paused. "Don't let them use me, Çelik. Either of them. Let me make a decision, for once in my life, that isn't a reaction to something someone else wants me to do."

"This is my job, MacBride. My ship. My command." *My mistake.*

"Commander Shaw, if you could please move."

Despite Raman's anger, despite his weapon, Tsagaan's request was polite. Composed. Shaw looked momentarily uncertain, but she took a reluctant step sideways, out of Raman's line of sight.

"Captain Çelik." She pronounced his name crisply, her consonants as clean as if she had been raised on Tethys next to him. "My life is forfeit to my own people. That I may feel some honor in the choice of how I leave this world is unimportant to them, but like Captain MacBride, this is my choice. I must respect him in his. And we can't give you ninety-seven lives. But for our two . . . we might buy three hundred."

"I don't care about MacBride's choices. This is down to me."

"You are not guilty, Captain Çelik. And you have a chance to do some real good here. These people—you can help them. MacBride could do nothing—he'd just end up a prisoner again."

"Which I won't accept," MacBride told him.

"The colonists don't matter to me," Raman said.

"I've seen you with Ruby. Even knowing that she betrayed you, that she led us to your ship, you've been kind to her."

"She's a child."

Tsagaan's eyebrows shot up. "Sentiment. She is no less culpable than any of them. So you will forgive me if I can't see you as revenge-mad."

"You're blind, then."

She took a step toward him then, and the barrel of his rifle pressed against her. If he fired, she would go up in flame and ash in an instant. " 'True revenge,' " she quoted, " 'isn't about killing. It's about destroying what your enemy has built.' "

His mother had told him that over and over again, when he felt angry and helpless about the bullies at school. He had seen, so often in his life, the truth of it. "You were used," he told her.

"We were."

"If you leave your people, they'll still be used."

"Not if you look after them, Captain Çelik."

"You want me to protect a pack of Syndicate raiders?"

"You've seen this colony, Çelik," MacBride said. "Small, underground, precarious, yes. But it's a community. A family. They've functioned all this time because of Tsagaan's tribe. Surely that's worth something."

"They have done nothing less than what I have asked of them," Tsagaan added. "They are good men and women. Your Central Gov may choose to prosecute them for what was done to your ship, and they will stand bravely in the face of whatever trumped-up justice you provide. But if you allow them to, they will stay here, and work with the colonists. This has been their home, as much as they've had one. I would ask you, Captain, to allow them the choice."

His people had had no choice. He had taken their futures away. They had stood, shoulder to shoulder, and died under his command. It was not the same; she had twelve left, perhaps fewer, and whether or not they had been part of the raid on *Exeter,* they were criminals. Career thieves. Their lives did not matter.

Twelve lives.

He lowered the nose of the rifle.

Tsagaan pulled off her hood and quickly stepped out of her suit as MacBride turned to Shaw. "I hate to ask, Commander," he said, "but this'll go more quickly if I have a proper toolkit." Wordlessly, Shaw unstrapped her spanner kit and handed it to him. As Tsagaan handed her suit to Raman, MacBride tugged his off and handed it to Shaw.

MacBride strapped the kit securely over the sleeve of his crumpled civilian clothes and turned to the terraformer. "I've no idea what it'll do once it syncs," he told them. "I've never seen a terraformer this powerful before. I don't know if the storms will disappear or get worse, but there's likely to be some kind of chain reaction. You'll want to get as far away from here as you can; preferably leeward."

"Of what?" Shaw asked, and Raman saw MacBride's face twitch into a grin.

"Point taken."

Raman watched as Tsagaan turned to MacBride, and then the two walked side by side toward the massive machine. Behind him, Shaw had a quick conversation with Foster; a moment later, Keita had dashed off into the rocks to where Raman assumed they'd left their ship. Foster turned to him.

"You should go with Keita," he said.

Raman didn't answer. "Do you agree with Tsagaan? That no one is responsible?"

And of course it was Shaw who answered him. "No, sir, I don't."

"You think we're all responsible."

"I think *Ellis* is responsible. And I think we made it easy for them."

Yes, he thought. *That's it.*

She put a hand on his arm. "We need to go, sir."

Tsagaan reached one of the terraformer legs and began scaling it, brisk and agile, MacBride at her heels. She swung herself onto the unit's first level, then walked around to the other side where they could not see her. MacBride followed, his steps steady and confident as he disappeared. They would be feeling it already, he supposed; bright and hot and unpleasant.

Not enough, he thought. *Never enough.* He let Shaw tug him back toward the raider ship.

Shaw took the pilot's seat. Raman levered himself onto one of the benches. He had half expected Foster to try to help him, but the man surprised him a second time that afternoon by studiously ignoring him. When he saw Foster slip automatically into the copilot's seat and start bringing up the ship's oddly configured dashboards, though, he understood: Foster was following his pilot's lead, performing long-familiar tasks. Raman's struggle to make his way across the floor of the raider's ship wasn't even on his radar.

"How fast can this thing go?" Shaw asked.

Foster scanned the unfamiliar indicators. "No idea."

"Strap in, Captain Çelik," she said.

"Shut up and fly," he told her.

She lifted them off, angling them upward toward the roiling clouds. Keeping them within thirty meters of the ground, she threaded the ship around hills and ruins, her eyes never leaving the schematic that showed the shelter ahead of them. Raman thought of the raider and MacBride, and wondered if he should have waited. If they failed, if the heat and the radiation killed them before they had a chance to link the units, Raman and the others would have to airlift as many as they could as quickly as possible, no matter what the colonists wished. It occurred to him, as he watched the bleak landscape streak past, that he had not expected to be returning from this trip. He had no idea what they would be facing back at the shelter. He had not thought of it at all.

He had not thought of anything.

He heard a distant thunderclap, and Shaw swore eloquently. "Hang on," she shouted to him, and opened the shuttle's throttle.

And before he had a chance to grip the side of the bench, they were hit with the percussion wave.

CHAPTER 51

Elena shot the little ship upward and away from the rocks, letting the blast of wind toss them violently back and forth as their guidance systems fought to keep them headed toward the shelter. She had a moment, as she bounced and jerked against her safety harness, to admire the build of the ship: it kept its orientation with much less navigational interference than she would have expected, the metal body flexing easily. She didn't expect the structure would have much shelf life—anything taking this sort of abuse would need replacing every five or six years at the most—but for the kinds of flying the raiders tended to do, it made a powerful, maneuverable little vehicle.

Which would shatter if they hit the rocks; but she had come to understand enough about the raiders to know that durability would not be a priority.

After about ten seconds the winds died down as the storm veered off to starboard, and she steadied the ship, settling back into her seat. "Captain Çelik?" she called.

"Here," Çelik replied. He sounded composed. "Nice flying, Chief."

She risked a glance at Greg. He was still gripping the console in front of him. He met her eyes, and slowly opened his hands, leaning back in his seat. "I forgot that you're a lunatic," he said.

She looked back out the window, watching through the ship's tactical overlay for the light indicating the shelter entrance. She caught herself grinning. "I forgot that you fly like my gran."

Another five minutes of buffeting winds brought them to the ruined town square, and chaos. Dee had landed *Orunmila*'s shuttle just outside the shelter entrance, which was wide-open, the yellow light streaming into the stormy atmosphere, dissolving in the rain and fog. There were several dozen people milling around, some of them moving toward the ship. By the shuttle's open door stood stacks of env suits, and people were carting them into the shelter by the armful. Dee was surrounded by colonists, speaking earnestly. He looked up as she landed the raider perpendicular to the shuttle, blocking as much as she could of the wind.

"What's going on?" she commed Dee as they all unstrapped themselves.

"They won't get in the ship," he told her, and he sounded exasperated. "They're waiting for repairs to be made."

Repairs. Good God. "What's going on down there?"

"They're on reserve battery power," he said. "But this guy's been telling me the ventilation system is struggling."

Not just struggling, she guessed, but drawing enough power to burn through their backups more quickly than they had anticipated. "We've got to get more battery power," she told him.

"As soon as you can get through to *Orunmila,* explain the situation to Captain Shiang and see if she's got some batteries she can spare."

"Where are you going?"

"I'm going to go down and see if I can help." She turned to Greg. "You've worked on terraformers, haven't you? I'm going to try to deal with their filtration system, but I need you to pull apart that terraformer and take out any batteries it's got. I don't know how good they'll be after all this time, but we need everything we can get."

"How much time do they have?" Greg asked her.

"From the backup system I saw," she said, "they've got maybe five hours left using nothing but essentials. If I can get the ventilation working, they'll be able to breathe, but they'll drain the batteries faster, too." She squinted at the sky. "Dee won't be able to get through to *Orunmila* for at least another forty minutes, and we don't know how that terraformer blowout is going to influence this storm system. But realistically, it'll be three or four hours before we can count on backup. If we can get more battery power, we should be able to make this work." She turned to Çelik and offered him her arm, and they followed Greg out.

The wind howled around them, even in the lee of the two ships, and she staggered more than once making her way down to the entrance. She kept her eyes on Greg, striding easily before her, seemingly untouched by the weather. The iconic hero, as always, even walking into a situation he knew nothing about. She felt a wave of relief so intense she stumbled again, and shoved the emotion aside as well as she could. Of course he was alive. Clearly he had not even been badly hurt. This was not like the last time, when she had nearly lost him. This was just another mission, and he would escape it unscathed if it killed her.

Which it still might.

At the bottom of the stairs, the situation was more chaotic. Most of the lights were out, and those that were still operational were at half strength, turning the whole place a dim, stony gray. More than a hundred people were clustered anxiously in the middle of the cavernous room, most of them focused on a trio of grim-faced women who were sorting through the env suits. They were discarding more than they were selecting, and handing each suit that passed the test to the closest colonist. Any second now, Elena realized, the crowd would rush the women, and all control would be lost.

"They need these suits more than we do," she told Greg, pulling off her hood and stripping off the rest as quickly as she could. She handed it to the person closest to her before he realized what she was doing. "Where's Ruby?" she asked, as he stared dumbly at the suit in his hands.

"I don't know," he said, looking worriedly from her to the suit. "She said she was going to fix the ventilators."

"What about the terraformer?"

"It shut down," he told her, "but we can't get ahead of the CO_2."

Elena turned to Greg and Çelik. Çelik had pulled off his hood and his jacket, and was maneuvering the suit's trousers around his mismatched boots. Greg had tugged off his hood and shrugged off his jacket, and the room began to still. *Oh, hell,* she thought. *His uniform.* Çelik was in uniform as well, but his was somewhat the worse for wear; and he was familiar here as a prisoner. Greg—tall, square-jawed, and slim, black hair buzzed close to his head, gray-black eyes alert and bright in the dim light—looked like something off a recruiting poster.

"Who are you?"

Elena craned her neck to see the speaker: Badenhorst. He pushed his way past the crowd to confront Greg. He was not, she noticed, wearing a suit yet.

Greg stared back at the raider. Badenhorst was shorter, but far more broadly built; he could have knocked Greg down with sheer momentum.

Greg stood firm.

"I am Captain Foster, of the CCSS *Galileo,*" he told the raider. "Who are you?"

But Badenhorst didn't reply. His eyes went from Greg to Elena, then back to Greg. "How many env suits did you bring?"

"Twenty-four."

Badenhorst considered a moment, then nodded shortly. "It's a help. Where's Tsagaan?"

It was Çelik who answered his question. "She's dead."

Elena had not seen Badenhorst in combat mode before. He slung his pulse rifle off of his shoulder in one quick movement, his face suddenly hard and angry. He aimed the rifle at Çelik's chest. "You killed her."

"He didn't," Elena said. "It was her choice. Hers and MacBride's together. She said her life was forfeit, that she had brought this on all of you. They shut down the terraformer network," she told him. "They saved us all." She didn't mention that the same action had depleted the only permanent power source they had.

But Badenhorst was unconvinced. "You came here to kill her," he told Çelik. "I heard you say it more than once. That she owed you ninety-seven deaths. Why should I believe any-thing you say?"

Çelik was still for a moment. Then he extended his arm, in which he had bunched Tsagaan's beaten, worn env suit. "She sent this back for you," he said. "She told me . . . she said that for their two lives, we might buy three hundred."

Badenhorst dropped the nose of the rifle and reached out to take the suit, staring down at it silently. Elena saw one of Tsagaan's dark hairs caught in the neckline. "How did she die?" he asked, not looking up.

"Exposure, or radiation," Çelik told him. "I can't say which would have killed her first. Fast enough, but not as fast as if I'd shot her."

Badenhorst looked up and met Çelik's eyes. Damned if he did not seem to be genuinely grieving. He turned to shout over his shoulder. "Angalia."

A woman pushed out of the crowd to stand at his side. She was smaller than he was, and not quite so thick-necked; but Elena was certain they were related, possibly twins. The woman frowned suspiciously at the three Corps soldiers; but then her eye caught the env suit in Badenhorst's fist. Her dark eyes widened, and her suspicious expression became sorrowful. She whispered some words in a dialect Elena didn't understand, then looked up at Badenhorst. "Are you sure?"

He nodded, apparently willing to take Çelik's word for it. "You're Tsagaan now, Angalia."

Angalia looked astonished, then briefly incredulous, and not-so-briefly annoyed. When her expression settled into resig-nation, Elena was reminded of Jessica. Angalia—Tsagaan—met Çelik's eyes. "Has she paid her debt to you?" she asked him.

Elena saw Çelik's jaw tighten. "She has."

"Then help us."

It was harder than she had thought it would be, sending Greg away. He had remained silent for most of this, his eyes sweeping the shelter, instinctively crouching in the low catacomb hallways. He had to have a thousand questions, but he knew as well as she did now was not the time.

"Keep going down that hall," she told him, pointing to the narrow, dark corridor. "It opens on the terraformer. There's a power access panel on the far wall, about a meter up from the floor. It's modular; you should be able to hook up any batteries you find through there. If you can't, bring them to me, and I'll hack them."

"Where will you be?" he asked, and she thought he didn't want to leave her, either.

"Up this hallway," she said, gesturing to the left fork of the corridor. "There's a utility room that holds most of their environmentals."

"You don't need a suit for that?"

"Not as much as you do."

He nodded, pulled the jacket of his env suit back on, and took off at a trot. She ran up the other corridor.

The hallways were deserted, the rest of the colonists having congregated in the common area, looking for a safe place to wait out the crisis. The dim lighting was eerie, but she was focused on the sound of the air vents, alternately laboring and nearly silent. *Not much time left.* She turned the corner, and the sound of machinery grew louder. Ducking into a room, she found Ruby hovering in front of a large, square machine, its front panel powered up and wide open, lit by an emergency light she was holding in her teeth. She looked up when Elena entered, then looked back down again, plucking the flashlight from her mouth. "We need at least three more to get ahead of it," she said. "What about the power?"

"Working on it," Elena told her. Mechanic's code for *That's the next disaster. Don't worry about it now.*

Ruby gestured over her shoulder. "There's another spanner kit on top of that one. I don't have another light."

Who needs light? Elena thought. *I've repaired a generator in circumstances far more dire than these.*

As she reached for the spanner kit, a loud alarm sounded. "What's that?" she asked, strapping the kit automatically to her arm.

Ruby's response was garbled by the flashlight between her teeth, but Elena was pretty sure she said "CO_2 warning."

Lovely.

The first unit she looked at was completely corroded, most of its usable pieces long since cannibalized for other ventilators. The second came apart as soon as she touched it, and she began to wonder if the time mattered at all. But the third seemed solid enough, and even coughed briefly to life as she ran its self-diagnostic. She settled in front of it, eyes on the familiar circuitry, tuning out everything but the task before her.

She soon had it activated and had already moved on to the next one when Ruby cursed behind her. "What is it?" Elena asked, not slowing down.

"I need a new driver circuit. This one's dust."

Elena opened the unit in front of her. The driver circuit appeared intact. "What's the capacity of that unit?"

"Ninety-seven meters per minute."

As big as three of the smaller units. A fair trade. Elena pulled the circuit and handed it to Ruby, then moved on to the next unit.

When she had three of them activated, she turned back to Ruby's unit. Crouching next to the smaller woman, she began piecing together the detritus that had been the ventilator's cooling system. No wonder it had overloaded: the system, designed to be relatively low-maintenance, was entirely clogged. She turned to the units she had just repaired, but pulling them apart wouldn't help the situation. Staring down at the tubing, she did the math. Assuming the weather pattern didn't deviate too much from the initial predictions, she could have parts from *Orunmila* in a few hours. She looked up at Ruby's deft fingers— she clearly knew what she was doing.

Elena wrapped her fingers around the coolant tubing, and yanked. With a few careful splices, she looped the cooling system onto itself, and the machine's regulator kicked on. Its harmonic was added to the cacophony in the room.

Ruby stepped back, standing next to Elena. The two women stared at the unit as the alarm sounded, loud and tireless, in their ears.

And then, when Elena was sure they had failed, there was silence.

Elena closed her eyes for a moment. She could swear that the air, still recycled, still tasting sour, seemed cleaner in her lungs. She opened her eyes and looked down at Ruby, expecting the woman to be grinning; instead, she was staring at the ventilator.

"You saved our lives," Ruby said.

"Of course we did," Elena told her.

And wished, in that moment, they'd said those words to each other eight years ago.

Greg had managed to graft three batteries to the circuitry in the wall. Based on the power draw, Elena thought they might last an entire week. Despite running more ventilators, the precipitous maintenance she and Ruby had done on the units had improved their efficiency somewhat—probably, she thought, just by cleaning. It wasn't much of a safety buffer, but a week would give them multiple weather windows they could use to evacuate the colony.

Except, of course, the colonists didn't want to leave.

"This is our home," the new Tsagaan explained to Greg again. It had been her only response to him, every time he had explained the precarious situation, the need for supplies, the unreliability of a battery-powered habitat under the ground on a planet as stormy and mercurial as this one. Elena could see Greg growing frustrated. He had not spent a day here, as she had, absorbing the bloody-mindedness of these people.

At one point, the situation was poised to grow ugly. "If you insist on trying to make us leave," Badenhorst said, "we will consider your presence an attack, and we will defend ourselves accordingly."

Greg had looked at the new Tsagaan, who had shrugged, not interested in contradicting Badenhorst. Greg had finally, at Elena's prompting, turned to Ruby for help.

"We don't trust you," she explained simply. "You can't come in here, recharge our batteries, and expect us to forget decades of Central duplicity."

He opened his mouth, but Elena just shook her head. *They're never going to believe it's not our fault.* He frowned with that formidable look he got when he was thinking, but at least he seemed to get the message.

"All right," he asked, "who do you trust?"

Ruby's eyes landed on Çelik. "Him," she said. "We trust your castoffs. They understand us."

Çelik actually laughed out loud. "You're crazy," he said flatly. "The first thing I got asked when I came back down here was whether I'd murdered Tsagaan and MacBride. Now you trust me?"

"More than we trust them."

Elena stood next to Greg as he pulled Çelik aside. "We're left in a bad position here," he said quietly. "If we leave without some kind of interim agreement, you can bet they'll dig in and never talk to us again. We need an ambassador."

"I told Tsagaan I'd advocate for her people staying here," Çelik said, "but that's it. I've got no interest in being any kind of ambassador."

Greg opened his mouth, and Elena laid a hand on his arm to stop him. "Just for a few days, sir," she said to Çelik. "Until we can figure out what sort of help they need, and how we're going to get it to them." Çelik kept frowning, and she added, "Captain Shiang is not going to be happy about helping a Syndicate tribe. To the extent that you have her ear . . . you're the only one who can help on that side of it, too."

Another snort of laughter. "You really think I can talk that woman into anything?"

"I think," Elena said, "you can explain the situation to her in a way that she will understand. If she can see this as a home for these people, she may be willing to see them as something other than ordinary Syndicate raiders."

"They *are* ordinary Syndicate raiders."

Elena let her eyes stray around the room. Twelve brown uniforms mixed seamlessly into the crowd of civilians. Were it not for the color, she would not be able to tell who was who. "Maybe," she conceded. "But maybe not." She turned back to him. "Either way, sir, you're the best chance they've got."

He shook his head. "She's going to think I've lost my mind."

"She's going to think we all did."

CHAPTER 52

Orunmila

Guanyin stood behind Foster and Shaw as the Corps officers spoke with their Admiralty back on Earth.

Çelik looked very much the worse for wear, but he had insisted on dealing with the admirals before heading to the infirmary. He sat draped over a chair, one arm in his lap, the other dangling over the side. He looked indolent and disdainful, but based on the angle of his leg, she thought he was simply making himself as comfortable as he could.

Not that he minds the assumption of arrogance.

Shaw and Foster stood side by side, half at attention, presenting a united front. Whatever had happened down on the planet, all of Foster's tense misery was gone, and as she watched him standing next to his mechanic, his eyes never leaving the comm vid, she was struck by the confidence he radiated. If he was at all concerned about the consequences of his actions, his superior officers would never know. She understood, at last, why he had the reputation he had, and why his Admiralty might have thought he could stumble into the Third Sector with only the barest of introductions.

Foster's chain of command was an odd pair: Admiral Waris, an ageless and handsome woman, blond-haired and pale as starlight, fairly vibrating with fury; and Admiral Herrod, a dark-skinned, aging man with the largest nose she had ever seen, wide-set eyes sharp and sardonic. Every word from Admiral Waris was cold and vaguely threatening. Herrod, on the other hand, sat mostly in silence, and now and then Guanyin thought those wide-set eyes looked amused.

"So what we have," Waris said, "is MacBride dead, without proof or vid of the incident, along with all of the raiders involved in the attack on *Exeter*. Is this correct?"

Shaw spoke up. "We also have the last two hundred and eighty-three survivors of *Canberra*."

"One is orthogonal to the other, Commander Shaw, and I believe you know that."

Guanyin very nearly shuddered at the look Waris gave the mechanic. There was a reptilian sharpness to Waris's exchanges with Shaw that worried Guanyin.

Captain Foster, ever unflappable, came to Shaw's rescue. "Respectfully, Admiral," he said, "the remaining raiders are aware that they have placed the colony at risk. They are willing to send a representative for trial, if we agree to help the colonists in good faith."

Before her, Waris's clasped hands tightened, but her voice was even. "This is not a negotiation, Captain. We will arrest them for trial, no matter what it takes."

"Are you willing to start a war over it?"

This was from Çelik, still sprawling over the chair, and Guanyin could tell from Waris's expression that his posture annoyed her. Almost as an afterthought he shifted, sitting straighter, resting his artificial foot on the ground next to the other one. "Admiral Waris, Canberra was always full of bloody-minded idealists who'd rather dig rocks for the rest of their lives then ask anybody for anything. This isn't a surprising move from them. And the raiders?" He gave an elaborate shrug. "We took out five of them, and they took out one themselves."

Waris opened her mouth, but this time Herrod held up his hand. "Captain Çelik, are you telling me you're satisfied the other raiders didn't know what was going to happen?"

"I am satisfied of nothing, sir." He took an uncharacteristic pause, and Guanyin wondered what he was thinking about. "But I do know that digging those people out of the ground is no decent memorial for my dead crew."

"They're harboring fugitives," Waris insisted. "They have no standing to resist us."

At that, Admiral Herrod cleared his throat tactfully. "I believe that matter is still up for discussion, Admiral," he said.

Guanyin stepped forward, and Foster and Shaw moved behind her. She saw Waris's eyes narrow at the implied deference. "You could gas them, I suppose," she said. "Easy enough, given what we have learned of their ventilation systems. Or you could send your infantry down after them, although given the limited access to the shelter, that would be riskier. I should point out, though, that you would lose a fair amount of goodwill in this sector if you choose such a course of action."

Waris's jaw set. "Is that a threat, Captain Shiang?"

"It is an observation," Guanyin said smoothly. "Most of the colonies here still see Central as a protector, if a frequently absent one." Waris bristled. "They will find it . . . curious that you should greet the discovery of disaster survivors with such inexplicable actions."

"Those raiders are fugitives," Waris said.

Guanyin nodded. "That is true," she conceded. "But there are twelve of them. Tell me: How much political capital are you prepared to spend for twelve people who may end up acquitted, especially when they have volunteered to send a representative for trial?"

Waris's fingers clenched again. This time, she tried a smile. "Captain Shiang," she said, some warmth in her voice, "I know that you are new to all of this, but—"

Oh, enough. "Admiral Waris." Guanyin interrupted the admiral, who by the look on her face was unused to such treatment. "As you know my name, you must also know that *Orunmila* is my domain. And perhaps you also know that I am currently the head liaison for all eight PSI ships in this sector."

Waris tried to regroup. "Of course, Captain. I only meant to suggest that you are not part of Central, and it's not reasonable for us to expect you to understand all of the political subtleties at play here."

"You misunderstand me, Admiral," Guanyin said. "I do not *need* to understand Central to understand Syndicate raiders. My people have been fighting them for centuries. In addition to that, *Exeter* has been our ally for fifteen years. The attack on her was an attack on us. If her captain tells us that the raiders responsible have been punished, we will believe him. Central and PSI have collaborated frequently over the last several decades, Admiral. I see no reason that will not continue." She leaned forward, her hands on the table. "But we will not support an operation we do not believe in, and we will certainly not be party to an attack on independent colonists who have done no one here any harm."

She wondered if Waris noticed she had stopped short of absolving the raiders of the rest of their crimes. She expected so; the woman would not be where she was if she were not observant. Çelik had told Guanyin of his promise to the dead raider leader, and she was still trying to figure out how to allow him to keep his word without letting the tribe run roughshod over her territory.

Perhaps it won't become an issue, she thought. *Perhaps these people have changed.*

It was not the most impossible thing she had considered that day.

"They're not your colony," Waris told her, the conciliatory tone gone. "PSI has no rights to Canberra, and no rights to tell us how to manage—"

"That's enough." This came from Admiral Herrod, who no longer appeared amused. Waris shot him a look, almost as chilling as the one she had given Commander Shaw, but Herrod was apparently impervious. "I'm not going to sit here while we threaten each other over what should be good news. You're right, Admiral Waris, that the issue of the survivors is independent of what happened to *Exeter,* and I won't see them conflated." He turned back to Guanyin. "Would you agree, Captain Shiang, to joint stewardship of the rebuilding mission on Canberra? PSI and Central, working together? That way, if the raiders become . . . creative again, we can share intelligence before deciding how to proceed."

Guanyin straightened, folding her hands over her stomach.

"I believe my people will be comfortable with joint stewardship, Admiral Herrod." *As long as Admiral Waris stays away from the operation.*

"There is one other issue," Admiral Waris put in. Her pale skin was blotched with red, but she seemed to have decided, for the moment, to keep her temper. "Commander Shaw, you are reporting that the terraformer failure was deliberate. That the part manufactured by Ellis Systems was purposefully faulty, causing the terraformer to accelerate atmospheric damage."

"Yes, Admiral."

"Why would anyone do that?" she asked, and Guanyin thought she was genuinely puzzled. "Why would they destroy an entire colony?"

"It's my guess," Commander Shaw said, "that this was a prototype. An experiment. That they weren't aware of the slave terraformer network the colonists added later, with the aid of materials bought or stolen from commercial shippers. The goal would not have been destruction of the entire colony, but to see how much damage they could inflict before detection. Which," she concluded, "turned out to be quite a bit."

Waris was still confused. "But where is the profit in it?"

"Weapons are always profitable, Admiral," Shaw said smoothly. "I would have thought we'd have all learned that last year."

Guanyin kept her eyes on Admiral Waris, whose lips were thinning again. But it was Admiral Herrod who spoke. "Is there proof, Commander?" he asked.

At that, Shaw looked resigned. "No, sir," she said. "We have the faulty part, and we could probably trace it back to Ellis. It's a smoking gun, certainly, but proving that the sabotage was deliberate, when it was just a single part in a long supply chain?"

Herrod nodded. "Very well. You can send the part to us by—"

"Forgive me, Admiral," Guanyin interrupted again. "But I believe PSI will retain possession of the faulty component."

Herrod frowned, but she thought she saw a hint of amusement in his eyes. "I thought we were allies, Captain Shiang."

"Just so," Guanyin told him. "And whatever we discover about this component, we will share with you."

Resigned, Herrod said, "Very well." Then he sobered. "Captain Shiang, if I may say—thank you for what you have done for *Exeter* and her crew. They are fortunate in their allies."

"As are we, Admiral."

"Please don't hesitate to let us know if anything else requires . . . clarification," he told her; and she thought, as he disconnected, she caught the flash of a smile.

The three of them stared at the space over the desk for a moment. Then Captain Foster said, "Wow."

She turned to him. "Did I surprise you, Captain?"

"Yes," he said bluntly.

"What he means," Shaw put in, "is that he's never seen anyone shut up Admiral Waris before. Not even me, and I've tried."

"Waris thinks she knows you, Shaw," Çelik said, from his chair. "She is not as quick on her feet with unknowns."

Guanyin caught herself grinning at them. "I have to admit, that was rather fun." She thought of Admiral Herrod, and sobered. "Admiral Herrod . . . he seems to be an ally, of a sort. But I believe he is far more dangerous than that icy, unpleasant woman. The easiest enemies are the ones who are up front about wanting you dead." She stretched, pressing a hand to the small of her back. "If you don't mind, Captain Foster," she said, "I am going to have someone write up a document outlining what we have agreed to here. If you could take it to your Admiralty when it is finished, I would be grateful."

Foster nodded. "I'd be honored. And—thank you, Captain Shiang."

"It is Guanyin," she told him. When he smiled, she decided his reputation for charm was not quite so incomprehensible after all.

CHAPTER 53

Greg made Jessica put Bob Hastings on the line.

"Is she supposed to talk?" he asked the doctor seriously.

"You do realize who you're asking about." Greg thought Bob's exasperation was feigned. He knew the doctor well enough to know how the reticent old man expressed affection. "No matter what I tell her she'll be talking to someone. Might as well be you."

That was all the permission Jessica needed. "You should have seen it, sir," she shouted, and Greg remembered she was still mostly deaf. "Everything on fire, we're all shooting like lunatics, and I'm positive—certain—we're all dead, and you're going to be so pissed off at me, when *Cassia* comes in out of nowhere and smokes that last raider."

He recognized the enthusiasm in her voice. Adrenaline and relief so often combined in a way that made the whole incident seem almost like fun. Within a day, the reality would hit her.

"It's a damn good thing she got to us when she did." Her voice became more subdued. "If she hadn't, Greg—that raider would have hit us. Even with all of our defenses, all our shuttles out there."

He glanced over at Elena, who was frowning, her anxiety for her friend looking like anger. "They won't fuck around with you anymore, will they, Jess?" Elena said.

Jessica laughed. "Probably not. Oh, sir—I invited Captain Vassily over for a drink. I hope you don't mind. She says she'll kill off your scotch supply for you."

The comms virus was still unraveling, but Mosqueda had routed all of the ship's comms through a shuttle that had been modified by Lieutenant Samaras. Streaming was still impaired—which was beginning to grate on people's nerves— and the low-bandwidth shuttle system meant direct-line Admiralty channels were blocky and distorted. Samaras, with Aida's help, had boosted everything through *Orunmila,* but Greg still lost words here and there.

Greg kept his opinion of Jessica's work to himself. She had taken a different route than he would have, and he was not entirely sure he approved, especially with her reliance on Admiral Herrod. But his ship and his crew were safe, and Jessica herself had stormed the front lines without hesitation. And now she was rattling on to him about raiders and Andriya Vassily with the confidence and enthusiasm of a seasoned officer.

He had known she would be good at this job, but he had hoped she wouldn't have to learn like this.

"As long as *Cassia*'s there," he told her, "I think you can rest for a while, Commander."

"I don't want to rest," Jessica shouted. "I want to run and jump and hug people. Does that happen to you, Greg, after a battle?"

Next to him Elena snorted, and he glanced over at her. He caught her eye, and she smiled at him. She was covered in dirt and oil, and her hair was tangled, drooping over her eyes, and her smile was the most beautiful thing he had ever seen.

"All the time," Greg told Jessica honestly.

He and Elena reached their quarters, and the door slid closed behind them. "You go first," Greg told her, nodding at the bathroom door. He was not sure he was in any better shape than she was, but she had been gone longer. And this would give him a chance to talk properly to Jessica.

Elena gave him a grateful smile and disappeared into the bathroom. After a moment he heard the water running, and he sat down on his bunk, closing his eyes against the last of the tension dissipating in his system.

"Is she really okay?" Jessica asked him.

"No idea." He rubbed his eyes, leaving them closed. "She's all adrenaline at the moment. But she's not hurt. Everything else will work out."

"Speaking of which. How is that going to go? They can't fix those terraformers. Is *Orunmila* going to take them on board? What about the raiders?" She had been thinking of the same things he had.

"Captain Shiang is sending down all the spare batteries she's got," he told her, "but those are only going to power them for two or three weeks. Her meteorologist is analyzing the new weather patterns, but it's going to take a few months, maybe more, before the influence of that terraformer burst dies out. What they'll leave behind is anybody's guess. It could be worse than what they've had. As for the raiders . . . ." He sighed. "That's going to be a tangle. Captain Shiang gets this polite look on her face when I talk about their contribution to the colony. PSI and the Syndicates have been enemies for too long for this to go smoothly. But I think she may at least be willing to listen to them."

"I do not understand the colonists, sir."

"What would it take to make you leave *Galileo*, Jess?"

"That's Elena's argument."

She was right. Elena would cheerfully die before she left her home. "Maybe," he allowed. "But I understand it. Some of those people—that woman, Ruby. She went back. There's something in the community they have. Whether it's good or just insular, I don't know, but it's a pretty strong pull for them."

"And Central's just going to let them squat there?"

"I don't know," he said. "But I will. And so will Captain Shiang. She's already coordinating with the other ships in the sector to get them supplies."

"So you guys are friends now?"

"After a fashion. She's . . ." He hesitated. "Flinty. Arrogant. Certain. Acts on instinct first, facts second."

"She sounds like you."

"Really?" He was not sure how he felt about that. "I was thinking Çelik."

"No comment, sir."

He grinned, knowing she couldn't see it. "Do not compare me to that man."

"I didn't, sir. You did." She grew quiet. "So what happens to him?"

At that, Greg sighed. "I don't know, Jess. He was pretty badly hurt down there. He'll never see active duty again."

"That's a waste."

"It's not our call, Jessie."

There was a quiet tone in his ear, and two words materialized before his eyes: *Admiral Herrod.* Jessica had heard the comm. "I'll let you go, sir," she said.

"It's Herrod." He tried to keep the knot of worry out of his voice. "Probably wanting to have a go at me without Waris on the line. I'll give him this; he's circumspect with his criticisms. I'll comm you later. And Jess?"

"Sir?"

"Well done, Commander. You and your crew."

He could hear the smile in her voice when she said, "Thank you, sir."

CHAPTER 54

Request permission to join your crew."

Guanyin had been reading in her quarters when Çelik came by, stiff and formal and strange. She had been anticipating some sort of awkward farewell—an apology, an admonishment, she was not sure—but this caught her off guard. He was staring straight ahead, at attention, weight balanced between his leg and the new prosthetic Xiao had attached. Xiao had told her his injuries were extensive, but would probably heal without incident. Even so, he would be in considerable pain for the next few months; now that the temporary prosthetic was becoming permanent, his physical therapy schedule was going to be punishing.

She pushed herself up out of her chair and walked over to him. Only when she was before him did he look down into her eyes, and she was surprised by the apprehension she saw there. This was not a joke, then, or an empty gesture: this was his wish, and what she said to him next would matter.

"You understand," she said, "what this will mean. You will not be a Corps soldier anymore."

"I don't want to be a Corps soldier anymore."

"Why not?"

This was the ritual: *Why? Why are you here? Why do you want to stay?* She thought she knew his answers. She needed to know that he knew them as well.

"They won't give me another ship. They won't let me fly."

"So you wish to join us so you can stay in space."

"Yes."

"There are other ways to do that."

His lips tightened, and his eyes went back to the wall. "I have fought since I was twenty-four years old," he told her. "I don't want to stop."

This was closer. "And Central will not let you fight?"

Say it, she thought.

"I can't be sure they are fighting a battle I want to share in anymore," he said at last.

"And we are?"

"Yes."

"What battle is that?"

He swallowed. "To help. To give people assistance. To allow them to survive. Grow. Thrive. To give them a chance to be human."

She realized, as she studied him, that she did not know if any other Corps soldier had ever joined PSI. She was certain that if anyone as high-profile as he was had done so, she would have heard. It was possible, she supposed, that some lower-ranked officers had joined, but Çelik's choice would cause problems. Central Gov would feel blindsided and worried. Shadow Ops would feel deceived. She would have to warn Greg and Elena, although she suspected they would not be surprised.

So be it. He was family now. Nothing else mattered.

"Kahraman Çelik," she began formally, "you have chosen to join the crew of the starship *Orunmila,* and to pledge your loyalty to your new family as part of PSI. Is this your free and independent wish?"

Çelik swallowed. "Yes, Captain."

"You will be trained for a period of six months. You must start with basic tasks. Here you have no rank. New members all start in the same place, children or adults. Your assignments will be tailored to the aptitude you show, nothing else. No one here will defer to you."

"I understand."

She stood as straight as she could. "Then from this moment forward, whatever you choose for your vocation, however you choose to live, whatever place you make your home, you are one of us, our family. No matter what our origins, we are all one blood. Do you agree to this?"

"Yes, Captain." No hesitation at all.

There was more she should say. There were probably official words she was not remembering. She had memorized it all, but that had been years ago, and she had never done this before. "At ease," she said gently. Çelik spread his feet out, but did not relax. "You are free to take a new name," she told him, "but I would recommend you keep the one you have."

That, of all things, caused him to make a face. "It's a stupid name. My mother thought it was noble."

" 'Iron Hero,' " Guanyin translated, and smiled. "It's quite appropriate, actually."

"For you," he said, "I will keep it."

Something seemed to be escaping from the corner of his eye.

She turned away. Samedi was curled up in the corner, his eyes half-open, weary but unable to let himself drop off. She was fond of creatures who did not know when to let go. "Do you like puppies, Raman?" she asked.

He blinked, then looked dubiously at the dog. "I don't know, Captain."

"Shall we see if they like you?" She crooked her finger and Samedi leapt to life, trotting over to her side and panting in anticipation. She met the dog's eyes, then nodded at Çelik. "Samedi, this is Raman. Raman, this is Samedi. I have many friends who are smarter than Samedi, but none that are more faithful."

Çelik raised a suspicious eyebrow, and for a moment a flash of his old arrogance returned. "Six children were not enough, then?" he asked. He held his fingers out, and Samedi extended his neck, sniffing Çelik's fingertips. After a moment he reached the limits of his puppy reserve, and started licking Çelik's hand with unrestrained enthusiasm.

She laughed, and Çelik looked surprised. After a moment he smiled at her, and his eyes filled again, and she thought, perhaps, that Çelik deserved a chance to be human as well.

CHAPTER 55

I should have known that was too easy.

Greg stared sightlessly at the bathroom door, the last of Admiral Herrod's words still echoing in his mind. On the other side of the door, Elena was still showering, still blissfully ignorant, still thinking they had won. Since they had returned from Canberra, he had felt reluctant to let her out of his sight; he had found, to his surprise, that she seemed to feel the same way. That had felt like victory as well.

And now he was going to lose all of it.

You're telling me, Greg had asked Herrod, incredulous, *that this is what we get for doing as they asked?*

No, Herrod had replied, and for the first time since they had met, he sounded tired and old. *It's the price you're paying for doing it your way instead of theirs.*

If you think for one minute we are going to pay for your fuck-ups, old man, you can go straight to hell. He had been furious. Desperate. Helpless.

And Admiral Herrod had laughed, a dusty, dead sound. *That, Captain, is a long-concluded journey.*

The bathroom door slid open and Elena emerged, barefoot, in clean shorts and black T-shirt. Her hair was unbraided, still damp, the dark, loose curls falling over her shoulders. She always looked different with her hair down: younger, more vulnerable, like some stranger, or some woman he had known years ago, when he was still a boy. He wished he had known her then, before Caroline, before the Academy, before the Corps. Before he had turned into the man he was.

"Sorry to be slow," she said, tugging her fingers through her hair. "I didn't think I was ever going to get the smell of that ventilated air off of my skin." She met his eyes, and instantly froze. "What is it?"

He had forgotten how easily she read him. "Elena." God, there were no words for this. "I just finished speaking with Admiral Herrod. He's—they're transferring you, Elena. They're pulling you off *Galileo.*"

Her hand dropped, and she stared at him, expression blank. He saw her eyes widen, just a little, with incomprehension. He might as well have been telling her of another death. She turned away, facing the window, wrapping her arms around her waist.

She said nothing.

He stood. "I don't have the paperwork yet, but when I receive it, I'll file a protest. That should buy us some time, at least. I shouldn't have any trouble coming up with a justification to keep you, especially if you log a protest as well. S-O isn't the whole Admiralty, after all. There are other people I can talk to—Chemeris, Overton, Turay—"

"Don't."

Her voice was calm, composed, her shoulders straight. She stood still, staring out the window, the faint starlight casting her gold skin blue. He could not read her expression. "I'm not going along with this, Elena," he told her, as if she had not understood.

"Yes you are."

That same level tone. Something cold coalesced in his stomach. After everything that had happened—could it be she wanted this? "If this is about me, Elena, we can do something about that. Something else. We could—"

She turned around, her shoulders still straight; but her eyes were bright and blazing. Furious. The ice in his blood vanished. "For God's sake, Greg," she snapped, annoyed, "this isn't about us. Don't you see? We never get it wrong until we forget that none of this is about us."

The anger rushed back. "Then how can you suggest we just take this? Just let them pull us apart? After everything we've been through, everything we've done, we just roll over and let them win?"

"This isn't about winning, Greg. Think about it." She brushed past him, and he caught the clean scent of her skin. "Everything we know about them. Everything we suspect. All the cards they could play, and this is what they choose."

"Don't you think it's enough?"

"I think it's hideous and spiteful, and I think they don't know you very well." She turned back to him. "But Greg—what's the worst thing that's within their power to do?"

This. But he began to see what she was saying. "They could have taken us both off."

"More than that, Greg, they could have decommissioned *Galileo* entirely. She's only halfway through her useful life, sure; but after what happened? How hard would it be to make the excuse? They could have shattered her entirely, and they didn't. Why do you think that is?"

He knew it. Even if half the Corps intelligence he had was false, he knew it. "They need her," he said.

"Exactly." She let her arms drop to her sides, but her hands were in fists. "They're doing this to punish you, to make you remember who's in charge, because you got around them. You disobeyed an order in a way they can't properly punish, because the end result is better than anything they could have come up with on their own. But they still need you, Greg, because *Galileo* doesn't function without you. They need that ship, and they need you at the helm."

"Fuck them," he told her. "They need me so bad, they can leave you where you are."

But she was shaking her head; he was still missing something. "That's the trouble, though. None of us know who the enemy is. We've all been operating like there's two sides. First it was us against S-O, then us and S-O against Ellis. But S-O isn't one side, it's about nine sides, and fuck if I want to be associated with any of them. And I'm not sure the Corps is cohesive enough to have a position on anything at all. Greg." She reached out and closed her fingers around his wrist. "You've got to let them think they've won this one. You've got to keep *Galileo* going, and stay in the loop. If you fight them, they shut you out, and we can't help anyone."

Damn. She was making sense, and all of his arguments were draining through his fingers. "So that's it?" he asked her. Her fingers were still on his arm; he wanted to trap her hand with his and refuse to let go. "The only way to fight is if we let them pull us apart?"

She stared back at him with those eyes of hers, dark and light all at once, boring into his thoughts. He remembered the first time she had looked at him like that, years and years ago, when they had first met: he had felt as if every thought and emotion and memory he had was laid open to her. He had been lost already, that early in their relationship, but it had taken him years to see it.

"Listen to me, Greg Foster," she told him. "They could throw me into some First Sector backwater horticultural survey. They could toss me onto a Seventh Sector exploratory ship, no comms, no stream, no contact with anyone, and it would not matter. They cannot separate us, do you understand?" Her fingers had tightened on his arm; there was desperation on her face as she willed him to believe her. "Nothing they do can separate us unless we let them. Do not let them, Greg. Promise me."

You don't understand, he wanted to say to her. *I cannot do any of this without you.* But it was fantasy, like the dreams he'd had as a child, before his mother died, when his heart was still innocent. He could do without her, and he would, because he had no other choice.

"I promise," he managed to choke out.

And she let go of his wrist, and flung her arms around his neck. After a moment he wrapped his own arms around her, pulling her close, feeling her damp hair against his cheek, inhaling her familiar fragrance. He closed his eyes, soaking in the warmth of her, and he thought, if he could commit it all to memory, he might manage to miss her less.

EPILOGUE

Orunmila

Jimmy looked at Dee almost cheerfully, as if he were glad to see a friendly face. Dee was not sure if he was pleased or disappointed. Jimmy had not changed at all, showed no signs of remorse or even regret that he had deceived the people who had trusted him and relied on him for so many years. Like a different species, Dee thought. Not even human.

That would make all of this much easier.

"Hey, Dee," Jimmy said easily. He was sitting on a cot in the back of the little cell, the text of a book floating half a meter in front of his face. It was not an uncomfortable room, Dee noticed. The cot was well-padded, and the bathroom was separate, although it had no door. There was a sink and what he thought was a refrigerator, and enough floor space for some minor exercises, should Jimmy be so inclined. Jimmy had never thought much of such things, though; most of his exercise, he always said, was from running after sick people during his shift. Dee used to tease him about it. A medic should care more about his own health. On the other hand, Dee had to admit it hadn't

509

done Jimmy much harm. Despite looking older than his thirty-five years, Jimmy was as lean and fit as he had been since Dee first met him. He was the only person Dee had ever known who had managed a Corps career untouched.

Dee glanced at the guard. Shiang had not compromised with this one; he was half a meter taller than Jimmy, and nearly as wide as Dee was himself. There was no way Jimmy would be running away under his watch. Even Dee would have some trouble, if he were so inclined.

"Can I go in?" he asked.

The guard gave him a look up and down. His eyes were careful, but not entirely without sympathy. He would understand, Dee thought, about years of joint service, about friendship. About the bounds of duty. The guard shrugged, and swiped at the wall to disable the room's force shield. Dee stepped over the threshold, and felt the subliminal electric charge in the air as the shield reactivated behind him.

Jimmy had swept his book away and stood. "Can I offer you a drink?" he asked, heading for the sink. Dee took a few steps in, looking around.

"No thanks," he said, "but don't let me stop you."

"I was wondering when you were going to come," Jimmy said conversationally. He opened the refrigerator and pulled out something that might actually have been beer. Dee supposed allowing prisoners to get drunk was some kind of human rights thing for PSI. They certainly seemed to be a kill-them-with-kindness people. He thought Shiang's kindness had been good for Captain Çelik; it gave him a sense of peace, on some level, thinking his captain was being looked after by someone like her. Captain Çelik did not have much experience with kindness. Dee had not expected him to respond to it the way he had.

"Not a lot of visitors, huh?" Dee prompted.

Jimmy actually laughed. "Nobody at all. I would have expected Elena by now, with one of her disapproving speeches. Kind of annoying to be a prisoner to that, I have to say. She's such a boor." He glanced back at Dee. "I suppose you never thought so."

Dee shook his head. "We understood each other," he said. They still did. He could read her as well as he always could. He thought she would be okay, would survive this. She survived everything. She had always been so much stronger than he was. He wished she was with him now; he could use some strength. With her strength, he might still turn and walk away from all of this.

Jimmy was grinning. "Oh, I doubt that," he said. He turned back to Dee, a drink in his hand, looking relaxed. Looking *liberated*. It occurred to Dee, then, that Jimmy was actually able to be himself now, possibly for the first time in his life. "She's so much better than we are, don't you know? She knows it, too. Always did. Too good for me, too good for Çelik. Too good for you, Dee, until you were falling apart. She cured you, and then she left. I'm guessing that's her habit."

She didn't cure me, Dee thought. *She forgave me.* But he didn't want to talk about Elena. "She's better than I am, sure," Dee agreed. "Not Çelik, though." He paused. "Don't you want to know why I'm here?"

"You mean you're not just looking up an old friend?" Jimmy's eyes grew hard. "Murov, can you give us a minute?"

Dee turned back to the guard, who gave him a speculative

look. *Could it really be this easy?* "I'm not going to release him, you know," Dee said. After a moment Murov nodded.

"I'm right outside the door," he told Dee. "Call if you need help."

Which would be satisfying, Dee thought; but the request would probably not be met the way he might hope. Murov slipped out of the room, and Dee felt briefly guilty.

"So." Jimmy's face relaxed again, and he took another sip of his drink. "Are you going to deliver Elena's lecture?"

Unable to hide his feelings, Dee scowled. "What the hell is wrong with you, anyway? *Lecture?* How about *you* tell *me* why the hell you sold us out? And you can skip the self-serving weasel words you told Foster."

"I didn't sell anyone out," Jimmy told him, unruffled. "All I did was suggest to Lawson he could get himself an in with Shadow Ops if he volunteered *Exeter* for transport. And I didn't make MacBride take that deal from Ellis. I just took a piece of it when it was made."

"This is for *money?*"

"What, do you think I did it for love?" He grinned again; Dee thought he was pleased to be talking about it. "Why not money? It's not like I was getting anything from the Corps."

"You didn't care about the work, about doing something useful? Why did you stay, then? You could have just quit."

"With what? I give them years and years of my life, I clean up after them, I sit through god-awful slaughters like Canberra, and I don't even have twenty centimes in the bank. You can live off of the pension, but who would want to? I retire, I live like a pauper."

"You could still be a doctor."

Jimmy's face twisted with revulsion. "Stupid, complaining bastards, patients. Whining over every little ache and pain. Dying like animals, instead of standing up like men. What's the point of trying to help them? You just make yourself a target, and they never listen anyway." He shot Dee a look of irritation. "You heard how Çelik spoke to me before that damned mission of his. If you'd told him to stay up here, he would have. Me? He talks to me like I'm an ensign, like I've been on the job a week. Why didn't you tell him to stay, anyway?"

There was no harm in explaining. "I wanted him to go," Dee said. "I wanted to see him get those raiders, to kill MacBride. I wanted revenge."

Jimmy looked confused, but still untroubled. "He'd have destroyed his career. Was that it? You wanted a command?"

Dee thought back. When he had joined the Corps, he had been twenty-two and fiercely stupid. He had thought to be a captain someday, to lead an intrepid force aboard a fine starship, to fight tyranny and starvation, to make the galaxy a better place. How long had it been since all of that had been burned out of him? How long would it be before the loss of it would stop hurting? "You don't believe I'd want MacBride dead?"

"I don't believe you'd let someone else do it, unless there was something in it for you."

"Maybe there was," Dee suggested. *Innocence, perhaps.*

But Jimmy wasn't buying it. "I don't think so." He put down his glass and walked back toward the cot. "You're a hands-on sort of man."

Indeed, Dee thought. "Did you know they were going to kill so many people?"

"I didn't think they'd be so . . . effective," Jimmy confessed. "I'd have planned to be off-duty, somewhere in the ship's interior. I came pretty close to getting killed myself. Not part of the plan."

"Do you have any sympathy for your ninety-seven crewmates who *did* get killed?"

Jimmy looked surprised again. "We all signed up for the same job," he pointed out reasonably. "Risk is part of it. They didn't get anything they hadn't earned."

He had needed nothing more than that. In one rapid movement Dee stepped forward, shoving Jimmy's back against the cell wall, his hand encircling his old friend's neck. He could feel Jimmy's pulse under his fingers, feel his Adam's apple as he swallowed. Jimmy looked startled, but not yet frightened, and his hands closed over Dee's arm, tugging at him.

"They were your friends," Dee hissed at him, staring into Jimmy's eyes. "Every one of them would have put themselves between you and death, and instead you *threw them away* because you felt *slighted*."

"Not like that," Jimmy managed to choke out.

"They wouldn't have believed it, you know?" Dee's mind flashed back to the battle, still fresh in his mind, lived and relived every night in his dreams, every moment he blinked, burned into the back of his eyelids. "They would have seen that ship coming, have known the guns failed, have still shot at it, one lousy cannon with no computer override, firing and firing because somehow a miracle would have happened. Someone would have hit the attacker. Someone would have saved us. They wouldn't have believed it, not when the ship filled the window, not when they knew beyond a doubt that it was going to tear right through our hull and burn us out. Even at that point, they would not have believed they were going to die. Because they were brave, and they were soldiers, and they stood with each other."

His fingers tightened, and he saw the first glimpse of fear in Jimmy's eyes.

"But you're going to know," he said clearly. "You're going to see it coming, and you are going to be afraid, like they never were, because I'm going to kill you, Jimmy. I'm going to choke you to death. And I'm going to do it slowly."

He felt the muscles in Jimmy's throat tense as he tried to shout for the guard, but Dee's grip was too tight.

"I want you to think about it while it's happening to you. The whole physiological process of your brain being deprived of oxygen. You can fight to stay awake all you want, but you know you'll fail. You'll get fuzzier and fuzzier, and more and more frantic. Your diaphragm will hitch, and all of your reflexes will kick and scream for air, and you'll get nothing. And the world around you will close in, get blurry, get dark, and you'll know that it doesn't matter. Fighting doesn't matter. Because you're going to die, and the last thing you're going to see is me looking at you, Jimmy. You are a fucking murderer, and this is my revenge."

Fear was clear in Jimmy's eyes now. He clawed more desperately at Dee's arm, and kicked at him futilely. Dee stared into his eyes, keeping his face close. He had thought he would find some comfort in this, even some exhilaration; but it felt like a chore, just one more mission. One last mission for *Exeter*, for his friends, for everything he believed in. One last chance at absolution.

Jimmy's scrambling grew weaker too quickly, and his eyes dropped closed at last. His limbs went limp. It would have been easier to snap his neck at that point, but instead Dee started a timer on his comm, and kept his hands around Jimmy's throat for ten full minutes. At some point he stopped feeling the pulse under his fingers, but he held on. He needed to be certain. There was no point in doing a job, after all, if it was not done properly.

When it was over he let go, and the body slumped to the ground. Dee backed up until he felt the opposite wall behind him, and he slumped to the ground as well. He sat, staring at his friend's corpse, and waited for the guard to return.

ACKNOWLEDGMENTS

A second book is a different animal than a first, no matter how of much of it you had in your mind when you started. I was privileged to work with the same team of people, who made it the best possible experience for both me and the book itself.

With thanks to:

My agent, Hannah Bowman, who kept me focused and talked me off an awful lot of ledges.

My editors, David Pomerico and Natasha Bardon, who poked at the story in all the right ways.

Rebecca Lucash, who answered my foolish questions with kindness and made everything run smoothly.

Caroline Perny, who watched after the first book so I could watch after this one and kept making me laugh.

And to my friends, who have put up with the worst of it:

Nancy Matuszak—there are not enough tater tots in the world to repay you for your friendship and wisdom.

Richard Tunley—for believing, especially on those days

when I couldn't. You kept me going on days when I thought it was impossible.

My incredible online folks—some of you I haven't seen in decades. Some of you I've never seen at all. You all make me laugh, and you make me less alone.

To my family, as always—my parents, who have put up with insane schedules and meltdowns and pleas for beta reads; and my brother, who finds all the good stuff for me. Thank you for propping me up.

To my husband, who has to live with me—thank you for still living with me!

And to my lovely girl. This is a sad story, and a happy story, and a tragic story, and a story of hope. Just like life. Stand up, open your arms, and embrace it.

ABOUT THE AUTHOR

Virginia Bonesteel

Elizabeth Bonesteel began making up stories at the age of five, in an attempt to battle insomnia. Thanks to a family connection to the space program, she has been reading science fiction since she was a child. She lives in central Massachusetts with her husband, her daughter, and various cats.

elizabethbonesteel.com

ACKNOWLEDGMENTS

A second book is a different animal than a first, no matter how of much of it you had in your mind when you started. I was privileged to work with the same team of people, who made it the best possible experience for both me and the book itself.

With thanks to:

My agent, Hannah Bowman, who kept me focused and talked me off an awful lot of ledges.

My editors, David Pomerico and Natasha Bardon, who poked at the story in all the right ways.

Rebecca Lucash, who answered my foolish questions with kindness and made everything run smoothly.

Caroline Perny, who watched after the first book so I could watch after this one and kept making me laugh.

And to my friends, who have put up with the worst of it:

Nancy Matuszak—there are not enough tater tots in the world to repay you for your friendship and wisdom.

Richard Tunley—for believing, especially on those days

when I couldn't. You kept me going on days when I thought it was impossible.

My incredible online folks—some of you I haven't seen in decades. Some of you I've never seen at all. You all make me laugh, and you make me less alone.

To my family, as always—my parents, who have put up with insane schedules and meltdowns and pleas for beta reads; and my brother, who finds all the good stuff for me. Thank you for propping me up.

To my husband, who has to live with me—thank you for still living with me!

And to my lovely girl. This is a sad story, and a happy story, and a tragic story, and a story of hope. Just like life. Stand up, open your arms, and embrace it.

ABOUT THE AUTHOR

Virginia Bonesteel

Elizabeth Bonesteel began making up stories at the age of five, in an attempt to battle insomnia. Thanks to a family connection to the space program, she has been reading science fiction since she was a child. She lives in central Massachusetts with her husband, her daughter, and various cats.

elizabethbonesteel.com